Jill Mansell lives with her family in Br̶ the field of Clinical Neurophysiology but now writes ƒu̶ll̶ ̶ She watches far too much TV and would love to be one of those super-sporty types but basically can't be bothered. Nor can she cook – having once attempted to bake a cake for the hospital's Christmas Fair, she was forced to watch while her co-workers played frisbee with it. But she's good at Twitter!

By Jill Mansell

The Unpredictable Consequences Of Love
Don't Want To Miss A Thing
A Walk In The Park
To The Moon And Back
Take A Chance On Me
Rumour Has It
An Offer You Can't Refuse
Thinking Of You
Making Your Mind Up
The One You Really Want
Falling For You
Nadia Knows Best
Staying At Daisy's
Millie's Fling
Good At Games
Miranda's Big Mistake
Head Over Heels
Mixed Doubles
Perfect Timing
Fast Friends
Solo
Kiss
Sheer Mischief
Open House
Two's Company

Jill Mansell

SHEER MISCHIEF

headline
review

First published in 1994 by Bantam Books,
a division of Transworld Publishers Ltd.

This edition published in paperback in 2014
by HEADLINE REVIEW
An imprint of HEADLINE PUBLISHING GROUP

25

Cataloguing in Publication Data is available from the British Library

ISBN 978 0 7553 3254 0

Printed and bound in Great Britain by
CPI Group (UK) Ltd, Croydon, CR0 4YY

Headline's policy is to use papers that are natural, renewable and
recyclable products and made from wood grown in sustainable forests.
The logging and manufacturing processes are expected to conform to
the environmental regulations of the country of origin.

HEADLINE PUBLISHING GROUP
An Hachette UK Company
338 Euston Road
London NW1 3BH

www.headline.co.uk
www.hachette.co.uk

To Lydia with my love

Acknowledgements

A huge thank you to Mum, as ever, for all those hours at the word processor; Dad, the only one who understands it; Tina, the babysitter extraordinaire; and Pearl, Sarah and Cino who all helped too.

Chapter 1

Running away from her boring old fiancé had seemed such a brilliant idea at the time. It was just a shame, Maxine decided, that running out of boring old petrol four hours later should be turning out to be so much less fun.

'Oh please, don't be mean,' she begged, but the middle-aged petrol-pump attendant remained unmoved.

'Look,' he repeated heavily, 'you've filled your car up with twenty pounds' worth o' petrol. Now you tell me you've only got seventy-three pence on you. You ain't got no credit cards, no cheque book, nor no identification. So I don't have no choice but to call the police.'

Maxine's credit cards, house keys and cheque book were back in London, lurking somewhere at the bottom of the Thames. Exasperated beyond belief by the man's uncharitable attitude, she wondered how and when the inhabitants of Cornwall had ever managed to acquire their reputation for friendliness. As far as she was concerned, it was a filthy lie.

'But I'll pay you back, I promise I will,' she said in wheedling tones. 'This is just silly. I don't know why you won't trust me . . .'

The attendant had a glass eye which glinted alarmingly in the sunlight. Fixing her with the bloodshot good one and evidently immune to the charms of hapless blondes with beguiling smiles, he exhaled heavily and reached for the phone.

'Because it's seven o'clock in the morning,' he replied, as if she were being deliberately stupid. 'Because you can't pay for your petrol. And because you're wearing a wedding dress.'

Janey Sinclair, peering out of her bedroom window overlooking Trezale's picturesque high street, was embarrassed. She'd had twenty-six years in which to get used to being shown up by her younger sister but it still happened. What was really unfair, she thought sleepily, was the fact that none of it ever seemed to faze Maxine.

'Sshh,' she hissed, praying that none of her neighbours were yet awake. 'Wait there, I'm coming down.'

'Bring your purse!' yelled Maxine, who didn't care about the neighbours. 'I need twenty pounds.'

What Maxine really needed, Janey decided, was strangling.

'OK,' she said, opening the front door and wearily surveying the scene. 'Don't tell me. You're eloping with our local policeman and you need the money for the marriage licence. Tom, are you sure you're doing the right thing here? Your wife's going to be furious when she finds out, and my sister's a lousy cook.'

Tom Lacey, Trezale's local policeman, had been married for ten months and his wife was due to give birth at any moment, yet he was blushing with pleasure like a schoolboy. Janey heaved an inward sigh and wished she'd kept her mouth shut.

Maxine, however, simply grinned. 'I did offer. He turned me down.'

Janey pulled her creased, yellow and white dressing gown more tightly around her waist. That was something else about Maxine, she always managed to upstage everyone around her. And although it was still relatively early on a Sunday morning, it was also mid-July, practically the height of the holiday season. Tourists, unwilling to waste a moment of their precious time in Cornwall, were making their way along the high street, heading for the beach but pausing to watch the diversion outside the florist's shop. They couldn't quite figure out what was going on, but it looked interesting. One small boy, deeply tanned and wearing only white shorts, deck shoes and a camera slung around his neck, was even taking surreptitious photographs.

'So why *are* you wearing a wedding dress?' she demanded, then flapped her arms in a gesture of dismissal. Maxine's explanations tended to be both dramatic and long-winded. 'No, don't bother. Here's the twenty pounds. Can we go inside now or are you really under arrest?'

But Maxine, having whisked the money from her sister's grasp and popped the rolled-up notes into her cleavage, was already sliding back into the passenger seat of the panda. 'My car's being held hostage,' she said cheerfully. 'Tom just has to take me to pay the ransom first, but we'll be back in forty minutes. Tom, are you as hungry as I am?'

'Well . . .' Tom, who was always hungry, managed a sheepish grin.

'There, you see. We're both absolutely starving,' declared Maxine, gazing with longing at the array of switches studding the dashboard and wondering which of them controlled the siren. Then, fastening her seatbelt and flashing her sister a dazzling grin, she added, 'But you mustn't go to too much trouble, darling. Just bacon and eggs will be fine.'

Tom, to his chagrin, was called away instead to investigate the case of the stolen parasol outside the Trezale Bay Hotel.

'Toast and Marmite?' Maxine looked disappointed but bit into a slice anyway. Rearranging her voluminous white skirts and plonking herself down on one of the wrought-iron chairs on the tiny, sunlit patio, she kicked off her satin shoes and wriggled her toes pleasurably against the warm flagstones.

'Why don't you change into something less . . . formal?' Janey, who was wearing white shorts and a primrose-yellow camisole top, poured the coffee. 'Where's your suitcase, in the car?'

Maxine, having demolished the first slice of thickly buttered toast, leaned across and helped herself to a second.

'No money, no suitcase,' she said with a shrug. 'No nothing! You'll just have to lend me something of yours.'

Janey had looked forward all week to this Sunday, when nothing was precisely what she had planned on doing. A really good lie-in, she thought dryly, followed by hours of blissful, uninterrupted *nothing*. And instead, she had this.

'Go on then,' she said as Maxine stirred three heaped spoonsful of sugar into her coffee cup and shooed away an interested wasp. 'Tell me what's happened. And remember, you woke me up for this so it had better be good.'

She had to concede, ten minutes later, that it was pretty good. Three years at drama school might not have resulted in the dreamed-of glittering acting career, but Maxine certainly knew how to make the most of telling a story. In the course of describing the events of the previous night her hands, eyebrows – even her bare feet – became involved.

'. . . So there we were, expected to arrive at this fancy-dress party in less than an hour, and bloody Maurice hadn't even remembered to tell me it was on. Well, being Maurice, he phoned his mother and she was round in a flash with her old wedding dress tucked under her skinny arm. It's a Schiaparelli, can you believe? So we ended up at this chronic company party as a bride-and-sodding-groom and everyone was sniggering like mad because the thought of us ever actually tying the knot was evidently too funny for words. And I realized then that they were right – I didn't want to spend the rest of my life pretending to be a dutiful banker's wife and having to socialize with a bunch of boring stuffed shirts. So I told Maurice it was over, and then I told the stuffed shirts and their smirking wives exactly what I thought of them too. Poor Maurice; as far as he was concerned, that really was the last straw. It didn't matter that I'd humiliated him, but insulting all the directors was too much. Janey, I've never seen him so mad! He dragged me backwards out of the hotel and told me I wasn't worth his mother's old slippers, let alone her precious wedding dress. I screamed back that as he was such an old woman *he* should be wearing the bloody dress! Then I kicked him because he wouldn't let go of me, so he called me a spoilt, spiteful, money-grabbing delinquent and chucked my evening bag into the Thames.' She paused, then concluded mournfully, 'It had everything in it. My favourite Estée Lauder eye-shadow palette . . . *everything*.'

All the toast had gone. Janey, reminding herself that it didn't matter, she was supposed to be on a diet anyway, cradled her lukewarm coffee in both hands and remarked, 'Bit daring, for Maurice. So then what did you do?'

'Well, luckily we'd taken my car. All my keys were in the river, of course, but I've always kept a spare in the glove compartment and the driver's door is a doddle – you can open it with a hair slide. I just jumped in, drove off and left Maurice standing in the middle of the road with his mouth going like a guppy. But I knew I couldn't break into the flat – he's got that place alarmed to the eyeballs – so I headed for the M4 instead. And because the one thing I *did* have was a full tank of petrol, I thought I'd come and visit my big sister.'

With a grin, Maxine ran her fingers through her tumbling, gold-blond hair and shook it back over her shoulders. 'I'm seeking sanctuary, darling. Just call me Quasimodo.'

'Don't call me darling,' grumbled Janey, who hated it. 'And whatever you do, don't call me *big*.'

But it was no good. Maxine wasn't going to go away. Neither – despite having driven all night from London to Cornwall – did she apparently have any intention of falling asleep.

Janey, who loved but frequently despaired of her sister, followed her upstairs and sat on the edge of the bed whilst Maxine carried out a brisk raid on the wardrobe. She wondered what Maxine had ever done to deserve a twenty-two-inch waist.

'These'll be fine.' Forcing another hole through the tan leather belt, she patted the size fourteen khaki shorts with approval and admired her reflection in the mirror. The white shirt, expertly knotted above the waist, showed off her flat brown midriff and her dark eyes sparkled. 'There, ready to face the world again. Or dear old Trezale, anyway. Where shall we go for lunch?'

'You don't have any money,' Janey reminded her with a sinking heart, but Maxine was already halfway to the bedroom door.

'I'll sort something out with the bank tomorrow,' she replied airily. 'They'll understand when I tell them what that pig of an ex-boyfriend of mine did with my cheque book. Now come along, Janey, cheer up and tell me where we can meet all the most gorgeous men these days. Is the Dune Bar still good?'

'He wasn't your boyfriend,' said Janey, wondering at the ease with which Maxine had apparently discarded him from her life. 'He was your fiancé.'

Maxine looked momentarily surprised. Then, waving her left hand in the air so that the large, square-cut emerald caught the light, she said gleefully, 'Of course he was! How clever of you to think of it. If the bank gets stuffy I can flog the ring, instead.'

'You think I'm a heartless bitch, don't you?'

They were sitting out on the crowded terrace of the Dune Bar. Janey tried not to notice the way practically every male was lusting after Maxine. Maxine, who genuinely appeared not to have noticed – it was a particular speciality of hers – sipped her lager and looked contrite.

'I *know* you're a heartless bitch,' said Janey with a faint smile. 'But at least you're honest about it. That's something, I suppose.'

'Don't try and make me feel guilty.' Maxine glanced down at her engagement ring. 'I didn't love Maurice, you know.'

'Surprise, surprise.'

'I liked him, though.' With a trace of defiance, she added, 'And I adored the fact that he had money. I think I managed to convince myself that ours would turn out to be like one of those arranged marriages, where love eventually grows. He was generous and kind, and I did so hate being broke . . .'

'But it didn't work out like that,' Janey observed, shielding her eyes with her forearm and gazing out over the sea. A pillarbox-red speedboat, skimming over the waves, was towing a water skier. Ridiculously, even after eighteen months, she still had to convince herself that it wasn't Alan before she could bring herself to look away.

'It might have worked, if Maurice hadn't been so boring.' Maxine shrugged, then grinned. 'And if I weren't so easily bored.'

Not for the first time, Janey wondered what it was like to be Maxine. Maybe her cool, calculating attitude to life wasn't such a bad thing after all. It might not be romantic, but at least it meant she spared herself the agonies of unrequited love and those endless, gut-wrenching months of despair.

I married for love, thought Janey, the cold emptiness invading her stomach as readily as it ever had. And look where it got me.

'Oh God,' cried Maxine, intuitively reading her sister's thoughts and grabbing her hand in consolation. 'I am a callous bitch! Now I've made you think about Alan.'

But Janey, managing a wry smile, shook her head. 'I think about him anyway. It's hardly something I'm likely to forget, after all.'

'I'm still an insensitive, clod-hopping prat,' insisted Maxine. Her expression contrite, she lowered her voice. 'And I haven't even asked how you're coping. Does it get better, or is it as hideous as ever?'

'Well, I'm not crying all over you.' Finishing her drink, Janey met her sister's concerned gaze and forced herself to sound cheerful. 'So that has to be an improvement, don't you think?'

'But it's still hard?'

'It *is* getting better,' she admitted. 'But the not knowing is the worst part of all. The awful limbo of not knowing what I am.' Pausing for a moment, she added bleakly, 'A widow or a deserted wife.'

Chapter 2

They were married on the first of May, the happiest day of Janey's life.

'I'm sure there's something I'm supposed to be doing today.' Alan, emerging from beneath the navy blue duvet with his blond hair sticking up at angles, sounded puzzled. 'What is it, the dentist . . .? Ouch!'

But Janey didn't let go of his big toe. 'Much worse,' she mocked. 'Much, *much* worse.'

'Aaargh, I remember now! The Registry Office. And you should be covering your eyes, you shameless female. You aren't supposed to see the blushing groom on the morning of his wedding.'

'Too late, I've already seen you.' Whisking back the duvet, she surveyed him solemnly. 'All of you.'

Alan grinned and reached out for her, pulling her back into bed and unfastening the belt of her flimsy dressing gown. 'In that case we may as well have a quickie. One last, glorious, pre-marital quickie. How many hours before we're married, Miss Vaughan?'

Janey glanced at her watch. 'Three.'

'Hmm,' he murmured, rolling on top of her and kissing the frantically beating pulse at the base of her neck. 'In that case, we might even have time for two.'

Once they'd torn themselves away from the bedroom to complete the formalities, Janey found she adored every moment and every aspect of being married. Each morning when she woke up she almost had to pinch herself to check that it was all real. But it always was, thank God, and the sheer joy of being Mrs Sinclair showed no signs of waning.

She enjoyed looking after their tiny flat, experimenting with new recipes and socializing with his surf-crazy friends. And because she was only twenty-five years old she enjoyed above all else knowing that they had the rest of their lives to spend together. Nothing need ever change.

No body was ever found.

'But something *must* have happened to him.' Janey, grief-stricken yet dry-eyed, simply couldn't believe that it hadn't. In an effort to convince the police, she uttered the words for what seemed like the hundredth time. 'He's my husband ... I know him ... he wouldn't just *disappear*.'

The police, however, whilst sympathetic, were less convinced. Every year, they explained, hundreds of people in Britain with no apparent problems or reasons to disappear, did precisely that, leaving behind them distraught families, endless unanswerable questions and countless shattered lives.

Janey's life was certainly shattered. On a sunny afternoon in July, after just fourteen months of marriage, her beloved husband had vanished without trace. Nothing had been taken from the flat and there were no clues as to the reason for his disappearance.

During the first few frantic days she'd pinned all her hopes on an accident, not serious enough to be life-threatening, just a bang on the head resulting in temporary amnesia. At any moment, she had fantasized helplessly, the phone would ring and when she picked it up she would hear his dear, familiar voice.

But although the discovery of Alan's body was what she'd most dreaded, as the weeks dragged into months she found herself almost beginning to wish that it would happen. She felt like a murderer, even thinking such a thing, but at least it would be conclusive. The torture of not knowing would be over. And – most deeply shaming of all – she would be spared the humiliation of thinking that her husband had vanished because he could no longer tolerate his life with her.

Nobody else had ever voiced this possibility aloud, of course, but whenever she was feeling particularly vulnerable Janey was only too easily able to imagine what was uppermost in their minds. As time passed she found herself, in turn, the object of macabre curiosity, whispered gossip and pity. And it was hard to decide which of these was worst.

Maxine drifted into the shop at ten-thirty the following morning, yawning and clutching a mug of tea. 'God your sofa's uncomfortable,' she grumbled, rubbing her back.

Janey, who had been up for over five hours, lifted an armful of yellow irises into a bucket and slid them into position between the gypsophila and the white roses. The shop had been busier than usual and she still had three wreaths to make up before midday.

'Sorry,' she replied wryly. It would never occur to

Maxine to bring her a cup of tea as well.

But Maxine was still massaging her back and pulling faces. 'I'll be a cripple by the end of the week.'

'Are you really planning to stay?'

'Of course!' She looked surprised. 'I'm not going back to Maurice-the-Righteous, and there's nothing to keep me in London. Besides,' she added dreamily, 'I'd forgotten how lovely it is down here. Much nicer than smelly old London. I think a summer by the sea would do me the world of good.'

'Hmm.'

'Oh come on, Janey. Don't look at me like that! It'll be fun; we can cheer each other up.'

Having consulted the notes on her clipboard, Janey began sorting out the flowers for the wreaths. 'You'll be too busy complaining about your back to have any fun,' she said brusquely. 'And having to listen to your endless whingeing is hardly going to cheer me up.'

'You don't want me to stay?' Maxine looked hurt and Janey experienced a twinge of guilt.

'I do,' she protested as the shop door swung open and Paula, having completed the morning's deliveries, dropped the keys to the van on the counter. 'Of course I'd like you to stay. It's just that the flat's so small, and I don't have a spare bedroom.'

'I see.' Maxine shrugged 'Well, that's OK. I'll go and see Mum.'

Janey looked doubtful. Their mother would only complain that nothing cramped one's style more effectively than a stray daughter hanging around the place. And Thea Vaughan's highly individual lifestyle didn't take kindly to cramping. She wasn't exactly the slippers-and-home-made-sponge-cake type.

But Maxine knew that as well as she did, so Janey didn't bother to voice these thoughts. Instead, she said, 'And you'd need some kind of job.'

'Oh God.' Maxine was looking gloomier by the second. Working had never been one of her strong points. 'I suppose I would. But what on earth can I do?'

Paula, who was a lot more thoughtful than Maxine, returned from the kitchen with two mugs of tea.

'Paula, this is my sister Maxine,' said Janey, seizing one of the mugs with relief. 'Now, take a good look at her and tell me what kind of work she might be able to cope with.'

Maxine, perched on the stool next to the counter with her long brown legs stretched out before her, gave the young girl an encouraging smile. But nothing fazed Paula.

'Here in Trezale, you mean?' As requested, she studied Maxine for several seconds. 'Well, selling your body's out for a start. Too many giggling girlies on the beach at this time of year, giving it away for free.'

Maxine burst out laughing. 'That's too bad.'

'Seriously,' protested Janey, weaving fronds of fern into the circular mesh base of the first wreath.

'Bar work?'

'Ugh.' Maxine cringed, rejecting the idea at once. 'Too hard on the feet.'

'Hotel receptionist?' suggested Paula, unperturbed. 'The Abbey's advertising in the paper this week.'

But Maxine shook her head. 'I'd have to be polite to ghastly tourists.'

'Nannying.' Paula looked pleased with herself. 'The family my mother cleans for is losing theirs. You could be a nanny.'

Maxine looked amused. 'Oh no I couldn't.'

But Janey's interest was aroused by this item of news. 'That's an idea!' she exclaimed, temporarily abandoning the wreath. 'You'd be able to live in. That way, you'd have a job and a place to stay. Max, it'd be great!'

'Apart from one small problem,' replied Maxine flatly. 'If there's one thing I hate more than tourists, it's children. Children and babies and nappies. Yuk!' she added with a shudder of revulsion. 'Especially nappies.'

'These two are a bit old for nappies,' said Paula, ever practical. 'Josh is nine and Ella's seven. I've met them a few times. They're nice kids.'

'And they'd be at school during the day,' put in Janey, her tone encouraging.

But Maxine, sensing that she was being ganged up on, pulled a face. 'I'm just not the nannyish type. I mean, for heaven's sake, do I look like Julie Andrews?'

Losing patience, Janey returned her attention to work. 'OK, you've made your point. You probably wouldn't have got the job anyway,' she added, unable to resist the dig. 'Most people prefer trained nannies and there'd be enough of those queuing up when they realize who they'll be working for.'

Needled by the insult, Maxine's brown eyes glittered. 'Why, who is it?' she demanded, ready to find fault with any prospective employer who wouldn't choose her.

'Guy Cassidy.' Janey shook droplets of water from the stems of a handful of yellow freesias. 'He moved into

Trezale House just over a year ago. He's a—'

'Photographer!' squealed Maxine, looking as if she was about to topple off her stool. 'Guy Cassidy,' she repeated faintly. '*The* Guy Cassidy? Janey, are you having me on?'

Bingo, thought Janey, exchanging glances with Paula and hiding her smile.

'Of course not.' She looked affronted. 'Why ever should I? And what difference does it make anyway? You hate kids. You just said so, yourself.'

'What difference does it make?' echoed Maxine, her eyebrows arching in disbelief. 'Janey, are you quite mad? It makes all the difference in the world. That man is *gorgeous* . . .'

Chapter 3

'God, this is hard work,' complained Guy, crumpling up yet another sheet of paper and lobbing it in the general direction of the wastepaper basket at the side of the bed. Fixing his son and daughter with a stern expression, he added, 'And it's too early in the day for this kind of thing. I don't know why you two can't write your own advert, anyway.'

Ella, squirming at his side, nudged his arm. 'Daddy, I can't spell!'

'And you hate those kind of adverts,' chided Josh, who was sprawled across the foot of the bed. Running his finger down the 'Help Wanted' columns of the slim magazine in which the finished advertisement would be placed, he found a shining example and began to read aloud in an exaggerated baby voice.

'Hello, my name is Bunty and I am two yearth old. I need thomebody to look after me whilst Mummy and Daddy are working. We live in a big houthe in Thurrey, with a thwimming pool. You muthn't thmoke . . .'

'OK, OK,' said Guy with resignation. 'So it wasn't one of my better ideas. Maybe I'll just put, "Two spoilt brats require stern battleaxe of a nanny to feed them cold porridge and beat them daily." How about that?'

Ella giggled. 'I don't like cold porridge.'

'You should say, "Widow with two children needs kind nanny",' suggested Josh, who had been giving the matter some thought.

'Widower,' Guy corrected him. 'Widows are female. Men are called widowers.'

'I know why you're a man,' Ella chimed in. Josh, at the foot of the bed, grinned.

It was too early in the day for this, too. Guy, closing his eyes for a moment and mentally bracing himself, said, 'Go on then. Why am I a man?'

'Because you haven't any bosoms on your chest,' declared his daughter with an air of importance. 'And you don't wear a bra.'

It was four-thirty when the doorbell rang. Berenice, the soon-to-be-married departing nanny, had taken Ella into St Ives for the afternoon on a shopping trip. Guy was busy in the darkroom, developing black and white prints, when Josh knocked on the door and informed him that he had a visitor.

'She said it was important,' he told Guy, his forehead creasing in a frown as he struggled to remember. 'I don't know who she is, but I'm sure I've seen her somewhere before.'

Maxine was standing before the sitting-room window, admiring the stupendous view of clifftops and sea. When she turned and smiled at Guy, and came towards him with her hand outstretched, he realized at once why his son had thought her familiar yet been unable to place her.

'Mr Cassidy?' she said demurely. 'My name is Vaughan. Maxine Vaughan. It's kind of you to see me.'

She was here in his house, thought Guy with inward amusement. He didn't really have much choice. But he was, at the same time, intrigued. Maxine Vaughan was an undeniably attractive girl in her mid-twenties. Her long, corn-blond hair was pulled back from her face in a neat plait, her make-up carefully unobtrusive. The dark green jacket and skirt were a couple of sizes too big for her and she was wearing extremely sensible shoes. It was all very convincing, very plausible. Guy was impressed by the extent of the effort she had made.

'My pleasure,' he replied easily, taking her proffered hand and registering short fingernails, a clear nail polish and – oh dear, first sign of a slip-up – a genuine Cartier wristwatch. 'How can I help you, Miss Vaughan?'

Maxine took a deep, steadying breath and hoped her palms weren't damp. She'd known, of course, that Guy Cassidy was gorgeous, but in the actual flesh he was even more devastatingly attractive than she'd imagined. With those thickly lashed, deep blue eyes, incredible cheekbones and white teeth offset by a dark tan, he was almost too perfect. But the threat of perfection was redeemed by a quirky smile, slightly crooked eyebrows and that famously tousled black hair.

He exuded sex appeal without even trying, she realized. He possessed an indefinable charisma. Not to mention a body to die for.

'I'm hoping we can help each other,' said Maxine. Then, because her knees were on the verge of giving way, she added, 'Would you mind if I sat down?'

'Please do.' Having concluded that she must be either a journalist or a model desperate for a break, Guy gently mimicked her formal style of speech. Either way, he would give her no more than ten minutes; he was all for a spot of personal enterprise but her unexpected arrival wasn't exactly well timed. He had work to do, phone calls to make and a nine-year-old son demanding to be taken for a swim before dinner.

He glanced at his watch. Maxine, sensing his veiled impatience, took another deep breath and plunged in. 'Right, Mr Cassidy, I understand you'll shortly be requiring a replacement nanny for your children. And since I myself am an experienced nanny, I'd like to offer my services.'

It was a good start, but the rest of the interview wasn't going according to plan, she realized several minutes later. And she hadn't the faintest idea why not.

On the surface, at least, Guy Cassidy was asking the appropriate questions and she was supplying faultless replies, but at the same time she had a horrible feeling he wasn't taking her seriously. Worse, that he was inwardly laughing at her.

'They're in Buenos Aires now,' she continued valiantly, as he studied the glowing references which she'd slaved for an entire hour to produce. 'Otherwise I'd still be with them, of course. The children were adorable and Angelo and Marisa treated me more as a friend than an employee.'

But her potential employer, instead of appearing suitably impressed, was glancing once more at his watch.

'I'm sure they did,' he replied. Rising to his feet, he

shot her a brief smile. 'And it was thoughtful of you to consider us, Miss . . . er . . . Vaughan. But I don't think you're quite what we're looking for.'

Maxine's guard slipped. 'Why not?' she wailed, remaining rooted to her chair. 'I've shown you my references. They're brilliant! What can possibly be wrong with me?'

Guy, enjoying himself, maintained a serious expression. 'You're too dowdy.'

'But I don't have to be dowdy,' said Maxine wildly. She knew she shouldn't have worn Janey's horrible suit. 'I'm not usually dowdy at all!'

'OK.' Gesturing for her to calm down, he continued. 'You're too prim and proper.'

'I am not prim!' Maxine almost shrieked. 'Please, you have to believe me. These aren't my own clothes . . . I'm not the least bit proper either and I *hate* these shoes!'

But Guy hadn't finished. Fixing her with his deadpan gaze, he said remorselessly, 'And you're a liar, Miss Vaughan. Which wouldn't set a particularly good example to my children. I'm afraid I can't employ someone who is dishonest.'

Maxine felt her cheeks burn. He was bluffing, he had to be. Stiffly, she replied, 'I don't know what you mean.'

'Don't you?' This time he actually smiled. 'In that case, wait here. I'll just go and find my son.'

He returned less than two minutes later with the boy in tow. Although nine-year-old Josh Cassidy had straight, white-blond hair in contrast to his father, Maxine was struck by the similarity of their extraordinary dark blue eyes.

'Hello, Josh,' she said, dredging up a brave smile and wondering why he was staring at her in that odd way.

But Guy was handing his son a large brown envelope. 'Here,' he said casually. 'I developed that film you gave me earlier. Take a look at these prints, Josh, and tell me how you think they've turned out.'

Maxine spotted the offending item a fraction of a second before Josh. Having tipped the photographs out of the envelope and spread them across the coffee table, he was still studying them intently, one at a time, when she let out a strangled cry and made a grab for it.

Guy, standing behind her, whisked the photograph from her grasp and handed it, in turn, to his son.

'Golly,' said Josh with a grin. Staring at Maxine, who was by this time redder than ever, he added, 'I thought I knew you from somewhere!'

'And the moral of this story,' she muttered sulkily, 'is never trust a member of the *paparazzi*.'

'You look different today.' Studying the glossy ten-by-eight at close quarters and looking pleased with himself, he said, 'I think I prefer you in the white dress. It's a good photograph, isn't it?'

It was a bit too good for Maxine's liking. No wonder Guy Cassidy had been able to recognize her. There she was, captured for posterity in that stupid wedding gown, laughing as she clambered out of the panda car and not even realizing that her skirts had bunched up to reveal white stocking tops and a glimpse of suspender. And the expression on Tom-the-policeman's face, she observed with resignation, didn't help. He was positively leering.

'Hang on a minute.' Josh was looking puzzled again.

'If you got married yesterday, why aren't you on a honeymoon?'

'I wasn't getting married,' said Maxine impatiently. '*Or* arrested. It was a fancy-dress party, that's all. Then I ran out of petrol on the way home and the policeman gave me a lift.' Fixing Guy with a mutinous glare, she added, 'It was nothing sinister, for heaven's sake.'

He shrugged. 'Nevertheless, I'm sure you understand why I can't consider you for the job. I'm sorry, Miss Vaughan, but I do have the moral welfare of my children to take into account.'

'At least I'm not dowdy and prim,' she muttered in retaliation.

'Oh no.' This time, as he drew a slim white envelope from his shirt pocket, he laughed. 'I'll grant you that. But I'm afraid I have work to do, so maybe I could ask my son to show you out. And Josh, I've written out the advert. If you run down with it now, you'll just catch the last post.'

'Well?' said Guy, when his son returned twenty minutes later.

'She gave me five pounds and a Cornetto.' Josh looked momentarily worried. 'Was that enough?'

Amused by his son's concern, Guy ruffled his blond hair. 'Oh, I'd say so. Five pounds and a Cornetto in exchange for a first-class stamp and an empty envelope. It sounds like a fair enough swap to me.'

Chapter 4

The response to the advertisement when it eventually appeared the following week wasn't startling, but it was manageable. Guy preferred to do his own hunting as a result of the futile experiences he'd had three years earlier when he'd tried using an agency. Having also learned to expect applications from star-struck girls and would-be second wives, he had omitted his name from the advertisement.

But last time he had struck lucky. Berenice, profoundly unimpressed by his celebrity status, had fitted the bill to perfection. Stolid, hard-working and not the least bit glamorous, what she lacked in sparkle she'd more than made up for in dependability. Guy, whose work required him to travel abroad at short notice, was able to do so without a qualm, safe in the knowledge that his children would be competently looked after by someone who cared for them and who would never let him down.

It had come as something of a shock, therefore, when Berenice had shyly informed him that she was shortly to be married, and that since her future husband had been offered a job in Newcastle, she would be leaving Trezale.

Guy hadn't even been aware of the existence of a man in her life, but discretion had always been one of Berenice's major attributes – as he had himself on numerous occasions had cause to be thankful for. The courtship, it appeared, had been conducted on her days off. And although she was sorry to be leaving, she now had her own life to pursue. She hoped he wouldn't have too much trouble finding a replacement.

Interviewing the half dozen or so applicants, however, was both tedious and time-consuming. What Guy wanted was a clone of Berenice with maybe a sense of humour thrown in for good measure.

What he got, instead, was a succession of girls in whom it was only too easy to find fault. Josh and Ella, dutifully trotted out to meet each of them in turn, were equally critical.

'She smelled,' said Ella, wrinkling her nose in memory of Mary-from-Exeter.

'She laughed like a sheep,' Josh observed bluntly when Doreen from Doncaster had departed.

Neither of them could make head nor tail of Gudren-from-Sweden's singsong accent.

'She's all right, I suppose.' Josh, referring to another contender, sounded doubtful. 'But why did she have a bottle of vodka in her handbag?'

They finally settled on Maureen-from-Wimbledon, a pale, eager-to-please twenty-five-year-old who was keen to move in and start work as soon as possible. Carefully highlighting her good points – she didn't smell, possess an irritating laugh or an incomprehensible foreign accent – Guy prayed the children wouldn't make mincemeat of her before she had a chance to find her feet. She barely seemed capable of looking after herself, but maybe she'd just been too nervous to create a dazzling first impression.

And at least, he thought dryly, recalling the very first candidate, she hadn't fluttered inch-long eyelashes at him, surreptitiously edged up her short skirt and treated him to a flash of emerald-green knickers each time she'd crossed and re-crossed her legs.

Janey was working in the shop when Guy Cassidy and his children walked in.

'I need some flowers,' he said without preamble, removing his dark glasses and surveying the myriad buckets lined up against the wall. 'For a wedding reception next Saturday. If I place the order now, would you be able to bring them to my house on the Friday afternoon and arrange them?'

'Of course I would.' Janey was delighted. Men for whom money was no object were definitely her kind of customer. Reaching for her clipboard she said, 'Tell me what type of arrangements you have in mind and which kind of flowers you think you'd like.'

Flowers, however, evidently weren't Guy Cassidy's strong point. Looking momentarily helpless, he frowned and said, 'Well, blue ones?'

'Berenice likes daffodils,' supplied Ella, tugging his white shirt sleeve. 'Remember? We picked her some for her birthday and she said they were her favourite.'

Janey had already guessed that the flowers were for

Berenice's wedding but now that Guy's daughter had given her the excuse she needed, she raised her eyebrows and said, 'You mean Berenice Taylor? Oh, I'm doing her bridal bouquet.'

'Put it on my bill,' said Guy casually, producing his wallet and pulling out a wad of twenties. With a self-deprecating smile he added, 'She's been our nanny for the last three years. Holding the reception at our house is my present to her.'

'How lovely.' Janey returned his smile, then gave Ella an apologetic shrug. 'I'm afraid daffodils are out of season now, but maybe we could see which flowers Berenice has chosen for her bouquet and work from there. I'll have to check to be sure, but I think she decided on a yellow and white colour scheme. Yes, that's it . . . white roses and sweet peas with mimosa.'

Guy Cassidy didn't even flinch when she eventually wrote down the estimated cost of the work involved.

'As long as it looks good,' he said good-humouredly, dealing the notes on to the counter. Then, as an apparent afterthought, he glanced down at his children and added, 'Actually, whilst we're here, why don't you two pick out a bunch of something-or-other for your new nanny? She's arriving tomorrow afternoon and some nice flowers will make her feel welcome.'

Josh liked the green, earthy smell of the shop but he was bored sick with flowers.

'They haven't got dandelions or deadly nightshade,' he said, his tone dismissive.

'Or stinging nettles,' put in Ella with a smirk.

Poor new nanny, thought Janey. Without speaking, she

selected a generous bunch of baby-pink spray carnations, wrapped them in pink-and-silver paper and calmly handed them to Josh.

Appalled, he said, 'Boys don't carry flowers,' and shoved them into Ella's unsuspecting arms.

Janey, watching the expression on his face, burst out laughing.

And Guy, who had in turn been watching her, said, 'Of course. You're Maxine Vaughan's sister.'

'Oh help!' said Janey. 'Not necessarily. Not if it means you cancelling the order.'

He looked amused. 'Don't panic, I don't think I could face the prospect of going into another shop and starting all over again.'

'But how did you know?' She flushed. 'We aren't a bit alike.'

Tilting his head to one side and studying her in greater detail, he disagreed. 'Physically, there are similarities. She's skinnier . . . blonder . . . wears more make-up than you do, but the resemblance is still there. And you have the same laugh.'

This must all be part of the famous Cassidy charm, thought Janey. By cleverly reversing the usual comparisons he had actually managed to make her sound more attractive than Maxine. What a neat trick.

'And at least you've managed to find a new nanny.' Changing the subject, she nodded at the gift-wrapped carnations. With an encouraging smile at Josh and Ella, she said, 'Is she nice?'

'She's a wimp,' replied Josh flatly.

'But honest,' Guy interjected, shooting him a warning

look before returning his attention to Janey. 'Unlike your sister.'

'Look, Maxine isn't as bad as you think,' she bridled, springing instinctively to her defence. 'She really wanted to work for you. And children adore her. If you ask me, you could have done a lot worse.'

'Of course children adore her,' drawled Guy. 'She bribes them with money and ice cream.'

Josh brightened. 'I liked her. The lady in the wedding dress, you mean? She was good fun.'

'She had good references too,' Guy remarked tersely, 'but that still doesn't make her ideal nanny material. Has she found another job yet?'

Janey shook her head. Maxine's efforts in that department had been half-hearted to say the least. 'Not yet.'

'Hardly surprising,' said Guy, his blue eyes narrowing with amused derision. 'Tell her from me, the next time she writes out her own references not to use violet ink. At least, not if she's planning to trot off to the interview with a smudge of it on the inside of her wrist.'

Chapter 5

Janey was leaning into the back of the van, stretching for the box of flowers which had slid up to the front and wedged itself behind the passenger seat, when Bruno gave her sticking-out bottom a friendly pat.

'You'll do that gorgeous body of yours an injury,' he said, nudging her out of the way and taking over. 'Come on, leave it to me.'

She flushed and smiled, and glanced quickly over her shoulder in case anyone was watching. Bruno, a notorious flirt, didn't mean anything by the playful gesture, but she still wouldn't like Nina to get the wrong idea.

Intercepting her glance as he carried the box into the empty restaurant, he winked. 'It's OK, she's still asleep.'

'*She* might be,' Janey protested. 'But you know what people are like for gossip around here.'

'Exactly. And they know what *I'm* like,' Bruno countered with an unrepentant grin. 'They'd be far more suspicious if I didn't lay a finger on you. Then they'd really know they had something to gossip about.'

He was pouring them both an espresso, as he invariably did when she arrived with the twice-weekly delivery of flowers for the restaurant.

It was ridiculous, thought Janey; since nothing had ever happened between them, there was no reason at all why she should feel guilty. But she felt it just the same, because no matter how many times she told herself that circumstances made him the most wildly unsuitable choice, her muddled emotions had taken charge and made the decision for her.

At the age of twenty-eight, she had developed a humiliating crush on Bruno Parry-Brent. And all she could do now was hope and pray that it would burn itself out before anything did happen.

In the meantime, however, it was so nice to feel human again, after all the endless months of aching deep-frozen nothingness. And Bruno was undeniably good company. A ladies' man in every sense of the word, he possessed that happy knack of being able to talk about anything under the sun. Even more miraculously he was a great listener as well, always genuinely interested in hearing other people's views. He paid attention, asked questions, never appeared bored.

It was, of course the great secret of his success with the opposite sex. Janey had watched him at work in the restaurant before now, weaving his magic in the simplest and most effective way possible. Real conversation with a real man was a powerful aphrodisiac and the women succumbed to it in droves, as Janey herself had done. But it was better this way, she felt, at least there was safety in numbers.

'New earrings,' he observed, bringing the tiny white cups of espresso to the table where she was sitting and leaning forward to examine them more closely. 'Very chic, Janey. Are those real pearls?'

'They're Maxine's.' Self-consciously, she fingered the slightly over-the-top earrings and prayed he wouldn't guess that he was the reason she was wearing them. Even Maxine had raised her eyebrows when she'd caught Janey digging around in her jewellery box. 'Earrings, lip gloss *and* mascara?' she'd remarked in arch tones. 'Darling, are you sure there isn't something you'd like to tell me?'

But diplomacy was another of Bruno's assets and, if he'd noticed such additional details himself, he was too nice to comment on them. Instead, stretching out in his seat and pushing his fingers through his long, sun-streaked hair, he said, 'I was going to ask you about Maxine. So you haven't managed to get rid of her yet?'

Janey pulled a face. 'She won't go, she won't look for work and she's so untidy: it's like living with a huge, unmanageable wolfhound.'

'But house-trained, presumably.' Bruno grinned. 'You haven't told me yet, what does she look like?'

'Maxine?' As she sipped her coffee, Guy Cassidy's words came back to her. 'Skinnier, blonder and noisier than me.' Then, because it sounded catty when she said it, she added shamefacedly, 'And much prettier.'

'Hmm. Well, we're pretty busy here at the moment. Maybe I could offer her a couple of evenings a week behind the bar.'

'She wouldn't do it,' said Janey hurriedly. 'Her feet, they'd ache . . .'

Bruno shrugged, dismissing the suggestion. 'Just a thought. But you'll have to bring her down here one evening, I'd like to meet her.'

Of course he would. And she could only too easily imagine Maxine's reaction when she, in turn, met Bruno Parry-Brent. They were two of a very particular kind.

'I will.' Janey tried not to sound unhappy, evasive. She had no intention of introducing them but Maxine had a talent for seeking out . . . well, talent, and Trezale wasn't a large town. It would surely be only a matter of time before she discovered Bruno for herself.

'Oh come on, cheer up.' He took her hand and gave it a reassuring squeeze. 'We all have our crosses to bear. Look at me, I have Nina!'

Janey tried not to laugh. He really was disgraceful.

'And where would you be without her?' she countered. Bruno and Nina made an odd couple, certainly, but after ten years together they still seemed happy enough in their own way. It wasn't something Bruno had ever discussed in detail but, as far as Janey could figure out, Nina didn't ask any questions and in return he was discreet. Indeed, although he was such a notorious flirt, she didn't even know whether he actually had affairs.

'Where would I be without Nina?' he repeated, teasing her. 'Probably in big trouble, because she'd have a contract out on me.'

Janey burst out laughing. Nina was the most placid woman she'd ever met. She doubted whether Nina could even summon the energy to read a contract, let alone organise taking one out.

'You'd be lost without her,' she told him in mock-severe tones. Rising to her feet, she smoothed her pink skirt over her hips. 'I'd better be getting back to the shop. Thanks for the coffee.'

Bruno grinned, unrepentant. 'Thanks for the pep talk. If you bring your sister down here maybe I'll be able to return the favour.'

'Hmm,' said Janey, renewing her vow to keep Maxine as far away from the restaurant as humanly possible. She could imagine what kind of favour he had in mind.

Maureen-from-Wimbledon wasn't on the four-o'clock train.

Guy, who had cut short a session in the darkroom and driven hell for leather in order to reach the station in time, couldn't believe it. If she'd missed the train at Paddington, she could have bloody well phoned and let him know, he thought furiously. And now what was he supposed to do, hang around on the platform and wait an hour for the next train to roll in?

But he hadn't waited and the would-be nanny hadn't phoned. By eight-thirty, when there was still no sign of her, he dialled the London number she had given him.

'Oh dear,' said Berenice, thankful that at least Ella, whom she had put to bed half an hour earlier, wasn't there to witness his language.

Josh, who was used to it, wondered if this meant his prayers had actually been answered. 'What is it, Dad?'

'No wonder she was in such a hurry to come and live down here,' Guy seethed, pouring himself a hefty Scotch and downing it in one go. 'I've just spoken to her mother. The lying, conniving bitch was arrested this morning and charged with credit-card-fraud! This is all I bloody need . . .'

'Does that mean she isn't going to be our nanny?' said

Josh, just to make absolutely sure.

Guy raised his eyes to heaven. 'I knew that expensive private education of yours would come in useful one day. Yes Josh, it means she isn't going to be your nanny.'

Hooray, thought Josh. Aloud he said, 'Oh. So what are we going to do?'

'Only one thing for it.' It was Wednesday night, Berenice was getting married on Saturday and he had to fly to Paris for a prestigious calendar shoot on Monday morning. 'We cancel Berenice's wedding.'

'You'll have to answer it,' said Maxine, when the doorbell rang. She was wearing bright orange toe separators and the crimson nail polish on her splayed toes was still wet. 'I look like a duck.'

'You look like a duck,' Guy Cassidy remarked when Janey showed him into the sitting room two minutes later.

Maxine, sitting on the floor with her bare legs stretched out in front of her, carried on eating her Mars bar. 'Just as well,' she replied equably. 'It means your insults roll off my back.'

Mystified by his unexpected appearance on her doorstep, Janey said, 'Would you like a cup of tea?'

'Thanks.' He smiled at her and lowered himself into an empty armchair. To Maxine, whose attention was fixed upon an old re-run of *Inspector Morse*, he said, 'Haven't you seen this one before? Lewis did it.'

Her gaze didn't waver from the television screen. With thinly veiled sarcasm she countered, 'Who's lying now?'

Janey fled to the safety of the kitchen.

'Go on then,' said Maxine eventually, when she had

finished the Mars bar and dropped the wrapper on to the coffee table. 'Tell me why you're here.'

There wasn't much point in beating around the bush. Guy said, 'The job. If you still want it, it's yours.'

'You've been stood up, then.'

He nodded.

'Gosh,' said Maxine, her expression innocent. 'You must be desperate.'

His mouth twitched as he allowed her her brief moment of triumph. 'I am.'

'And here am I, such an all-round bad influence . . .'

'You might well be,' he replied dryly, 'but your sister put in a few good words on your behalf and for some bizarre reason my son has taken a liking to you.'

'And you're desperate,' Maxine repeated for good measure, but this time he ignored the jibe.

'So are you interested, or not?'

'We-ll.' Tilting her head to one side, she appeared to consider the offer. 'We haven't discussed terms, yet.'

'We haven't discussed your funny webbed feet either,' he pointed out. 'But live and let live is my motto.'

Janey had been eavesdropping like mad from the kitchen. Unable to endure the suspense a moment longer, she seized the mugs of tea and erupted back into the sitting room.

'She's interested,' she declared, ignoring Maxine's frantic signals and thrusting one of the mugs into Guy Cassidy's hand. 'She'll take the job. When would you like her to start?'

Chapter 6

Guy Cassidy was twenty-three years old when he met Véronique Charpentier. It was the wettest, windiest day of the year and he was making his way home after a gruelling fourteen-hour shift in the photographic studios where his brief had been to make a temperamental forty-four-year-old actress look thirty again.

Now the traffic was almost at a standstill and his car was stuck behind a bus. All he could think of was getting back to his flat and sinking into a hot bath with a cold beer. In less than two hours he was supposed to be taking Amanda, his current girlfriend, to a party in Chelsea. It wasn't a prospect that particularly appealed to him but she had insisted on going.

There was no room to overtake when the bus came to a shuddering halt and began to spill out passengers. Guy amused himself by watching them scurry like wind-blown ants across the pavement towards the relative shelter of the shop canopies lining the high street.

The last passenger to disembark, however, didn't make it. As her long, white-blond hair whipped around her face she struggled to control her charcoal-grey umbrella. At the exact moment the umbrella flipped inside out, she stumbled against the kerb and crashed to the ground. Her carrier bag of shopping spilled into the gutter. The inverted umbrella, carried by the wind, cartwheeled off into the distance and a wave of muddy water from the wheels of the now-departing bus cascaded over her crumpled body.

By the time Guy reached her, she was dragging herself into a sitting position and muttering 'Bloody Eenglish' under her breath.

'Are you hurt?' he asked, helping her carefully to her feet. There was a lot of mud, but no sign of blood.

Her expression wary, she shook her wet blond head, then cast a sorrowful glance in the direction of the spilled carrier bag lying in a puddle. 'Not me. But my croissants, I theenk, are drowned. Bloody Eenglish!'

'Come on.' Smiling at her choice of words, he led her towards his car. When she was installed in the passenger seat inspecting the holes in the knees of her sheer, dark tights, he said, 'Why bloody English?'

'Eenglish weather. Stupid Eenglish umbrella,' she explained, gesticulating at the torrential rain. 'And how many kind Eenglish people stopped to 'elp when I fell over? Tssch!'

'I stopped to help you, he remarked mildly, slipping the engine into gear as a cacophony of irritated hooting started up behind them.

The girl, her face splashed with mud and rain, sighed. 'Of course you did. And now I'm sitting in your car and I don't even know you. It would be just my luck, I theenk, to get murdered by a crazy person. Maybe you should stop and let me out.'

'I can't stand the sight of blood,' Guy assured her. 'And I'm not crazy either. Why don't you tell me where you live and let me drive you home? No strings, I promise.'

She frowned, apparently considering the offer. Finally, turning to face him and looking puzzled, she said, 'I don't understand. What ees thees no strings? You mean like in string vests?'

Her name was Véronique, she was eighteen years old and she lived in an attic which had been shabbily converted into a bedsitter but which had the advantage – in daylight at least – of overlooking Wandsworth Common.

As a reward for not murdering her on the way home, Guy was invited up the five flights of stairs for coffee. By the time his cup was empty he had fallen in love with its maker and forgotten that Amanda even existed.

'Let me take you out to dinner,' he said, wondering what he would do if Véronique turned him down. To his eternal relief, however, she smiled.

'All wet and muddy, like thees? Or may I take a bath first?'

Grinning back at her, Guy said, 'I really don't mind.'

'It is best if I take a bath, I theenk,' Véronique replied gravely. Rising to her feet, she gestured towards a pile of magazines stacked against the battered, dark blue sofa. 'I won't be long. Please, can you amuse yourself for a while? They are French magazines, but maybe you could look at the pictures.'

The tiny bathroom adjoined the living room. Guy smiled to himself as he heard her carefully locking the door which separated them. The magazines, he discovered, were well-thumbed copies of French *Vogue*, one of which contained a series of photographs he himself had taken during last spring's Paris collections. The thought of Véronique poring over pages which bore his own minuscule by-line cheered him immensely. It was, he felt, a good omen for their relationship.

But the magazines were also evidently a luxury for her. The bedsitter, though charmingly adorned with touches of her own personality, was itself unprepossessing and sparsely furnished. The sofa, strewn with hand-embroidered cushions, doubled as a bed. Strategically situated lamps drew the attention away from peeling wallpaper and the posters on the wall, he guessed, were similarly positioned in order to conceal patches of damp. Neither the cinnamon-scented candles or the bowls of pot pourri could eradicate the slight underlying mustiness which pervaded the air.

And there was no television; a box of good quality writing paper and a small transistor radio seemed to comprise her only forms of entertainment. Guy, exploring the meticulously tidy room in detail, greedy to discover everything there was to know about Véronique Charpentier, felt an almost overwhelming urge to bundle her up and whisk her away from the chilly, depressing house, to tell her that she no longer needed to live like this, that he would take care of her . . .

And when she emerged from the bathroom twenty-five minutes later, he actually had to bite his tongue in order not to say the words aloud. Mud-free, simply dressed in a thin black polo-necked sweater, pale grey wool skirt and black tights, she looked stunning. The white-blond hair, freshly brushed, hung past her shoulders. Silver-grey eyes regarded him with amusement. She was wearing pastel pink lipstick and *Je Reviens*.

'OK?' she said cheerfully.

'OK!' Guy nodded in agreement.

'Good.' Véronique smiled at him. 'I theenk we shall have a nice evening.'

'I know we will.'

She blew out the cinnamon-scented candles and picked up her bag. 'Can I make a confession to you?'

'What?' Guy's heart sank. He couldn't imagine what she was about to say. He didn't want to hear it.

But Véronique went ahead anyway. 'I theenk I begin to be glad,' she confided, lowering her voice to a whisper, 'that I fell off the bus in the rain. Maybe Eenglish weather isn't so bloody after all.'

Oliver Cassidy wasn't amused when his son informed him, three weeks later, that he was going to marry Véronique Charpentier.

'For God's sake,' he said sharply, lighting a King Edward cigar and not bothering to lower his voice. 'This is ridiculous. She's eighteen years old. She's French. You don't even know her.'

'Of course I do!' Guy retaliated. 'I love her and she loves me. And I'm not here to ask your permission to marry her, because that's going to happen anyway. I've already booked the Register Office.'

'Then you're a bloody fool!' Oliver glared at him. 'She's in love with your money, your career; why on earth can't you just live with her for a few months? That'll get her out of your system fast enough.'

'There's no need to shout,' said Guy. Véronique was in the next room.

'Why not? Why can't I shout?' His father's eyebrows knitted ferociously together. 'I want her to hear me! She should know that not everyone is as gullible as you obviously are. If you ask me, she's nothing but a clever, scheming foreigner making the most of the opportunity of a lifetime.'

'But I'm not asking you,' Guy replied, his tone icy. 'And Véronique isn't someone I want to get out of my system. She's going to be my wife, whether you like it or not.'

Oliver Cassidy turned purple. 'You're making a damn fool of yourself.'

'I'm not.' His son, sickened by his inability even to try to understand, turned away. 'You are.'

They were married at Caxton Hall and Véronique accompanied Guy on a working trip to Switzerland in lieu of a honeymoon. Upon their return, she moved her few possessions into his apartment, gave up her job in a busy north London delicatessen and said, 'So! What do we do next?'

Joshua was born ten months later, a perfect composite of his parents with Guy's dark blue eyes and Véronique's white-blond hair. With no family of her own, Véronique said sadly, 'It's such a shame. Your father hates me, I know, but he should at least have the chance to love his grandson.'

Guy, though not naturally vindictive, wasn't interested

in a reconciliation. 'He knows where we live,' he replied in dismissive tones. 'If he wanted to see Josh, he could. But he clearly doesn't want to, so forget him.'

The arrival of Ella two years later brought further happiness. Contrary to Véronique's plans that this time the child should have silver-grey eyes and dark curly hair, she was a carbon copy of Josh. Guy, his career sky-rocketing, took so many photographs of his family that they had to be stored in suitcases rather than albums. It wasn't until he received a large Manila envelope through the post, addressed to him in familiar handwriting and containing a selection of the choicest photographs, that he realized Véronique had sent them to his father. 'Don't ever do that again,' he said furiously, hurling the envelope to the ground. 'He doesn't deserve anything. I've told you before . . . just forget him!'

But Veronique could not forget. All children were supposed to have grandparents, and her enduring dream was that her own children should know and love the only living grandparent left to them. As the years passed and the rift remained as deep and unbridgeable as ever, she became quietly determined to do something about it. Both her husband and her father-in-law were clearly too proud to make the first move but for Josh and Ella's sakes she was prepared to take the risk. If Oliver Cassidy were to come face to face with his grandchildren, she reasoned, the rift would instantly be healed. It would be a *fait accompli*, following which human nature would take its course and all would be well.

Knowing that her fiercely protective husband would never allow her to make the initial move towards reconciliation, however, she planned her campaign with secretive, military precision. Oliver Cassidy was at that time living in Bristol, so she waited until Guy was away on a two-week assignment in New York before booking herself and the children into an hotel less than a mile from her father-in-law's address.

By the time of their arrival at the station, Véronique's head was pounding and she was feeling sick with apprehension, but there was no backing out now. For the sake of Josh and Ella she struggled to maintain a bright front. At their hotel, overlooking the Clifton Suspension Bridge, she treated them to ice-cream sundaes on the sweeping terrace and said gaily, 'Eat them all up, and don't spill any on your clothes. We're going to see a very nice man and he might not be so impressed with chocolate ice-cream stains.'

Josh, six years old and enjoying the adventure immensely, said, 'Who is he?'

But Véronique, whose headache was worsening by the minute, simply smiled and shook her head.

'Just a very nice man, my darling, who lives not far from here. You'll like him, I'm sure.'

Josh wasn't so sure he would. The big house to which his mother took them was owned by a man who didn't look the least bit pleased to see them. In Josh's experience, very-nice-people smiled a lot, hugged you and, perhaps, gave you sweets. This man, with fierce grey eyebrows like caterpillars, wasn't even saying hello.

'Mr Cassidy,' said Véronique quickly. It was an unpromising start and her palms were sticky with perspiration: 'I have brought Josh and Ella to see you

. . . I thought you would like to meet them . . . your family—'

Oliver Cassidy didn't like surprises. Neither did he appreciate emotional blackmail. A man who seldom admitted that he might be in the wrong, he saw no reason to revise his opinion of his only son's French wife. In her flowered dress and with her straight blond hair hanging loose around her shoulders, she still looked like a teenager, which didn't help. And as far as he was concerned, the fact that she thought she could simply turn up out of the blue and expect some kind of fairytale reunion proved beyond all doubt that she was either stupid or staggeringly naïve.

'What's the matter?' he said coldly, eyeing her white face with displeasure and ignoring the two children at her side. His gesture encompassed both the Georgian house and the sloping, sculptured lawns. 'Afraid they'll miss out on all this when I'm gone?'

'No!' Appalled by her father-in-law's cruelty, Véronique took a faltering step backwards. 'No,' she cried again, pleading with him to understand. 'They are your grandchildren, your family! This isn't about any inheritance . . .'

'Good!' snapped Oliver Cassidy as Ella, clinging to her mother's hand, began to cry. 'Because they won't be seeing any of it anyway.'

'I feel sick,' Ella sobbed. 'Mummy, I feel—'

'And now, I have an urgent appointment.' He glanced at his watch in order to give credence to the lie. Then, with a look of absolute horror, he took an abrupt step sideways.

But it was too late. Ella, who had eaten far too much chocolate ice-cream, had already thrown up all over her grandfather's highly polished, handmade shoes.

It wasn't until they were back at the hotel that Véronique realized she was ill. The headache and nausea which she had earlier put down to nervousness had worsened dramatically and she was aching all over.

By early evening a raging fever had taken its grip and she was barely able to haul herself out of bed in order to phone downstairs and ask for a doctor to be called. Summer flu, she thought, fighting tears of exhaustion and the shivers which racked her entire body like jolts of electricity. Just what she needed. A fitting end to a disastrous visit. Had she been superstitious she might almost have believed that Oliver Cassidy had cast a malevolent jinx in order to pay her back for her impudence.

The doctor, however, took an altogether more serious view of the situation.

'Mrs Cassidy, I'm afraid we're going to have to get you into hospital,' he said when he had completed his examination.

'*Mais c'est impossible!*' Véronique cried, her fluent English deserting her in her weakened state. '*Mes enfants . . .*'

But it wasn't a suggestion, it was a statement. An ambulance was called and by midnight Véronique was being admitted to the neurological ward of one of Bristol's largest hospitals. The hotel manager himself, she was repeatedly assured, was contacting her husband in New

York and had in the meantime assumed full responsibility for her children who would remain at the hotel and be well looked after for as long as necessary.

By the time Guy arrived at the hospital twenty-seven hours later, Véronique had lapsed into a deep coma. As the doctors had suspected, tests confirmed that she was suffering from a particularly virulent strain of meningitis and although they were doing everything possible the outlook wasn't good.

'Mummy said we were going to see a nice man,' said Josh, his dark eyes brimming with tears as Guy eased the truth from him 'But he wasn't nice at all, he was horrid. He shouted at Mummy, then Ella was sick on his shoes. And when we came back to the hotel Mummy wasn't very well. Daddy, can we go home now?'

It was as Guy had suspected. He didn't contact his father. And when Véronique died three days later without regaining consciousness, he saw no reason to change his mind. Oliver Cassidy might not have caused Véronique's death but he had undoubtedly ensured that her last few waking hours should have been as miserable as possible. For that, Guy would never forgive him.

Chapter 7

Guy watched from the kitchen window as Maxine's Jaffa-orange MG screeched to a halt at the top of the drive.

'I don't know,' he said, looking doubtful. 'I'm still not sure about this. Somebody tell me I'm not making a big mistake.'

Berenice followed his gaze. The girl climbing out of the car was wearing white shorts and a sleeveless pale grey vest with MUSCLE emblazoned across her chest. She also possessed a great deal of gold-blond hair and long brown legs.

'Just because she doesn't look like your idea of a nanny,' she replied comfortably. Then, secure in the knowledge that by this time tomorrow she would be a married woman, she added with a slight smile, 'She certainly doesn't look like me.'

There really wasn't any diplomatic answer to that; the differences between the two girls were only too evident. But Berenice had been such relaxing company, thought Guy, and it had never occurred to anyone who'd met her that there might possibly be anything going on between the pair of them.

The arrival of Maxine Vaughan, on the other hand,

was likely to engender all kinds of lurid speculation.

'I don't care what she looks like.' His expression was deliberately grim. Above them came the sound of thunderous footsteps as Josh and Ella hurled themselves down the staircase. 'I just want her to take care of my kids.' He was about to continue but his attention was caught by the scene now taking place on the drive.

'OK,' Maxine was saying, leaning against her car and surveying the two children before her. 'Just remind me. Which one of you is Ella and which is Josh?'

Josh relaxed. She wouldn't, he was almost sure, force them to eat cold porridge. He had high hopes, too, of being allowed to stay up late when his father was away. Berenice had always been a bit boring where bedtimes were concerned.

'I'm Ella,' said his sister, meeting Maxine for the first time and struggling to work out whether she was being serious. 'I'm a girl.'

'Of course you are.' Maxine grinned and gave her her handbag. 'Good, that means you can carry this for me whilst I get my cases out of the boot. Isn't your dad here?'

'He's in the kitchen,' supplied Josh. 'With Berenice.'

'Hmm. Nice of him to come out and welcome me.' With a meaningful glance in the direction of the kitchen window, she hauled the heavy cases out of the car and dumped them on the gravelled drive. She'd been so serious about the live-in aspect of the job that she'd been up to Maurice's flat in London to collect all her things. 'Well, he can carry them inside. That's what men are for.'

By the time Janey arrived at Trezale House in the van,

Maxine appeared to have made herself thoroughly at home. Her enormous bedroom, flooded with sunlight and nicely decorated in shades of pink, yellow and cream, was already a mess.

'Berenice has given me a list of dos and don'ts,' she said, rolling her eyes as she tossed an armful of underwear into an open drawer and kicked a few shoes under the dressing table. 'She seems incredibly organized.'

'Nannies have to be organized,' Janey reminded her.

'Yes, well. I pity the chap she's marrying.'

'And you're going to have to be organized,' continued Janey remorselessly. 'If these children have a routine, they'll need to stick to it.'

Maxine gazed at her in disbelief. 'We never did.'

This was true. Thea, engrossed in her work, had employed a cavalier attitude to child rearing which involved leaving them to their own devices for much of the time, whilst she, oblivious to all else, would lose herself in the wonder of creating yet another sculpture. Janey, in the months following her own marriage, had traced her love of domesticity and orderliness back to the disorganized chaos of those early years when she had longed for order and stability. It had never seemed to bother Maxine, however. More adventurous by nature, and less interested in conforming than her elder sister, she positively embraced chaos. Janey just wished she could embrace the idea of work with as much enthusiasm.

'That's different,' she said sternly. 'At least we had a mother. Josh and Ella don't. It can't be easy for them.'

'It isn't going to be easy for me.' Maxine looked glum

and handed over the list, painstakingly written in neat, easy-to-read capitals. 'According to this they get up at six-thirty. And I'm supposed to give them breakfast!'

'Oh please,' sighed Janey, exasperated. 'You wanted this job! You were desperate to come and work here. Whatever's the matter with you now?'

'I wanted to work for Guy Cassidy.' Maxine stared at her as if she was stupid. 'But he's just been going through his diary with me and from the sound of it he's going to be away more often than he's here. Whilst he's leaping on planes and jetting off all over the world, I'm going to be stuck here in the wilderness with the kids like some frumpy housewife.' She paused then added fretfully, 'This wasn't what I had in mind at all.'

Guy emerged from his study as Janey was putting the finishing touches to the flowers in the hall. Crossing her fingers and praying that it wouldn't pour with rain overnight, she had garlanded the stone pillars which flanked the front entrance to the house with yellow and white satin ribbons, and woven sprays of mimosa and gypsophila between them. Together with the tendrils of ivy already curling around the bleached white stone they would provide an effective framework for the bride and groom when they stood on the steps to have their photographs taken by none other than one of the country's best-known photographers.

'It looks good.' Standing back to survey the overall effect with a professional eye, he nodded his approval. 'You've been working hard.'

'So has the hairdresser,' Janey observed, as a car drew

up and Berenice stepped out, self-consciously shielding her head from the light breeze coming in off the sea. Her mousey brown hair, pulled back from her face and teased into unaccustomed ringlets, bounced off her shoulders as she walked towards them.

'How are you going to sleep tonight?' said Guy, and Janey glimpsed the genuine affection in his eyes as he admired the rigid style.

Berenice, turning her head this way and that, said, 'Upright,' then broke into a smile as she inspected Janey's work. 'This is gorgeous; it must have taken you hours!'

'I think we all deserve a drink.' Placing his hand on her shoulder, Guy drew her into the house. When Janey hesitated, he added, 'You too.'

Berenice said, 'Where are the children?'

'Upstairs with the new nanny.' He grinned. 'And a pack of cards. I heard her saying she was going to teach them poker.'

'Enjoying yourself?' asked Guy, coming up to Janey in the sitting room the next day. She was perched on one of the window seats overlooking the garden, watching Maxine flirt with the best man.

'It was nice of Berenice to invite me,' she replied with a smile. 'And even nicer for her, being able to have the reception here. She's terribly grateful – she was telling me earlier that otherwise they would have had to hold it in the skittle alley at the Red Lion.'

He shrugged. 'No problem. Weddings and bar-mitzvahs a speciality. And forty guests is hardly over the top.'

'You'll miss her,' said Janey, nodding in Berenice's direction.

'The kids certainly will. We were lucky to keep her as long as we did.' He hesitated, a shadow coming over his face. 'She's been with us since my wife died.'

Weddings were an integral part of Janey's job but she still found them difficult to handle at times. They invariably brought back memories of her own marriage to Alan.

'It can't be easy for you,' she said, guessing what would be uppermost in his own mind. Out in the garden, Berenice and Michael were posing with their arms around each other's ample waists whilst Josh, his expression exquisitely serious, finished up yet another roll of film. Through the open window they could hear him issuing stern commands: 'Don't laugh . . . stay still . . . just look happy . . .'

Moving her half-empty wine glass out of the way, Guy eased himself down next to Janey and stretched out his long legs.

'Not easy, but bearable,' he said, his tone deliberately even. 'I don't resent other people's happiness. And Véronique and I had seven years of it, after all. That's more than some.'

More than I had, thought Janey sadly, but of course he didn't know anything of her own past. Since she wasn't about to try and compete in the tragedy stakes, she said nothing.

Now that the subject had been raised, however, Guy seemed to want to continue the line of conversation.

'Other people's attitudes are harder to cope with,' he

said, breaking the companionable silence between them. 'In the beginning I just functioned on automatic pilot, doing what had to be done and making sure Josh and Ella suffered as little as possible. Everybody was so concerned for us, everywhere you turned there were people being helpful and sympathetic . . . I couldn't do a thing wrong in their eyes. Then, after about six months, it was as if I couldn't handle any more sympathy. I kicked against it, went back to work and started, well, it was a pretty wild phase. Subconsciously, I suppose, I was looking for a replacement for Véronique but all I did was pick up one female after another, screw around like it was going out of fashion and get extremely drunk. All I managed to do, of course, was make an awful lot of people unhappy. Including myself. And everyone who'd been so sympathetic in the early days changed their minds and decided I was a real bastard instead. Sleeping with girls and dumping them – deliberately hurting them so they'd understand how *I* felt – seemed like the only answer at the time but all it did was make me more miserable. In the end, I came to my senses and stopped doing it.' With a rueful smile and a sideways glance at Janey, he added, 'I suppose I was lucky not to catch anything terrible. At the time, God knows, I deserved to.'

Janey, who had read books on the subject of coping with grief, said hesitantly, 'I don't know, but I think it's a fairly normal kind of reaction. Probably men are more likely to go through that kind of phase than women, but once it's out of their system they . . . settle down again. What's it like now? *Do* you feel more settled?'

It was an amazingly intimate conversation to be having

with someone who was, after all, a virtual stranger. But she was genuinely interested in finding out how he had coped and was continuing to cope. She wondered too whether she would ever enter a promiscuous phase . . .

Guy didn't appear in the least put out by her questions. Reaching for a bottle of white wine, he refilled both their glasses. 'There's still the problem of other people's attitudes.' His eyes registered mild contempt. 'Not that I particularly care what they think, but it can get a bit wearing at times. After three years, it seems, I'm expected to remarry. And the pressure's always there. Nowadays, every time I'm introduced to some new female at a dinner party I know it's because she's a carefully selected suitable candidate. Sometimes I half expect to find a tattoo on her forehead saying "Potential Wife". The next thing I know, everyone's telling me how marvellous she is with children and saying how hard it must be for poor Josh and little Ella, at their ages, not having a mother.' He shuddered at the unwelcome memory. 'God, that's happened to me so many times. It's like a recurring nightmare. And it's a bigger turn-off, of course, than a bucketful of bromide.'

'What's bromide?' said Ella, and they both jumped.

Guy, recovering from the surprise of her unexpected appearance, said, 'It's a kind of cold porridge. You wouldn't like it.' Then, pulling her on to his lap, he added, 'And what you need is a cowbell around your neck. Have you been eavesdropping, angel?'

'No.' She shook her head so vigorously that her white velvet headband slipped off. 'I was listening to you. Daddy, when can *I* get married?'

He assumed a suitably serious expression. 'Why? When would you like to get married?'

'Tomorrow.' Ella giggled and smoothed her lilac cotton dress over her knobbly knees. 'I'm going to marry Luke.'

Luke was eight years old and Berenice's nephew.

'I see.' Guy looked thoughtful. 'Well, tomorrow sounds OK to me. But maybe I should have a word with him first.'

Ella frowned, anxious that he shouldn't hear about the glass of lemonade she had accidentally spilled into a handbag left open and unattended in the kitchen. Biting her lower lip and looking dubious, she said, 'Why?'

'Marriage is a serious business,' Guy told her. 'I'd definitely need to speak to Luke, man to man. Apart from anything else,' he added severely, 'I have to ask him about his future prospects.'

'You seemed to be getting on rather well with my boss,' said Maxine, polishing off a slice of seafood quiche and sounding faintly put out. 'What were you doing, giving him the rundown on my sordid past?'

'Not at all.' It was early evening now and they were sitting outside on a wooden bench enjoying the light breeze. For most of the day the temperature had been up in the eighties. Janey, examining her arms for signs of sunburn and hoping she wouldn't wake up tomorrow with strap marks, said, 'I was the one who stuck up for you, remember? I'm hardly likely to scare him to death by telling him what you're really like. He might drag me into court and sue me for misrepresentation.'

'So what *were* you talking about?'

Despite having wolfed down at least half a dozen sausage rolls and a slice of wedding cake as well as the quiche, Maxine's lipstick was still immaculately in place. Shielding her eyes from the sinking sun, she was surreptitiously watching Guy Cassidy as he stood at the far end of the terrace talking to Berenice's new mother-in-law.

'He was telling me how fed up he gets, being chased by women hell-bent on becoming the next Mrs Cassidy.' Janey's tone of voice was casual but she felt it necessary to point out this fact, both to save her sister from making a fool of herself and to ensure that Guy wouldn't dispense with Maxine's services. Now that she had her flat to herself once more she wanted to keep it that way.

But Maxine only laughed. 'They can't have been very good at it then. The whole point of chasing a man – and catching him – is to make sure he doesn't realize it's happening. It's a delicate process, Janey! Practically an art form in itself.'

'Well, it sounds as if he's had plenty of practice at being on the receiving end.' Janey, having at least made her point, changed the subject. 'And you seemed to be getting on rather nicely with the best man anyway,' she observed. 'What was his name, Colin? He looked keen.'

'He was.' Maxine, licking her forefinger and dabbing at the crumbs of pastry on her plate, sounded gloomy. 'And I may as well change my name to Cinderella. Guy wants me to stay here for the rest of the weekend so the kids have a chance to get used to me before he leaves for Paris on Monday morning. Then I'll be here on my own with them until he gets back on Friday. I'm allowed next weekend off, apparently, but by that time Colin will have left on a cricket tour.' She shrugged. 'We did try, but we couldn't seem to get ourselves synchronized. At this rate my social life looks set to have all the sparkle of a squashed snail.'

'Welcome to the real world,' said Janey shortly. Her own social life had been practically non-existent for the past eighteen months.

Maxine cast her an impatient glance. 'Yes, but it's all right for you,' she replied with characteristic lack of tact. 'You're used to it.'

Chapter 8

The heatwave continued. On Sunday morning Janey packed a canvas holdall and headed down to the beach. It would be packed solid but she could amuse herself by guessing, according to the various shades of pallor, redness and tan, how long the holidaymakers had been in Trezale. And eavesdropping on their conversations – bickering couples were a particular favourite – was always entertaining.

The beach *was* crowded but the tide was on its way out, which helped. A lot of sandcastles were being constructed along the stretch of damp sand, leaving more room for the serious sunbathers on the dry sand. Janey chose a promising spot where she could stretch out, make a start on the latest Danielle Steel novel and simultaneously overhear the lively argument already in progress between a pair of big, sunburnt Liverpudlians who couldn't decide whether to go for cod and chips later or splash out on a proper Sunday lunch at that posh place in Amory Street. She wondered idly whether to tell them that the posh place, Bruno's, was closed on Sundays, but it seemed a shame to interrupt them. Uncapping her bottle of Ambre Solaire she smoothed the lotion haphazardly over the bits of her most likely to burn and promptly fell asleep instead.

She awoke with a start some time later. Ice-cold liquid was being dripped into her navel.

Grinning, Bruno held the Coke can aloft.

'It should be Bollinger of course,' he said, admiring her exposed body in the brief, fuchsia-pink bikini, 'but sometimes one just has to improvise. Can I sit down?'

'I don't know.' Shielding her eyes from the sun, Janey deadpanned, 'Can you?'

'OK. May I be permitted to share a corner of your towel?' He lowered himself down beside her anyway and offered her the Coke. 'You're looking rather gorgeous, I must say. I hardly recognized you at first, without your clothes on.'

Behind them, the Liverpudlian couple tittered. Janey tried hard not to flinch as Bruno ran a hand lightly across her stomach. It was a disturbingly pleasant sensation; she just wished her diet had been a bit more of a success.

But he wasn't stopping. 'Don't,' she protested, pushing his hand away. 'I'm too fat.'

'Rubbish!' replied Bruno firmly. The female predilection for dieting was a source of constant irritation to him, particularly when they tried to do it in his restaurant. 'Everyone else is too thin.'

Out of sheer desperation, she said, 'Where's Nina?'

'Gone to visit her parents.' He gave her a soulful look. 'She comes back on Tuesday morning. I'm all alone for two whole days.'

'You poor thing.' Janey smiled at the expression on his face. 'Whatever will you do with yourself?'

He knew what he'd like to do, but he also realized that he would have to tread very carefully indeed. Janey Sinclair was one of those rare females who seemed genuinely unaware of her own attractions. Since getting to know her, he had been struck by the aura of sadness surrounding her, and impressed by her refusal to seek sympathy from those who knew what she had gone through.

She was certainly no holiday bimbo. If she had been, he would have seduced and discarded her long ago. As it was, however, the sense of intrigue and interest had been maintained. She was, in a way, forbidden fruit. Time and again Bruno had told himself that in view of his own track record he should simply leave it at that and not get involved, but the attraction was definitely there and he was expert enough to know that it was mutual. Behind the awkward, diffident exterior he sensed Janey's own interest. It was heady stuff, all this self-denial and surface badinage. It had been years since he had experienced the pain and pleasure of such a slow-burning, tentative friendship. But at the same time Sunday and Monday stretched emptily ahead and he was certainly no saint . . .

'I'm too hot,' he said, finishing off the Coke and eyeing her glistening, Ambre-Solaired body. 'And if you stay here you're going to burn. Come on, let's go and get some lunch.'

It was a tempting offer. Hungrier than she'd realized and delighted at the prospect of company, Janey raised herself up on her elbows and said, 'Where?'

'My place.'

'Oh.' Nina wasn't there. She wasn't sure she should. 'But—'

'Oh dear,' he mocked, sensing her doubt. 'Now I've got you worried and you're desperately trying to think of a diplomatic way to say no.'

Janey, floundering, felt her cheeks redden. 'Well . . .'

'For heaven's sake,' said Bruno, sounding faintly exasperated. 'Live a little. All I'm talking about is a spot of lunch. I'm not inviting you to have wild sex with me.'

Embarrassed, she replied, 'I didn't think you were.'

'Oh yes, you did.' He grinned and helped her to her feet. 'But there's no need to panic; you'll be quite safe. Come on, let's go.'

Like Janey, Bruno and Nina lived above the shop, but whereas her own flat was tiny, their apartment was both spacious and stylish.

Janey, who had never visited it before, was impressed. Immaculate white rugs on the tiled floors offset the lavender and green décor. Modern, semi-abstract paintings were ranged around the walls and well-tended plants spilled out of white porcelain pots. The main ceiling was palest lavender, exactly matching the two three-seater leather sofas, and the cat occupying the one closer to the windows was white with luminous green eyes.

'You're surprised,' said Bruno, handing her an ice-stacked Pimm's.

'A bit,' she admitted. The almost clinical perfection of the apartment was so at odds with languorous, faintly hippyish Nina.

But once again he seemed able to read her mind. 'This

is me. Nina isn't bothered about interior design; she just goes along with my ideas.' As far as Janey could make out, Nina went uncomplainingly along with most things. Following him into the well-equipped kitchen, she leaned against the wall and watched Bruno prepare lunch. There was something almost irresistible about a man who could cook and talk at the same time. Before she had a chance to put down her empty glass, he had refilled it and added an extra dash of gin for good measure.

The unaccustomed strength of the drink went straight to her head. By the time they sat down to eat, her knees were like cotton wool and she was feeling deliciously uninhibited.

'Why aren't you two married?' she asked, intrigued.

'I don't make promises I can't keep.'

'So you aren't faithful to Nina.' Gosh, she couldn't believe she'd actually said that. To make up for it, Janey tried to look disapproving, although the effect was slightly spoiled when she attempted to fork up a frond of radicchio and it slipped, landing on the pale green tablecloth instead.

This time his smile broadened. 'Actually, I was thinking of the for richer, for poorer bit.'

'Oh.' She wondered if he was joking. It was difficult to tell, with Bruno.

But this time, it seemed, he was serious. 'Nina's the wealthy one,' he explained guilelessly, the sweep of his arm encompassing both the apartment and the restaurant below. Then he shrugged. 'She bought this place, I run it, and the arrangement suits us both. But if she didn't have any money, well . . .'

'That's terrible,' Janey protested, but Bruno wasn't in the least put out.

'No it isn't. It's honest.' Finishing his omelette and pushing his plate to one side, he lit a cigarette. 'There are trade-offs in every relationship. Ours simply happen to involve money. And Nina does realize this,' he added, pausing to execute a perfect smoke ring. 'She understands. If she decided she didn't like it she could always kick me out.'

The Brie omelette and tomato salad were delicious but Janey had lost her appetite. It was all very well for Bruno. He made it sound so simple and natural, but as far as she was concerned his theories were too unnervingly close for comfort. She wasn't wealthy by any means, but after meeting Alan she had worked hard and long enough to acquire the lease on her own small shop and the flat which went with it. He, on the other hand, had been falling behind with the rent on his own shared apartment and taking on casual work only when it became absolutely necessary in order to eat. Surfing and water skiing, his two great passions in life, weren't exactly profitable. During the moments of dark despair following his disappearance, Janey had wondered uneasily whether she had ever been more than a convenient stop-gap, supplying bed and board to a man whose love she'd only imagined.

But she was here now, with Bruno, and she damn well wasn't going to cry. He and Nina had an understanding: they were more of a business partnership than a real couple, and they weren't even married. Taking another gulp of Pimm's, she felt her own resolve weakening. She'd been alone for eighteen months, mourning the loss of her husband and wondering if life would ever be truly enjoyable again. Maybe it was time she had a little fun. Maybe she should take the plunge and find out.

'So your life is perfect,' she said, her smile deliberately provocative. 'You have everything you want.'

'Pretty much.' He nodded in agreement, those devastating bedroom eyes roaming lazily over her body. Janey shivered with sudden longing; it had been so long since she'd felt *wanted*.

Bruno certainly wanted her, but he had no intention of doing anything about it. Not yet, anyway. Tempting though the thought was, he knew that Janey had her preconceived ideas about him and that if he lived up to them this afternoon she would undoubtedly have her regrets by tomorrow. And he didn't want their relationship prematurely curtailed by a guilt attack. Where Janey Sinclair was concerned, he had decided, a single afternoon of pleasure simply wouldn't be enough.

Janey, walking home several hours later, didn't know whether to be relieved or disappointed. Her virtue was still intact, which was good in one way, but at the same time her ego had taken a bit of a knock. For Bruno, true to his word, had behaved like a perfect gentleman. Lunch had been followed by coffee on the sunny balcony, easy conversation and absolutely no untoward moves whatsoever. When she had succumbed to the effects of the Pimm's and closed her eyes, he had brought cushions for her head and left her to doze whilst he dealt with the washing up. When she awoke, it was to the muted strains of Vivaldi emanating from the stereo and the sight of

Bruno, sitting opposite her, quietly reading the *Sunday Times*. Glancing up, he'd grinned and said, 'Oh good, you can help me with the crossword. I'm stuck on eight across.'

Chapter 9

Over at Trezale House Maxine found herself on the receiving end of a similar lack of interest, but in Guy Cassidy's case it was entirely genuine. Spending his working life surrounded by some of the most beautiful women in the world, she decided sourly, had evidently had some kind of immunizing effect. Instead of the admiration to which she was accustomed, she was only too well aware that when he looked at Maxine Vaughan all he saw was the new nanny. And when he had observed the haphazard way in which she tackled the ironing, he'd been even less impressed.

'I can't do it if you're standing there watching me,' she'd said defensively, seizing Ella's fiendishly difficult pink cotton dungarees and realizing that she should have checked the pockets before chucking them into the machine earlier. Shreds of blue paper tissue clung to the bib like burrs.

'Don't worry,' he'd replied, backing out of the kitchen in horror. 'I can't bear to watch.'

And now here she was, stuck in the rotten kitchen with the beastly ironing, feeling more like bloody Cinderella than ever. Outside, Guy was fooling around with Josh and Ella, threatening them with the garden sprinkler. Ella, shrieking with laughter and making a desperate bid for freedom, tripped and landed in the flowerbed. As she scrambled to her feet once more, Maxine sucked in her breath; the clean white tee-shirt and jeans were clean no more. And no prizes for guessing who would have to deal with them.

Josh, skidding into the kitchen, grabbed a carton of orange juice from the fridge and emptied the contents into a mug, rubbing ineffectually with his muddy toes at the drops spilled on the floor.

'Why don't you come out and play?' he asked kindly when he had gulped down the orange juice in one go. 'We're having fun.'

'Fun?' Maxine echoed, glancing out of the window at Guy. Her voice heavy with irony, she said, 'Oh dear, I'd better not then. Your father wouldn't approve of that.'

Josh looked troubled. 'Don't you like it here?'

Softening, she turned and smiled at him. It was hardly his fault, after all, that coming to work for Guy Cassidy wasn't turning out as she had expected.

'Of course I do. I'm just not that keen on ironing.'

'You aren't going to leave then?'

Maxine, reminding herself that she didn't really have anywhere else to go, shook her head. 'No.'

'Good,' he said not bothering to hide his relief. 'I know Dad's a bit strict sometimes, but we like you.' Brightening, he added, 'And he's going out tonight, so we'll be able to have fun without him. We can play poker again. For real money, if you like . . .'

In the event, the evening was more entertaining than she had anticipated. Guy, preparing to go out, was in a good mood. To Maxine's utter amazement, he had even asked her if she'd like him to bring back an Indian takeaway.

'Where's he gone?' she said, when the cream Mercedes had disappeared down the drive. Josh was sitting cross-legged on the floor, practising his shuffling technique. Ella, curled up next to her on the sofa wearing red spotted pyjamas and furtively sucking her thumb, was engrossed in a video re-run of Friday night's *Coronation Street*.

'Dad?' Josh shrugged. 'Seeing one of his girlfriends, probably.'

'*One* of his girlfriends?' Maxine's spirits plummeted. Despite having got off to a not-terribly-promising start, she still entertained fantasies of her own in that department. The ridiculously handsome widower and the pretty nanny, living and working together and eventually falling in love had a certain ring to it. But this was the first she'd heard of any girlfriends. When Guy had remained un-partnered during yesterday's wedding reception, she'd assumed the field was clear.

Josh, however, was more interested in mastering the art of the shuffle. 'He's got lots,' he said vaguely. 'I expect it's Imogen tonight, because she phoned up this morning.'

Pushy, thought Maxine. Aloud, she said, 'Is she nice?'

Coronation Street had finished. Ella, who was humming along with the theme tune, took her thumb out of her mouth and said, 'I like Imogen. She's pretty.'

Hmm. Maxine decided she couldn't be that fantastic. Guy had said he'd definitely be home by eleven.

'She's *quite* pretty,' Josh corrected his sister. 'But Tara's better.'

'Tara can sit on her hair,' agreed Ella happily, confirming Maxine's suspicion that the girl in question was Tara James, currently one of the most sought-after models in Europe. Hell, she thought gloomily. Talk about competition.

Josh was now painstakingly dealing out the cards. Looking up and glimpsing the expression on Maxine's face, he said in matter of fact tones, 'They're OK I suppose. But none of them is as good as Mummy. She was prettier than anyone.'

'Really?' Maxine was intrigued. 'I'd love to see some photos of her.'

'We've got loads,' said Josh cheerfully. 'I'll bring them downstairs later and show them to you.'

She looked hopeful. 'We could do it now.'

'We have to play poker first,' he replied firmly. 'And I need to buy some new batteries for my Gameboy tomorrow, so we can't stop until I've won at least two pounds.'

It took some deft manipulation on Maxine's part, but she managed; a respectable forty minutes later, Josh was two pounds and twenty pence up and he hadn't noticed the sleight of hand which had been necessary in order to achieve it.

'Well done,' said Maxine, clearing away the cards with some relief. 'Go on then, run upstairs and find those albums. I love looking at other people's photographs.'

Particularly when they belonged to Guy Cassidy. And there were hundreds of them, depicting his life over the past decade. Josh steered her through the albums, pointing with pride to the many pictures of Véronique.

'That's Mummy with Ella, just after she was born. This is me with Mummy in Regent's Park when I was four. And this one's Mum and Dad at a party in St Tropez. He's laughing because Sylvester Stallone just asked her for a dance and she said no.'

Véronique Cassidy had certainly been beautiful. Maxine pored over the close-ups which revealed stunning blond good looks in all their glory. Even more dauntingly, she had been a natural beauty, never over-embellishing herself, simply allowing the exquisite basics to speak for themselves.

But what shone through most of all was happiness. Maxine knew instinctively which of the photographs of his wife had been taken by Guy. And those featuring the two of them together were almost unbearably poignant. Their obvious love for each other shone out; it was almost a tangible thing.

Quite uncharacteristically, she felt tears pricking at the back of her eyelids. Something approaching envy curled in her stomach; not for Véronique, but for their shared happiness. Looking at them with their arms around each other, Maxine was reminded that she herself had never been in love, not really. Her own experiences were of a string of tumultuous and usually short-lived relationships where lust had figured high on the agenda. Instinctively drawn to men whose volatile personalities mirrored her own, it was almost as if she was ensuring that the affairs wouldn't last. For all their similarities, she and her partners never seemed to have much in common in so far as ordinary, day-to-day living was concerned. Within weeks of the initial dazzling attraction, boredom would set in and she would find herself looking for a way out. Invariably, the way out involved another man.

Yet she was, it seemed, doomed to failure. In a deliberate attempt to break the sad and sorry pattern she had got herself involved with Maurice Stanwyck and that, thought Maxine ruefully, had turned out to be the biggest mistake of all. Poor, pedantic Maurice, hellbent on conforming to his mother's ideas of success, simply hadn't been able to cope with a wayward fiancée. And she in turn had tried to conform, she really had, but all she'd managed to do in the end was to hurt and humiliate him.

Returning to London last week to pick up her belongings, she had attempted to apologize. The meeting, however, had been an awkward one. Maurice, his stiff upper lip super-glued into place, had initially betrayed no emotion at all. Then, after twenty minutes of following her around whilst she packed her cases, his guard had dropped. Maxine had been forced to endure the far more harrowing ordeal of listening to him as he begged her to change her mind. At one point he had been on the verge of tears. All she'd been able to do was to remind him how miserable she would undoubtedly have made him if she'd stayed, and what a disaster she would have been as a corporate wife.

Poor Maurice, she thought now, gazing numbly down at the photographs of Guy and Véronique in her lap. She hoped he'd put the experience behind him and find himself another more suitable girlfriend soon.

Josh, meanwhile, was still sorting through the piles of

photos which hadn't made it into the albums. Thrusting a selection into Maxine's hands, he said in matter-of-fact tones, 'This is us after Mummy died. That's me when I was seven, on my new bike. That's Ella's birthday party when she was five. And these are some of Dad's girlfriends.'

It was as if Guy had deliberately chosen women who in no way resembled his wife. Véronique, with her straight blond hair and Madonna-like beauty, couldn't have been more different from these gypsy-eyed, dark-haired females who pouted and smiled for the camera and who were evidently trying too hard to impress.

The difference in Guy, she observed, was equally apparent. Just as earlier she had been able to tell at a glance which photographs of Véronique had been taken by him, so now she could have guessed which of those featuring him had been taken after her death. It was almost indefinable, but there nevertheless; a hardening of the expression in the eyes . . . the loss of carefree pleasure . . . concealed sorrow reflected in the wryness of his smile.

Feeling uncomfortably as if she was intruding upon his private grief, Maxine bundled the photographs together and handed them back to Josh. Ella, still sucking her thumb, had fallen asleep at her side.

'They're lovely.' Maxine smiled as Josh replaced them with care in the cardboard box. 'You're lucky to have so many pictures of your mum.'

'Yes.' The boy looked thoughtful for a moment. 'I wouldn't have forgotten what she looked like but Ella might have. She was only young when it happened.'

She wondered how he felt about the string of subsequent girlfriends but sensed that she had done enough prying for one night. Outside, it was growing dark. It was past both children's bedtime. Tugging tentatively at Ella's thumb, Maxine found it plugged into the rosebud mouth as firmly as a sink plunger.

'Come on, I'm still on parole. Your father will shoot me if he finds out how late I've let you stay up. You take the photographs back upstairs and I'll carry Ella.'

They Think It's All Over was about to start on TV. Josh said jealously, 'What will you do when we've gone to bed?'

Maxine gathered Ella into her arms. She was only small but she weighed an absolute ton. 'What else?' she countered, with a long-suffering sigh. 'The rest of the rotten ironing.'

True to his word, Guy was back by eleven with the Indian takeaway. Maxine, having watched *They Think It's All Over*, switched the television off and the iron on the moment she heard his car pull up the drive and promptly assumed the kind of saintly-but-weary expression which indicated that whilst he'd been out enjoying himself with one of his floozies, she had been hard at work for hours.

Her mouth watered as he unwrapped the brown carrier bag and lifted the cardboard lids from their foil containers. Prawn korma, scented and golden, was piled over pilau rice. Massaging her back for good measure, she switched the iron off.

'What time did they get off to bed?' said Guy, turning his attention to the lamb dhansak and naan bread.

'Nine o'clock.'

He grinned. 'That means ten.'

'Well . . .' It was on the tip of her tongue to ask him

what time he'd gone to bed, but she didn't want to risk spoiling his good mood. 'Ella fell asleep on the sofa and Josh thinks he's the Cincinnati Kid. At this rate I can see my entire salary disappearing into his piggy bank.' She pulled a face. 'I wish now I'd never taught him how to play poker.'

'If it makes you feel any better,' said Guy, deadpan, 'you didn't. I did. Last Christmas.'

For the first time, Maxine realized, they were actually sitting down and discussing the children rather than engaging in a battle of verbal wits. The sparring subsided, she began asking suitably intelligent questions about Josh's education and the atmosphere, helped along by a bottle of Sancerre, grew positively relaxed.

Before she knew it, she was asking Guy the question she hadn't felt able to ask Josh.

He frowned. 'Why? What's he been saying?'

'Nothing really.' She crushed a poppadum and licked her fingers. 'Just that you have lots of girlfriends, but none of them is as pretty as his mother was.'

'I see.' The dark blue eyes registered amusement. 'Well, he's probably right about that. Although I don't know about the actual number. "Lots" sounds pretty alarming.'

'Aren't there?' Maxine cast him an innocent look. 'Lots, I mean.'

'One or two.' He shrugged. 'I've tried to keep it low key, for the kids' sakes. On the other hand, I'm only human. And they've never seemed to mind the occasional . . . visitor.'

'Children are adaptable,' agreed Maxine, reassured by his reply. 'And it isn't as if you went through a traumatic divorce. At least they know you were happily married.'

'I hadn't thought of it like that.' Guy looked pensive. 'Maybe it does help.'

Pleased with herself for having said the right thing, she nodded. 'I'm sure it does.'

'I could show you photographs of Véronique, if you're interested.'

Maxine wondered if this was some kind of test. She didn't want him to think of her as morbidly curious.

'There's no hurry,' she replied easily, getting to her feet and taking his empty plate from him. 'Maybe Josh and Ella will show them to me whilst you're away.'

And then it was all spoiled. By the time she returned from the kitchen Guy was standing by the sofa with his back to her. When he turned around, she saw the crumpled photograph in his hand and the look of disdain on his face.

'Why did you lie?' he said coldly. 'I wouldn't have minded if you'd told me you'd already seen them. But why the bloody hell did you have to lie?'

The photograph of Véronique must have slipped down the side of the sofa when she had lifted the sleeping Ella and taken her upstairs. Since then, she had been sitting on it.

'I'm sorry . . .' began Maxine. To her horror, she saw that it was not only crumpled, but torn.

'Don't be sorry,' Guy replied, his tone curt. 'Just be careful, that's all. These pictures might not mean much to you, but they do to us. They're all we have left.'

Chapter 10

Never at her best at the ludicrously early hour of seven in the morning, Maxine propped herself up on her elbows at the breakfast table and wondered how on earth Janey managed to get up at five in order to visit the flower market. It simply wasn't natural.

And as for having to cope at the same time with two starving children and their picky, irritable father, she thought as she battled to stay awake, it was downright unfair.

'There's a pink elephant in my Sugar Puffs,' squealed Ella, waving the plastic toy in Maxine's face and sprinkling her with milk.

'Eat it. It's good for you.'

'Don't forget we've got to go and buy my batteries today,' Josh reminded her, speaking through a mouthful of toast and blackberry jam and jingling the money in his shorts' pocket for added emphasis. 'Maxine, open your eyes. I said we've got to buy new batteries for my—'

'Gameboy,' she supplied wearily. 'I heard you. And don't talk with your mouth full – you look like a cement mixer in overdrive.'

'You shouldn't have your elbows on the table,' Josh

retaliated, unperturbed. 'Berenice says it's rude. Doesn't she, Dad?' He turned to his father for confirmation. 'Berenice says elbows on the table are rude.'

Having to get up at six-thirty evidently didn't bother Guy Cassidy. Fresh from the shower and wearing a white linen shirt and faded Levi's, he was looking unfairly good for the time of day. Although it was all right for him, thought Maxine mutinously; he was zipping off to Paris. Whilst she spent the week looking after his monsters, he would be surrounded by beautiful semi-naked models only too eager to show him their version of a really good time.

He was standing by the dresser painstakingly checking the cameras he would be taking with him and piling rolls of film into the small case which would accompany him on to the plane. Ignoring Josh, he turned that unnervingly direct dark blue gaze upon Maxine.

'Now, are you sure you're going to be able to cope whilst I'm away?'

She wished she'd had time to brush her hair before stumbling downstairs. 'Don't worry, I'll manage,' she replied evenly, thinking that he'd be stuffed if she said no. 'And you'll have Paula's mother coming in to keep an eagle eye on me in case I'm tempted to do anything drastic, like tape their mouths up and lock them in the cellar.'

'We haven't got a cellar.' Ella, dive-bombing the elephant into her cereal bowl, looked triumphant.

'In that case, it'll just have to be the attic.' Maxine confiscated the elephant. For the first time that morning, a glimmer of a smile crossed Guy's face.

'There you go then,' he warned. 'You'd better behave yourselves. A week in an attic wouldn't be much fun, would it?'

Ella, who was devoted to *Coronation Street*, said, 'I wouldn't mind if I could have a television up there.'

'Oh, you could have a TV set,' Maxine exclaimed, cheering up and buttering herself a slice of toast. 'But no plug.'

The next week, despite Maxine's misgivings, was a greater success than either she or Guy had anticipated. After one or two inevitable power struggles as the children tested the limits of her patience and she in turn exerted her own particular brand of authority, they settled into a routine of sorts and began to enjoy each other's company. Josh and Ella could be noisy, argumentative, boisterous and infuriating but Maxine, retaliating in kind, found she didn't hate them after all. In some ways, she realized with amusement, they reminded her quite a lot of herself.

'Yuk, I don't like cauliflower,' declared Ella, her tone fractious.

To the child's astonishment Maxine replied, 'Neither do I,' and promptly lobbed the offending vegetable out through the kitchen window. 'Let's have frozen peas instead.'

'We like Big Macs,' said Josh hopefully the following evening.

Maxine, who had been burrowing through the contents of the freezer in search of fish fingers, because she knew how to cook them, closed the door with relief.

'OK,' she said to Josh's amazement and delight.

Berenice had always been a stickler for proper, home-cooked meals. 'But don't tell your father.'

Guy phoned every evening. Maxine, hovering unseen in the doorway, eavesdropped shamelessly whilst his children sung her praises. Nannying wasn't so bad once you got the hang of it, she decided, priding herself on her success. And letting the children stay up until midnight had been a stroke of genius; no more horrendous six-thirty starts. She couldn't imagine why more households hadn't cottoned on to such a perfect scheme.

'Everything all right?' Guy would enquire, when she was summoned to the phone for interrogation.

'Perfect!' Determined to impress the hell out of him to pay him back for ever having doubted her, she boasted, 'They've been absolute angels.'

Josh and Ella, sitting on the stairs, collapsed in giggles.

'Hmm,' said Guy, not believing her for a second. 'In that case you've got the wrong children. Return them to the spaceship and make sure the real ones are home by the time I get back.'

'You didn't tell Dad you'd reversed his car into the gatepost,' Josh reminded her when she had replaced the receiver.

Maxine's smile was angelic. 'Don't you remember, darling? That stupid man in the Reliant Robin drove into the back of the car whilst we were parked on the seafront.'

'No he didn't. You reversed into the gatepost.'

'Fine.' She picked up the phone once more. 'I'll call and tell your father now. Oh, and maybe you'd like to explain to him how you managed to smash the kitchen window with your sister's Sindy doll . . .'

Josh's shoulders sagged and he waved his hands in a gesture of defeat. He might have known he didn't stand a chance against an expert like Maxine. 'OK, OK. Put the phone down. You win.'

But whilst being with the children was fun, it had its restrictions. Maxine found herself yearning for adult company. By Thursday she realized she was even looking forward to Guy's phone call from Paris, and felt absurdly put out when he spoke to Josh and Ella, then hung up.

'He was in a hurry,' Josh explained. 'He said some people were waiting for him and he had to go out.'

'How nice for him,' said Maxine sourly. It was five o'clock and the evening stretched ahead interminably. All she had to look forward to was beating Josh and Ella at Monopoly and maybe the added thrill of washing her hair.

Janey, who enjoyed washing her hair, was in the bath when the phone shrilled at six o'clock. Inwardly cursing but unable to leave it to ring – there was always that infinitesimal chance that it might be Alan, after all – she climbed out of the bath and made her way, naked and dripping bubbles, into the sitting room.

'Big favour,' Maxine beseeched, on the other end of the line. 'Big, big favour. How would you like to save your poor demented sister's life?'

'Not very much.' If Maxine was planning a moonlight flit from Trezale House, Janey didn't want her flitting back to the flat. With a trace of suspicion she said, 'I thought Guy was away this week.'

'Exactly,' declared Maxine, then giggled. 'What a strange thing to say. I wasn't asking you to play hired assassin.'

That was a relief, Janey supposed. Shifting from one foot to the other, she watched the bath bubbles melt into the carpet. 'So what do you want?'

'I'm suffering from cabin fever,' cried Maxine with suitable drama. 'If I don't get out of here for a couple of hours I won't be responsible for my actions. And Colin's just phoned, inviting me to have a drink with him.'

'I'm in the bath,' complained Janey.

'No you aren't, you're in the sitting room. Sweetie, it's not too much to ask, is it?' Maxine switched into wheedling mode. 'Josh and Ella would absolutely love to see you again. And you know how brilliant you are at Monopoly . . .'

It really was a gorgeous house. Janey, kicking off her shoes and stretching out across the long sofa, gazed around appreciatively at the beamed ceiling, matte burgundy walls and glossy, rug-strewn parquet floor. Maxine and her incurable mania for clutter had reduced her own small flat to chaos but Trezale House was evidently large enough to handle it. The style of the sitting room was elegant but at the same time relaxed. The paintings hanging on the walls vied for space with a selection of framed photographs, expertly lit. Thanks to Jessica Newman, Paula's mother, the antique furniture was lovingly polished, the indoor plants immaculately tended. Janey was pleased to see that her own flower arrangements were still looking as fresh as they had the previous Saturday.

But it was midnight, the children were in bed and she was starving. 'Help yourself to anything,' Maxine had declared, the expansive sweep of her arm encompassing the contents of the entire kitchen. That had been at seven-thirty when Janey hadn't been hungry. Now, checking her watch and marvelling at her own gullibility – Maxine had promised faithfully to be back by eleven at the very latest – she padded barefoot into the kitchen and opened the fridge. Josh, who was the most appalling cheat, had beaten her at Monopoly and a girl deserved some compensation, after all.

Abandoning her diet, she'd just finished piling a dinner plate with French bread, pâté and a hefty slice of Dolcelatte when a car snaked up the drive, its headlights dazzling her as she peered out through the kitchen window.

Maxine was back at last. Too hungry to stop now, Janey gave her a wave and picked up the already opened bottle of red wine which had been left balancing precariously on the edge of the windowsill. She wouldn't have bothered if she'd been on her own, but now that Maxine was here they might as well finish it up between them.

By the time the front door opened, Janey was comfortably ensconced once more on the sofa. Through a mouthful of pâté she called out, 'And about time too! Come in here this minute and tell me what you've been doing to that poor defenceless cricketer. I hope you haven't been tampering with his middle wicket . . .'

'Absolutely not,' said a cool male voice behind her, and Janey turned pale.

'Oh God, I'm s . . . sorry,' she stammered, hideously

embarrassed at having been caught out. The attempted witticism had been feeble enough anyway, but at least Maxine would have laughed.

Guy Cassidy, however, wasn't looking the least bit amused. Janey's complexion, unable to make up its mind, promptly reddened. The dinner plate clattered against the coffee table as she shoved it hurriedly away from her, like a shoplifter caught in the act. It was ridiculous, she told herself; she had a perfect right to be here. She just wished Guy wouldn't look at her like that.

'Well,' he said finally, glancing at the two brimming glasses of wine on the table and at the almost empty bottle beside them. 'You appear to have made yourself at home. Aren't you going to offer me a drink?'

Bastard, thought Janey. To add insult to injury, her hand shook like a leaf as she silently passed him the nearest glass.

'And I suppose I don't need to ask where Maxine is. Screwing some unfortunate cricketer, from the sound of it.' Collapsing into one of the chairs opposite her, he consulted his watch. 'It's past midnight. Is this a regular occurrence?'

'What?'

'You, doing the babysitting. Has it been going on all week?'

'Of course not!' Janey retaliated. Outraged by the unfairness of the suggestion, she took a great slug of wine. There was really no need for him to take his irritation out on her. 'I thought you weren't supposed to be flying back until tomorrow, anyway,' she said in accusing tones, wishing she didn't feel at such a disadvantage. He must have been travelling for hours, but in his olive-green cashmere sweater and white jeans he still looked as fresh as if he'd just got up, whereas she was only too conscious of the fact that she was wearing an ancient grey tee-shirt and leggings, and no make-up at all.

'Maybe I wanted to check up on what happens when I'm away,' he countered evenly, those unnerving dark eyes boring into her as she emptied her glass. 'I hope you enjoyed that.'

By this time thoroughly fed up, Janey responded with a belligerent stare. 'It was OK.'

He nodded 'So it should be. That was a bottle of seventy-eight Châteauneuf du Pape. It cost two hundred and forty pounds.'

Chapter 11

Swarming tourists were all right in their place but unless they were prepared to put their money where their mouths were, Thea Vaughan was a lot happier when she had her beloved studio to herself.

All day long she'd smiled and silently suffered the endless stream of visitors who'd trooped in and out of the gallery. Most had temporarily tired of the beach and were simply seeking a diversion out of the sun. Some, treating Thea as if she didn't exist, openly criticized her sculptures. Others, feigning interest, admired her work and engaged her in pointless, time-wasting conversation. Occasionally they fell in love with a particular piece and only balked when they saw the price tag.

So far this week she hadn't sold a single sculpture. With the rent overdue, it was especially demoralizing. All those wasted smiles and dashed hopes. She was tempted to tell the next influx of ignorant, sunburnt visitors to get stuffed, just for the hell of it.

'I'm sorry, did you say something?'

The visitor, a lone male in his early sixties, turned enquiringly in Thea's direction as she emerged from the back of the gallery where she had been making a fresh pot of coffee.

'Not a word,' Thea lied smoothly, having glanced down at his shoes. No holiday flip-flops these, but polished brown leather brogues of the very highest quality worn with traditional lighter brown trousers, a brown and cream checked shirt and a Harris tweed jacket. In these temperatures the man had to be on the verge of heat-stroke. One simply didn't tell the owner of such an outfit to get stuffed.

It was one of her better decisions.

The prospective customer was standing in a pool of sunlight beside the open window, thoughtfully stroking his moustache as he studied one of the sculptures of which Thea was particularly proud. The almost life-sized figure of a ballerina, sitting on the floor to tie the ribbons on her shoes, was priced at £3,000. Earlier in the day a skinny Welshman had elbowed his wife in the ribs and said loudly, 'There now, Gwyneth, maybe I could put you in your slippers, dip you into a tank of concrete and flog you in some fancy gallery.' The wife had cackled with laughter and Thea had gritted her teeth, longing to punch them both down the stairs. To add insult to injury the sniggering couple had left Starburst wrappers strewn across the bleached wooden floorboards. Oh, the joys of cretinous bloody tourists . . .

But this man, even if he was a tourist, which she doubted, was in a different league altogether. Anxious not to put him off, Thea decided to wait for him to initiate any conversation. Resuming her seat before the half-finished figure upon which she was currently working, she rinsed her fingers in the bowl of water next to it and continued moulding the clay over the wire base of the torso.

Within the space of a minute she became aware of the fact that the man was now watching her. Calmly ignoring him, she concentrated instead upon the job in hand. The naked female required breasts and she had to decide on an appropriate size for them. It was also tricky ensuring they didn't end up looking like improbable silicone implants. The figure was of a middle-aged woman; they had to have the correct amount of droop.

Oliver Cassidy, in turn, was studying the interesting outline of Thea Vaughan's breasts beneath her ivory cheesecloth blouse. She was wearing several heavy silver necklaces and no bra, and as far as he was concerned her figure was admirable.

He was drawn, too, to the strong facial features of the woman who seemed so absorbed in her work. With those heavy-lidded dark brown eyes and that long Roman nose, she looked almost like a bird of prey. The swirl of white hair, caught up in a loose bun, contrasted strongly with her deep tan, but although he estimated she must be in her late forties, the lines on her face were few.

Observing her clever, capable hands as they moulded the damp clay, he said, 'Did you do all these?'

Thea glanced up and responded with a brief smile. 'Yes.'

'You're very good.'

'Thank you.'

Intrigued by her apparent lack of interest in engaging him in conversation, Oliver Cassidy thrust his hands into his trouser pockets and surveyed the ballerina once more.

'I particularly like this one.'

'So do I,' said Thea easily. Leaning back and resting

her wrists on her thighs, careful not to get clay on the full, navy blue cotton skirt, she added, 'It's for sale at three thousand pounds.'

She liked the fact that he didn't even flinch. She liked it even better when he frowned and said, 'What's the matter, are you trying to put me off? Don't you want to sell it?'

'I'm an artist, not a saleswoman.' Narrowing her eyes and tilting her head to one side in order to survey the figure currently in progress, she said, 'And since three thousand pounds is a great deal of money, I doubt very much whether anything I say would have much impact either way. I couldn't persuade you to buy something you didn't want, so why on earth should I even try?'

Accustomed to the cut-throat machinations of the property business which had made him his fortune and rendered him impervious to the hardest of hard sells, Oliver Cassidy almost laughed aloud. Instead, however, and much to his own surprise, he heard himself saying, 'But I do want it. So persuade me.'

Thea, enjoying herself immensely, replied, 'No.'

'Why not?'

'Because you might not be able to afford it. I couldn't live with my conscience if I thought I'd inveigled you into buying something you couldn't afford.'

In fifty-one supremely selfish years she had never yet been troubled by her conscience, but he didn't need to know this. Her eyes alight with amusement, she shook her head.

'Do I look,' demanded Oliver Cassidy in pompous tones, 'as if I can't afford it?'

This time she gave him a slow, regretful smile. 'I wouldn't know. As I said, I'm not a saleswoman.'

He replied heavily, 'I can tell.'

The ensuing silence lasted several seconds. Thea, determined not to be the one to break it, carried on working.

'I'll buy it,' said Oliver Cassidy finally. 'On one condition.'

She raised her eyebrows. 'Mmm?'

'That you have dinner with me tonight.'

Openly teasing him now, she said, 'Are you sure you can afford both?'

For the first time, Oliver Cassidy smiled. 'I think I can just about manage it.'

'Oh well then, in that case it's an offer I can't refuse. I'd be delighted to have dinner with you, Mr—'

'Cassidy. Oliver Cassidy. Please, call me Oliver.'

For buying the ballerina I'd call you anything you damn well like, thought Thea, struggling to conceal her inner triumph. Rising to her feet, she wiped her hands on her skirt. What did a few clay stains matter, after all, when you'd just made a mega sale? The contract was sealed with a firm handshake.

'Thank you! It's a deal, then. Oliver.'

Chapter 12

'He's a pig,' said Janey, who still hadn't forgiven Guy for his snide comments of the previous night. Overcome with a sudden need for companionship she had arrived at Thea's house at eight only to find her mother getting ready to go out.

Thea, wearing her favourite crimson silk shirt over a peasant-style white skirt, was doing her make-up in the mirror above the fireplace. With an ease borne of long practice, she swept black liner around her eyes, enlarging and elongating them just as she had done for the past thirty years.

'You mean that photographer chap?' she said vaguely, having been only half listening to her elder daughter's grumbling. 'I thought he was supposed to be rather gorgeous.'

'That's beside the point.' Janey, immune to Guy Cassidy's physical attractions, threw her a moody glance. 'And that stupid bottle of wine was just about the last straw. It was Maxine's fault, of course, but he automatically assumed I'd opened it.'

Thea completed her make-up with a dash of crimson lipstick and treated herself to an extra squirt of Mitsouko for luck. Chucking the bottle into her bag, she said briskly, 'Well, he isn't your problem. And I'm sure Maxine can deal with him. She's always been good with difficult men.'

Luckily, Janey hadn't expected motherly support and reassurances; they simply weren't Thea Vaughan's style. Now, listening to her airy dismissal of the problem which as far as her mother was concerned wasn't even a problem, she managed a rueful smile.

'Speaking of difficult men, who are you seeing tonight?' Is all this really in aid of Philip?'

Thea froze with her bag halfway to her shoulder. Her eyebrows lifted in resignation. 'Oh, sod it.'

Philip Slattery wasn't difficult at all. One of Thea's long-standing and most devoted admirers, he was as gentle as a puppy. Janey liked him enormously, whereas her mother took him almost entirely for granted, seeing him when it suited her and ditching him unmercifully whenever somebody more interesting came along. As, presumably, somebody now had.

'You mean, Oh sod it, you *were* supposed to be seeing Philip but you'd forgotten all about him,' she said in admonishing tones. Then, because Thea was showing no sign of reaching for the phone, she added, 'Mum, you'll have to let him know. You can't just stand him up.'

Thea pulled a face. 'He's going to be awfully cross with me. He's holding a dinner party at his house. Now I suppose he'll accuse me of lousing up the numbers.'

'Mum!' Janey protested, dismayed by this act of thoughtlessness. 'How could you possibly forget a dinner party? Why don't you just cancel your other date?'

'Out of the question,' declared Thea, picking up the

phone and frowning as she tried to recall Philip's number. Her own, it went without saying, was practically engraved on his heart. 'I sold the ballerina this afternoon.'

'So?'

'He invited me to have dinner with him, on the strength of it. Darling, he's seriously wealthy, not to mention attractive! This could be so *important;* I'd have to be a complete idiot to turn him down.'

Poor, faithful Philip and cruel, mercenary Thea. Janey listened in silence to her mother's side of the phone call as she blithely excused herself from the dinner party which he had undoubtedly spent the past fortnight planning to the nth degree.

'Who is he, then?' she said when Thea had replaced the receiver.

Her mother, whose memory was notorious fickle, checked her reflection in the mirror and smoothed an eyebrow into place. 'Oliver. Kennedy, I think.' With a vague gesture, she dismissed the problem in favour of more important details. 'He wears extremely expensive shoes, darling. *And* drives a Rolls Royce.'

'You mean he's a chauffeur.'

Thea gave her daughter a pitying look. 'Janey, don't be such a miserable spoilsport. He's rich, he's interested, and I like him. I mean this is the kind of man I could even be persuaded to *marry.*'

It was the kind of lifestyle she could easily get used to, the kind she had always felt she deserved. Hopeless with money herself, however, Thea had got off to a poor start when, at the age of nineteen, she had met and fallen even more hopelessly in love with Patrick Vaughan. Big, blond and a dyed-in-the wool Bohemian, he was the mercurial star of his year at art college, adored by more women than even he knew what to do with and a dedicated pleasure-seeker. Within six weeks of meeting him, Thea had moved into his incredibly untidy attic apartment in Chelsea, embracing with enthusiasm the chaotic lifestyle of her lover and encouraging him in his work.

But Patrick only embraced her in return when no other more interesting women were around. Incurably promiscuous, his wanderings caused Thea such grief that, looking back over those years, she wondered how she'd ever managed to stand it. At the time, however, she had loved him so desperately that leaving had been out of the question. When Patrick, laughing, had told her that fidelity was bourgeois, she'd believed him. When he'd told her that none of the others meant anything anyway, she'd believed him. And when – quite seriously – he'd told her that he was going to be the greatest British artist of the twentieth century she'd believed that too. She was lucky to have him, and nobody had ever said that living with a genius would be easy.

It wasn't. The never-ending supply of eager women continued to troop through their lives and turning a tolerant blind eye became increasingly difficult. Furthermore, Patrick Vaughan only painted when he felt like it, which wasn't often enough to appease either the buyers or the bookmakers.

Gambling, always a passion with him, fulfilled yet another craving for excitement. And although it was fun when he won, the losses far outweighed the gains. As his addiction spiralled, Thea began to realize that maybe love wasn't enough after all. The all-consuming intensity with which Patrick gambled might divert his attention from the numerous affairs but it scared her. Patrick, still laughing, told her that worrying about money was even more bourgeois than fidelity but this time she had her doubts. Neither the promised luxurious lifestyle nor his glittering career were showing any signs of materializing and the novelty of being poor and perpetually cheated on was beginning to wear off.

Unable to find a market for her own work she had reluctantly taken a job in a Putney craft shop, but Patrick was spending everything she earned. Bailiffs were knocking on the door. She deserved more than this. It was, she decided, time to leave.

Fate, however, had other ideas. Discovering that she was pregnant threw Thea into a flat spin. She was only twenty-two, hopelessly unmaternal and deeply aware of her own inability to cope alone. All of a sudden Patrick-and-all-his-faults was better than no Patrick at all.

To everyone's astonishment Patrick himself was delighted by the news of the impending arrival. Never having given much thought to the matter before, he was bowled over by the prospect of becoming a father and didn't – as all his friends had secretly imagined – do one of his famous runners. He had created a son who would inherit his artistic genius, good looks and charisma, he told everyone who would listen. This was his link with immortality. What could be more important than a child? At Patrick's insistence, and to his friends' further amazement – they had assumed he would think it far too bourgeois – he and Thea were married at once. The wedding was funded by a timely win on the Derby. Fascinated and inspired by his new wife's condition, he resumed painting with a vengeance, insisting that she sit for him whilst he captured her voluptuous nakedness in oils. The paintings, among the best he'd ever done, sold easily through a West London gallery. Gradually the creditors were paid off. And if Patrick was still seeing other women, for once in his life he exercised discretion. For Thea, the months before the birth were some of the happiest she had ever known.

Janey, when she arrived, was a monumental disappointment to both of them. Squashed and ugly, not only did she bear no resemblance whatsoever to either parent, she was entirely the wrong sex.

With all his visions of Madonna and child shattered and the reality of fatherhood failing abysmally to live up to fond expectations, Patrick promptly reverted to type. The painting ground to an abrupt halt, the gambling and womanizing escalated to new and dizzy heights, and in order to escape both the noisy wails of his daughter and the silent tears of his wife, he spent less and less time at home.

Maxine, born twenty-two months later as a result of a last-ditch attempt at reconciliation, failed to do the trick. Another daughter, another shattering disappointment. Knowing that it was hopeless to go on trying and by this time so miserable that it was hardly even a wrench, Thea packed her things, gathered up the two girls and left.

Not wanting to stay in London, she moved to Cornwall in order to start a new and happier life. From now on, she vowed, she would learn by her mistakes and Patrick's example. Being a doormat was no fun; selfishness ruled. Never again would she let herself be emotionally intimidated by a man. She was going to make damn sure she kept her self-respect and enjoyed the rest of her life.

For twenty-five years she had kept her promise to herself. Bringing up two young daughters single-handed wasn't easy, but she'd managed. And whilst it would have been easy to let herself go, she deliberately didn't allow this to happen.

Janey and Maxine learned to fend for themselves from an early age, which Thea felt was all to the good and the only sensible way to ensure that they would grow up with a sense of independence. She wanted them to realize that the only person one could truly rely on was oneself.

She had been divorced, now, for over twenty years and never been tempted to remarry. Patrick had disappeared to America, leaving her with nothing but his surname, and although alimony would have been nice, it wasn't something she'd ever expected from him. Managing on her own and struggling to balance her meagre finances had become a matter of pride.

And, on the surface, she was content with her modest lifestyle. Now that her children were grown up, the struggle had eased. Her home was small but comfortable. The studio where she created and sold her sculptures was rented. She made just enough money, as a rule, to enjoy herself, and when business was slow there was always Philip, happy to help out in whichever way he could. Not a wealthy man himself, he was nevertheless heartbreakingly willing to dig into his own pockets when the need arose. He really was a very nice man, as devoted to Thea as she had once been to Patrick. Sadly for him, she was unable to prevent herself treating him as badly as Patrick had once treated her.

But Oliver Cassidy was in a different league altogether. After years of struggling and making do, Thea was ready to be spoiled by a man who wasn't afraid to wave his wallet. And although she'd only just met him, she knew instinctively that here was a man who wasn't afraid of anything at all.

It had been a dazzling evening. Arriving in the Rolls less than five minutes after Janey had left, Oliver had picked her up and taken her to the five-star Grand Rock Hotel where he was staying. The hotel restaurant, one of the best in Cornwall, was as impressive as she had hoped. And her dinner companion, Thea decided as she sipped her cognac, had definitely exceeded all expectations.

'How long are you staying down here?' she asked, having already learned that he lived in Bristol.

Oliver Cassidy shrugged, adjusting snowy shirt cuffs. 'A week, maybe two. I've been looking at properties in the area, thinking of moving down here.'

Better and better, thought Thea happily, admiring his discreet gold cufflinks and breathing in the scent of Penhaligon cologne. 'Well, I'm pretty familiar with the area. Perhaps I could help you there.' Pausing, she broke into a smile. 'Helping other people to spend their money is a great hobby of mine.'

As far as Oliver Cassidy was concerned, her bluntness made a refreshing change. Over the years he had become something of an expert on the subject of gold-digging females and what he'd discovered was that, to a woman, they would tear out their own professionally manicured fingernails rather than admit that his money held any interest for them or that it could make any difference to their attraction towards him. It was all so tiresome, so bloody predictable.

Thea Vaughan, on the other hand, was making no secret whatsoever of her interest in both him and his money, and he found her honesty quite disarming. He wanted to get to know this charming, teasing woman; she interested him more than anyone else had done for years. He also, quite urgently, wanted to take her up to his suite and make love to her. Ever the perfect English gentleman, however, he felt he should allow her to finish her cognac first.

It wasn't difficult to read his mind. Thea was looking forward to the hours ahead just as much as he was. Beneath the immaculate, dark blue suit and white shirt she could only too easily imagine the contours of his body. Oliver Kennedy – no, Cassidy – had the erect stance of a guardsman and he'd kept himself in remarkably good shape. His chest was broad, his stomach flat and he sported an impressive tan. Going to bed with him, she thought as her fingers idly caressed the stem of her brandy glass, would be fun.

But there was no hurry. No hurry at all.

'Go on then,' she said with a provocative smile. 'I've told you all about my miserable marriage. Now it's your turn.'

'Which particular miserable marriage did you have in mind?' Oliver, after puffing meditatively on his cigar, leaned back in his chair and signalled for the waiter to replenish their drinks. If she could wait, so could he. 'There are three to choose from.'

'All of them,' said Thea cheerfully. 'In chronological order. And I want to hear the gory details . . .'

Since picking wives had never been one of his strong points, there were plenty of those, too. Over the next half hour he regaled her with hair-raising tales of his three scheming, volatile wives. If Thea suspected that he was bending the facts in order to present himself in a blameless light, she didn't voice such thoughts aloud. And it was riveting stuff anyway, better than any soap opera. According to Oliver – trusting, innocent Oliver – he had been bamboozled in turn into matrimony by Liza, Milly and Fay. All three, it appeared, had been blonde, beautiful and absolute hell to live with. They made Macbeth's witches look cute.

None of the marriages had lasted longer than three years. Each wife had departed in a flurry of recriminations and alimony. Following the third divorce, Oliver had vowed that he would stick to mistresses. They might be expensive but they were a damn sight less expensive than greedy, vengeful wives.

'And there were no children?' said Thea, totally engrossed and not in the least put out by the declaration. She couldn't imagine anything more thrilling than being an expensive mistress. This kind of scenario was right up her street.

Oliver looked momentarily uncomfortable. 'I have a son by my first wife,' he replied, after taking another puff of his cigar. 'But we had . . . er . . . a disagreement some years ago. I'm afraid we haven't been on speaking terms since then.'

With a directness which so often made her elder daughter cringe, Thea rested her chin on her clasped hands and said, 'Really? What happened?'

'I tried to stop him making the same mistake I had.' Oliver Cassidy didn't make a habit of admitting that he could have been wrong. He still wasn't entirely convinced that in the matter of Véronique he might have been, but her untimely death had come as a great shock to him nevertheless. 'I'd been through three disastrous marriages and realized too late that my wives were only interested in my money. My son was living in London, doing very well for himself in his own career. Then, when he was twenty-three, he met a young French girl. She was eighteen years old and penniless. He was besotted with her. Within a few weeks of meeting her, he brought her down to Bristol and informed me that they were planning to get married.' He paused, remembering the ensuing argument as plainly as if it had happened yesterday. 'Well. To cut a long story short, I told him he was a bloody fool, and he went ahead and married her anyway. They had two children, and a few years later she died. I attempted to contact my son afterwards, but I'm afraid he wasn't able to forgive me for disapproving of the marriage in the first place.'

'But that's terrible!' cried Thea, suffused with indignation on his behalf. 'You only had his best interests at heart. You were trying to help him!'

'I know, I know. But my son had ideas of his own. You know how stubborn children can be.'

'So you've never ever seen your grandchildren?' Thea persisted, her dark eyes sympathetic.

Oliver shook his head. There was no need to mention that fateful afternoon when Véronique had brought them to his house. The encounter wasn't something of which he was particularly proud.

'Never.'

'It's a tragedy,' she declared expansively. 'And those poor children . . .'

Smiling, he leaned closer. 'Between ourselves, that's one of the reasons I'm thinking of buying a house down here. They moved to Trezale a year ago. I'm not getting any younger.' He spread his hands and added sorrowfully, 'I'd like the chance to get to know them.'

Her emotions heightened by Chablis and champagne, Thea was on the verge of tears. She took his hand in hers. 'You know, you really are a very nice man.'

Oliver Cassidy's plush suite was decorated in peacock blues and greens, and subtly lit.

Unashamed of her body, Thea removed her clothes with neither coyness nor ceremony, then crossed the bedroom to stand naked before him.

'Who's seducing who?' he said, appreciating her lack of artifice.

Thea, loosening his tie, looked amused. 'Does it really matter? We're adults. I think we both know why we're here . . .'

He removed his jacket and watched her capable fingers unfastening the buttons of his white shirt. She was still smiling, evidently enjoying herself. And she was right, of course; any further games were unnecessary.

Aroused by her straightforward attitude, as well as by the proximity of her unclothed body, Oliver realized that it was years since he had wanted a woman this badly. He put his arms around her, drawing her against him. He was sixty-one years old and his life wasn't over yet.

'Yes,' he said, inhaling her warm scent and pressing a kiss to her temple, where white hair met tanned, enticingly perfumed skin. 'And I think you are a very nice woman.'

'You're so right.' Closing her eyes, Thea slid her hands inside his unbuttoned shirt. 'I am.'

Chapter 13

'If you don't eat your Weetabix,' said Maxine, hating the sound of her own voice and frantically casting about for an appropriate threat, 'I'll—'

'What?' Josh challenged her, his eyes narrowing. In the two days since his father had been back from France, Maxine had definitely changed for the worse. No longer any fun, she had taken to bossing them around, ruthlessly rationing their television time and insisting they do boring school work even though it was still the middle of the summer holidays. If she hadn't demanded to see his exercise books he would never even have found the squashed Mars bar in the side pocket of his satchel, so the fact that he wasn't hungry was all her fault anyway. 'If I don't eat my Weetabix,' he repeated mutinously, 'you'll what?'

Hell, thought Maxine, who couldn't have cared less whether or not he ate his stupid breakfast. All she was trying to do was prove to Guy Cassidy that she could do the job he so obviously didn't think her capable of, and all she was doing was making everyone miserable, including herself.

And Guy, damn him, wasn't even paying attention. Buried behind his paper, apparently engrossed in the racing pages, he was drinking strong black coffee and ignoring his young son's act of rebellion. Maxine, who had been so determined to impress him, wondered why she even bothered.

'I shall begin by shaving your head,' she replied sweetly, because Josh was inordinately proud of his spiky blond hair. She had also observed the first furtive flickerings of interest in ten-year-old Tanya Trevelyan, whose parents ran the local post office. 'And then I shall paint red spots all over your face with indelible felt pen. Then I'll tell Tanya that you're madly in love with her!'

Ella screamed with laughter. Josh, turning purple, shot Maxine a look of fury.

'You wouldn't!'

'Oh yes, I would.'

Grabbing Guy's arm, he wailed, 'Dad, tell her she can't do that! She can't tell Tanya I love her . . .'

But Guy, who appeared to have other matters on his mind, wasn't interested. 'Of course she won't.' His tone brusque, he glanced at his watch and stood up. 'Damn, I'm going to be late. I'll be back this evening at around nine.'

'Make her promise not to say anything to Tanya,' Josh begged, still mortified by the prospect of hideous humiliation.

'Make him promise to eat his Weetabix,' said Maxine, imitating his nine-year-old whine.

Guy merely looked exasperated. 'For heaven's sake!'

'Thanks for your support,' muttered Maxine, seizing the bowl of beige mush and clattering it into the sink. 'You're a great help.'

Ella, who detested having her hair washed, tugged at her sleeve. Her eyes shining, she said hopefully, 'Maxine? If I'm naughty, will you shave *my* head?'

Since attempting to instil discipline and show Guy what a treasure she was had been such a dismal failure, Maxine left the children to their own devices for the rest of the morning. If non-stop TV cartoons were all they wanted to watch, why should she care?

Having washed up the breakfast things and gazed morosely out at the rain sweeping in from the sea, she sat down at eleven o'clock with a big gin and tonic and the portable phone. To cheer herself up and get her own back on Guy for being so stroppy, she was going to phone all her London friends for a good gossip. The fact that it was peak time and would cost him an absolute fortune only made the prospect more enjoyable.

'You make him sound like an ogre,' exclaimed Cindy, from the opulent comfort of her four-poster bed in Chelsea. Recently married to a rich-but-ugly industrialist, some twenty-five years older than herself, whose vast stomach, thankfully, was a serious impediment to their sex life, she couldn't imagine what Maxine had to moan about. 'I met Guy Cassidy at a party last year and he was absolutely charming. All the women were drooling like dogs! Maxi, you have to admit he's sensationally attractive...'

'Looks aren't everything,' Maxine drawled, jiggling the ice cubes in her glass and tucking her bare feet beneath her on the sofa. Then, relenting slightly, she added casually, 'Well, he's not bad I suppose.'

'Don't give me that,' crowed Cindy, who knew her

too well. 'What are you trying to tell me, that you've had your hormones surgically removed? You must fancy him rotten!'

Maxine grinned. Cindy, in London, was a safe enough confidante.

'OK,' she admitted, taking a slug of gin. 'So maybe I do, a bit. But I'd fancy him a lot more if only he'd show a smidgeon of interest in return. You have no idea how demoralizing it is, slapping on the old make-up and making myself generally irresistible when he takes about as much interest in me as he does in the bloody milkman.'

'Sometimes make-up isn't enough,' replied Cindy, ever practical. 'Sometimes you just have to rip off your pinny and get naked.'

'You mean I should seduce him?' At such an awesome prospect, even Maxine blanched.

'Works every time,' Cindy said happily. Maxine doubted whether Cindy would even recognise a pinafore if it leapt up and strangled her. She'd certainly never worn one in her life.

'It wouldn't work with Guy.' Gloomily contemplating her almost empty glass, she imagined the scenario. She had a horrid feeling he would laugh his handsome head off. Before firing her, naturally.

'Why?' countered Cindy. 'Have you got fat?'

'I've got Guy Cassidy as a boss,' Maxine sighed. 'So far, he's seen through everything I've tried, and all he does is sneer. He's too smart to fall for an old trick like that.'

'You're losing your nerve, girl. Living out in the sticks is doing something to your brain. Isn't he worth taking a chance on?'

'It's all right for you.' As Maxine spoke, the doorbell rang. 'All you did was meet him at a party. You want to try living with him.'

'Darling, I'd be there like a shot!' Cindy, her interest aroused, sounded excited. 'Now *there's* an idea. You could invite me down for a weekend. If you're too chicken, I'll have a crack at him myself!'

'I'll have to go.' Maxine, uncurling herself, realized that her left leg had been seized by pins and needles and was now completely numb. 'There's someone at the door.'

'Oh pleeease,' Cindy urged. 'I'm your friend, aren't I? Go on, invite me!'

'No,' said Maxine bluntly. 'You're married.'

'Don't be so boring,' protested Cindy. 'At least I'm not chicken!'

Cindy didn't understand, thought Maxine as she made her way awkwardly to the front door, clinging to furniture as she went. She wasn't chicken either, she just wasn't prepared to make a complete prat of herself and lose both home and job into the bargain. And she would have her wicked way with Guy Cassidy eventually, she was quite determined on that score. It was simply a matter of timing and technique. And pouncing on him buck-naked, Maxine decided with a small, wry smile, didn't exactly rate highly in terms of finesse.

She needn't have bothered to stop en route and grab a handful of fivers from the tin in the kitchen, because it wasn't the milkman after all.

'Yes?' said Maxine, staring at the woman on the doorstep and mentally noting the style and quality of the clothes she wore. She'd bet her last Jaffa cake it wasn't the Avon lady either.

'Is Guy here?' The visitor eyed Maxine in turn, instantly homing in on the blackcurrant jam stain which, courtesy of Ella, adorned her yellow tee-shirt.

The rain was still bucketing down, driven in from the sea by a ferocious wind and hammering against the windows like gravel. Anyone else, caught out in such a storm, would have looked like a scarecrow.

But this woman, wrapped in a long, lean leather coat the colour of toffee apples, worn over a cream and toffee-apple striped silk shirt and cream trousers, seemed impervious to the weather. Screamingly elegant from her short, sleek black hair to her beige Ferragamo shoes, she simply wasn't the kind of female whose mascara ever ran. Maxine couldn't bear people like that. Most ominous of all, however, was the fact that in her elegant hand she carried an elegant suitcase. Naturally, it matched the outfit.

Feeling very down-at-heel by comparison, Maxine replied with a trace of belligerence. 'He's away on a shoot in Wiltshire. We aren't expecting him back until late this evening. He may even decide to stay there overnight.'

The woman, however, simply shrugged and smiled. Even her teeth were elegant. 'So much for surprises.'

Deeply engrossed in her telephone conversation with Cindy, Maxine hadn't heard an approaching car. Now she realized there wasn't one.

'I came by taxi,' said the woman, intercepting her glance in the direction of the drive.

'Don't worry.' Maxine stepped aside and gestured her

to step inside. 'I'll phone for another one. I'm sorry you've had a wasted journey, but if you'd like to leave a message for Guy I'll make sure he gets it. As I said, he probably won't be back tonight . . .'

'It's quite all right,' said the woman easily, making her way past Maxine into the hall and dismissing her offer with a nonchalant wave of her wrist. Indicating the suitcase in her other hand, she added, 'This isn't a fleeting visit. I'm down here for a week at least.'

Bugger, thought Maxine. It hadn't worked. 'Really? How nice,' she said aloud.

Her name was Serena Charlton and in confined spaces the reek of her scent was positively overpowering. One of Guy's ruthlessly slender model 'friends', she was showing every sign of making herself at home.

'We're extremely good friends, she told Maxine as she slithered out of the leather coat and handed it to her. 'I expect Guy's told you all about me.'

Not so much as a syllable, thought Maxine, taking comfort from the fact. It was going to be interesting seeing Guy's reaction when he returned and found an uninvited guest comfortably installed in his home. What fun if he booted her out . . .

'Then again,' said Serena, observing her deliberately blank expression, 'he always did like to keep his private life to himself. And gossiping with the household staff isn't quite the done thing, after all.'

'Of course not.' No m'lady, sorry m'lady, Maxine silently mocked, only just resisting the urge to tug her forelock and bob a fetching little curtsey. She was expected, it seemed, to hang the coat up. To amuse herself, she dumped it instead over the back of the nearest chair.

But Serena appeared genuinely unaware of the fact that her words might have given offence. Making herself comfortable on the sofa, she smiled across at Maxine and said, 'A cup of tea would be nice. White with two Hermesetas, please.'

Having heaped at least a hundred calories' worth of brown sugar into the cup, Maxine felt a little better. When she carried it through to Serena in the sitting room she said, 'Josh and Ella are playing upstairs. Shall I tell them you're here?'

Serena was undoubtedly beautiful but she hadn't featured in Josh's list of favourite females, which was another bonus. Maxine soon found out why.

'The children are here?' Serena's face fell. Her tone of voice registered distinct lack of enthusiasm. 'Why aren't they at school?'

'Summer holidays.' Maxine had to work hard to suppress a grin. Serena Charlton, presumably, was childless.

'Oh. No, don't worry about getting them down here. No need to disturb them. You carry on with your work, um . . . Maxine. I'll just sit here and enjoy my tea in peace.'

And get fat into the bargain, thought Maxine smugly, remembering the amount of sugar she'd put in. Dying to get the low-down on Serena, she raced upstairs to interrogate Josh. The lack of enthusiasm, it transpired, was entirely mutual.

'She's staying for a whole *week*?'

Reaching for the remote control, Maxine reduced the volume on the television.

'She thinks she is. Why, don't you like her?'

'Her face is quite pretty,' said Ella helpfully. 'And she's got really short hair.'

'She's OK I suppose.' Josh was making an effort to be fair. 'She brought us some sweets once. But she'd rather be with Dad than us. We've only met her a few times and she always thinks we should go outside and play.' He pulled a face. 'Even when it's raining.'

Their earlier row forgotten, Maxine retorted indignantly. 'And what does your father have to say about that?'

Sometimes Josh seemed wiser than his years. His gaze drifting back towards the television screen, where Tom was beating hell out of Jerry, he replied absently, 'Most of Dad's girlfriends make too much of a fuss over us because they think it'll make him like them more, and then maybe he'll marry them. I think Dad likes Serena because she doesn't do that. He says at least she's honest.'

Nifty reasoning, though Maxine appreciatively. On both sides.

'If I go and get the scissors,' said Ella, 'will you cut my hair off now?'

Chapter 14

Thanks to the appalling weather, business in the shop was slow. Few people, it seemed, were interested in buying flowers when it was pouring with rain. Janey and Paula, guiltily eating cream cakes from the bakery next door, passed the time by doing the crossword in the local paper and taking it in turn to make endless mugs of tea.

'What's a nice chap like me doing in an advertisement like this?' Paula read aloud as Janey emerged from the back of the shop with yet more tea.

'How many letters?' Janey asked, easing herself back onto her stool and peering across at the paper. 'Could it be Jeremy Beadle?'

'God forbid!' Paula grinned and pointed to the next page. 'I'm on to the Personal column. Don't you ever read it?'

'No.' Pulling a face, Janey followed Paula's index finger and read the rest of the advert. ' "I am a good-looking male, thirty-four, with a whacky sense of humour." Hmm, probably means he's into serious spanking. "Fun-loving partner required, five feet three or under." Ah, so he's an extremely short spanker. "Age, looks and marital status unimportant." That means he's totally desperate.'

'OK,' said Paula, conceding the point. 'He doesn't sound great, I'll admit.'

'Great? He sounds like a nerd.'

'But they aren't all like that. How about this one? "Divorced male, forty, own home and car, new to the area. Likes dining out, theatre, tennis, long walks . . ." What's wrong with him?'

Janey said unforgivingly, 'BO I expect.'

'Don't be mean! Why are you so suspicious?'

'I don't know.' She shrugged. 'If he's so terrific, why does he need to advertise in the Lonely Hearts?'

'He's new to the area and he doesn't want to cruise the bars picking up girls,' said Paula, springing to his defence. 'Because the type of girl he likes doesn't hang around bars waiting to be picked up. There's nothing weird or sinister about advertising in the Personals,' she added firmly. 'Sometimes it's just the most sensible thing to do.'

Janey had never thought of it like that. Neither would she ever have imagined that Paula would argue the case so strongly. Her curiosity aroused, she said, 'Have you done this kind of thing yourself?'

'No, but a friend of mine tried it once. And it worked for her.'

'What happened?'

The younger girl broke into a grin. 'She met a tall blond airline pilot. Within six weeks, they were married. And they're amazingly happy.' Paula, who could give Maxine a run for her money where bluntness was concerned, added, 'You should try it.'

Startled, Janey laughed aloud. '*Me?*'

'It's been two years now since Alan . . . disappeared.'
Paula fixed her with a steady gaze. 'I know it's been hard
for you, but you really should be starting to think about
the rest of your life. You're only twenty-eight, Janey. You
need to start going out, meeting new people . . . having
fun . . .'

'And you seriously think this is the answer?' Deeply
sceptical, Janey said, 'That by answering a few crazy
adverts in the local paper I'll change my life?'

'I don't know.' Paula, having made her point, crossed
her fingers beneath the counter and prayed that Janey
would never find out she'd made up the fairytale romance
between her friend and the pilot. Reaching for the paper
and returning her attention to the crossword, she added
casually, 'But if you don't try it, you'll never know. Now,
have a look at fourteen across. Do you think it could be
pfennig?'

Paula had a way of saying things which stuck in the mind.
As she tackled a pile of ironing that evening, Janey found
herself recalling their earlier conversation and beginning
to wonder if she had a point after all. Having overcome
her initial misgivings, she now conceded that for some
people, circumstances beyond their control made it hard
for them to socialize in the traditional manner. When she'd
pressed Paula for further details about her friend, for
example, she'd explained that as an airline pilot, Alistair
had been so busy flying all over the world, he simply
hadn't had time to meet any girls in his own country.
Not interested in the air hostesses with whom he worked,
he had placed an advert instead, in *Time Out*, and received

sixty-seven replies. The first date hadn't worked out and Geraldine, Paula's friend, had been the second. True love had blossomed almost instantaneously and the remaining sixty-five females hadn't had a look-in.

Janey hadn't believed this story for a moment. Even if Paula hadn't own-goaled herself, calling the pilot Alistair one minute and Alexander the next, she would have seen through the enormous fib, but that didn't mean it couldn't happen. Janey herself had read magazine articles detailing such meetings and subsequent marriages. Paula had undoubtedly been right when she'd declared that sometimes it was simply the most sensible thing to do.

Abandoning the ironing before she wrecked something she was particularly fond of, Janey switched on the kettle. Her stomach was rumbling and she could have murdered a bowl of spaghetti but the cream cakes that afternoon had probably used up her calorie quota for the next three weeks.

Gloomily surveying the contents of the fridge, she set about making herself a boring salad sandwich instead.

'Widower, 62, seeks the company of a lively lady 45-60, for friendship and old-time dancing. Resilient toes an absolute must.'

He sounded lovely. Janey was only sorry she wasn't old enough for him. Wondering if maybe she couldn't get away with lying about her age, she read on.

'Lonely vegan (Sagittarius) wishes to meet soulmate,' pleaded the next ad. 'Non-smoking, teetotal young lady required. Capricorn preferred.'

Aaargh, thought Janey. Oh well, it took all sorts. And who knew, maybe there was a soulmate out there somewhere, reading this advert and experiencing a leap of joyous recognition.

'Gentleman required for plumpish but well-preserved divorcee, 55. Fond of walking, gardening, cooking and dancing.'

That was nice, she could pair up with the foxtrotting widower.

'Discreet businessman seeks ditto lady, 30-50, for mutually pleasurable meetings, afternoons only.'

A typographical error, surely, thought Janey with a grin. Didn't he mean 'matings'?

'Tall, presentable, divorced male, 35, would like to meet normal female.'

She paused and re-read the words, attracted by their simplicity and intrigued to know more. Had his wife been spectacularly abnormal? How tall was tall? And did 'presentable' mean a bank-managerish grey suit with accompanying dandruff, or clean jeans and a tee-shirt that had actually been ironed?

Twenty minutes later, after having absently flipped through the rest of the paper and finished her sandwich, Janey found herself back once more at the Personal column. With a guilty start, she realized she was studying the advertisement placed by Mr Presentable. Even more alarming she was actually giving it serious consideration.

'You should try it,' Paula had said in her uncompromising way. 'You need to meet new people. If you don't try it, you'll never know what you might be missing.'

If the Sagittarian vegan was anything to go by, Janey suspected she did. But maybe . . . just maybe Paula had a point. Mr Presentable didn't sound weird and there was always the chance that he might turn out to be genuinely nice. There was, after all, an undeniable gap in her life, and a cautious toe in the water – nothing too alarming, perhaps a brief meeting in a wine bar for a lunchtime drink – would satisfy her own curiosity and at the same time show Paula that she had at least been willing to make some kind of effort on the man-front.

Or more aptly, the unmanned front.

Although there was Bruno, of course, whom Paula didn't know about. Janey wasn't sure whether he really counted. In addition, knowing how she would have felt if Alan had cheated on her, she hated the thought of getting involved and upsetting Nina. Bruno had assured her that theirs was an open relationship but she was, after all, only hearing his side of the story.

If she was being honest, her attraction towards Bruno was yet another good reason why she should consider replying to the advert. Any real involvement with someone like him could only eventually end in tears. What she really needed to do, Janey decided, was to diversify.

'I don't believe it!' cried Maxine, who had only phoned up in order to relieve her own boredom and have a good moan about Serena. Riveted by the news of Janey's decision, she quite forgot her own irritations. 'Darling, what an absolute scream! I know, we could both answer a few ads and compare notes afterwards. Marks out of ten for looks, brains and bonkability!'

'It isn't a joke.' With great firmness, Janey interrupted her. Her sister, of course, was about the last person in the world in whom she should have confided. Maxine simply couldn't comprehend the idea that meeting new men wasn't always easy. She could scarcely take five paces without tripping over likely contenders in nightclubs, on the street, at supermarket checkouts, even on one occasion in Asprey's. The man in question had been in the company of his girlfriend at the time, choosing from a selection of wildly expensive engagement rings. Maxine, broke as usual and shamelessly trying on jewellery for the hell of it, had fallen into conversation with the two of them and came away with the bridegroom-to-be's phone number in her jacket pocket. When you were Maxine, Janey remembered, men were there for the taking. They practically queued up to be taken, in fact. Usually for everything they had.

'What do you mean, it isn't a joke?' Maxine demanded. 'Of course it's a joke. You can't seriously be serious!'

Janey had known she was making a big mistake. Patiently, she said, 'Why not? If I was looking for a new car, I'd see what was being advertised in the paper. If I wanted to move house I'd find out what the estate agents had on their books. Why should looking for a new man be any different?'

I sound like Paula, she thought with amusement. Maybe we should forget selling flowers and set up a dating agency instead.

'I don't believe it,' repeated Maxine, as close to being struck dumb as it was possible for Maxine to get. 'You *are* serious!'

Having made up her mind, Janey had no intention of allowing herself to be bulldozed out of it now. Before

Maxine had a chance to get her teeth into a really below-the-belt argument on the subject, she said, 'OK, OK. You're right, it was a bad idea.'

'About the worst you've had since you decided I should come and work at the Hotel Cassidy,' declared Maxine, remembering why she had decided to phone her sister in the first place. 'As if I wasn't enough of a skivvy already, some ghastly tarty girlfriend of Guy's rolled up earlier today with wagonloads of cases and announced that she was here for the week. All she's done is sit on her fat bum watching television and demanding endless cups of tea.'

'Funny, that's what you do when you visit me.' Janey grinned to herself. 'Has she really got a fat bum?'

'She soon will have, by the time I've finished with her.' Maxine spoke in self-satisfied tones.

'And she's tarty? I wouldn't have thought that was Guy's style at all.'

This time she was almost able to hear Maxine's shoulders slump in defeat.

'OK, so maybe she isn't tarty. If she were, I might not hate her so much.'

'Ah, so she's a threat,' Janey teased. 'You had your designs on Guy and now she's put your nose out of joint.'

Gloomily, Maxine said, 'She even has a designer nose.'

It was cheering to discover that even Maxine could feel inadequate when the odds were stacked against her. Janey, who knew only too well how it felt, said, 'Is she really stunning?'

'Hmm.' Maxine sounded resigned. 'Come up and see us sometime, then you might understand what I'm up against.'

'Isn't your sparkling personality enough?'

'Don't be stupid, of course it isn't. Men like Guy aren't interested in personalities.' Maxine paused, then added, 'I mean it, Janey. Come over tomorrow morning, then you can see for yourself.'

'I can't just turn up,' protested Janey. 'That really would look stupid.'

'Florists deliver flowers, don't they?' Maxine spoke with exaggerated patience. 'So, if you're going to be boring about it I'll place an order. How about a nice bouquet of deadly nightshade?'

'Oh dear.' Janey grinned. 'Are you sure you wouldn't prefer a wreath?'

It was eleven-thirty by the time Guy returned home, and to Maxine's disappointment he didn't boot Serena unceremoniously out into the night.

Staying put in her armchair, she eavesdropped like mad on the reunion out in the hall. If she twisted round and craned her neck all the way over to the left she could have watched them through the crack in the door, but that would have been too tacky. Besides, Guy would probably catch her at it.

He sounded surprised, though not unhappy, to find Serena waiting for him at the front door. Maxine heard her say, 'Darling, Thailand was cancelled so I found myself with a free week. I've been here since about midday.'

Maxine was only too easily able to envisage the accompanying embrace; Serena was the lithe, wrap-around type. The kiss that went with it, thankfully, wasn't audible.

'You should have phoned,' said Guy, eventually.

'It doesn't matter now. I'm just glad you decided not to stay away overnight after all.'

Maxine winced. Guy didn't miss a trick.

'Has Maxine been looking after you?' she heard him say. There was a faint edge to his voice She winced again, this time in anticipation.

'Mmm,' Serena replied vaguely. 'Well, in her own way I suppose. She served up the most extraordinary supper, a kind of fish pie made with instant mashed potato.'

She made 'instant' sound like maggot-infested. Maxine heard Guy say, 'The children like it.'

'And it was positively teeming with garlic.'

All the better to repel you with, my dear, thought Maxine happily. With six whole cloves of the stuff to contend with, she doubted whether Guy had much enjoyed his welcome-home kiss.

'Yes, well. Maxine's culinary techniques are . . . interesting,' he replied dryly. 'Where is she now, in bed?'

'In the sitting room.' Serena didn't bother to lower her voice. 'Darling, is it wise to allow the nanny the run of the entire house? She's been there all evening, hogging the most comfortable chair and the remote control. And she's been helping herself to your gin.'

Maxine turned and smiled at Guy as he entered the room. Since there wasn't much point in pretending not to have overheard, she said brightly, 'Only one gin. Oh, and a splash of tonic and two ice cubes. You can deduct them from my wages.'

'Don't be silly. Are the children all right?'

'Bound, gagged and manacled to their beds.' She

beamed. 'Don't worry, they can't escape.'

'Good.' He gave her a brief smile. Serena, as she had anticipated, clung lovingly to his arm. 'Well, we're off to bed now. Don't forget to turn everything off before you go up.'

With any luck, thought Maxine, I did that when I mashed six cloves of garlic into the fish pie.

Chapter 15

Janey saw what Maxine meant when she turned up at Trezale House the following morning. The storms had cleared, Cornwall was bathed in glorious sunshine once more and Serena Charlton was sunning herself topless in the garden. Observing the sheer flawlessness of her long, lean body and deeply envious of such perfect breasts – the pert kind, which wouldn't dream of sliding down to nestle in each armpit as her own unruly pair invariably did – Janey was glad she didn't share her sister's need to compete. When the opposition was this stunning, it was a daunting prospect to say the least.

'For me?' said Guy, coming into the kitchen behind her and spotting the cellophane-wrapped bouquet of lemon-yellow roses in her arms. 'How kind. Nobody's given me flowers for years.'

He seemed to be in a good mood. Janey, moving out of the way as he reached into the fridge for a bottle of milk, tried not to stare at his naked torso. All he wore was a pair of Levi's and delicious aftershave. Yet another faultless body, she thought enviously. Such dazzling perfection was almost too much to bear.

'Maxine ordered them. She's gone to track down a vase.'

'Who?' Rubbing his wet hair with a green towel slung around his neck, he said cryptically, 'Ah, you mean our in-house saboteur.'

Janey's heart sank. 'What's she done now?'

But Guy merely grinned. 'I'm sure she'll tell you. When she does, perhaps you would let her know that it didn't work.' When Janey continued to look blank, he added enigmatically, 'Tell her that for lunch yesterday I had chicken Kiev.'

'Found one,' said Maxine, coming into the kitchen with a slender, very elongated smoked-glass vase. 'It looks like Serena, don't you think? Except that the vase has a higher IQ. Oh . . . sorry!' Spotting Guy and not looking the least bit apologetic, she stood the vase on the table. 'I thought you were still in the shower.'

Guy raised his eyebrows in good-humoured disbelief. Turning to Janey, he said, 'Do me a favour, will you? Take her out somewhere tonight.'

'Can't afford it,' said Maxine promptly. 'I've got to get the clunking noise in my car sorted out before the wheels fall off. I thought I'd stay in and save my pennies.'

Serena, taking a break from sunbathing, appeared in the kitchen doorway. The gauzy white blouse she had thrown on over her bikini was virtually transparent. Up close, Janey thought with a twinge of envy, she looked even more stunning than she had at a distance.

'I'd like a cup of tea,' she announced with a brief, pointed glance in Maxine's direction. 'And this time, maybe I could have Hermesetas in it instead of sugar.'

'Of course you could,' Maxine replied smoothly, filling the lookalike vase at the sink and busying herself with the task of flower arranging. 'The kettle is that round metal object next to the toaster. The teabags are in the cupboard.'

Exchanging yet another glance with Janey, Guy said, 'I've changed my mind. Take her away with you now.'

Maxine, thrilled at the prospect of almost a whole day off, protested, 'But I can't afford to go anywhere . . .'

'Here.' With a look of resignation he reached for his wallet. Peeling off eighty pounds, he handed the notes to Janey. 'Have fun. On one condition.'

Janey, who didn't trust conditions, looked wary. 'What's that?'

'You have to promise not to send her back before midnight.'

'It's a deal.' Maxine, cheered by her success, promptly abandoned the flowers in the sink.

Serena, frowning as Janey pocketed the money, said, 'I've never heard anything so ridiculous in my life.'

'Don't worry about it,' riposted Maxine, her smile angelic. 'I'm worth every penny. Just ask Guy . . .'

'Down here on holiday then, girls? Come on, don't be shy, we'll buy you a drink. Come and sit down with us.'

At Maxine's insistence, because 'you said you wanted to meet some men', they had set out at seven in the evening on a seafront bar crawl. And there was no doubt about it, thought Janey with a suppressed shudder: they were certainly meeting some men.

'Don't let them do it,' she whispered frantically in Maxine's ear, at the same time tugging her in the direction of the door. But Maxine, for someone so lacking in bulk, was surprisingly untuggable. She was also flashing the kind of smile that meant they were staying put.

Within seconds, two glasses of house white had materialized and the short one with the beer belly stretching a salmon-pink Lacoste shirt to its limits was leading Janey to the table. Maxine, brown eyes gleaming as she settled herself into one of the vacant chairs, was already nose to nose with his far better-looking friend.

'I'm Phil and he's Ricky,' said the little fat one, before diving enthusiastically into his pint and downing it in seconds. Having wiped the moustache of froth from his upper lip, he returned his attention to Janey. 'So how long are you down here for? Where d'you come from? What kind of work d'you do and what's your name?'

Janey stared at him. Fat Phil roared with laughter. 'Hey, it's a joke! Time is money, babe, and why waste time getting to know each other when we could be having fun? That's what I say!'

'I couldn't agree with you more.' Janey, suppressing a shudder, handed him her untouched glass of wine. 'And I hope you have lots and lots of fun, I really do. But I'm afraid I have to go now. The babysitter's expecting me back at nine and she'll kill me if I'm late—'

'What *is* the matter with you?' Maxine cried indignantly, catching up with her thirty seconds later. 'You wanted men, I got you men. Janey, you didn't even give him a chance!'

'Are you sure he was a man?' Janey countered, stung by her sister's insensitivity. 'He looked seven months pregnant to me. *And* he had breasts.'

'But he had a kind face.'

Maxine's ability to point out redeeming features in the most hopeless of cases never failed to amaze Janey. Provided, of course, that they were somebody else's hopeless cases and not her own.

'Maybe.' It was no good, she wasn't going to feel guilty. 'But I can't pretend to be interested in people. It just isn't me. Besides, he was a pillock.'

'You don't have to fall in love with him.' Maxine was trying hard to understand but it was an uphill struggle. 'You aren't supposed to take men like that seriously. They're just good to practise on, until the real ones turn up.'

This time Janey laughed because nobody would ever change Maxine. She had her own strategy in life and it would never even occur to her to question it. And why should she want to, anyway? As far as Maxine was concerned, it worked.

'OK, I'm sorry. What shall we do now?'

Maxine, straight-faced, said, 'I know. Back to your place, into our woolly dressing gowns and slippers. We'll watch that nice cookery programme on the telly and take it in turns to make the cocoa. If you're really good, I'll teach you how to crochet a tea cosy that looks like a thatched cottage.'

'Or?'

'Blow the money on a stupendous meal,' Maxine replied promptly. 'I'm starving.'

Janey threw her a look of disbelief. Whilst she'd been working in the shop all afternoon, Maxine had been out on the patio, sunbathing and stuffing herself with food. An entire tub of Häagen Dazs rum and raisin had vanished from the freezer and when she'd gone out to clear up at six o'clock, empty crisp packets and Coke cans had littered the wrought-iron table.

But since it didn't even occur to Maxine that she shouldn't be hungry now, she misinterpreted the expression on Janey's face.

'Oh, all right! I absolutely promise not to talk to any strange men for the rest of the night.'

Janey doubted whether she was physically capable of such a feat, but it was a noble offer. Beginning to relax, she said, 'OK. How about La Campagnola?'

'Boring,' declared Maxine. 'The cricketer took me there last week and it was practically empty. No, I asked Guy about restaurants. He said the best one was in Amory Street. I think it's called Bruno's.'

'Janey, my gorgeous girl!' shouted Bruno when he saw her coming through the door, and Maxine's eyebrows shot up in amazement.

Janey, praying she hadn't turned red, explained hurriedly, 'He says that to all the girls.'

'Hasn't said it to me,' murmured Maxine as Bruno made his way across the restaurant to greet them. 'Hmm, and very nice too. Is he gay?'

'Is the Pope Jewish?' countered Bruno, who possessed 20-20 hearing. Embracing Janey and at the same time studying Maxine over her shoulder he murmured, 'Darling, what have you been telling this poor girl?'

'She isn't a poor girl, she's my sister.' As if Bruno hadn't already guessed, Janey thought morosely. Hadn't she, after all, been complaining to him about Maxine for the past fortnight?

'Maxine Vaughan,' said Maxine, gazing with interest at possibly the only man on the planet capable of making Janey blush. He wasn't what you'd call startlingly good-looking but the eyes were the greenest she'd ever seen and the grin was irrepressible. He was, she decided, one of those men with an indefinable aura of attractiveness about them . . . a wonderfully wicked, *tantalizing* aura of attractiveness.

Janey, in turn watching Maxine survey Bruno, prayed she hadn't made a hideous mistake in agreeing to come here. On the one hand, Bruno's attentions were always guaranteed to boost her morale, and whenever Maxine was around, God knows, it needed boosting.

On the other hand, however, just introducing Bruno and Maxine was playing with fire. A bloody great bonfire, thought Janey ruefully, for already the inevitable sparks of interest were there. She could almost predict what would follow. Maxine and Bruno, both brimming with confidence and rapier-like repartee, were a perfectly matched pair. Whilst she, in dismal contrast, could practically feel herself melting into the wallpaper.

As she had known he would, Bruno ushered them to the most favoured table in the restaurant, next to the window.

'Come on, forty minutes over coffee is long enough,' he informed the diners already seated there. Whisking away cups and liqueur glasses and signalling to one of the waitresses to bring fresh linen and cutlery, he added briskly, 'Time's up, off you go, don't forget to leave an enormous tip.'

'Charming,' muttered the younger of the two men.

Bruno, winking at Janey and Maxine, slipped an arm around their waists and gave them both an appreciative squeeze.

'Charming isn't the word, sir. These ladies are stupendous . . . magnificent . . . the jewels in my own personal crown. And just think, if you hadn't spent practically a week's wages earlier on that ludicrously expensive bottle of wine, you might even have been able to afford to take them home with you for the night.'

'Hmmph,' snorted the older man, eyeing Maxine's bare legs with disdain as he rose to his feet.

'And hmmph to you too,' said Bruno cheerfully, guiding them towards the door. 'Goodbye, gentlemen. Have a wonderful evening. See you again very soon.'

'Gosh,' said Maxine, watching with admiration as Bruno waved them off the premises. 'Is he always like this?'

Janey, who was studying the menu, nodded. 'All the time.'

'But doesn't he lose an awful lot of customers?'

Janey shrugged. 'Bruno says it keeps them on their toes. And the ones he doesn't kick out are so grateful they leave bigger tips.'

Maxine was clearly impressed. When Bruno returned to their table with a bottle of Pouilly Fumé and pulled up another chair, Janey was surprised she didn't offer to sit on his lap.

'I love this place,' Maxine declared, her expansive gesture encompassing the green and white decor, the latticed ceiling and the spectacular view from the window. 'Thank goodness we didn't go to La Campagnola! And why on earth hasn't my big sister brought me here before?' Having given Janey a look of mock reproach, she returned her attention to Bruno. 'She's a sly one, I must say. She told me she didn't know any interesting men in Trezale.' With an arch smile, she added, 'And to think that you were here all the time.'

Janey, who would have torn out her own tonsils rather than come out with such a line, stared at her in disbelief. Was she being serious? Did other women really say things like that and get away with it? Had Maxine no shame?

The answer, it seemed, was no. If anything, her sister was looking more entranced than ever. The thin straps of her indigo camisole were slipping off her shoulders now and she was making no attempt to pull them up again. Her dark eyes, illuminated by candlelight, were bright with unconcealed interest.

'But how do you know each other?' she was asking Bruno, her chin cupped in one hand and the camisole top gaping to reveal more chest than ever.

In reply, he touched the arrangement of lilac and white freesias in the centre of the table. 'She brings me flowers.'

Maxine grinned. 'How romantic.'

'Come on, pay attention,' said Janey firmly, thrusting the menu into her free hand. 'You're the one who was so hungry. I'm having the seafood risotto and the lamb.'

By the time their food arrived, Maxine was in her element. Having discovered as much about Bruno Parry-Brent in the space of thirty minutes as Janey had learned in a year, she was now regaling him with her own life history. By the time they had moved on to the coffees, she was launching into a bitchy attack on Guy Cassidy.

'He's the one paying for this meal tonight,' Janey pointed out in Guy's defence.

Maxine looked scornful. 'Only because he wanted me out of the way.' Turning back to Bruno, she went on, 'You wouldn't believe this girlfriend of his. I didn't think anyone could treat me worse than Guy, but at least he's been known to say the odd please and thank you. Serena Charlton's a living nightmare; I can't believe what terrible taste in women some men have.'

Janey couldn't resist it. 'Maxine's only saying this because Guy isn't interested in her,' she explained. 'She had visions of moving into Trezale House and dazzling him, and it hasn't happened. It's been a great disappointment to her.'

'Oh, crushing,' Maxine agreed with a trace of mockery.

'But her ego, of course, won't allow her to admit it.' Janey smiled. Two could play at bitchery. Besides, Maxine had been showing off for long enough. She deserved it.

'He comes in here quite often,' said Bruno, aware of the undercurrents and of Janey's irritation with her sister. It didn't take a genius, he deduced, to figure out the reason for it. 'Brings some spectacular women with him, too.'

'His harem.' Maxine gave a dismissive shrug and spooned brown sugar into her coffee.

'So are you going to stick it out?' Bruno grinned. 'Or leave?'

Maxine hesitated. Rattling on about Guy's pigheadedness was one thing, but she had no intention of jacking in her job.

'He's a pain,' she said with a brave smile, 'but the kids

are OK. It wouldn't be fair to leave them.'

Janey pulled a face. 'My sister, the patron saint of children.' Turning to address Bruno once more, she said evenly, 'Take it from me, nothing interests Maxine more than a man who isn't interested in her. As long as Guy puts up with her, she'll stay. She doesn't give up on anyone without a fight.'

'So how long have you had this raging crush on Bruno?' said Maxine, on the way home.

Janey concentrated on driving. The lane leading up to Trezale House was narrow and unlit. 'Don't be silly,' she replied, her manner offhand. 'He's a friend, that's all.'

'And I'm your sister,' declared Maxine, not fooled for a moment by her apparent lack of interest. 'Come on, Janey! First you don't even mention him, then you have a go at me, deliberately putting me down in front of him. Why else would you do it?'

'You were showing off.'

Maxine shot her a triumphant grin. 'I'm always showing off. What's so interesting is the fact that this time you minded like hell. Darling, it's nothing to be ashamed of . . . there's no reason on earth why you shouldn't fancy him! He's an attractive man. I thought he was lovely.'

'I know you thought he was lovely,' said Janey in cutting tones. In her less-than-serene state, she crunched the van's gears. 'The entire restaurant knows you thought he was lovely. I just don't understand why you have to be so obvious.'

'Because that's the way I am.' Maxine shrugged. 'But

we're getting away from the point. The reason I asked you about your own little crush was because I wanted to know how serious it was. If you're madly in love with him, I'll do the decent thing and steer clear. After all,' she added infuriatingly, 'I wouldn't want to waltz in and snatch away the first man you've been interested in since Alan.'

Janey gritted her teeth, sensing that they were on the verge of their first real quarrel for years. Even more annoying was the fact that, deep down, she knew she was the one at fault. She was also in serious danger of cutting off her nose to spite her face.

As they approached Trezale House, she took a deep steadying breath. 'OK, I do like him. He *is* the first man I've been interested in since Alan, and the reason I didn't tell you about Bruno was because I didn't want you to say anything embarrassing when you met him.' She drew the van to a halt, switched off the engine and gazed out into the darkness ahead. 'There, so now you know.'

'Well, hallelujah!' Maxine retorted. 'I don't know why you couldn't have said all that in the first place. Darling, it's no big deal. Sometimes you're just too proud by half!'

Unlike Maxine, thought Janey, who had no pride at all. She still wasn't entirely happy, either. The last thing she needed was to be patronized by a younger sister who thought the entire situation too amusing for words.

'You needn't worry,' Maxine assured her now. 'From this moment on, he's all yours. I shall treat Bruno like a brother. We shall be friends.' She grinned. 'And I shan't even *try* to imagine what he looks like naked.'

Janey was tired. She sensed, too, that Maxine was still

poking gentle fun at her. 'It's past midnight,' she announced pointedly. 'You're allowed back into the house now. And I have to be up at five.'

But Maxine was still prattling on about Bruno. 'He is fun, though. I still can't believe he practically booted those customers out into the street just so we could sit at the best table. You have to admit, darling, that takes style!'

'Oh, please,' sighed Janey. 'Don't tell me you fell for that old routine. Nick and Tony run the antique shop next door to the restaurant. Bruno does that to them every night.'

Chapter 16

In for a penny, in for a pound. Having given the matter a great deal of thought, Janey replied to the advertisement in the paper, posted it at once so she couldn't change her mind, then began drafting out an ad of her own. The chances of Mr Presentable turning out to be Mr Ideal might be slim, but if she received a dozen replies she would at least have a selection to choose from. And if eleven of them were duds it wouldn't even matter, because number twelve could be perfect and *one* perfect male was all she needed.

It really was extraordinarily difficult, though, describing oneself in just a few brief sentences. If she exaggerated the facts she risked ridicule when she eventually came to face it out. The prospect of being greeted with a look of horror and a derisory 'I thought you said you were attractive', was positively bone-chilling. The bald facts, however, – 'plumpish, blondish deserted wife' – might be so off-putting that no man would even be tempted to reply.

It took longer than filling out a tax return and was about as harrowing. Every time a customer came into the shop she jumped a mile and shoved her writing pad under the counter. When Paula returned from making the morning deliveries, Janey was so engrossed she hardly heard her words.

'I've had a brilliant idea.'

The pad was hidden but the pen was still in Janey's hand. Twiddling it frantically between her fingers and pretending she'd been writing down an order, she managed, 'What?'

'If you placed one of those ads yourself, you could arrange to meet each man somewhere busy and ask them to wear a white carnation in their buttonhole.'

'So?'

Paula, looking pleased with herself, pulled herself on to the spare stool and swung her legs. 'So, all we have to do is sit here and wait for men to come in asking for a single white carnation. You'll be able to have a good look at them first, incognito. And if they're too hideous for words you wouldn't have to bother turning up.'

'Cruel!' protested Janey, starting to laugh.

'Sensible. Not to mention good for business.' Paula threw her a sidelong glance. 'Do you think you might advertise, then?'

Paula was trustworthy, but some items of gossip were just too good to pass up. Her mother worked at Trezale House and Janey was determined that Maxine shouldn't find out about this. Now, more than ever, she needed to keep the last vestiges of her self-confidence intact.

'Maybe when I'm fifty,' she replied with tolerant amusement. 'But for now, I think I'll give it a miss.'

Maxine, unable to understand why she couldn't simply

scrawl the names on with pink Magic Marker, was struggling ill-temperedly to sew name tapes into Josh's school shirts. Guy hadn't helped, earlier, when he had remarked, 'Not that anyone else is likely to mistake Josh's shirts for their own, the way you iron them.'

He had said it jokingly, but Maxine had detected the dig. And although she'd been sewing for the last two and a half hours the pile of new school clothes still waiting to be attacked seemed more mountainous than ever.

'Dad's taking photographs of Serena,' Josh reported from his position in the window seat overlooking the back garden. He frowned. 'She doesn't have very big bosoms for a grown-up.'

Maxine suppressed the memory of what she'd imagined working for Guy would be like. In her innocence she'd envisaged organizing games of hide-and-seek for the children, accompanying them to the pantomime and in her free time socializing happily with Guy. In her more elaborate fantasies, she was the one being endlessly photographed. And because Guy was so famous and respected, interest in his stunning new model would spread like wildfire . . . the life of a super model beckoned . . . she would become wealthy, a celebrity, loved by everyone . . . especially Guy Cassidy.

'But then your bosoms are only little, as well,' said Josh, who had been studying her with a critical eye. 'Your sister has much bigger ones than you.'

'A word of advice.' Maxine clenched her teeth as she bit off a length of thread. 'You'll find life a lot easier if you don't go through it telling people what small bosoms they have.'

'Bosoms' was currently his favourite word. Josh smirked.

'And don't you think you should be getting changed into something more suitable?'

Guy and Serena were supposed to be taking both Josh and Ella into St Ives for lunch and it was one o'clock already. Maxine, who had set her heart on an afternoon of serious sunbathing, was beginning to wonder if they'd forgotten.

Josh shrugged. 'Oh, we aren't going now. Dad's taking Serena to meet some of her friends instead. They've got a yacht moored at Falmouth.'

Maxine's heart sank. Bang went her peaceful afternoon. She wondered whether Serena had done it on purpose.

'So we're staying here with you,' said Josh cheerfully. Then, in conversational tones he added, 'Why do you keep pricking your fingers, Maxine? I hope all that blood's going to wash out.'

Maxine was battling with the washing machine, which was making alarming noises like a jailer rattling his keys, when the doorbell rang. Glancing out through the kitchen window she saw a silver-grey Rolls Royce parked majestically in the drive. What fun, she thought, if the visitor was yet another of Guy's ritzy model girlfriends, complete with sneer and a bootful of suitcases. He could install her in the other spare bedroom and visit them on alternate nights like some Arab sheik.

But just as the identity of the last unexpected caller had turned out not to be the milkman but Serena, so this one appeared not to be a pouting, leggy model at all.

Wrong again, thought Maxine, realizing that she was grinning inanely at the visitor on the doorstep. What a good job she hadn't set her heart on a career as a fortune teller.

'Good afternoon,' said the man, and although she was certain they hadn't met before, he looked vaguely familiar. Hastily rearranging the grin into a more suitable smile, Maxine shook his outstretched hand and wondered if he might know something about erratic washing machines.

'You must be Maxine, the new nanny,' he continued warmly. 'I'm Oliver Cassidy.'

Realization dawned. 'I spoke to you on the phone earlier,' she said, recognizing the deep, well-bred voice. 'How nice to meet you, but I'm afraid Guy isn't back yet. We aren't expecting him home until this evening.'

'I know.' Oliver Cassidy looked a lot like his son but Maxine felt he possessed a great deal more charm. Now he shrugged and smiled. 'But it seemed a shame to pass up the opportunity to see my grandchildren. It's been quite a while, you see, and I'm only down here for the afternoon.'

Delighted to see him and mightily impressed with his car – which even had personalized plates – Maxine said at once, 'Come in! Of course you couldn't miss seeing the children. They're playing in the summer-house at the moment; shall I go and call them or would you prefer to take them by surprise?'

'Oh, surprise, I think.' Guy's father winked at her. He really was tons nicer than Guy, she decided. She'd never really gone for older men before, but he was almost enough to make her think again.

'Can I get you a drink?' she said brightly, but Oliver Cassidy shook his head.

'That's kind of you, my dear, but I'd better not. I'm driving.'

'It's a beautiful car,' said Maxine.

'My great pride and joy.' He nodded, acknowledging her admiration. 'I thought Josh and Ella might enjoy a ride in it before I leave. If you have no objections, that is.'

'Of course not!' Maxine's reply was almost vehement, her approval of Guy's father was increasing in leaps and bounds. And now she would be able to sunbathe in peace after all.

'Take them out for as long as you like,' she told him happily. 'I'm sure they'd love a trip in your car. What a shame, though, that you'll miss seeing Guy.'

'I cannot . . . simply *can not* believe you could be so stupid!'

He was more furious than Maxine had ever imagined possible. 'Fury' wasn't enough to describe his emotions. 'Rage' wasn't good enough either. Guy simply looked as if he wanted to kill her.

This is it, she thought numbly. Now I really am out of a job and on to the streets.

Almost more galling, however, was the fact that Serena appeared to be on her side.

'Look,' said Maxine, struggling to defend herself and willing herself not to lose her temper. 'I've already said I'm sorry, but how on earth was I supposed to know I was doing the wrong thing? He just turned up on the doorstep like any normal grandfather and said he'd come to see Josh and Ella. From the way he acted, I assumed he was a regular visitor. And he seemed perfectly nice—'

'Yes, darling,' put in Serena, her tone soothing.

Her defence of Maxine's actions was wholly astonishing as far as Maxine was concerned, and coming from any other quarter it would have afforded her some small comfort to know that she wasn't as negligent as Guy was making out.

'It isn't Maxine's fault that you and your father aren't on speaking terms,' Serena went on. 'If you didn't want him to see the children you should have told her.'

His eyes glittered. 'He's seen them once before. Only once, when he wasn't given any alternative. So it was hardly likely that he'd turn up.'

Serena shrugged as if to say, *Well, there you are then,* but Guy hadn't finished.

'Besides, that's hardly the point.' Turning back to Maxine, he said icily, 'He could have been anybody. Josh and Ella could have been kidnapped, held to ransom . . . murdered.'

'He wasn't a kidnapper,' shouted Maxine. 'He was your father.'

'You mean he told you he was my father.'

Stung by his derisory tone, she snapped back. 'He looked like you. Only better.'

'Oh, for God's sake!'

Maxine had had enough. It wasn't as if Josh and Ella had been at all harmed, anyway. True to his word, Oliver Cassidy had taken them out in the Rolls, given them afternoon tea at one of the better beach-front hotels and delivered them back safely at five o'clock, as promised. He had even left them each clutching a crisp fifty-pound note because, as he'd explained to Maxine, it was hard to know what to buy children these days now that train sets and dolls were passé. It wasn't until after he'd left that she'd made the alarming discovery that Josh and Ella didn't actually know their grandfather. Although being on the receiving end of fifty-pound notes certainly went some way towards persuading them that they should.

'Go on then,' she said abruptly, rising to her feet and glaring back at Guy. 'You're dying to do it, so sack me. Find yourself a new nanny who'll safety-pin the children to her ankles and shoot any strangers on sight. In the meantime, I'm sure Serena would just adore to stay on for a few more weeks and look after them herself.'

Too late she remembered that Serena had been sticking up for her, although it hardly mattered now. If she was out on her ear she'd never see either of them again anyway.

As far as Serena was concerned, however, the bitter jibe was too true to be offensive. 'I've got work lined up,' she said hurriedly. 'My agent would kill me if I tried to cancel anything now.'

Guy crossed to the drinks tray and poured himself a stiff Scotch. Part of him still wanted to kill Maxine but he was making an effort to calm down. Since even Serena had defended Maxine's actions, he realized now that the hatred he bore his father had led him to overreact. Maxine undoubtedly had her faults, but the fact remained that Josh and Ella adored her. And although he still didn't have the faintest idea why his father had turned up out of the blue, they had enjoyed themselves. Josh had only been six and Ella four when Véronique had taken them to meet him and even if they dimly recalled the events of that day they clearly hadn't connected them with this afternoon's surprise visitor. Both children had thoroughly enjoyed themselves and Josh, who was smitten with expensive cars – not to mention crisp new bank notes – was already asking when they might see him again.

As far as Guy was concerned, 'when hell freezes over' was the phrase that sprang most readily to mind, but it was a reply he'd kept to himself. And he supposed that, given the circumstances, Maxine couldn't really have been expected to refuse entry to an *apparently* charming relative visiting his much-loved grandchildren.

Draining his Scotch, he turned back to find Maxine, the picture of belligerence, still glaring at him. With her blond hair ruffled, she looked like an indignant parakeet.

'Oh cheer up,' he said with a trace of exasperation. 'I'm not going to sack you. Just take a bit more care in future, OK? They might not be the best behaved kids in the world but they're all I've got, so I'd quite like to hang on to them if I could.'

Chapter 17

It was all happening amazingly quickly. Janey, who had envisaged a wait of at least a fortnight before hearing anything back from Mr Presentable, had been caught so off-guard by his phone call that before she could gather her wits she heard herself agreeing to meet him that evening. Profoundly grateful that Paula wasn't in the shop at the time, she added hurriedly, 'Why don't you wear a carnation? Then I'll be able to recognize you.'

'Why don't you just look out for a tall, dark-haired man in a navy blue blazer and grey flannels?' he countered, sounding faintly amused. 'I'm not really the carnation-wearing type.'

'Oh.' Crestfallen, and on behalf of florists everywhere, Janey said, 'Why not?'

'Every time I put one in my buttonhole,' he replied, 'I find myself getting married.'

His name was Alexander Norcross and he had two ex-wives, a dark blue Porsche and a small cottage on the outskirts of Trelissick. Janey also suspected that his refusal to wear a carnation was due to the fact that it would have meant buying one.

'No, we decided against children,' he explained, over lukewarm coffee in a quiet bar away from the seafront which Janey had suggested because nobody she knew ever went there. 'They cost an absolute fortune. My wives tried to make me change my mind, of course, but I wasn't having any of it. There's no way I could have afforded to keep the Porsche on the road and bring up kids as well.' Leaning across the table he added confidentially, 'So I got out each time they started hankering, before they had a chance to pull the old "Oops, how did that happen?" routine. It isn't as if they really wanted children, after all. They just saw their friends doing it and didn't want to miss out. It didn't even occur to them to consider the expense.'

It was truly astounding, thought Janey, that someone so mean with money should be so generous with his aftershave. Great wafts of Old Spice were whooshing up her nose. It even seemed to have invaded her cup of coffee, which hadn't tasted great in the first place. She wondered how soon she could decently leave.

But meeting Alexander was an education, at least. He wasn't bad looking, he had a nice voice and he was tall. The packaging, she decided, was as much as anyone could possibly hope for. The only let-down was the fact that it belonged to a complacent, penny-pinching bore.

But there was also the irresistible challenge of discovering just how awful he could be. Summoning up a Maxine-ish smile and working hard not to inhale too much Old Spice, she said, 'So has advertising been a success? I expect you've met lots of girls.'

'Ah, but it's quality that counts.' Alexander gave her a

knowing look. 'Not quantity. I've found the initial telephone conversations to be revealing, Jane. All some of these females are interested in is a free meal, which is when I make my excuses. That's why I was so interested in meeting you,' he added happily. 'As soon as I read your letter, I felt we had something in common. And when you suggested we meet for a quick drink, I knew I was right.'

'Thank you,' murmured Janey, by this time struggling to keep a straight face. 'After all, why should people need to eat in order to get to know one another?'

'Exactly my point!' Alexander looked positively triumphant. Finishing his cold coffee, he pushed the cup and saucer an inch or two in her direction. 'And when you consider the ridiculous prices restaurants charge for an omelette . . . well, I call it money down the drain. I'd rather stay at home and know I wasn't being ripped off. How about you Jane?' he added, gazing at her with renewed interest and approval. 'Do you cook?'

Thanking her lucky stars she hadn't pinned all her hopes on Alexander Norcross, Janey was longing to tell someone the story of the brief encounter which – bizarrely – had gone some way towards restoring her own self-confidence.

'It was so ghastly it ended up being funny,' she said to Bruno the following morning, grinning as she recalled the way Alexander had complained to the bar manager about the price of a cup of coffee. 'He was so awful, but he really thought he was Britain's answer to Mel Gibson. If you could have seen the look on his face when I said I wouldn't be seeing him again—'

'Was he handsome?'

'Oh yes, but such a jerk! When I got back to the flat I was dying to phone Maxine to give her all the gory details, but I'd already decided not to tell her anything about answering the ad. I shouldn't be telling you, either.' Janey tried to look repentant, and failed. 'You're just as likely to make fun of me as she is. But it *was* funny, and I had to tell someone.'

'It certainly seems to have cheered you up,' remarked Bruno, inwardly appalled that she should have been driven to reply to a newspaper advert in the first place. 'But Janey, aren't you taking a bit of a risk? You don't need to do that kind of thing. A gorgeous girl like you could take her pick of men.'

Colouring at the compliment, even if it was only Bruno saying what he would no doubt say to anyone under the age of ninety, she resorted to flippancy. 'Yes, well. The neighbours were starting to complain about the queues outside my front door so I thought I'd try going about it another way.'

'Hmm.' Bruno, who wasn't stupid, surveyed her through narrowed eyes. 'Or does it have something to do with that noisy, pushy sister of yours?'

Janey could have hugged him. She'd been so sure he would be entranced by Maxine. Her self-confidence rose by yet another notch. 'Not at all,' she lied, relaxing visibly but still not quite daring to admit that she'd placed an advertisement of her own. 'I just thought I'd give it a go. It didn't work out. End of story.'

'I should bloody well hope so.' Bruno glanced at his watch and saw that he'd have to get a move on if they were to open for lunch. Janey *was* gorgeous, he thought. She deserved a hell of a lot better than a guy with a Porsche and a padlocked wallet. 'Look, I could get away early tonight.' As he spoke, he began unpacking the box of flowers she had brought to the restaurant, pink carnations and sweet-smelling lilac today to match the new tablecloths. 'If you aren't doing anything, why don't we go out for something to eat?'

'Oh!' Janey looked astonished. After a moment's hesitation, she said, 'But this is your restaurant. Shouldn't we eat here?'

'That would make it business.' Bruno gave her one of his most irresistible smiles. 'What I had in mind was pleasure.'

'But you're—'

'I'm not married,' he reminded her. 'And I don't argue with bar managers about the price of coffee, either.'

'But—'

'No more excuses,' said Bruno, his tone firm. 'I'll pick you up at ten.'

'Oh, but—' said Janey, torn between delight and the hideous prospect of having to get up at five o'clock tomorrow morning.

'Stop it,' said Bruno, very firmly indeed. 'It'll be fun.' Then he winked. 'Besides, better the devil you know . . .'

The drawback to being picked up at ten o'clock in the evening was that it left one with far too much time to get ready. Instead of flinging on the first decent thing that came to hand, Janey found herself racked with indecision. None of the more casual skirts and tee-shirts she wore for work would do; Bruno had seen them all a hundred times. The black sequinned dress was wonderfully slimming but it would be way over the top, and the only other really decent outfit she owned, a violet crêpe-de-Chine affair with no back and swirly skirts, made her look like something out of *Come Dancing*.

Clothes littered the bed as she tried on and discarded one outfit after another. A white, dripping-with-lace blouse resembled nothing so much as an overdone wedding cake. The black trousers were too tight, her favourite red silk shirt had a hole in the sleeve and Maxine had spilt make-up down the front of her cream lambswool sweater.

Finally settling for a sea-green shirt and white jeans, Janey did her make-up and fiddled with her hair. After putting it up, experimenting with combs and taking it down again because the combs wouldn't stay in anyway, it was still only eight-thirty. When the phone rang fifteen minutes later she almost hoped it would be Bruno calling to tell her he couldn't get away after all. Her stomach could only stand so many jitters. She had been looking forward to the evening far more than was good for her. Bruno might not be married to Nina but he still wasn't properly single, either.

'Janey? Now listen to me. Get out of that old dressing gown and do yourself up this instant!'

Maxine was shouting into the phone to make herself heard above a background of loud music and roars of male approval.

'Where are you calling from?' said Janey. 'It sounds like a strip-joint.'

'What? We're down at the Terrace Bar of the Manderley Hotel. My lovely cricketer's come back to Cornwall and he's brought the rest of the team with him, so I'm hopelessly outnumbered. They're calling for reinforcements, Janey, and as soon as I mentioned a fancy-free sister they insisted I get you down here.' She giggled. 'In fact they carried me to the phone.'

Janey, listening to the ear-splitting whistles of eleven over-excited cricketers, said, 'I can't, I'm going out.'

'Who with?'

'A friend.'

'Who?' demanded Maxine.

'Nobody you know.'

'That means nobody at all! Darling, don't be so *boring*. You wanted to meet new men and here I am, granting your wish with a dazzling selection . . . they're dying to meet you and now you're chickening out. Oh, look what you've done to them. They're starting to cry.'

From the chorus of boo-hoos now drowning out Maxine's protests, it certainly sounded as if they had a collective mental age of around seven. Janey could only wonder at the amount of beer they must have consumed.

'I really can't,' she repeated patiently. 'I'm meeting a friend for a quick drink and then I must get an early night. I have to be—'

'—up at five o'clock in the morning to go to the flower market,' chanted Maxine, who had heard it all before. 'Janey, how many times do I have to tell you, there are more important things in life than getting enough sleep? These boys are *raring* to go. You're missing out on the opportunity of a lifetime here!'

'Then I'll just have to miss out,' she said firmly, so that Maxine wouldn't be tempted to persist. 'And I'm sure you can handle them all beautifully without my help. I'll ring you tomorrow to see how your hangover is, but I really do have to go now. Bye.'

'If I'd known we were coming here I would never have worn jeans,' whispered Janey for the third time as they were finishing their meal. The black sequinned dress wouldn't have been OTT after all, she decided, glancing around at the other diners. And she wouldn't have needed to fumble under the tablecloth surreptitiously in order to loosen her belt three more notches. 'Heavens, I haven't eaten so much in years. This food is perfect!'

'But not too perfect,' said Bruno, who liked to keep an eye on the opposition. Looking pleased with himself, he said, 'The mange-touts were a fraction overdone and the Bordelaise could have used a touch more black pepper. This Burgundy's good though,' he admitted, twirling the stem of his glass and sniffing the wine appreciatively. 'Very nice indeed. I may have to order some of this for the restaurant. Nick and Tony would go into raptures over it.'

Janey, mindful of the last time Bruno had plied her with wine, was rationing herself severely. Determined that tonight she was going to stay in control – and awake – she shook her head as he held the bottle towards her.

'Maxine was most impressed with the way you kicked them out the other night.'

'Ah, well. I expect it made her feel important.' Bruno looked amused. 'I imagine it's the kind of thing she enjoys.'

'It's what she lives for,' said Janey dryly. Then, glimpsing the expression on his face, she added, 'I know I'm being bitchy and disloyal, but I don't care. Sometimes Maxine goes too far.'

'No need to apologize.' Calmly, Bruno leaned forward and examined the slender gold chain around her neck. 'I've only met her once but it was enough to put me in the picture. I don't think I'd walk too far out of my way for one of her dazzling smiles.'

It was reward enough to know that just one man was impervious to Maxine's charms. That the man in question should be Bruno was positively blissful. Like a puppy yearning to have its ears tickled, Janey moved fractionally closer so that the fingers investigating her necklace could brush against her skin. When they did so, she experienced once again the delicious tingle of anticipation only Bruno's touch could evoke.

'I thought you'd adore her,' she confessed, trying to sound matter-of-fact.

'Then you don't know me as well as you think you do.'

'I suppose not.'

The green eyes glittered. 'So in future, maybe you should leave it up to me to decide whom I adore.'

It was only Bruno, she reminded herself breathlessly, coming out with his usual banter. She wasn't expected to take it seriously. He didn't mean it.

It seemed, however, that he hadn't lost the knack of reading minds, either. Trailing his fingertips along her collarbone he said, 'Come on Janey, have a little faith.'

She gulped. 'In what?'

'Me. You never know, I might just be serious.'

It was what half of her longed to hear. Yet it was nerve-racking too. Relieved to spot the waiter approaching with their bill, she said, 'You're never serious.'

'Never say never.' Bruno remained unperturbed. 'Who gave you that necklace anyway?'

'My husband.'

'Still miss him?'

Janey opened her mouth to say yes, because that was the standard reply, the one she'd been trotting out for the past eighteen months. But was it still true?

'Sometimes,' she amended. 'It isn't as unbearable now as it used to be. Whenever anyone said time heals all wounds, I wanted to punch them.'

Bruno grinned. 'Good.'

'Why, do you think I should have punched them?'

'No.' He shook his head. 'It's good that you only miss him sometimes. You're getting back to normal.'

Right now, Janey wasn't feeling the least bit normal. She was hopelessly attracted to Bruno and she was sure it wasn't wise. And since it was by this time almost midnight she wasn't likely to be feeling too normal when she woke up tomorrow morning either.

'Here, let me pay half,' she said, reaching for her handbag as he placed a credit card over the folded bill. She couldn't bear to think how much such a spectacular dinner must be costing him.

'Because you don't think you deserve to be taken out for a decent meal?' Raising his eyebrows, Bruno gave her a knowing look. 'Put that purse away, for God's sake. My name isn't Alexander Norcross.'

'Oh help,' murmured Janey minutes later as they were leaving. Almost wrenching Bruno's arm out of its socket, she dragged him behind one of the magnificent marble pillars flanking the main entrance to the hotel. 'That's my mother over there.'

'Pity.' Bruno grinned. 'For a moment I thought my luck was in.'

'Sshh.'

'Why the panic anyway?'

'You don't know my mother.' Janey pulled face. 'She'd interrogate you.'

'She's over-protective?'

'No, just incurably nosey. Before you knew it, she'd be asking when we were going to get married.' Edging a cautious inch away from the pillar, she peered across at the man with her mother. 'I don't believe it, they're holding hands! This must be the new chap she was so excited about the other week, the one with the Rolls.' Really, she thought with a trace of despair; if her mother had taken to frequenting five-star hotels the least she could do was wear a bra. That glossy white shirt was practically transparent.

'He must be sixty at least,' said Bruno, watching as they picked up their room key and headed for the lift. Grinning, he added, 'Isn't it reassuring to know that old people can still enjoy sex? When I was younger I was always terrified it might stop at thirty.'

'I'm sure I've seen him somewhere before,' whispered Janey, who could only see his profile. 'I can't place him, but he definitely looks familiar.'

'He's certainly familiar with your mother.' Bruno's grin

widened as the lift doors slid shut. 'He's got his hand inside her shirt. Janey, did you notice that your mother isn't wearing a bra?'

Chapter 18

Back at Janey's flat, Bruno pointed out the splash of red wine on the knee of her white jeans.

'You should soak them in cold water. Go and take them off,' he said matter-of-factly. 'I'll make the coffee.'

Janey, standing in the bedroom and gazing at her reflection in the wardrobe mirror, wondered what on earth she was supposed to do now. Slip into something more comfortable? Lever herself into another pair of jeans and pray the zip would stay up? Envelop herself in her oldest towelling dressing gown and furry slippers, surely the most effective contraceptive known to woman?

By the time she emerged from the bedroom Bruno had made the coffee, switched off the overhead light in the living room in favour of a single table lamp, and mastered the stereo. Ella Fitzgerald was crooning in the background and the cushions had been rearranged on the sofa.

Feeling absurdly self-conscious, Janey sat down at the other end.

'That's better.' He nodded approvingly at her pale pink shorts. 'You should show off your legs more often.'

Janey immediately wished she'd settled for the dressing gown and slippers after all. When all you were wearing were a pair of shorts, trying to hide your legs was a physical impossibility.

'They're fat.'

'They're the best legs in Trezale,' Bruno replied evenly. 'What you mean is, they aren't a pair of matchsticks like your sister's.' He gave her a sidelong, knowing look. 'Janey, we're going to have to do something to get you over this ridiculous complex. You're a gorgeous girl and you don't have to compare yourself unfavourably with anyone, least of all Maxine.'

It was nice that he should say so, but the belief was so deeply ingrained that she couldn't take him seriously. Scatty, extrovert Maxine, forever embroiling herself in drama and emerging unscathed, was the beautiful slender sister to whom all men were drawn like magnets. Janey, hard-working and about as scatty as Margaret Thatcher, was the one best known for the fact that her husband had disappeared without trace. What a riveting claim to fame.

'Won't Nina be wondering where you are?' Compliments embarrassed her anyway. And it was almost one o'clock.

'No,' said Bruno simply. Then his face softened. 'OK, no more pep talk. Why don't you just move over here instead?'

When Janey stayed put, he smiled and edged his way slowly towards her instead. 'Well, if the—'

'—mountain won't come to Mohammed?' guessed Janey, when he hesitated. 'That's what you were going to say, wasn't it? But you thought I'd be offended if you called me a mountain.'

'Don't be so silly.' Bruno slid his arms around her waist. As he pulled her towards him, his mouth brushed her ear. 'Take it from an expert, sweetheart. You're not fat. If anyone should be envious of their sister, it's Maxine.'

It had been so very long since she had last been made love to. It sometimes seemed more like eighteen years than eighteen months and Janey had wondered if she would remember how it was done.

But magically . . . miraculously . . . she was remembering now, and the reality was even more blissful than the memories. Bruno, the self-acknowledged expert, was proving to her that he wasn't all mouth and no trousers, and she had no complaints at all. She no longer even cared that it was ridiculously late, and that she had to be up early. Just for once, the flowers could wait. She was having the time of her life and she had no intention of asking him to hurry such delicious proceedings along . . .

The hammering at the front door downstairs sounded like thunder, making them both jump.

'What the . . . !' exclaimed Bruno, rolling away from her and cracking his ankle against the leg of the coffee table. 'Ouch. *Bloody* hell!'

Janey froze as the hammering started up again. As she scrambled to her feet a loud, authoritative voice from the street below shouted: 'Open up! Police. This is an emergency.'

'Oh my God, what is it?' She stared fearfully at Bruno. Her knees were trembling and all she was wearing was her jewellery.

'Police. Open up!' repeated the voice outside.

Running to her bedroom, Janey grabbed her dressing gown and threw it on, fumbling to tie the belt as she made her way downstairs. An emergency could only be a bomb scare or a major gas leak, she thought frantically, her mind whirling as she considered the possibilities. Unless something terrible had happened to Maxine.

As soon as she unlocked the door it crashed open.

'Surprise!' yelled Maxine gleefully. Clinging to the arm of one of her companions, who was six and a half feet tall and built like Arnold Schwarzenegger, she ricocheted off the open door and clutched Janey's shoulder with her free hand.

Before Janey could react, four more men piled through, squeezing themselves into the narrow hallway and chorusing: ''Ello, 'ello, 'ello, what 'ave we 'ere then?'

'This wallpaper, Constable,' barked one of them. 'Arrest it immediately.'

'What about the dressing gown, Detective Inspector?' demanded another.

'Arrest the wallpaper first, Constable. Charge it with being pink.'

'Aye, aye, sir. And the dressing gown, sir? What shall I charge that with?'

'Easy peasy,' yelled Maxine, by this time almost helpless with laughter. 'Grievous bodily harm!'

Each of the cricketers was over six feet tall. Janey had never felt so small in her life.

'OK, very funny,' she said evenly. 'Now get out.'

'Can't get out, only just got in,' protested the man she had seen at Berenice's wedding, the one who was with Maxine. Behind him, his even taller friend was solemnly addressing the wall: '. . . but I have to warn you that anything you do say will be taken down and used in evidence.'

'*Out*,' repeated Janey, her voice firm.

'In-out-in-out, shake it all about,' chanted the other two. To her absolute horror they were pushing past her, hokey-cokeying towards the stairs.

'She said you'd make us a cup of coffee,' explained Maxine's cricketer with what he no doubt thought was a beguiling grin. 'Oh come on, Janey, don't be cross. We won't stay long. We aren't really arresting your wallpaper.'

Frantic with worry that any minute now they were going to come face to face with Bruno – there wasn't even room for him to hide in her wardrobe – she wrenched the front door open again and glared at Maxine as ferociously as she knew how.

'No! You're all drunk and you aren't getting any coffee. Now *leave*.'

Maxine, unperturbed by the lack of welcome, simply giggled. 'Gosh, Janey, has anyone ever told you you're beautiful when you're angry? And we're not drunk, just . . . merry. I've told you a million times, don't exaggerate.'

This was awful. Janey considered bursting into tears to show them she meant it.

But Maxine was on a mission and she wasn't about to allow an unco-operative elder sister to put her off. 'One quick coffee,' she insisted, attempting to prise Janey away from the door. 'Well, one each would be even better. You see, darling, we felt sorry for you . . . no man, no social life . . . so we thought we'd come and cheer you up. Now isn't that a kind gesture?' She broke off, observing Janey's stony expression, and pouted. 'Oh cheer up, Janey. You could at least be a teeny bit grateful.'

Janey would have preferred to be a teeny bit violent. The next moment she swung round in panic. The hokey-cokeyers, after several wobbly false starts, had actually made it up the staircase. As she watched them lurch towards the door at the top of the stairs, one of them bawled: 'Open, sesame!'

And to her horror, it did.

'I say, what a brilliant trick,' said Maxine. Then, as Bruno appeared in the doorway, she did a classic double-take. 'Oh I *definitely* say! No wonder you didn't want to let us in. Two's company, seven's a crowd. Or an orgy . . .'

Bruno's pink-and-grey striped shirt and grey trousers were only slightly crumpled, and he had combed his hair. Having had time to compose himself, he was also looking amazingly relaxed.

'I've made the coffee,' he said, meeting Janey's petrified gaze. 'But there's no milk left, so it'll have to be black.' Pausing to survey the state of the astonished, bleary-eyed cricketers, he added pointedly, 'Under the circumstances, maybe it's just as well.'

'So now we're getting down to the nitty gritty,' crowed Maxine when Bruno had made his excuses and left. The cricketers, having piled into the tiny kitchen, were trying to remember whether or not they took sugar. Maxine, sitting cross-legged on the floor, was avid for details. 'The secret life of Janey Sinclair! Not only is she having a rip-roaring affair with a practically married man, but she has the confidence to do it in a ten-year-old towelling dressing gown.'

'I am not having an affair with Bruno.' Janey struggled to remain calm. If she lost her temper, Maxine would know for sure she'd struck gold. She had to be plausible. 'If I was,' she added, improvising rapidly, 'I wouldn't *be* wearing this dressing gown, would I?'

'Hmm. I wouldn't put it past you,' retorted Maxine, still looking deeply suspicious. 'In that case, why are you wearing it?'

'We went out for a meal. I spilled red wine on my jeans.' This, at least, was the truth. Gesturing towards the bathroom she said, 'They're soaking in the basin, if you'd like to check for yourself. Or maybe you'd prefer to send them off to Forensic.'

'So you went out to dinner and came back here afterwards for a nightcap? You sat here chatting and didn't notice the time? I'm sorry darling, but I don't believe you.'

Inwardly close to despair, Janey said. 'Well you're just going to have to. Because if I was having an affair with Bruno I'd tell you. But I'm not, so there's nothing *to* tell. Got it?'

'Don't be-lieve you,' repeated Maxine in a singsong voice.

'Oh for God's sake, it's the truth! Why can't you see that?'

Maxine unravelled herself and leaned slowly forwards. 'Because I'm the untidy sister,' she said joyfully, 'and you're the efficient, organized one.'

'What?'

Reaching under the sofa, Maxine pulled out the primrose bra which Janey had been wearing earlier and which Bruno had missed when he'd bundled up the rest of her clothes and slung them on the bed. 'Exhibit number one, m'lud,' she said, her expression triumphant. 'And no need for further cross-examination. Leaving items of lacy underwear beneath the settee? Janey, it just isn't you.'

Chapter 19

Elsie Ellis, who lived above the bakery next door and who thrived on gossip, wasted no time the following morning. Bustling into Janey's shop with a self-important air and exuding as she always did the aroma of chocolate doughnuts, she was scarcely able to contain her impatience as Janey served the customer who'd beaten her in there by thirty seconds.

The customer was Serena Charlton, looking very chic in a midnight-blue off-the-shoulder tee-shirt, slender white skirt and navy-and-gold shoes. 'It's my mother's birthday tomorrow,' she explained, flipping a credit card on to the counter. 'It's so hard to know what to get them, isn't it? And I've left it rather late. As a matter of fact, it was Maxine who suggested I came to you.'

At the mention of Maxine's name, Elsie's chins began to wobble. Janey, steadfastly ignoring her and thinking that putting a bit of business her way was the least Maxine could do to make up for last night, took out her order pad and uncapped a biro.

'Something around the fifty-pound mark,' Serena continued vaguely, gazing around the shop in search of inspiration. 'Oh I don't know. Flowers aren't really my thing. Any kind, as long as they're white.'

Fifty pounds, white, wrote Janey. Lifting her head she said, 'And the message?'

Serena cast around for further inspiration. Finally, it came. 'Happy Birthday, Love Serena.'

My word, thought Janey. You ought to write a book.

When Serena had finished reciting her mother's address she added, 'Oh yes, I nearly forgot. Maxine wanted me to ask you how you're feeling this morning. She mentioned something about a late night.'

Elsie's chins exploded into life once more. This time she couldn't control herself. 'Funny you should mention Maxine,' she said, dying to know exactly what had happened and equally curious to discover the identity of the glamorous, dark-haired girl. 'I could hardly believe it when that incredible racket started up at two o'clock this morning. All that hammering on your front door and thumping around . . . nearly fell out of bed with the shock of it, I did!'

'Really?' Serena looked faintly amused. 'And what was it?'

Janey, saying nothing, gazed at Elsie.

'Well, I peeped out of my window.' Elsie's chest now swelled with self-importance as she turned to address Serena. 'It was dark, mind you, and I didn't have my glasses on, but I could see enough. It was young Maxine herself, with a whole bunch of plain-clothes policemen, and they said it was an emergency. Looked to me like she'd been arrested.'

Janey, who didn't see why she should have to explain anything, simply gave Elsie an unhelpful smile.

'So that's why I felt I should pop round and find out if you were both all right,' said Elsie, disappointed by the lack of response. 'It's only natural, after all, to worry when something like that happens. I just hope Maxine isn't in any *serious* trouble.' she concluded with relish.

'There's no need for you to worry about anything,' Janey assured her, running Serena's credit card through the machine and giving her the slip to sign. 'It's all been sorted out now, and Maxine is fine. It was nice of you, though, to be so concerned.'

Serena watched Elsie leave the shop. 'Well,' she said, calmly sliding the credit card back inside an expensive purse, 'you can say one thing about Maxine.'

Janey could think of several but they weren't wonderfully polite. Instead she said, 'What's that?'

Senena smiled. 'She certainly lives life to the full.'

When the cricketers had departed to play cricket somewhere in the north of England, Maxine had been briefly despondent. Only briefly, though. The very next day, whilst walking along the beach with Josh and Ella, she had encountered Tom.

'Bleeeuchh!' yelled Tom, coming awake with a jolt. Josh, who had been running, had stumbled against an abandoned shoe and inadvertently sent up a fountain of sand. Tom, spitting it out of his mouth, glared at Josh.

'Gosh, sorry,' said Josh. 'I didn't mean to do it.'

'It was my fault.' Maxine, removing her sunglasses, grinned down at the body on the sand. It was quite the nicest body she'd seen in . . . ooh, twenty-four hours. 'If I hadn't been chasing him, he wouldn't have tripped.'

She was wearing a pastel pink bikini and her long, blond hair was tied back with a pink scarf. Tom's mood improved almost at once.

'It doesn't matter.' Ruefully wiping his cheek, he said, 'It's a long time since anyone kicked sand in my face.'

'I should think it was.' Maxine admired his biceps. 'Do you weight-train?'

'Three times a week.' Tom was intensely proud of his physique. 'Have to,' he added, because he was also an incurable show-off. 'When you're out in the lifeboat it might mean the difference between life and death.'

'The lifeboat?' gasped Maxine, playing it to the hilt and deciding that Josh had earned himself an ice cream at the very least. The dazzling smile came into play. 'Goodness, you must be incredibly brave . . .'

But going out to dinner with a man who carried a beeper had its drawbacks. Maxine, who had worked long and hard on Guy in order to wangle another night off, and who had promised to babysit for the next three evenings to make up for it, was dismayed when she realized what was happening: one minute they were in Bruno's restaurant, about to dive into great bowls of mussels swimming in garlic butter sauce, and the next minute Tom was responding to his beeper as if he'd been stuck with an electric cattle prod.

'You're leaving now?' Maxine stared at him as he leapt up from the table. He could at least stay to finish his first course, surely.

Everyone in the restaurant had by this time turned to stare at the source of the beeping. Tom loved it when that happened. He felt just like Superman.

'Vessel in distress,' he said, just loudly enough for them all to hear. Snatching up his car keys he added, 'Every second counts. Sorry, love. I'll be in touch.'

That's what you think, Maxine thought moodily. Whilst she appreciated the urgency of the situation, she still wasn't happy about it. She'd never been stood up in the middle of dinner before. Even more disturbing, it looked as if she was going to be stuck with the bill.

'Bugger,' she said aloud, pouring herself another glass of wine and now wishing she hadn't chosen such an expensive bottle.

'Oh dear.' Bruno materialized at the table as the door swung shut behind Tom. 'Lovers' tiff?'

Maxine, poking at the mussels with her fork, gave him a wry smile. 'Saving lives, apparently, means more to him than my scintillating company and your stupendous food.'

'Some people have no sense of priority.'

'If he only knew what a struggle I had, getting the night off,' she went on with a trace of irritation. 'I wouldn't have bothered if I'd thought this might happen. What a waste!'

'Some people are so selfish,' Bruno mocked. Interestingly, he observed, she was no longer bothering to flirt with him as she had done on her previous visit. Since discovering him in Janey's flat, presumably, she had decided he was off-limits.

'You'd better go and tell the chef to stop cooking the steaks,' said Maxine. 'I can't afford to pay for them as well.' Gloomily she added, 'I don't even have enough cash on me for a taxi home.'

But Bruno was hungry and the Scotch fillets this week were superb. 'Please,' he said, in the same wry tone. 'You'll have me in tears next. I'll eat with you, if you like. If you're good,' he added with a brief smile, 'I'll even give you a lift home.'

If the mussels had been great the steaks *au poivre* were even better. Maxine, demolishing hers with enthusiasm, soon cheered up. 'Tell me all about it then,' she demanded, when the party at the table closest to theirs had left. 'How long have you been sleeping with Janey? And why on earth was she so desperate to keep this ravishing little item of gossip from me?'

'I think you've just answered that one yourself.' Bruno raised an eyebrow as he picked up his glass. 'Janey's hardly the type to enjoy being an item of gossip.'

'Oh you know what I mean,' said Maxine crossly. 'But she could at least have told me. I'm her sister! It isn't as if I'd go rushing out, broadcasting the news to all and sundry. I can be discreet, you know. When I have to be.'

Having heard all the lurid tales of Maxine's past conquests, Bruno didn't doubt it. But he was more interested right now in discovering whether she really knew why Janey had been so determined to keep their relationship a secret.

'In that case,' he said mildly, 'there must have been other reasons.'

Maxine, however, just looked puzzled. 'What other reasons?' she demanded. 'Your girlfriend? Her absent husband? She could still have told *me*.'

'Don't be dense,' sighed Bruno. '*You're* the reason she didn't want to tell you.'

'What?'

'You make her insecure. She thinks you're more attractive than she is,' he said bluntly. 'On her own, she's fine. When she's with you, she loses all faith in herself.'

Maxine looked appalled. 'You mean she doesn't trust me?'

She genuinely hadn't known. Bruno smiled slightly. 'I don't know, maybe I'm the one she doesn't trust. I don't have the greatest reputation in the world . . .'

'And that's why she didn't want us to meet in the first place,' said Maxine, her tone thoughtful. 'She thought you might prefer me.'

'Of course she did.' With a trace of exasperation, Bruno said, 'I can't believe it's never occurred to you. How can you not notice something like that?'

'Easy.' She drained her glass and inspected the bottle. 'I'm selfish and thoughtless, aren't I?'

'So what are you going to do now?'

'That's easy, too.' She smiled. 'See if I can't persuade you to open another bottle of wine.'

As he drove her back to Trezale House, Maxine said, 'You still haven't told me how long it's been going on.'

'You mean how long I've been sleeping with your sister?' There was a note of irony in his voice. 'Why don't you ask Janey?'

Maxine shrugged. 'She isn't speaking to me at the moment.'

'And I'm not telling you,' said Bruno. With a sideways glance in her direction, he added, 'There, doesn't that prove how discreet I can be?'

'It certainly proves how bloody infuriating you can be.' Peering into the darkness ahead, she said, 'Next turning on the left, just past that big tree. I know you didn't believe me earlier, but I can keep the odd secret . . . no, I said next left.'

Bruno, who knew the country lanes well, ignored her. A couple of hundred yards further along the road he turned the car into a gateway.

'This isn't next left,' said Maxine, as he switched off the ignition.

'We haven't finished talking yet. There's something I'm curious about.'

'What's that?'

The sky was inky black and sprinkled with stars, but the moon was almost full. The darkness wasn't total; she could see Bruno's white shirt and green eyes. She could also see that he was smiling.

'I've told you what Janey was afraid of,' he said in conversational tones. 'But you haven't asked me whether or not she was right.'

'Oh.' Maxine thought for a moment, aware of what he might be leading up to. 'OK then. Was she?'

'Janey's an attractive girl.' Bruno shrugged. 'Who needs her self-confidence building up.'

'And?'

'I think you already know how attractive you are.'

Maxine half-smiled. 'But when you first saw me, did you like me more than you like Janey?'

'I like you both, very much,' he said slowly. 'But you and I are more alike. We understand each other. And as I said before, I'm very discreet.'

Maxine didn't bother to look surprised. Bruno Parry-Brent was every bit as unscrupulous as she had suspected. They might be alike in many ways, she thought, but even she wasn't that two-faced. 'I see,' she murmured, pushing back her hair with her fingers. 'You mean, what Janey doesn't know about won't hurt her?'

'Exactly. You said you could keep a secret when you had to.' His smile broadened, his teeth gleaming white in the darkness. It had evidently not even crossed his mind that she might turn him down. 'It could be fun. A lot of fun. You and I.'

Charisma was a powerful aphrodisiac, and Bruno had more than his fair share of it. He really was amazingly attractive, thought Maxine. But then he had to be. Only men at the very top of the league in the attractiveness stakes could expect to get away with this kind of thing. And most of the time, presumably, they did.

Wishing, now, that she hadn't worn four-inch heels – although at least she was only a quarter of a mile from home – she ran her hand lightly over the soft leather upholstery.

'Do these seats go right back?'

Bruno grinned. 'All the way.'

'Hmm,' said Maxine. 'Somehow I thought they would.'

'Where are you going?' he protested as she opened the passenger door and climbed out of the car.

Yuk, thought Maxine as her heels sank into three inches of mud. So this was her reward for making a noble stand. No wonder she'd never bothered in the past.

'Home,' she said, her tone brisk. 'I realize this may come as a bit of a shock to you, but you aren't totally irresistible. And if you really want to know, I think you're a complete shit.'

'Maxine—'

'Poor Janey,' she continued, slamming the door shut and addressing him through the open window. 'What chance does she have, falling for a two-faced bastard like you?'

'OK,' said Bruno, making calm-down gestures with his hands. 'I get the message.'

'And here's another message,' Maxine snapped. 'I may not be perfect, but did you seriously think I'd play a dirty trick like that on my own sister?'

Bruno sighed good-naturedly, 'Spare me the moral lecture. It was just a suggestion, after all. Some girls would take it as a compliment.'

'My God, you're amoral!'

'And you're some kind of saint?' Bruno was grinning once more. 'Come on now, there's no need to make this much of a fuss. All you had to do was say no.'

'I don't care about me,' Maxine said icily. 'I care about Janey. You're going to hurt her.'

'I'm rehabilitating her,' he protested. 'Where's the harm in that? I haven't made any false promises.'

'You're just incredible.' She shot him a look of disdain. 'When I tell Janey what you've said to me tonight . . .'

'Now that really would hurt her,' said Bruno reasonably.

Maxine, who had already worked that out for herself, glared at him. She knew she couldn't tell Janey but she still didn't see why Bruno should escape scot-free.

'Come on, sweetheart,' he said again, patting the seat

beside him. 'No hard feelings. Now you've got that little outburst out of your system, I'll drive you home.'

Maxine, however, hoisted the strap of her evening bag over her shoulder and shook her head. 'I'd rather walk.'

'Why?'

Because I've just dropped an opened bottle of traffic-light-red nail polish on to the passenger seat, thought Maxine, still gazing at him through the wound-down window. And I don't want to get it all over my nice white skirt. Explain that one away to your girlfriend tomorrow morning, sweetheart.

'I'd just rather walk,' she said, straightening up and stepping away from the car. 'Don't worry, I'll be safe.'

'I'm sure you will,' murmured Bruno, realizing that he had well and truly blown it and switching on the ignition once more. Well and truly, he mused as he reversed out of the muddy gateway. And what on earth was that peculiar smell . . . ?

Chapter 20

Oliver enjoyed watching Thea at work in her studio. Never having considered himself a suitable candidate for retirement, taking it easy for the first time in forty years had come as a pleasant surprise. Now, with the sun streaming through the windows and nothing to do but relax, he found it extraordinarily soothing simply to sit and admire her skill.

And Thea was such good company, too. She didn't indulge in idle gossip. If she had something worth saying, she said it. If she didn't, she kept quiet. As far as Oliver was concerned, the companionable silences, together with her down-to-earth attitudes and innate sensuality, made her about as perfect as any woman could be. Now that he had found her, he had absolutely no intention of letting her go.

'I wish you'd marry me,' he said, but all Thea did was smile and reach into the bucket beside her to rinse her hands.

'I thought you might have learned your lesson by now.'

Each of his three ex-wives had squealed with delight when he had proposed, the pound signs glowing practically neon in their eyes as they accepted. Thea, however, calmly continued to fashion a jawline from clay, studying it intently as a cloud passed over the sun, altering the shadows on the semi-constructed face.

Moving over to where she sat, Oliver stood behind her and rested his hands on her shoulders. 'They were the wrong women. You're the right one. Thea, you know how I feel about you.'

She knew, she knew. And if she had been young and foolish she would have married him in a flash, as recklessly as she'd once married Patrick. But independence was sweet, and learning both to achieve and enjoy it had taken half a lifetime. Thea was superstitious enough to believe that if she married Oliver their relationship would be spoiled. Furthermore, like snakes and ladders, she would then be forced to start all over again . . .

'I do know how you feel about me,' she said, tilting her head and smiling up at him. 'And I love you, darling. But we're allowed to feel this way. We don't need a vicar to give us permission.'

'I want us to be together,' he protested. 'Properly together.'

'And you think a silly scrap of paper would do the trick?' She leaned back, sounding amused. 'I'm not going to say yes, Oliver. I'll be your mistress but I won't be your wife. Just think, people might call me Mrs Kennedy the fourth. I'd end up feeling like the consolation prize in a raffle.'

She was always doing that, getting his name wrong. 'Cassidy,' he corrected her with mock severity.

'Of course.' Thea grinned, then looked puzzled. 'Why is that name so familiar?'

'It belongs to the man who wants to marry you. If you weren't so bloody obstinate, it could be your name!' Faintly exasperated, he added, 'Then you'd have to remember it.'

But her expression had cleared. 'Of course. Guy Cassidy, the photographer. That's the chap my younger daughter works for. You've probably heard of him, darling . . . I believe he's rather famous.'

'Ah.' Oliver, who had been waiting for some time for her to make the connection, realized he may as well get it over with. Clasping Thea's hand in his, he took a deep breath. 'As a matter of fact, I have heard of him . . .'

'One question,' said Thea, when he had finished. 'Was I part of this plan? Did you know I was Maxine's mother when you came into the studio that day?'

'No.' Oliver shook his head. 'You definitely weren't part of the plan. Just a glorious, unexpected bonus.'

Thea smiled, satisfied he was speaking the truth. 'That's all right then, and I suppose you'd rather I didn't mention any of this to Maxine?'

'It might be best.' He kissed her teasingly on the forehead. 'Not until the wedding, at least.'

'How have the children been?' asked Guy, sitting down at the kitchen table and watching Maxine wash up. Serena had left for a fashion shoot in Barcelona and he'd spent the day in London after seeing her off at Heathrow.

'Wonderful.' Maxine, immeasurably cheered by Serena's departure, grinned at him. 'I took them to the supermarket this morning. When we got back here I found a packet of Jellytots in Ella's pocket. I felt like Fagin.'

Guy frowned. 'I hope you told her off.'

'Told her off? I stood in front of her and ate every last one. And I've told her that next week she has to go back, apologize to the manager and hand over two weeks' pocket money. If she's lucky he won't send her to prison.'

'She won't do that again in a hurry, then.' He looked amused.

'She won't speak to me again in a hurry either,' said Maxine. 'According to Ella, it was my fault for not allowing her to buy any Jellytots in the first place.'

Guy rose to his feet and picked up a tea towel. When he started drying the plates she'd washed, Maxine knew at once something was up.

'But they do speak to you,' he said, his tone casual. 'Tell me, what do they think of Serena?'

Uh oh. It hadn't escaped Maxine's notice that Serena had arrived with four suitcases and only left with two. She might have known she shouldn't get her hopes up. 'Why? Are you thinking of marrying her?'

'I'm just interested in hearing anything you may have picked up,' said Guy.

Serena had stuck up for her, Maxine remembered, when he had bawled her out over the Oliver Cassidy incident. She'd also given her a Monopoly board-sized box of expensive make-up, an unwanted gift which she said she'd never use. In her own vague way, Maxine supposed, she wasn't really that bad. Not scintillating, but bearable.

'They think she's OK,' she replied, washing a teaspoon with care. 'They don't dislike her, anyway. She doesn't really talk to them that much.'

Guy raised an eyebrow. 'Is that it?'

Maxine handed him the teaspoon. 'As far as Josh is concerned, most of your girlfriends go so far over the top they're practically in orbit. At least Serena doesn't do that. She doesn't gush over them.'

'Hmm.' He paused, then said, 'And how about you?'

She gave him an innocent look. 'I don't gush either.'

'What's your opinion of Serena?'

He wasn't being very fair. If she said anything remotely bitchy it could only go against her. With a trace of resentment, Maxine said, 'Why are you asking me? My opinion hardly counts. You're old enough to make up your own mind about whether or not you like her.' Furthermore, she thought grumpily, she couldn't for the life of her understand why he should be so apparently taken with Serena and so uninterested in herself.

'I know.' There was a glimmer of a smile on his face. 'I have. But it is going to affect you. Serena's sold her flat in London and she's going to be moving in with us when she gets back from Barcelona.'

Oh hell, thought Maxine. If Guy and Serena were going to play happy families, did that mean she was out of a job? Aloud, she said, 'Permanently?'

He shrugged. 'We'll see how it goes. She was looking at other flats, but completion on her own went through more quickly than expected, so it seemed an appropriate time to . . . well, try it.'

Maxine turned, gave him a look and said nothing.

'I know, it's hardly the romantic gesture of the decade,' hedged Guy, 'but it's tricky, with the children . . . I just don't want to make any mistakes.'

'And what do Josh and Ella think of all this?' she countered. 'They haven't said anything about it to me.'

'I'm speaking to them this evening.' He smiled. 'I asked you first.'

'What for, my permission?'

'Your opinion.'

Maxine dried her hands on a tea towel. 'Don't their opinions matter?'

'Of course they do,' Guy retorted. 'If they really couldn't handle it, Serena wouldn't move in. And this isn't a cue,' he added severely, 'for you to put the boot in behind my back.'

She kept a straight face. 'Would I?'

'Of course you would.' He raised an eyebrow. 'That's why I'm saying don't even think of it. This is important to me.'

Me too, thought Maxine. Leaning against the sink and folding her arms she said mildly, 'If Serena's moving in, does that mean you won't need me any more?'

'Good God, of course not!' Guy looked astonished. 'Is that what you thought? No, Serena has her career . . . she travels abroad more often than I do. You'd still be needed to look after the children.' He paused, then added, 'If anything, I was more concerned that you might decide to leave.'

It was the nicest thing he'd ever said to her, Maxine decided. Heavens, it was practically a full-scale compliment. 'Does that mean you really *want* me to stay?' she said, milking the situation for all it was worth.

But Guy wasn't that easily fooled. 'The children do,'

he replied neatly. 'But then they don't know about the incident the other night outside your sister's flat.'

'Oh, but I hadn't really been arrested—'

'I know.' He looked amused. 'I'm just saying there isn't much point in fishing for compliments. There's such a thing as pushing your luck too far.'

'If you want to marry someone, why don't you marry Maxine?' said Ella, as if that solved the problem. 'Then Serena wouldn't need to move in.'

Guy tried to imagine what was going on in her seven-year-old mind. Ella's memories of her mother were becoming sketchy. She had been cared for by nannies – first Berenice, now Maxine – for over three years.

'I'm not marrying Serena,' he replied carefully. 'We just thought it might be nice if she came to live here.'

Ella frowned. 'But she's your girlfriend. Does that mean she'd be sort of like a mummy?'

Guy didn't know the answer to that. In darker moments during the past year or two when other people had made pointed comments and guilt had mingled with the weight of parental responsibility, he had wondered whether he should simply find himself a wife, a suitable stepmother for the children, and stop waiting for *it* to happen. It, he thought, was taking its time. Love didn't grow on trees. There had been more than enough willing candidates, God knows, but the ones who would have made ideal stepmothers had never captured his interest and those with whom he had become briefly involved had on the whole been wildly unsuited for the task.

And it was a hell of a task for any woman; he knew

that. But of all of them, at least Serena had had the guts to be honest with him from the start. Young children weren't something she was familiar with. She was sure Josh and Ella were perfectly nice but if he didn't mind she'd prefer to take her time getting to know them. Besides, she had added, who knew how their own relationship would work out? There didn't seem much point in getting too emotionally involved with the kids if all they ended up doing was splitting up. That would only cause them more unnecessary pain.

It might be a pessimistic attitude, but it was practical. Guy was willing to give it a go. Just because he had fallen in love with Véronique within minutes of meeting her didn't mean it always had to happen that way. Maybe this time with Serena, it would simply unfold at a gradual pace.

Ella, wearing pale pink pyjamas and Mickey Mouse slippers, was curled up beside him on the sofa. Reaching for the doll she had been playing with earlier she began replaiting its blond nylon hair.

'No, Serena's just . . . Serena,' said Guy cautiously, in reply to her question. 'She's a friend.'

'So we aren't going to be a whole family?' Ella gazed up at him, eyes serious.

He gestured towards Josh, sitting on the floor in front of them. 'The three of us are a family, sweetheart. You know that.'

'Serena's just Dad's girlfriend.' It was Josh's turn to explain the situation to his young sister. 'She isn't part of our family because she isn't related to us. The only way she can get related is if Dad married her, but even then she'd only be a distant relation.' Glancing at Guy for confirmation, he added cheerfully, 'Like that man who gave us the money the other week, our grandfather. He's a distant relation too. It means they can buy you presents but they aren't allowed to tell you off.'

Guy hesitated, then nodded. This particular matter had yet to be sorted out. All he'd got so far each time he'd attempted to call his father was the answering machine.

Ella, however, brightened. 'He was nice! When are we going to see him again?'

'I don't know, sweetheart. We'll have to see. Now, are you happy about Serena moving in? Is there anything else you'd like to ask me?'

She shrugged. 'I don't mind. As long as she isn't allowed to tell us off.'

'That's what Maxine does,' said Josh earnestly. 'It's her job.'

Ella finished fiddling with the doll's springy hair. 'And teaching me how to do plaits,' she said with pride. 'Daddy, will Serena sleep in the same bed as you when she starts living here?'

Guy nodded once more. For the sake of appearances, Serena had been occupying the guest room for the past week. From now on, however, the subterfuge was going to have to come to an end. 'Yes sweetheart, she will.'

'Poor Serena,' said Ella with a sigh. 'She's really going to hate it when you snore.'

Chapter 21

The trouble with liking the sound of someone from the letter they had written in reply to an advert, Janey decided, was that it didn't tell you everything about them. Certain vital details only emerged later, when it was too late to say you'd changed your mind after all and that although you hadn't even got to know them yet you just knew it wasn't going to work out.

If James Blair had only mentioned in passing that he had a laugh like a donkey on helium, for example, she would have crossed him off her list faster than you could say snort. As it was, he only hit her with the awful reality of it after introducing himself in person, in the foyer of the theatre where they had arranged to meet prior to seeing a play in which his sister had a starring role.

He wasn't afraid to use it either. To her dismay, Janey realized that the play was billed as a comedy. All James had done so far was buy her a gin and tonic prior to curtain-up, and he'd laughed five times already. Everyone was turning to stare. One poor woman, standing unsuspectingly with her back to him, was so startled by the incredible noise that she'd spilled her drink down her blouse. It was a loud laugh that erupted abruptly, exploded out of all control and didn't know when to stop. If James Blair had wanted to forewarn her about it in his letter, he could have described it as: Bleugh-huuu . . . eek . . . bleugghh-huuu . . . eek eek eek . . . blaaaahhhuuu-huuu . . . eek. Now she was stuck with it for the next ninety minutes at the very least. She didn't know which was worse, the sound of the laugh or the curiosity and barely concealed amusement of every other theatre-goer within earshot.

I'm a shallow, spineless person, Janey reprimanded herself, and James is probably a very kind man. Just because he doesn't laugh like other people, there is absolutely no reason at all to wish I was anywhere in the world but here.

But it was no good. James was still laughing, people were still staring and the play, now due to start in less than three minutes, was described in her programme as 'rip-roaring, rib-tickling, fun, fun, fun!'

'Marvellous play,' declared James, taking her arm in order to steer her back towards the bar when it was over. 'I can't remember when I last enjoyed myself so much. Didn't you think it was marvellous, Janey?'

'It's awfully late.' Damp patches of perspiration had formed under Janey's arms; she could feel them as she glanced at her watch. 'I really think I should be making a move.'

'Oh, but I told my sister we'd meet her for a drink after the show. You can stay for another ten minutes, surely?'

He looked so crestfallen she hadn't the heart to refuse. He wasn't her type, but he was undeniably decent.

'OK,' she heard herself saying out of sheer guilt, 'just a quick drink. Then I'm afraid I really will have to leave.'

'Jolly good!' James beamed, his boyish face alight with such enthusiasm that she felt guilty all over again. If she hadn't been feeling so ashamed of herself she would never have allowed him to slide his arm in a proprietorial manner around her waist. 'What'll you have then, a quick gin? Or a slow one? Sloe gin . . . geddit? Bleugh-huuu . . . eek . . . bleugghh-huuu . . . eek eek . . .'

Janey could have died on the spot when she saw Guy Cassidy ahead of her at the bar. All evening she'd been consoling herself with the thought that at least she hadn't bumped into anyone she recognized. It might be shallow and spineless of her, but it was a comfort nevertheless. Or it had been, up until now.

'Hello, Janey.' Breaking off his conversation with a balding middle-aged man, he turned and smiled at her. Perspiration prickled once more beneath her arms and down her spine as for a fraction of a second his gaze flickered to James, still caught up in the throes of his own unfunny joke.

Feeling sicker than ever, because he was also bound to relay every detail to Maxine, Janey made an effort to return his smile. 'Guy, what a surprise!'

'I know,' he replied with mock solemnity. 'I don't make a habit of visiting the theatre but I'd heard such great things about this production . . .'

'What he means,' explained his balding companion, 'is that he was dragged here against his will because we've been friends for years and I happen to be the play's director. I told him he had to suffer first if he wanted dinner afterwards.'

Guy grinned. 'I felt like a girl out on a blind date.'

Janey felt herself go scarlet. James, who had been listening to the exchange with interest, guffawed. 'Like a girl out on a blind date? Oh I say, that's jolly funny, bleugh-huuu . . . eek eek eek . . .'

'Why don't you like me?' said Serena suddenly.

Guy was upstairs saying goodnight to Josh and Ella. Maxine, who was busy stuffing clothes into the washing machine, hadn't even realized she was no longer alone in the kitchen. She looked up, surprised.

'Who says I don't like you?'

'I'm not stupid,' said Serena calmly. Pulling out a chair, she sat down and examined her perfect fingernails. Maxine, who thought that anyone capable of spending one and a half hours buffing and manicuring their nails had to be stupid, didn't reply.

'Is it envy?'

'I don't dislike you,' Maxine protested, because the situation was bordering on the embarrassing. She half smiled. 'And no, I'm not envious. I've always liked being five feet six and blond.'

'I'm used to being envied for my looks.' As if to prove it, Serena ran a hand through her sleek dark hair then fixed her unswerving gaze on Maxine, who was still kneeling on the floor with a box of Persil in one hand and an armful of Ella's socks in the other. 'But that isn't what I meant.' Slowly she added, 'I'm talking about Guy.'

'Guy!'

'He's an attractive man.' Serena smiled slightly. 'Please, Maxine. Don't tell me you hadn't noticed.'

'And you think I'm jealous because you're living with him,' cried Maxine, outraged. This was too much. Of course Guy was attractive, but the fact that she had been secretly lusting after him for weeks didn't even enter into it. If Serena hadn't been so distant and stand-offish from day one, things might have been different. If, Maxine thought crossly, she'd made even the slightest attempt to fit in, it might have helped – regardless of her own small crush on Guy. But Serena, it appeared, had eyes only for Guy and no interest at all in either his children or herself. Maxine knew only too well that she wasn't the most likely nanny in the world but she'd grown extremely fond of Josh and Ella, who were friendly, cheerful and endlessly entertaining. Serena's persistent and total disregard for them, she now felt, was downright weird.

'Yes, I think you're jealous.' Serena picked up and investigated a half-full cup of tepid coffee.

If she asked me to make a fresh pot, thought Maxine, she'll get it over her head.

'Well you couldn't be more wrong!' she snapped back. 'OK, he might not look like Quasimodo, but as far as I'm concerned Guy Cassidy is irritable, moody and not a great deal of fun to work with. I came here because I wanted to stay in Trezale and I needed a job.' Shovelling the last of the laundry into the washing machine – which ran a lot more smoothly now that her spare set of car keys had been removed from the outer drum – she added crossly, 'And if I was really interested in chasing after your boyfriend, you'd know about it.'

Serena merely raised an immaculate eyebrow. 'No need to lose your temper,' she observed, her tone mild. 'Maxine, I don't *want* us to be enemies. What I'm trying to say is that if you are interested in Guy, I can understand that. Personally, I'd be amazed if you weren't.'

'Well I'm not,' lied Maxine. Serena sounded like a benevolent schoolmistress; the urge to act like a five-year-old and stick out her tongue was almost overwhelming.

'All right.' Serena, looking more tolerant then ever, said soothingly, 'We'll leave it at that then, shall we? I truly didn't mean to upset you, Maxine; all I was going to say was that if you were hoping some kind of relationship might develop, well . . . I'm afraid it isn't really on the cards.'

This was getting crazier by the minute. Maxine, shaking with suppressed rage, spoke through clenched teeth. '*What?*'

'I discussed the matter with Guy,' explained Serena, unperturbed. 'He told me that you absolutely weren't his type.'

Chapter 22

The cliff path leading down to the cove was stony and narrow but worth the effort. The beaches at the heart of Trezale would, at eight o'clock in the evening, still be overrun by holidaymakers, whereas Shell Cove, on the outskirts of the town, was virtually empty. Few people could be bothered to stray the mile or so from the shops and bars; fewer still could face the prospect, at high tide, of clambering back up the steeply sloping track to the road at the top of the cliff.

Which was really just as well, thought Janey, since it enabled Maxine to rant and rave as loudly as she liked without fear of alarming the tourists.

'. . . so Serena said, "We'll say no more about it,"' Maxine spat furiously, continuing the monologue which had started 300 feet up, 'and walked out of the kitchen. I had plenty more to bloody say about it, I can tell you!'

'But you couldn't tell her so you're telling me instead.'

They had reached the bottom; rocks and crumbling gravel gave way to fine dry sand. Janey removed her shoes and wiggled her toes in its delicious warmth.

'Damn right I'm telling you,' said Maxine, pushing her hair away from her face with an indignant gesture.

'It's the only way to make sure I don't explode. The bloody nerve of that woman!'

'She was right, though.' Jancy, who hadn't completely forgiven her sister yet for barging into the flat the other week, couldn't resist pointing it out. 'You *are* after Guy.'

'Not any more.' Maxine's dark eyes glittered with disdain. Then, catching Janey's sidelong glance, she added forcefully, 'And it isn't because Serena says he isn't interested, either. I wouldn't have anything to do with a man who had anything to do with her. I can't for the life of me imagine what he even sees in her, anyway.'

'We've been through this before,' Janey pointed out. 'Perfect face, perfect body . . .'

'Oh that!' Maxine threw her a look of derision. 'Physically, she's perfection on a sodding stick. But mentally she's nothing, no personality whatsoever. Half the time it's like trying to hold a conversation with a bowl of fruit.'

'You mean she isn't temperamental.' Janey grinned. 'Like you.'

'I mean I've never seen her laugh,' snapped Maxine, aiming a kick at a heap of seaweed. 'Josh was telling her jokes yesterday and I swear she didn't even get them. And then she has the nerve to discuss me with Guy, for God's sake!'

Janey was struggling to hide her amusement. 'At least that means they have conversations.'

'But you should have heard the way she said it,' howled Maxine. Kicking a bundle of seaweed along the shoreline was no longer enough; picking up the largest pebble within reach she hurled it into the sea. 'She was so bloody superior and all the time I was having to bite my tongue because she thinks that now she's moved in with Guy she's home and dry. Except that I know,' she added darkly, 'what he's really been getting up to whilst she's away.'

'Oh?' This was more like it, Janey, whose attention had begun to wander, looked interested.

'Exactly,' Maxine declared with an air of triumph. 'Those other women of his haven't given up on him yet. They still phone up, and he didn't come home on Tuesday night until gone three. That would wipe the smirk off Serena's face, if she only knew.'

Tuesday, thought Janey. That was when she had bumped into him at the theatre. Innocently she asked, 'Why, who was he with?'

'Which particular female, you mean?' countered Maxine, her voice awash with sarcasm. 'Well, it was one of them, and that's all that matters. When I asked Guy he told me it was none of my business and not to be so damn nosey, so I knew he'd been up to no good.'

If Guy had walked out of the sea at that moment, Janey would have thrown her arms around him and covered him with kisses. Tempted though she'd been to beg him not to mention their chance meeting to Maxine, she hadn't had the nerve to do so. But Guy hadn't said a word about it anyway. Her shameful secret was safe.

'Maybe there's an innocent explanation,' she suggested cheerfully, but that wasn't what Maxine wanted to hear.

'What's the matter with you?' Seizing another pebble and tossing it into the waves, she almost decapitated a passing seagull. 'Taking his side all of a sudden? Give me a break, Janey – he has more women than he knows what to do with and he was hardly going to spend the night playing Monopoly. The man's about as innocent as Warren Beatty, and the least he could do is have the decency to let me in on the agenda. After all, I'm glad he's seeing somebody else. Anyone's better than that smug bitch Serena.'

'Perhaps he thinks you might run off and tell her,' said Janey.

'If I thought it would get rid of her, and if it didn't mean risking my job,' Maxine replied crossly, 'I bloody would!'

As children they had always taken the same route around the cove. Now, reaching the rock pools, they made their way across the slippery boulders to their favourite pool, the one that always contained the most interesting wildlife and which provided two comfortable seats worn into the rock by centuries of tides.

Maxine, having finally run out of invective, dabbled her bare feet in the sun-warmed water, and watched two miniature crabs skitter out of the way in alarm. 'You haven't been very sympathetic,' she grumbled, casting a sidelong glance at Janey's fuchsia toenails. 'What's the matter, are you still mad because we invaded your flat and spoiled your fun with Bruno?'

It was the first time the subject had been mentioned. Janey had been waiting for it to come up. She had also decided that there was no longer any point in holding back. 'Don't worry,' she replied cheerfully, 'we've made up for it since then.'

'Oh. So you're still seeing him.'

Maxine sounded disappointed. This had to be a first for her, thought Janey with a flicker of triumph. Two attractive men, neither of them the least bit interested in ever-popular, oh-so-irresistible Maxine Vaughan. Not what she was used to at all.

'I am,' she said with pride.

'Hmm.'

Now it was Janey's turn to be annoyed. 'Such enthusiasm,' she snapped. 'You were the one who nagged me to find myself a man, and now I have. Couldn't you at least pretend to be pleased?'

Maxine sighed. Although diplomacy had never been one of her strong points, she recognized that she would have to tread with care. 'But he's somebody else's man,' she said, her tone even. 'Janey, is this wise? What about the girl he's living with?'

Janey's mouth narrowed. This was rich; couldn't-careless Maxine was giving her a moral lecture. Talk about double standards.

'Look, Nina knows what he's like and she accepts it. If she doesn't mind, why should I?'

'Oh, so you've asked her.' Maxine threw her a challenging stare.

'Of course I haven't asked her.' Beginning to feel cornered, Janey retaliated crossly, 'And I can't believe I'm hearing this holier-than-thou rubbish from someone who once had an affair with a man because she'd "forgotten" he was married!'

'That was me,' said Maxine, forcing herself to keep calm. 'I'm different. But darling, sneaking around with a married man simply isn't your style. You're too *nice* . . .'

'Bruno isn't married.'

This was Janey's mantra, the phrase with which she endlessly comforted herself in order to justify her actions. Of course the situation wasn't ideal, of course she wasn't proud of herself, but at least Bruno was not married.

'She's his common-law wife,' Maxine continued remorselessly. 'They've been together for years.' Then she softened. 'Oh Janey, that isn't why I'm against it. I just don't want you to end up getting hurt, and I'm so afraid you will. Bruno isn't your type of man. He's—'

'You mean he's your type,' Janey countered bitterly. 'And you don't want me to have fun. Well I've spent the last twenty months not having any fun and I'm not going to go back to that again. I like Bruno and he likes me. A lot.'

For the first times their rôles had been reversed. Maxine, struggling to keep her older sister on the straight and narrow, and to prevent her from being hurt, realized that she wasn't making a roaring success of the operation. It wasn't as simple, she thought ruefully, as Janey had always made it look. But if she told her exactly what Bruno had suggested the other night she would only splatter Janey's fragile self-confidence and probably lose her friendship into the bargain. Hell, it was hard being a good guy.

'I'm sure he likes you,' she said cautiously. 'But I still don't think he's the right man for you, sweetheart.'

'Stop it!' Janey had had enough. With a look of disdain she rose to her feet. 'I know it's come as a shock to the system but you're just going to have to face up to it. Bruno prefers me. And you're jealous.'

* * *

Life at the moment, Maxine decided, wasn't being very fair. Returning to Trezale House, she ran into Guy at the foot of the stairs.

'I've been trying to work,' he said, gesturing with a handful of contact prints in the direction of the darkroom, 'and the bloody phone keeps ringing. Someone called Bruno has rung three times asking to speak to you. He wants you to phone him back as soon as possible.'

Serena's car was parked on the driveway outside. Glancing at it through the hall window, Maxine said, 'Can't Serena answer the telephone?'

'She's in the bath.'

Josh and Maxine had taken to laying bets on the duration of Serena's famous baths. The longest so far had been an hour and forty minutes. Maxine hoped Josh was upstairs, timing this one. Keeping a straight face, she said, 'Oh, right.'

'She also tells me that you lost your temper with her this afternoon.'

Maxine's dark eyes flashed. 'And did she happen to mention why?'

Guy nodded. For a moment she thought she detected a glimmer of a smile.

'OK, maybe she went a bit far but there was still no need for you to fly off the handle like that. We all have to make allowances if we're going to get on together.'

'Nobody else does,' Maxine retorted sulkily. 'I don't see why I should have to be the one who makes all the allowances around here.'

'You aren't the only one,' he countered, his tone brisk.

'I've answered the phone three times this evening, haven't I? And I'm passing on the message, even though I don't approve of what you're up to.'

'What I'm up to?' She looked astonished. 'Tell me, what am I up to?'

'Oh come on,' Guy drawled. 'It isn't too difficult to figure out. Bruno, I presume, is Bruno Parry-Brent. I might not know him that well, but I've heard enough to know what he's like. And now he's panting down the phone after you. Or as near as dammit.'

'It's none of your business why he's ringing up,' Maxine countered furiously.

'Of course it isn't. I just thought you might have had a bit more sense than to get involved with a married man. He's hardly ringing up to check table reservations, is he?'

'He isn't married,' hissed Maxine. This was ridiculous, now she sounded like Janey. 'And I'm not involved with him! I don't even like the man.'

'Oh please.' At this, Guy rolled his eyes. 'If they're male, you like them. If they're female, Bruno likes them. Let's face it Maxine, the two of you are a perfectly matched pair.'

'Come out with me tomorrow night,' said Bruno.

'No, I don't want to go out with you tomorrow night.' Maxine, who had deliberately waited until Guy was in the room before returning Bruno's call, spoke the words slowly and clearly. For good measure she added, 'Or any other night. Bruno, I've told you before; I'm just not interested.'

'I know.' He sounded amused. 'But I am. And the

harder you play to get, the more interested I become.'

Maxine shot a triumphant glance at Guy, who was reading the paper and eating the children's Jaffa cakes. 'The answer's still no.'

Guy, apparently engrossed in his horoscope, didn't react.

At the other end of the line Bruno laughed. 'Hasn't anyone ever told you that the saintly act doesn't suit you? Come on now, you owe me one night out at least. Have you any idea how much it cost me to get the nail varnish cleaned off that car seat?'

'Serves you right,' said Maxine briskly. 'And no, I don't owe you anything. If you're so determined to go out tomorrow night I suggest you take Nina.'

Guy ate another Jaffa cake.

'She's gone to stay with her sister in Kent.'

Maxine almost blurted out: 'Take Janey, then, instead,' though why she should bother to protect her gullible sister's reputation from Guy she didn't know. Instead, she said smoothly, 'Well, I'm sure you'll be able to find someone else to keep you company.'

'I'm sure I will,' Bruno replied good-naturedly. 'It's just that you were my first choice.'

'What a shame you aren't mine,' Maxine retorted. 'Goodbye.'

When she hung up, Guy lifted his head from the paper. Returning his gaze with pride, Maxine said, 'There.'

'Totally believable,' he remarked dryly, shaking the last Jaffa cake out of the box. 'The best piece of acting I've seen in years. Who were you talking to, the speaking clock?'

Chapter 23

Sunday mornings were funny creatures, Thea decided. Waking up alone on a Sunday morning, as far as she was concerned, was downright depressing. In the first months after the break-up of her marriage, she had spent each week dreading those few hideous hours above all others. Solitary Sunday mornings, like solitary Christmases, were the absolute pits.

And then there were the other kind . . .

'What are you thinking?' asked Oliver, leaning across and brushing a croissant flake from her cleavage.

Thea smiled at him. 'That there really isn't anything more wonderful than lying in bed on a Sunday with fresh croissants, lots of newspapers and a superb lover.'

'Does that mean I trail in third?' he protested. 'Behind food and *The Times*?'

'No.' As she kissed his cheek, the newspapers crackled between them. 'They're nice but they aren't crucial. Having you here is what makes it so wonderful.' Her smile widening, she pushed back her long white hair. 'And of course there is the even more wonderful added bonus . . .'

Oliver smirked. 'That I'm a superb lover.'

'Actually,' said Thea, 'it's that you're so good at crosswords.' She chuckled in delight. It was the most gorgeous day but she didn't even want to venture outside. Oliver was here with her and that was all that mattered.

Oliver, however, was still hungry. 'If we'd stayed at the hotel we could have called room service,' he grumbled.

Remembering to buy the croissants and a jar of black cherry jam had stretched Thea to the domestic limits. Never having been the type to keep a fridge bursting with cold roast chicken, smoked ham, good wine and strawberries, she knew with certainty that the only items currently in occupation were three opened jars of mayonnaise in various stages of senility, a Body Shop eye mask for hangovers, and a mango. But what the hell, she decided comfortably. I'm an artist. I'm allowed to be a slob.

'I don't have any more food, we shall have to starve,' she told Oliver, lifting her face to his for another kiss. 'There, you see? A prime example of why I must never marry you. I'm hopeless in the kitchen. Within weeks you'd be a shadow of your handsome former self and screaming for a divorce.'

'I would not!' He looked astonished. 'We'd have a housekeeper.'

'To cater for our every whim?' Thea mocked. 'How exotic!'

'I'm being serious. And meanwhile . . .' Picking up the phone beside the bed, he punched out the number of his hotel.

'How marvellous,' Thea sighed, when he had spoken to the restaurant manager and arranged for two three-course lunches to be sent over by taxi within the hour. 'The power of the favoured customers.'

'The power of money.' Oliver dismissed it with a shrug. 'It's not such a big deal.'

'It's a big deal when it means you get to eat rack of lamb with fennel instead of dial-a-pizza,' Thea said happily. She might not cook but she still adored exquisite food.

'If you're that easily impressed,' Oliver retorted, 'I don't know why you won't marry me. Then you could eat whatever you liked, go wherever you liked . . .'

As Thea sat up, the sheet dropped away, revealing her nakedness. Trailing the back of her hand across Oliver's cheek, she felt the bristly soft texture of his moustache against her skin. 'Don't be cross with me,' she chided, her tone gentle. 'If I said yes, people would wonder if I'd married you for your money. I would wonder if I'd married you for your money! But this way it doesn't matter, because I love you anyway. I'm already where I want to be and I'm doing exactly what I want to do. As far as I'm concerned, this is as perfect as it gets.'

Oliver was in the shower when the doorbell rang. Thea, only vaguely decent in an embroidered black silk robe which showed off her splendid bosom, and with her long white hair still hanging loose down her back, was padding barefoot around the kitchen in search of matching cutlery.

As she headed for the front door, her stomach rumbled. Lobster mousse, rack of lamb, fresh fruit salad and two bottles of Chardonnay were going to go down very well indeed. But three figures were silhouetted through the patterned glass and none of them appeared to be carrying trays of sumptuous food.

One outline was instantly recognizable, the other two were short. Thea groaned. It was too late to shrink back and pretend not to be at home. Whilst she hesitated, she heard a young girl enquire in high-pitched tones, 'So if she's your mother, does that mean she's really old?'

'Ancient,' Maxine replied. 'Over forty.'

Thea took a deep breath and opened the door. 'But young at heart,' she declared, praying that Oliver wouldn't choose this moment to break into song upstairs. 'Darling, how lovely to see you, but you really should have phoned. I'm in a tearing hurry, about to go out . . .'

'Just five minutes then.' Since it hadn't for a moment occurred to Maxine that she might not be welcome, she was already halfway through the door, ushering her two small charges into the hallway ahead of her. 'Mum, this is Ella, and this is Josh, and am I glad you're home. We've walked all the way from Trezale House and I forgot to bring any money with me. If you could lend me a fiver for cold drinks . . .'

'I'll go and find my purse,' said Thea, backing away. 'Wait here.'

'. . . and if Ella could just run upstairs and use the bathroom,' Maxine went on, scarcely pausing for breath. 'She's had her legs crossed for the last twenty minutes. It's been painful to watch.'

Damn, thought Thea, glancing down at the small blond girl whose knees were pressed tightly together. 'Right, um . . . give me a couple of minutes first.'

'Is that the shower?' Maxine, listening to the distant

sound of running water, gave her mother an enquiring look. 'Who's upstairs?'

'No one.' Thea gathered her black robe around her and moved towards the staircase. 'I was just about to jump in. I'll go and turn it off.'

'Out,' she hissed moments later, grabbing Oliver's soapy arm and dragging him out of the shower. 'My daughter and your grandchildren are downstairs, waiting to use the loo. You'll have to hide in the bedroom.'

'Bloody hell!' Shampoo cascaded down his face and chest, half blinding him. Stubbing his toe against the edge of the door he cursed once more beneath his breath as Thea pushed him naked on to the landing. 'I knew we should have stayed at the hotel. How long are they here for?'

'As long as it takes to pee.' Thea, stifling laughter, steered him towards the bedroom. 'Don't worry I'll get rid of them. Stay in here. And whatever you do, don't sneeze.'

By the time she returned downstairs, Maxine and the children had moved into the front room. Maxine, glancing out of the window, said, 'If you ordered a taxi to pick you up, it's already here. Shall I go out and tell the driver he'll have to wait?'

'I'll do it.' Thea hurried towards the door but the taxi driver was already out of the car, reaching into the back seat and sliding out a vast wicker hamper.

'Can I go to the bathroom now?' cried Ella, frantic with need.

'First left at the top of the stairs,' Maxine replied absently, her gaze still fixed on the driver as he struggled up the path with the hamper. 'Mum, what's going on? Have you adopted a puppy?'

'I've invited someone to dinner.' Thea looked shamefaced. 'He doesn't know I can't cook and I wanted to make a good impression so I ordered the food from a restaurant.'

'Good heavens,' said Maxine, because Thea had never worried about making a good impression before. 'I hope he's worth it.'

'Don't worry.' Thea smiled to herself, because Oliver was worth millions. 'He is.'

'Do you know, Maxine, your mother wasn't telling the truth?' Josh remarked as they made their way back along the beach.

Maxine licked a blob of chocolate ice-cream from her wrist. 'No?'

'She hadn't had a shower when we got there,' he continued seriously, 'and her hair was dry. But when I went up after Ella, there were wet footprints all along the landing and blobs of shampoo on the bathroom carpet.'

'Gosh.' Maxine looked shocked. 'You mean—?'

Josh, who was deeply interested in becoming a detective when he grew up, nodded. 'Somebody else was upstairs.'

'I knew that,' Ella piped up, anxious not to be outdone. 'I went into the wrong room by mistake and there was someone hiding under the duvet in a big bed.'

Josh was a particular fan of Inspector Poirot. His expression serious, he said, 'Were they dead?'

'Well, I could hear breathing.'

'That's a relief then,' said Maxine cheerfully. 'At least he was alive.'

Josh stared at her. 'Why did you say he? How do you know it was a man?'

She grinned. He wasn't the only one to be intrigued. For the first time in her life Thea was being secretive and there had to be a particularly good reason why.

'I don't know,' she told Josh. 'Lucky guess.'

Chapter 24

Janey, hampered by the tray of flowers in her arms, was about to push open the door of the restaurant with her bottom when it was done for her. She tried not to look too taken aback when she saw that it was Nina.

'Oh . . . hi,' she said quickly, terrified that her voice sounded artificial. Nodding down at the tray, brimming with delphiniums, pinks and snowy gypsophila, she added stupidly, 'Just delivering the flowers.'

'Bruno told me to expect you,' Nina replied. 'One of the waitresses dropped twenty-eight dinner plates last night so he's gone out to get replacements.'

She was wearing a long, droopy dress of pale blue cheesecloth, several silver necklaces and flat, hippyish sandals laced around the ankles with leather thongs. No matter how many times Janey had tried, she simply couldn't envisage Bruno and Nina in bed together. She couldn't even imagine them sharing the same laundry basket.

'Heavens!' Putting the tray down, she wondered how quickly she could arrange the flowers and get away. 'He must have been furious. He'll be looking for a replacement waitress.'

'It wasn't her fault.' Nina, lighting a cigarette and sitting down to watch Janey at work, appeared unconcerned. 'She was taking the stack of plates down from a high shelf in the kitchen and Bruno pinched her bum. She screamed and dropped the lot. Under the circumstances, there wasn't a great deal he could say.'

Here, thought Janey, was the opportunity she'd been waiting for. This was her chance to assuage her own conscience, to gain first-hand proof of the understanding shared by Nina and Bruno, to prove without a shadow of a doubt that what she was doing wasn't wrong.

'Doesn't it bother you?' she said, her tone ultra-casual, her fingers trembling only slightly as she pushed cones of bottle-green oasis into each of the vases. 'Bruno, I mean, flirting with other women?'

Nina, looking amused, blew a perfect smoke ring.

'By that I presume he's been flirting with you.'

'No . . .' Flustered, Janey felt the colour rising in her cheeks. 'Well, maybe a bit, but not me in particular.'

'Of course not,' Nina replied mildly. 'Just you and every other woman he sets eyes on. That's Bruno's way, I'm used to it by now . . . and it is only flirting, after all. Harmless enough stuff.'

Janey felt her stomach begin to churn. What she and Bruno had been doing went way beyond a harmless flirtation. Was Nina bluffing, playing the part of the tolerant partner, or had Bruno been lying to them both? Not having the nerve to ask outright, however, she resorted to lies of her own.

'My husband was the same,' she said, improvising rapidly, 'but I found it harder to cope with than you do. I kept wondering if, well, if that was all it was.'

'You thought he might be having an affair?' Nina looked interested. 'And was he?'

Despising herself, Janey shook her head. 'I don't know. If he was, he disappeared before I could find out.'

'Of course.' Remembering, Nina nodded. The next moment she added unexpectedly, 'But you only felt that way because you were jealous.'

Janey looked up at her. 'Aren't you?'

'I have no reason to be jealous.' Leaning forward, Nina stubbed out her cigarette. Clasping her hands together in her lap, she said simply, 'I love Bruno. I trust him. And I know he would never be unfaithful to me.'

This was no bluff. Her calm belief in him was staggering. Feeling sicker by the minute, Janey said, 'What would you do if he was?' Hastily she added, 'In the future, I mean.'

Nina gave the hypothetical question some thought. 'I'd be devastated,' she said at last, and smiled. 'Goodness, it's not something I've ever really considered. Bruno's my whole life. It would mean he'd betrayed me and my love for him.' She paused, then said, 'I could never forgive him for that.'

Janey wanted to cry, because Bruno had betrayed them both and because her own newfound happiness had been nothing but a sham. She too had trusted him, had believed him when he told her he loved her. For the first time in almost two years she had felt like a human being, experiencing emotions she'd thought she might never feel again.

And it had all been an illusion because Bruno didn't have an understanding with Nina and had lied to them both in order to satisfy his own selfish craving for adulation and sex. Janey wondered how many other gullible woman had fallen into the same trap. Most of all she hoped Nina would never find out.

But ignorance was bliss and whilst her own world crumbled around her, Nina's train of thought was moving on to more relevant matters. Happily lighting up another cigarette and flicking back her long straight hair, she settled herself more comfortably in her seat. 'Come on, Janey, cheer up. No use dwelling on the past. You're coming to Bruno's party on Friday night, aren't you?'

Dumbly, Janey nodded. Her name was already on the guest list. She wouldn't go, of course, but a last-minute excuse was easier than coming up with something plausible just now.

'It's going to be great fun,' said Nina with more enthusiasm than Janey had known she possessed. Then she sighed and added plaintively, 'The trouble is, I haven't a clue what to get him for his birthday. I'm hopeless at choosing presents. What do you think, Janey? Any ideas?'

A monogrammed chastity belt, thought Janey. And a muzzle. Aloud, she said, 'I don't really know. How about aftershave?'

'Oh!' Nina started to laugh. 'I think Bruno's worth a bit more than that, don't you? He is my life partner, after all. I was thinking more along the lines of a new car.'

During the next two days, Janey didn't have a chance either to see or speak to Bruno. By Friday night she was in a turmoil about whether or not to go to the party. The thought of turning up, being sociable towards Bruno and

Nina, and allowing him to think that nothing had changed seemed hideously hypocritical.

But on the other hand, and for purely selfish reasons, she was tempted to go anyway. Bruno's famous birthday parties were a social landmark in Trezale, enormous fun and always riotously successful. His friends, glitzy and glamorous and all at least as extrovert as Bruno himself, descended from all corners of the country for the event which invariably carried on into Saturday. Last year the gossip columns had been full of the stories about the playboy racing driver, water-skiing naked at dawn across Trezale Bay and eloping the next day with the only just divorced young wife of a particularly pompous Tory MP. The marriage had lasted seven months and six days, which was seven months longer than anyone who knew either of them had predicted. Earlier in the week Bruno had shown Janey the fax sent by the same racing driver accepting his invitation to this year's party: 'Me and my skis say yes, yes, please,' he had scrawled across the top of the page. Below it, he had written out fifty times: 'And this time I must not elope.'

Oh sod it, thought Janey, throwing down the evening paper and switching off the television. She'd been looking forward to this party for weeks. The prospect of sitting alone in her flat mourning the loss of a bastard with whom she should never have got involved in the first place and consoling herself with a hefty bar of Cadbury's fruit and nut was too depressing for words. She was going to do herself up, take herself along to the party, flirt with strangers and have an all-round bloody good time. Telling Bruno to get stuffed could wait until next week.

And who knew whom she might meet, Janey decided, daydreaming as she turned on the bath taps and tipped in at least half a pint of peach bubble-bath. As long as she maintained a positive attitude the possibilities were endless. And if the worst came to the very worst, there was always the water-skiing racing driver . . .

By eight-thirty she was almost ready and for once, to her immense relief, everything seemed to be going right. The black sequinned dress she so seldom had the opportunity to wear looked as good as it always did, enhancing the curves she wanted enhanced and discreetly skimming over those she preferred to keep to herself. Wickedly expensive but worth every penny, it imbued Janey with self-confidence and glittered like coal when she moved.

Her hair, too, had decided to behave this evening; the bronze combs holding it up at the sides were staying firmly in place and even the loose blond tendrils at the nape of her neck were falling naturally into place instead of sticking out at silly angles as they so often did when she tried to look chic.

Bronze eyeshadow, black mascara, a bit of eyebrow pencil and two coats of pinky-bronze lipstick later, Janey was done. Stepping back and surveying her reflection in the mirror, she decided that if she said so herself, she looked pretty damn good.

She was going to the party and she was ready for anything.

Except maybe water-skiing at dawn, she thought ruefully. At least, not in this dress . . .

Chapter 25

The restaurant had been transformed. Tonight, minus its twenty-five tables, with wild music pulsating from loudspeakers and the lighting subdued, it looked more like a nightclub. And although it wasn't yet ten o'clock the place was already heaving with glamorous bodies intent on having a fabulous time.

Bruno, wearing a new, raspberry-pink silk shirt, monopolized what was now the dance floor. With a bottle of Remy Martin in one hand and a fetchingly dishevelled brunette in the other, he was performing the lambada and simultaneously carrying on a shouted conversation with a tall blond actor, star of a long-running series of coffee commercials. Watching him as he laughed, joked and didn't miss so much as a single move of the complicated dance, Janey realized that this was Bruno's speciality; here, as if she needed it, was yet another example of his ability to have it all. He wanted to dance and he enjoyed talking to his friends, so why waste time doing first one thing, then the other? And when he liked two women, why miss out, she thought bitterly. Why not have both?

Gazing around, she realized she couldn't see Nina

anywhere. All the women were amazingly done-up, there wasn't a shred of sprigged Laura Ashley cotton in sight. The next moment, in mid-gyration, Bruno saw her. Whispering something in the giggling brunette's ear, he pressed the bottle of cognac against her cleavage and turned her in the direction of the actor. As he made his way over to Janey she felt the familiar tug of longing in the pit of her stomach. The man was a liar and a cheat but sexual attraction didn't automatically evaporate into thin air. Willing herself to overcome it, she returned his welcoming grin with a brief smile and urged herself to remain in control. She supposed she ought to feel honoured that he had abandoned the brunette in order to come and see her instead.

'Janey, you look incredible! Mmm, and you smell of peaches . . .'

As she submitted awkwardly to his embrace, Bruno murmured, 'Sweetheart, relax. It's my birthday; I'm expected to kiss my guests.'

'Here's your card.' Taking a step backwards, she pulled it from her bag. Then, eyeing the table stacked with elaborately wrapped gifts she added, 'I didn't buy you a present.'

'Don't worry, you can give it to me later.' Bruno winked. 'Upstairs.'

He simply didn't care, thought Janey. He wasn't even bothering to lower his voice. Taking another step back, she flinched as her high heel landed on someone else's foot. Behind her, more and more guests were arriving, piling in through the double doors like customers on the first day of Harrods' sale. The stifling, perfumed heat combined with the green and gold decor gave the place a jungle atmosphere. Over to her left a tall woman screeched with laughter like a parrot. The place was noisy and chaotic but Bruno, she thought crossly, shouldn't assume he couldn't be overheard.

'. . . absolutely gorgeous,' he continued, sliding an appreciative forefinger along her exposed collarbone. 'Janey, you should do yourself up like this more often. I can hardly wait to unwrap you. Happy birthday to me, happy birthday to—'

He was, Jancy realized, well on the way to getting drunk. She hadn't seen him like this before. Removing his hand from her shoulder before it could weasel its way anywhere embarrassing, she said abruptly, 'Where's Nina?'

'Nina?' Bruno laughed. 'Do I know a Nina? Come on sweetheart, make my day. Tell me you're wearing stockings underneath that delicious dress.'

'Don't be stupid.' Trying to sound brisk, Janey slapped away the errant hand now threatening to slide down her thigh. 'Where is she?'

'I say, you sound just like my old headmistress.' Bruno gazed at her in admiration. 'Now there's an idea.'

'Where is Nina?' repeated Janey, loudly enough for those around her to hear. People were beginning to stare. 'I need to speak to her.'

'Her grandmother's been taken ill.' He grinned once more, totally unrepentant. 'She was rushed into hospital this morning. Nina's gone up to Berkshire to see her. She won't be back until tomorrow night at the earliest.'

So that was why he wasn't bothering to be discreet,

thought Janey. Feeling sorry for Nina she said, 'Is it anything serious?'

'Chronic affluence.' Bruno helped himself to a glass of pink champagne from the table behind her and raised it in mock salute. 'Dear old Granny Bentley. Seriously wealthy and ninety-three to boot. Well past her sell-by date, wouldn't you say?'

At first Janey didn't say anything at all. At that moment her task became easier. To Bruno it had simply been a flip one-liner, but as far as she was concerned it was downright cruel. And wonderfully, miraculously off-putting.

'My grandmother is ninety-four,' she lied, her tone icy. 'Maybe you think she's past her sell-by date, too.'

André Covel, who owned the hugely successful surf shop where Alan had spent most of Janey's hard-earned money, and who had been a particular friend of his, refilled Janey's glass with white wine. Glancing across at Bruno, who was now back on the dance floor with the stunning Italian wife of a well-known rock singer, he raised his sun-bleached eyebrows and said, 'You seem to know Bruno rather well. Anything going on that I should be told about?'

Definitely not, thought Janey with a suppressed shudder. She liked André but he was the most appalling gossip. And he knew *everyone* . . .

'No.' She made it sound as if the idea was an amusing one, because anything the least bit emphatic would only bring out the Sherlock Holmes in him. 'Not my type, thanks.'

'Bruno?' Jan, André's girl friend, had been only half listening. With a giggle she said, 'Everyone's *his* type, though, lecherous old sod! D'you know, last Christmas he tried to seduce me in the kitchen of this very restaurant? It was right at the end of the evening but there were still three tables of customers out here. Bruno invited me through to the back to see his Sabatier knives and told the washer-up to take a ten-minute coffee break. I told Bruno to take a running bloody jump,' she declared with pride. 'I mean to say, ten minutes!'

Bruno's reputation was evidently common knowledge. Janey, who had never known of it until now, realized that she simply hadn't been mixing in the right circles. Gossip, it appeared, had its uses after all.

But anger and humiliation churned inside her. She just wished she could have had this conversation six weeks ago, before falling blindly into Bruno's arms and kidding herself that it was love.

'That's nothing,' André was saying, oblivious to the effect his revelations were having. As he offered Janey a cigarette, he lowered his voice to a conspiratorial whisper. 'Remember Natasha, the blonde with the tattoo on her bum who came to work for me last year? Bruno had an affair with her mother. Fifty years old and the manageress of that building society in Pink Street. She was totally besotted with him, apparently. Natasha said she only just managed to persuade her not to have a face lift.'

'Fifty!' squealed Jan, who was twenty-four. 'Practically old enough to be his mother. Yuk, totally gross.'

Janey had heard more than enough for one night. The white wine wasn't going down too well; her stomach felt like a nest of snakes. Moving away in search of food, hoping it might help, she found Nick and Tony, the antique dealers from next door, who were admiring the splendid buffet. Tony, wearing a magenta cravat and a new, extremely glossy toupee in a startling shade of chestnut, was piling his plate with scampi tails and endive salad. Nick, who had been greedily envying the whole fresh salmon, slipped his arm around Janey's waist and gave her a welcoming peck on the cheek. He smelled of Penhaligon's cologne and garlic, and Janey smiled because at least it was safe to assume that neither of them had ever slept with Bruno. They were devoted entirely to each other.

'Here you are, my darling. Teeny Cornish potatoes coated in breadcrumbs, deep-fried and rolled in garlic butter.' Nick popped one into her mouth, selected another for himself and rolled his eyes in appreciation. 'Sheer heaven. Better than sex.'

'Lovely,' agreed Janey, when she had swallowed. With a grin she added, 'So Bruno hasn't thrown you out yet.'

'Too busy philandering,' Nick remarked, with a nod in Bruno's direction. Following his gaze, Janey saw that Bruno and a blonde appeared to be playing pass-the-orange without the orange.

'Bless him,' said Tony with an indulgent smile. 'He works hard; he's just letting off steam. If you can't philander on your birthday, when can you?'

According to André, Bruno had been doing it day in, day out throughout most of his adult life. He practically made a career out of it. Reminded once more of her own gullibility, she said, 'He's getting too old to be a philanderer. Before long he's not going to find it so easy to impress the girls.'

'Ah, but he has charm,' Tony observed through a mouthful of salmon. 'Charisma. Mark my words, that boy will always get by.'

Nick and Tony adored Bruno. Janey couldn't decide which was the most painful, being regaled with André's scurrilous gossip or having to endure this paeon of praise. Belatedly, she wished Maxine could have been here with her tonight. Maxine, who didn't yet know the sordid truth, had sensed instinctively what Bruno was really like and had tried to warn her away from him.

I was wrong and she was right, thought Janey wryly, sipping her drink. *Ouch.*

It would have been nice to have company, too. Doing herself up and telling herself that the party would be fun was all very well, but now she was actually here Janey was beginning to feel conspicuously single. Most of the guests were from out of town and she didn't know as many people as she had imagined she would. Sometimes even being driven to distraction by Maxine's over-the-top chat-up lines was preferable to standing alone and wondering who to talk to next.

Chapter 26

The next moment, just to prove she looked as solitary as she felt, a male voice behind her said, 'Speak of the devil's sister. Hello, Janey, all on your own tonight?'

Turning, she saw that it was Guy Cassidy, looking ridiculously handsome in a black dinner jacket and white shirt. Next to him stood a tall, titian-haired woman wearing a strapless topaz silk evening dress. Janey smiled as Guy, making no mention of Serena, introduced her as 'Charlotte, a friend of mine'. From what Maxine had told her, he had almost as many female friends as Bruno.

'I was just telling Charlotte about Maxine's latest adventure,' Guy went on, his tone dry. 'She got on to Josh's skate-board, shot down the lane at the end of our drive and landed up in the back of a milk float. The milkman almost had a heart attack.'

Janey winced. 'Was she hurt?'

'No, but she spent the rest of the afternoon washing strawberry yoghurt out of her hair. And the milkman, in a state of shock, ran over the skate-board.'

'Poor Josh.'

'Poor Maxine! Very poor Maxine, in fact. As soon as her hair was dry, Josh dragged her down to the shops and made her buy him a new one.' With a grin, he added, 'It cost thirty-eight pounds. When I found out what he'd done I didn't have the heart to tell her he'd bought the old one in Oxfam for a fiver.'

This time Janey laughed. Grateful that Guy hadn't asked her where laughing-boy James was tonight and eager to keep him away from the subject, she said, 'When she was seven, Maxine rode her bike into a fish pond and ended up covered in frogspawn. You'd think she would have learned her lesson by now.'

Guy stepped to one side as a man wearing a crash helmet, white silk boxer shorts, a tropical suntan and a pair of water skis made his way past. 'This party would suit Maxine down to the ground,' he observed. 'She could have brought Josh's new skate-board along and challenged that chap to a race.'

'She'd certainly enjoy herself.' Janey wondered where Serena was. 'Is Maxine at home with the children?'

'I thought it would be safer,' Guy replied enigmatically. 'Bruno invited her, of course, but I told her it was her turn to babysit and for once she didn't kick up a fuss.'

Surprised and faintly put out because she hadn't realized Maxine had been invited to the party by Bruno, Janey said, 'Oh.'

Charlotte, who was gazing with fascination at the water-skiing racing driver, drawled, 'Do you know, those boxer shorts are completely see-through.'

'Enthralling.' Guy returned his attention to Janey. 'We hadn't planned to come here ourselves; Charlotte pressganged me into partnering her at a charity dinner at some castle in Bodmin but it was so Godawful we escaped at half-time.'

'Between the main course and the sweet.' Charlotte, gazing fondly up at Guy, slid her hand into his.

'I didn't particularly want to come here, either,' said Guy. 'Bruno Parry-Brent isn't one of my favourite people but he knows how to throw a party. And at least the food's edible.'

Janey raised her eyebrows. 'Does this mean you're gate-crashing?'

'Oh, I was invited too.' He looked amused. 'Probably because I'm a good customer and Bruno felt I deserved to be thanked.'

Charlotte, who evidently felt that Guy was spending too much time talking to a rival female, gave his arm a possessive tug. 'Come on, darling, we're missing all the fun.'

'Hooray,' said Guy. On the dance floor the water-skier had now been joined by a fat man in a bikini with a surfboard under his arm. 'Why don't you go and dance with them?'

'I've got a much better idea.' Charlotte wasn't about to give in. Her green eyes glittered. 'Why don't you come and dance with me?'

'Oh look, there's Suzannah.' Embarrassed and terribly afraid that Guy was only staying because she was on her own and he felt sorry for her, Janey waved at a girl she barely knew. With a brief smile she said, 'Do excuse me, I must go and say hello.'

At least Suzannah didn't mention Bruno. 'My boyfriend's buggered off to Ibiza,' she pouted. 'Men, honestly. He didn't even have the nerve to tell me to my face! All I got was a message left on my answering machine saying he'd be back in three weeks. How about you, Janey? Are you seeing anyone at the moment?'

Out of the corner of her eye Janey glimpsed Bruno, murmuring into the ear of yet another blonde. The next moment he was kissing her neck.

'No,' she replied firmly. 'Nobody at all.'

Suzannah, who was also blonde, and whose parents owned the largest yacht in Cornwall, didn't work. Getting her hair highlighted and zipping around in her open-top jeep evidently occupied all her time.

'Ah, but it's all right for you,' she told Janey. 'You're running your own business. At least you've got something to take your mind off not having a man.'

'Of course.' Janey managed to hide her smile. 'It's a great help.'

'You're really lucky,' sighed Suzannah. 'I sometimes wonder if I should think about getting a little job.'

How about Governor of the Bank of England, thought Janey. But at least she was talking to someone, even if it was only Suzannah. At this moment she couldn't afford to be choosy. Feigning interest, she said, 'What kind of work are you interested in?'

'God, I don't know.' Suzannah flicked back her hair with a tanned arm and half a dozen solid gold bangles jangled in unison. 'Something easy, I suppose. Like your job.'

Janey tried to envisage Suzannah getting up at five every morning, working flat out for twelve hours a day and settling down at night to do the books. Determined to keep a straight face even if it killed her, she said, 'I didn't realize you were interested in floristry.'

'Oh, I love flowers.' To prove her point, Suzannah gestured vaguely in the direction of a frantically gyrating girl whose purple taffeta dress was patterned with enormous yellow daisies. 'They're so . . . um . . . pretty, aren't they?' Then, brightening, she added, 'In fact my boyfriend bought me a big bouquet of flowers for my birthday. *And* he got them from your shop.'

'Really?' Every cloud, thought Janey. Men, incapable of coming up with anything more imaginative for the women in their lives, were what kept her in business. 'What were they?'

'Red ones,' said Suzannah, pleased with herself for having remembered. 'Roses, I think. With bits of funny white stuff mixed in.'

'Cocaine?'

'What?'

'Sorry.' Biting her lip, Janey said, 'It's called gypsophila.'

'Oh, right.'

'Did the roses last a long time?' Janey couldn't help it. She always wanted people to get the very best out of their flowers. 'If the heads start to droop after the first week you can re-cut the stems and plunge them into boiling water for a few seconds. It works wonders.'

'Really?' Suzannah looked blank. 'I forgot to put them in water when he gave them to me. When I woke up the next day they were all dead.'

The dedicated revellers were moving up a gear. People were stripping off to reveal swim suits beneath their party clothes, ready for a moonlight dip at high tide. A state-of-the-art camcorder ended up in a bowl of punch and one of the male guests, suspected of working on behalf of one of the more down-market tabloids, was handcuffed to a tree in the restaurant garden, his hairy ankles tied together by the reel of exposed film from his camera.

For Janey, introduced by Nick and Tony to an hotelier who *was* interested in flowers, the evening was turning out to be not so bad after all. He needed regular arrangements for his foyer and sitting rooms and a deal was struck over two hefty measures of cognac, both of which were drunk by the hotelier.

'Sign here,' said Janey, having written out details of the agreement on one of Bruno's linen napkins. 'You may not remember this tomorrow. I want something I can jog your memory with.'

'You sound like my wife,' he grumbled goodnaturedly. 'I still don't remember asking her to marry me. She just woke me up the next day and told me I had.'

'Don't worry.' Janey grinned as he scrawled a haphazard signature across the bottom of the napkin. 'This isn't going to tie you down nearly as much as a wife.'

Bruno caught up with her as she was on her way to the loo.

'I saw you,' he murmured, catching her around the waist and pulling her towards him. 'You've been talking to Eddie Beresford for the last twenty minutes.'

'I'm amazed you even noticed.' Bruno reeked of Shalimar. Janey tried to pull away, but he was stronger than she was. Now he was drawing her back towards the dance floor.

'I notice everything.' With a derisory glance in Eddie Beresford's direction, he drawled, 'He could hardly take his eyes off your cleavage.'

'Don't worry,' said Janey in pointed tones. 'I'm sure he's faithful to his wife.'

But Bruno didn't make the connection. 'He's so ugly I shouldn't think he could find anyone to be unfaithful with. Anyway, it's my turn now.' His green eyes glittered as he studied Janey's rigid face. 'And don't think I've forgotten about my birthday present either. How about a couple of dances to put us in the mood, then you head on up the stairs and make yourself . . . comfortable? I'll have a quick drink with Guy Cassidy and the redhead, and follow you up five minutes later. If anyone spots you on the way, just tell them you feel faint.'

He'd got her as far as the dance floor but Janey wasn't moving. Causing a major scene was the last thing she wanted.

'I see,' she said carefully. 'But what should I do if the bed's already occupied?'

Bruno laughed. 'Sweetheart, the keys to the flat are right here in my pocket. I'm hardly going to rent out my own bedroom to whoever fancies a quickie!'

'It's *your* quickies I'm talking about.' It was no good, she hated Bruno about as much as she despised herself for having been so weak-willed in the first place and she couldn't contain herself a moment longer. With icy disdain she said, 'I can't seem to spot the blonde you were dancing with earlier. Are you sure she isn't still up there, hunting for her knickers and hoping for a repeat performance?'

'Oh dear.' He gave her a mock-sorrowful look. 'Are we jealous?'

Janey, who'd said it but hadn't meant it, realized with a sickening jolt that she'd been right.

'I'm not jealous.' The urge to punch him was almost overwhelming. 'I just can't believe it's taken me this long to find out what you're really like. I can't believe I've been so stupid. Believe it or not, I actually trusted you . . .'

Bruno, who liked Janey a lot and who found her innocence particularly appealing, decided that he could bluff his way out of this one. True, she was upset, but only because she didn't realize the sacrifices he'd made since their relationship had begun.

'Sweetheart, there's no need for this.' Still smiling, he tried to draw her towards him. It was like dragging a child into the dentist's chair. 'You can trust me. OK, so maybe I've played the field a bit in the past, but if you only knew how many women I *haven't* slept with since we've been together . . . I'm a reformed character, truly I am!'

'Liar,' hissed Janey. 'I spoke to Nina. You don't have any kind of understanding.'

Bruno, determined to chivvy her out of her mood, gave her a disarming look. 'OK, call it an unspoken agreement. Whichever, she's hardly likely to admit it to you.'

'And what about all the others?' Janey countered bitterly. 'My God, I don't know when you find time to sleep! Let go of me . . . !'

This was more than a mood, he realized. Janey meant business. Oh well, it had been good fun while it lasted.

'So what are you saying?' He released his grip on her arms so abruptly that she almost staggered backwards. 'That you don't want to meet me upstairs in ten minutes after all?'

'You arrogant bastard.' Without her even realizing it, Janey's eyes had filled with tears. 'I never want to meet you again anywhere. I never want to see you again!'

Bruno's relationships ended when he wanted them to end. He had never been dumped in his life. And if Janey thought she could get away with doing it in public, with making a fool of him at his very own party, she could suffer the consequences in return.

At that moment, by chance, the dance music which had been blaring through the speakers came to a halt. The tape had finished.

'Oh dear,' Bruno drawled into the ensuing silence. 'And there I was, doing my good Samaritan bit and thinking you'd be grateful for the attention. I'm beginning to realize now why your husband might have wanted to disappear. Is that what you yelled at him, Janey? Did you tell him you never wanted to see him again?' He paused for a second, then added with a cruel smile, 'If you ask me, the poor sod probably couldn't believe his luck.'

Chapter 27

It was a nightmare. A nightmare with an audience. With tears streaming down her face, Janey turned and searched frantically for the way out. All she could see was a blur of faces. Mascara stung her eyes and she didn't know where the hell she'd left her handbag. Her face burned with shame as she pushed her way through the crowd of riveted partygoers in what she prayed was the direction of the door.

The next moment a pair of strong arms were guiding her. Behind her a voice murmured reassuringly, 'It's OK, I've got your bag. Just keep walking.'

Janey stumbled on the steps outside the restaurant and the arms tightened their grip on her shoulders, keeping her upright. When they reached the pavement she turned to face her rescuer.

'I'm all right. Thanks . . . I'll be f-fine now . . .'

Her voice wavered and began to break as a fresh wave of humiliation swept over her. Fumbling blindly for her bag, she tried to hide her blotched face, cruelly exposed by the bright spotlighting outside the restaurant. She must look a complete wreck; this was almost more awful than having to endure Bruno's sneering jibes.

'Don't be so bloody stupid,' said Guy, handing over

her bag but keeping a firm hold on her arm. 'You aren't all right at all and you're certainly in no state to drive home. Come on, give me your car keys.'

He might have come to her rescue but he wasn't being wildly sympathetic. Still sobbing, Janey said, 'I'm not drunk.'

He sighed. 'I know you aren't drunk, but you can't see where you're going, either. Why don't you just give me the keys and let me drive?'

'Because the van isn't here.' She sniffed loudly. 'I walked.'

For some reason he seemed to find her reply amusing. Turning her around and leading her briskly across the road towards his own car, he said with a brief smile, 'Fair enough.'

'You can't take me home.'

'Why not?'

Janey wiped her wet face with the back of her sleeve. Sequins, like miniature knives, grazed her cheeks. 'What about . . . thingy? Charlotte?'

'Oh, thingy will understand.' This time he grinned. 'Besides, you only live half a mile away. All I'm doing is giving you a lift home; we aren't eloping to Gretna Green.'

It was dark inside the car, which was a relief, but Janey still flinched each time another vehicle passed them, beaming sadistic headlights over her face. She couldn't seem to stop crying, either; the harder she tried not to think about Bruno and the degrading scene back in the restaurant, the more insistently the tears slid down her face. She hoped Guy Cassidy couldn't see them plopping into her lap.

The journey took all of two minutes. Janey was free of

her seat belt and reaching for the door handle before the car had even drawn to a halt outside the shop.

'It's customary to invite the man in for a coffee, you know,' he observed, when she had mumbled her thanks and scrambled out on to the pavement.

Janey, who had been about to slam the passenger door shut, forgot to avert her swollen eyes. 'Look, you've been very kind but I'd really rather be on my own. Don't you think I'm embarrassed enough as it is?'

But Guy had switched off the ignition and was already stepping out of the car. 'I think it wouldn't be fair to leave you on your own bawling your eyes out.' His tone of voice was more gentle now, and reassuringly matter of fact. 'Come on, we can't stand here arguing in the street. People will think you're Maxine.'

'She said you were a bully,' Janey grumbled, realizing that he wasn't going to go away. 'And what about Charlotte, anyway? You took her along to the party. She won't be very pleased with you if you don't go back.'

'She'll survive.' Guy dismissed the protest with a careless gesture. Taking the keys from her trembling hand, he opened the front door and guided Janey into the hallway ahead of him. 'Besides, rescuing damsels in distress is as good a reason as any for escaping. I grew out of those kind of parties years ago, and I've already told you I don't much care for Bruno Parry-Brent.' With a brief sidelong glance at Janey, he added, 'That's something we appear to have in common, at least.'

So much for looking great, thought Janey, gloomily surveying her reflection in the bathroom mirror. Having scrubbed her face, soaping away every last vestige of make-up, it no longer looked like a ploughed field but it was certainly in a sorry state. The whites of her eyes were pink and her cheeks, normally pink, were white. Her eyelids remained hopelessly swollen too, despite her best efforts with a cold flannel. And somewhere along the line she had managed to lose one of the combs holding her hair back at the sides. All in all, she looked like a lop-eared rabbit.

But since she wasn't about to run off to Gretna Green, as Guy had so caustically reminded her earlier, what did it matter? Pulling a face at herself in the mirror, chucking the other bronze comb on to the windowsill and running her fingers through her no longer perfect hair, Janey unlocked the bathroom door. Guy was in the kitchen making coffee. If he was so hellbent on hearing her side of the unflattering story behind Bruno's contemptuous outbursts tonight, she would give it to him. She had no reason to want to impress him; he was only another rotten man anyway.

'You're looking better.' Guy, having made the coffee and brought it through to the sitting room, handed her the pink mug with elephants round the side. Stretching out in the chair by the window, he added, 'Not wonderful, but better.'

'Thanks.' He certainly had a way with words, thought Janey. Flattery like that could turn a more susceptible girl's head.

'So what was it all about?'

She shrugged. There was no reason on earth why Guy Cassidy should be interested in hearing this, yet he was certainly giving a good impression of an agony aunt. One of those brisk, no-nonsense ones, Janey decided, who wouldn't hesitate to tell you what a prat you'd been.

'Well, Marje,' she began with a rueful smile, 'I suppose you could say I got myself involved with the wrong kind of man. I fell for the old chat-up lines, and even managed to convince myself that we weren't doing anything wrong.'

'Don't tell me. He said his wife didn't understand him.'

'Quite the reverse. He said Nina understood him only too well, and that she didn't mind.'

'Of course.' Guy's dark eyebrows twitched with suppressed amusement. 'And you believed him.'

'I don't make a habit of getting involved with attached men,' Janey protested. 'I know what you must be thinking, but I'm really not like that. I suppose I believed him because I wanted to. And he was plausible,' she added defensively. 'I'm not trying to excuse myself, I'm just explaining how it happened. It simply didn't occur to me that he might not be telling the truth.'

'Until tonight, presumably, when you learned otherwise.'

'I found out a couple of days ago,' Janey admitted. 'I asked Nina.'

'Good God.'

'I didn't tell her!' she said crossly. 'I'm not that much of a bitch.'

'OK. So what happened after you'd made your momentous discovery?'

'You were there.' To her shame, she felt fresh tears on her cheeks. 'You heard the rest. I told Bruno what I thought of him and he retaliated.' Fumbling for a tissue, she took a deep breath. 'He . . . he hit back where it hurt. I wasn't expecting him to say what he did.'

'About your husband?' Once again, Guy's tone was reassuringly matter of fact. 'I didn't even know you'd been married. How long ago were you divorced?'

'I'm not divorced,' said Janey, her voice beginning to break. 'My husband . . . disappeared. We hadn't had a fight or anything like that. He just went out one day and n-never came b-b-back. Nobody knows what happened to him . . . We don't even know if he's alive or d-d-dead.'

It should have been embarrassing, breaking down in tears all over again in front of a man she barely knew. But Guy took it all in his stride, allowing her to get all the pent-up despair out of her system, making more coffee and showing no sign at all of wanting to slope off.

'Stop apologizing,' he said calmly when Janey, lobbing yet another sodden tissue into the waste paper basket, mumbled 'Oh hell, I'm sorry' for the fifth time. 'You haven't exactly just had the best two years in the world. You're entitled to cry.'

'I don't usually talk about it,' she admitted in a small voice.

'You should. It helps to talk.'

'Did you?' Janey hesitated, wondering if he would be offended. 'Talk, I mean. After your wife died.'

'Probably bored a few close friends rigid,' said Guy. 'But they were kind enough not to let it show.'

'And now here I am, boring you.'

'Not at all.' He grinned across at her. 'If I was hearing it for the twentieth time and knew the words off by heart, then I'd be bored. But I'm being serious, Janey. It doesn't help, bottling it all up. You really need to get it out of your system.'

'I know, I know.' The tears had dried up now, making it easier to speak. 'But it's so . . . unfinished. If I knew what had happened, it would help. If Alan had wanted to leave me, why didn't he just say so? Sometimes I think . . . oh hell, it doesn't matter—' Mindful of Guy's own past experience, she bit her tongue before the shameful words could spill out. But he was already nodding in agreement, having understood exactly what she was about to say.

'Sometimes you think it would be easier if he were dead.'

Plucking at the sequins on her dress, Janey nodded.

'Of course it would be easier,' he continued gently, 'but you can't put your life on hold while you wait to find out one way or the other. You could carry on like that indefinitely and still not get an answer.'

Beginning to feel like one of those novelty dogs in the backs of cars, Janey nodded again. Guy's voice was wonderfully soothing and now that her nose was no longer blocked from crying she was able to taste the hefty measure of brandy he'd added to her coffee.

Guy, however, was really getting into his stride. 'I'm going to be brutal,' he said, fixing her with his unnervingly direct gaze. 'If Alan is dead, he's dead. If he's alive, it means he did a particularly cowardly runner. Either way, the marriage is over.'

He wasn't telling her anything she didn't already know, but Janey still winced. Having clung so fiercely in those first few weeks to the total-amnesia theory, she had never been able to discard it from her subconscious.

'Yes,' she replied obediently. 'I know that.'

'So what you have to do is put it behind you anyway and rebuild your life.'

Janey managed a brief smile. 'That's what I was trying to do. With Bruno.'

'Heaven help us.' With a rueful shake of his head, Guy said, 'Now that's what I call choosing the wrong man for the job. Tell me, who would you go to if you needed brain surgery? A lumberjack?'

'Don't. I think I must need brain surgery.' This time she laughed. All of a sudden, the Bruno fiasco didn't seem quite so terrible. Guy had certainly been right when he'd said it helped to have someone to talk to.

'OK, so now you forget him,' he declared briskly. 'He's an unscrupulous little shit and he'll get his comeuppance sooner or later. With any luck,' he added suddenly, 'it'll be with Maxine. Punishment enough for any man, I'd have thought. Even a bastard like Parry-Brent.'

By the time Guy rose to leave it was gone three o'clock. Janey, opening the front door for him, found herself suddenly and unaccountably overcome by shyness.

'Well, thank you.' Clutching the door handle for support, she shifted from one stockinged foot to the other. 'For um . . . bringing me home. And for staying to talk.'

'No problem,' said Guy easily. 'I've enjoyed myself.'

Without her high heels, she was dwarfed by him. And since he'd seen her lose both her dignity and her makeup, Janey realized, there wasn't a great deal of point in being shy. She owed him so much for having come to her rescue, the very least she could do was reach up on tiptoe and give him a quick kiss on the cheek.

But her courage failed her, and she remained firmly rooted to the carpet. Some people, like Maxine, did that kind of thing all the time but she herself just wasn't the quick-kiss-on-the-cheek type. Besides, thought Janey, how awful if Guy thought she was making some kind of amateurish pass at him . . .

'I'm glad you decided to sneak away from the charity dinner, anyway,' she said hurriedly, before he could read her mind.

'Not half as glad as I am.' He grinned. 'It was pretty dire.'

'And I hope Charlotte isn't too furious with you for abandoning her at the party.'

'Well at least you've managed to stop apologizing,' said Guy, sounding amused. 'All you have to do now is stop feeling guilty on my behalf. If I'm not worried about Charlotte, I don't see why you should be.'

'Oh, but isn't she—'

'Absolutely not. She's a friend, but that's as far as it goes. And shame on you,' he added in mocking tones, 'for even thinking otherwise. What has your fiendish sister been saying about me?'

'Nothing at all,' lied Janey. 'I'm sorry. It was just me, getting it wrong as usual. I suppose it was because Charlotte seemed so . . . well, so keen.'

'She did?' Guy looked genuinely surprised. Then he shrugged. 'I'm not encouraging her, anyway. As I told you once before, I gave up behaving like Bruno Parry-Brent a couple of years ago. It isn't worth the hassle.' He paused, then added severely, 'And whilst we're on the subject of faithfulness, who was that chap I saw you with at the theatre the other week? I don't suppose you mentioned him to Bruno.'

Aaargh, thought Janey, blushing in the darkness. Just when she thought she'd got away with it. 'Oh, him. He wasn't worth mentioning,' she said, her tone off-hand. 'I hadn't even met him before that night. A so-called friend set me up on a blind date.' She shuddered. 'I could have killed her; I'd never been so embarrassed in my life.'

'Until tonight,' Guy reminded her. 'And I'm afraid you're really going to have to learn not to feel guilty on your own behalf.'

Janey's blush deepened. 'What do you mean?'

'After you'd left, I was introduced to your blind date's sister,' he replied evenly. 'She told me he'd met you through a Lonely Hearts column in the local paper.'

'Oh God,' sighed Janey, mortified.

'I don't know why you're so embarrassed,' Guy continued briskly. 'He might have a loud laugh but he can't be as much of a bastard as Parry-Brent. You need to make up your mind about what you really want.'

Now he'd managed to make her feel deeply ashamed of herself. Was there no end to this man's talents?

'Sleep, I think.' Janey glanced at her watch. It was three-fifteen.

'I'm going. Just one more thing.'

Eyeing him warily, she said, 'What?'

'Something you said earlier.' Guy broke into a broad grin. 'It's been bothering me. Do you really think I look like Marje Proops?'

Chapter 28

'Oh please,' Maxine begged, thrusting the letter into Guy's hands. In her excitement she'd almost torn it in two. 'Look, the audition's tomorrow! I'll just die if I can't go up for it . . . and think how thrilled Josh and Ella would be if I was chosen! They'd be able to see me on television . . .'

'Sitting on the loo,' said Guy acerbically, having scanned the contents of the letter. 'Maxine, this is an audition for a toilet-roll commercial. It's hardly *Macbeth*.'

'You mustn't say that word; it's always referred to as the Scottish play,' she replied in lofty tones. Then, because she didn't want to irritate him, she waved her arms in a gesture of apology. 'But you can call it anything you like.'

'I still call this a toilet-roll commercial.' Guy remained unimpressed. 'And I can't imagine why you should even want to do it. What's happened, have they run out of puppies?'

Maxine was practically hopping up and down with frustration. It was all right for him, she seethed; he was already successful and famous.

'It's a brilliant opportunity,' she explained, struggling to control her impatience and giving him a beseeching

240

look. 'It means I'd be seen by millions, and that includes other directors. A break like this gets you known. And the pay is fabulous too. All those repeat fees!'

'It's still only an audition.' Guy frowned. 'I don't know what makes you think you stand a chance anyway.'

'I do,' said Maxine happily. 'The casting director's a friend of mine. Oh please say I can go! It isn't too much to ask, is it? If I catch the eight o'clock train tomorrow morning I can be home again by six.'

'And I'm flying out to Amsterdam tonight. What are you planning to do with Josh and Ella, cart them up to London with you?'

He was being deliberately unhelpful, Maxine decided, because he didn't want her to win the part, get famous and leave him with the task of finding a new nanny. How selfish could a man be?

'Serena's here,' she reminded him. 'She isn't doing anything tomorrow. Why can't she look after the kids?'

'I'm not a kid,' declared Josh, wandering into the kitchen and looking cross. 'I'm nine years old and a half. Maxine, we're still hungry. Could you make some more peanut-butter-and-jam sandwiches?'

'You aren't a kid,' Maxine retaliated briskly. 'You're nine years old and a half, and I'm busy arguing with your father. Make your own horrible sandwiches.'

'What are you arguing about?'

'I want to audition for a TV commercial.' Maxine looked sorrowful. 'And your father won't let me take the time off to do it.'

'How long does it take?'

She sighed. 'Only a few hours.'

Josh's eyes lit up with excitement. Turning to Guy he said, 'Oh Dad, say yes! If Maxine's on television I can tell all my friends at school. They'll be dead jealous ... *please* say she can go to the audition!'

Maxine crossed her fingers behind her back, assumed a saintly expression and silently vowed never to tease Josh about Tanya Trevelyan again.

Guy, looking suspicious, addressed Josh. 'Is this a set-up? Did she tell you to come in here and say that?'

'No.' Bewildered, Josh said, 'What's a set-up?'

'OK.' Returning his attention to Maxine he said wearily, 'But only if Serena agrees. And you'll have to ask her yourself.'

Maxine could have kissed him. Instead, more prudently, she said, 'Thank you thank you thank you,' flashed him a dazzling smile, and made a dash for the kitchen door before he could change his mind. 'I'll go and speak to her right away ...'

Josh caught up with her at the top of the stairs.

'My angel,' cried Maxine, picking him up and showering kisses on his blond head.

'Yeeuk!' said Josh. 'Put me down. Kissing's for cissies.'

'You were *brilliant.*'

'I know I was.' He wiped his hair, then grinned. 'You aren't the only one around here who can act, you know. Come on Maxine, hand over the ten pounds.'

It wasn't that Serena actively disliked children, she had simply never found much use for them. An adored only child of parents who had themselves been only children, she had wanted for nothing and enjoyed their undivided attention to the full. Extended networks of brothers and sisters and cousins, as far as the young Serena could make out, only meant having to share your toys and wear hand-me-downs. And if there were four children in one family, she deduced, each child could only receive a quarter of the love. She couldn't understand for the life of her why any parents should ever want more than one.

Those had been Serena's thoughts throughout her own childhood. People change, however, and by the time she reached her early twenties she had revised her opinions. The prospect of having to endure pregnancy in order to produce a baby had become more and more off-putting. Not only would it mean putting her career on hold for almost a year, but there was no sure-fire guarantee that you wouldn't turn into a blimp and lose your figure for good. Besides, there was no rule that said you had to bear offspring anyway. She could go one better than having one child, she concluded happily. She needn't have any at all.

And, as time passed, Serena looked around at her friends and saw that she had made absolutely the right decision. Children were expensive, time-consuming and inconvenient. As for their table manners . . . well, they could be positively grotesque.

But then along had come Guy, a coveted catch by any standards, and Serena, who up until now had made a point of steering well clear of men-with-children, realized that he was simply too good an opportunity to pass up. Josh and Ella were something of a drawback but at least there was no neurotic ex-wife lurking in the background. And Guy employed a full-time nanny, which Serena decided was another bonus. She wouldn't actually be expected to look after them herself.

'Serena, Josh has got his toast jammed in the toaster and there's all smoke coming out of it.'

Serena, who had been reading *Harpers & Queen* with her fingertips carefully splayed, suppressed a sigh of irritation. As children went, Ella and Josh weren't bad – and their table manners, at least, were faultless – but they certainly knew how to pick their moments.

'Tell him to switch the toaster off,' she said. 'I can't do anything now. My nails are wet.'

Ella gazed enviously at Serena's glistening nails, the exact colour of pink bubble-gum.

'Could you paint my nails for me?'

'Your father wouldn't like that.'

'Daddy isn't here. He's in Holland.'

'I think you're too young for nail polish.' Serena's attention was drifting back to Galliano's autumn collection. Darling John, one of her favourite designers, had such an eye for colour and line. Those velvet jackets were divine . . .

'When your fingers are dry, will you do my hair in plaits then? With ribbons threaded through them?'

Serena raised her gaze from the glossy pages. Ella was shifting from foot to foot in front of her, looking hopeful.

'What?'

'With pink and white ribbons threaded all through them, like when Maxine does it for me.'

Serena had observed this ritual on numerous occasions during the past weeks. Even Maxine, with her practised, nimble fingers, couldn't complete the complicated procedure in less than twenty minutes.

'Sweetheart, your hair looks fine as it is,' she said in soothing tones. 'It's much prettier hanging loose. Now why don't you run back into the kitchen, and tell Josh to switch off the toaster? Your father isn't going to be very pleased if he sets the kitchen on fire.'

The result of such lack of interest was that by mid-afternoon Ella was deeply bored. Josh, addicted to computer games and taking full advantage of Maxine and Guy's absence, was closeted in his bedroom with his beloved Gameboy, going glassy-eyed over Pokémon. Normally limited to thirty-minute sessions, he was in heaven. Guy always confiscated the batteries when half an hour was up. Maxine, even more infuriatingly, swiped the whole thing and started playing the game herself.

'Go away,' he told Ella, who was perched on the end of his bed kicking her heels.

'Can't I have a turn?'

'No. I've got fourteen thousand points.'

Ella stuck out her bottom lip. 'But Jo-osh—'

'And stop kicking the bed, you're making me blink.'

Ella kicked the bed harder. Josh, putting the game on pause, leaned across and shoved her on to the floor.

'Look, you make me blink and I haven't got *time* to blink. Just go away and leave me alone.'

'I hate you,' whined Ella, but Josh wasn't going to be drawn into a fight. Fourteen thousand points was his highest score ever and he had no intention of stopping now.

'Good,' he murmured as Ella flounced towards the

bedroom door. 'I hate you too.'

If she couldn't have her hair in plaits and she couldn't play with Josh, Ella decided, she should at least be allowed to buy sweets instead. It was only fair.

Serena, who had finished with *Harpers & Queen*, was now engrossed in the *Tatler*. Several of her more glamorous friends were featured in this month's edition and it was always fun seeing who'd been doing what. Even better, the fact that they were often caught unawares by the camera meant there was always the chance of spotting an unflattering expression, an exposed bra strap, even a lethal hint of a double chin . . .

'Can we go down to the shop and buy some sweets?'

Glancing up from the pages of Bystander, Serena saw that Ella was back. This time she was clutching a yellow purse shaped like a banana.

'Of course you can, darling.'

'I've got eighty pence.'

'How lovely.' Serena gave her a benevolent smile.

When she showed no sign of moving from the sofa, however, Ella tried again.

'Can we go now, please?'

As realization dawned, Serena's smile faded. 'Isn't Josh going with you?'

'He won't. He's playing his stupid Gameboy game. It isn't far away, though.' Ella gave her a pleading look. 'And it's stopped raining now so we won't get wet.'

Trudging half a mile down a muddy lane overhung with dripping chestnut trees wasn't Serena's idea of fun, although it was gratifying to think that Ella wanted her company. 'Thank you, darling,' she replied, her tone soothing, 'but I'm not really in the mood for a walk right now. Maybe tomorrow.'

Ella was by this time thoroughly confused. Serena appeared to be saying no to the walk, but she hadn't said no to the sweets. Desperate for Rolos and Maltesers, she said in hesitant tones, 'Does that mean I can go down to the shop?'

'Of course you can,' Serena replied absently, her attention captured by a familiar face amongst the guests at a recent society wedding. Good heavens, she hadn't seen Trudy Blenkarne for years and now here she was, complete with nose job, collagen-inflated lips and an ugly Texan husband to boot . . .

It absolutely wasn't fair, thought Josh, shaking the Gameboy and willing the batteries to surge back to life. Just when there was nobody to stop him playing, they'd had to run out. And it was all Maxine's fault, he decided crossly. She was the one who'd kept confiscating the game and playing it instead of doing the ironing. Now she'd used them up.

Feeling vaguely remorseful for having driven Ella away earlier, he went in search of her. His sister's bedroom was empty, however, and when he got downstairs he found Serena alone in the sitting room, drinking orange juice and watching television.

'Oh,' said Josh, surprised. 'I thought Ella was down here with you.'

A girl was abseiling down the side of a tall building. Serena, evidently enthralled, waited until she'd reached the ground before turning to smile at Josh.

'I'd probably be sick if I had to do that, wouldn't you? No . . . I haven't seen Ella for a while. Perhaps she's upstairs.'

He frowned. 'I've already looked in her room.'

'Oh well.' Serena shrugged, sipped her orange juice and glanced up at the grandfather clock. 'She's around somewhere. Go and find her, Josh, and ask her what she'd like for tea. It's either fish cakes or poached eggs on toast.'

When Josh returned to the sitting room ten minutes later, Serena still hadn't moved.

'She isn't anywhere,' he said, his voice taut with worry. 'I've looked all over the house and in the garden and she isn't anywhere at all.'

Serena sighed. 'Well when did you last see her? What time did she get back from the shop?'

'What shop?'

'The newsagent's,' said Serena patiently. 'She went to buy sweets.'

Twitching with agitation, Josh stared at her. 'On her own?'

She stared back. 'Of course on her own. She said you wouldn't go with her because you were playing with that silly Gameboy machine.'

'But Ella isn't allowed to go to the shop without someone with her.' Abruptly, Josh's eyes filled with tears. 'Because of strange men. She's only seven years old.'

Chapter 29

Having waved Paula off, Janey closed the shop at five o'clock and settled down to the fiddly business of constructing a fourteen-foot flower garland, commissioned by a local dignitary to festoon the buffet table at his wife's sixtieth birthday celebrations. Linen bows, stiffened with flour-and-water paste and sprayed silver, were to be interspersed along the swagged length of the garland and the flowers – summer jasmine, champagne roses and stephanotis – needed to be wired painstakingly into place. It was a time-consuming but rewarding task and the end result, Janey hoped, would be spectacular. The party, too, sounded very much a keeping-up-with-the-Joneses affair and could bring plenty more business her way, so long as the dignitary's wife didn't try and pass off the flower garland as a little something she'd knocked up in her own spare time.

She was up to her elbows in damp sphagnum moss, packing it securely around the wire which formed the basis of the garland, when the phone rang.

'Janey, is that you?'

It was a young voice and at first she didn't recognize it. 'Yes, it's me. Who's that?'

'Josh. Josh Cassidy. Maxine gave me your number in case anything was ever wrong, and she's not due back home until tonight . . .'

He sounded very scared. Janey, her heart racing, wiped her wet hands on her sweater and said, 'It's OK, Josh. I'm here. What's the matter?'

'Dad's away.' His voice was high and strained, as if he was struggling to hold back tears. 'Serena's been looking after us today but Ella went down to the shop an hour and a half ago on her own and she hasn't come back. I said we should phone 999 but Serena thinks I'm making a fuss about nothing. She says I mustn't call them and that Ella will be back soon, but she isn't even supposed to go out on her own and I'm worried about her. Janey, what do you think I should do?'

Janey's blood ran cold. Was Serena out of her mind? 'Darling, don't worry,' she said urgently, as memories of Alan's disappearance flooded back. 'I'm sure Ella will be just fine, but to be on the safe side I'll phone the police myself.'

'What about Serena? She'll be cross with me.'

His voice began to break. Janey, trying to sound as reassuring as possible, said, 'Don't you worry about Serena. As soon as I've phoned the police I'll come on over. You've done absolutely the right thing, Josh. Just hang on for a few minutes and I'll be there with you. And you needn't say anything to Serena if you don't want to. I'll speak to her myself.'

Abandoning the flower garland on the shop floor, Janey drove the van faster than it had ever been driven before in order to reach Trezale House before the police did. Thankfully, Tom Lacey had been on duty when she'd phoned and explained the situation, and he was on his way.

Serena opened the front door. From the expression on her face Josh had evidently spoken to her after all.

'Have you really called the police?' she said, frowning at the sight of Janey in her unflattering work clothes. 'I must say you're making an extraordinary fuss about this. Ella's probably bumped into a friend.'

'And maybe she's bumped into a maniac with a penchant for attacking little girls,' Janey retorted, only managing to keep her voice down because she'd spotted Josh hovering white-faced in the hallway behind her. 'For God's sake, Serena. How long were you planning to wait before you did anything . . . a few *days*?'

'But this is Cornwall.' For the first time Serena began to look worried. 'If we were in London . . . well, OK, there are weirdos about . . . but it's different down here.'

'That is the most pathetic excuse I've ever heard in my life,' Janey replied icily, pushing past her and reaching for Josh. Flinging his arms around her waist, he buried his blond head in the folds of her sweater in order to hide his wet face.

'You can't let the police try and blame me for this,' Serena protested. 'No one told me Ella wasn't supposed to go out alone. It isn't my fault if something's happened to her.'

Josh's whole body was trembling. Having led him gently into the sitting room, Janey pulled him on to her lap whilst Serena remained outside. 'Nothing's happened to Ella,' she murmured, cradling him in her arms as he choked back tears. 'I expect she's just wandered off and forgotten the time.'

'But I t-told her to leave me alone,' Josh sobbed. 'She said she hated me because I was playing with my Gameboy and I said I hated her back. What if she's run away for ever?'

It was a fear with which Janey was only too painfully familiar. In the distance she heard the sound of a fast-approaching car. At the same moment the rain started up again, giant droplets splattering noisily against the windows.

'Ella knows you don't hate her,' she said in soothing tones. 'You might have said it, but you didn't mean it any more than she did. Come on now, sweetheart, use this handkerchief and blow your nose. Tom's here. What you have to do now is try and think where Ella may have gone, so we know where to start looking. What about schoolfriends living nearby . . . ?'

Tom Lacey, himself the proud new father of six-week-old twin boys, questioned Josh with kindly understanding and attention to detail. When he'd finished, he put away his notebook and stood up.

'Right then, all you have to do it wait here. I'll check out the addresses of those names you've given me, and call in at the shop on my way. If young Ella turns up back here in the meantime, you can phone the station and they'll contact me on the car radio.'

The thought of staying at the house and doing nothing, however, was too much for Josh.

'Can't we come with you?' he pleaded, but Tom shook his head.

'Best not,' he said gently.

'But I want to help look for her!'

Sensing his need to do something, Janey squeezed his hand.

'If she's gone to a friend's house, Tom will find her.'

'And if she's run away, he won't,' said Josh. 'Will you come out with me, Janey? I want to look for her too.'

The rain was torrential by the time the two of them set out on foot to investigate the wooded areas bordering the narrow lane which led away from the house. The woodland, dark and forbidding, separated the lane from the clifftop a quarter of a mile away. Janey, who had borrowed one of Maxine's hopelessly impractical jackets, was soaked to the skin within minutes.

'If we move too far away from the road we won't be able to hear Tom sounding his siren,' she warned. This was to be the signal that Ella had been found.

But Josh, already clambering over fallen branches and pushing his way through the woody undergrowth, didn't stop. Turning, he glanced up at her from beneath his drooping yellow sou'wester. 'If she was close to the road she would have come home.'

Janey wiped the rain from her face. The trees grew more densely here and there were no clear paths, yet Josh was moving purposefully on ahead. She almost said, *Do you come here often?* but caught herself in time. Instead, catching up with him, she turned him back round to face her once more. 'Josh, do you know where you're going?'

For a second, the dark blue eyes flickered away. Josh

drew a breath. 'Well, we've been through here a few times. It's a short cut to the top of the cliffs, but Dad told us we weren't allowed to come through the wood, so . . .'

He shrugged, his voice trailing away.

'. . . So you know this area like the back of your hand,' Janey supplied, giving him a brief smile and refusing even to think about the clifftop ahead. 'Don't panic, I'm not going to tell you off; come on, Josh, lead the way.'

They found Ella fifteen minutes later, lying in a small crumpled heap against a fallen tree. Cold and extremely wet, her face was streaked with mud and tears.

So relieved she found it hard to breathe, Janey said unevenly, 'Here you are then. We wondered where you'd got to.'

But for Josh, who had been fearing the worst and blaming himself, relief took another form. Unable to control himself, he shouted, 'How dare you run away! I didn't mean what I said . . . How could you be so *stupid*!'

When Janey tried to help her to her feet however, Ella let out a piercing shriek. 'I didn't run away, I tripped over a blackberry branch and hurt my ankle . . . ouch, it hurts!'

Carefully investigating the ankle, Janey saw that it was badly swollen but probably not broken. 'It's OK, sweetheart. Put your arms around my neck and let me lift you up.'

'Stupid,' repeated Josh, choking back fresh tears. 'Serena's mad as hell, and we called the police in case you'd been murdered.'

Ella, clinging to Janey, shouted, 'Well I wasn't murdered and I hate Serena anyway. I went to the shop and bought some sweets and on the way back I saw a rabbit going along our secret path so I followed it, to give it some chocolate. But then I fell over and the rabbit ran off and it started raining. If you hadn't told me to go away,' she added, her voice rising to a piteous wail, 'we could both have gone to the shop and I wouldn't have been all on my own when I fell over.'

The Waltons it wasn't.

'OK, OK,' Janey said soothingly, struggling to get a secure grip on Ella and mentally bracing herself for the trek back through the woods. 'Stop arguing, you two. Josh, you'll have to go before me and hold the branches out of my way. And Ella's very cold; why don't you take off your oilskin and drape it round her shoulders?'

'Because I'll get wet.'

'He's a pig,' sniffed Ella. 'It's all Josh's fault anyway. I still hate him.'

'And you're a litter-bug,' Josh retaliated, pointing an accusing finger at the Rolo wrapper and shreds of gold foil on the ground. 'I'm going to tell the policeman you left that there. You'll probably have to go to prison.'

The time had come to be firm. Janey, whose arms were aching already, said, 'All right, that's enough. Josh, pick up that sweet wrapper and stop arguing this minute.'

'I'm c-cold,' whimpered Ella, whose blond, raindrenched hair was plastered to her head.

'And take off that oilskin. Your sister needs it more than you do.'

'I thought you were nicer than Maxine.' Obeying at the speed of mud, Josh gave her a sulky look. 'But you aren't.'

* * *

Maxine returned to the house at eight-thirty, by which time Tom Lacey had left, the local doctor had also been and gone and the only physical reminder of the afternoon's events was a neat white pressure bandage encasing Ella's left ankle, of which she was fast becoming inordinately proud.

'What's going on? Why's Janey's van parked outside?'

Looking puzzled, Maxine dropped her coat over the back of an armchair. Serena, hogging the sofa as usual, was apparently engrossed in a frantic game show on the television. An ancient skinny man, having evidently just won himself a vacuum cleaner and a weekend at a health farm, was leaping up and down in ecstasy.

'Nothing's going on.' Serena finally turned to meet her gaze. 'Ella sprained her ankle, that's all. Your sister has been making an incredible amount of fuss over a simple accident.'

Maxine stared back. 'Janey doesn't make incredible amounts of fuss unless there's a damn good reason for it. What kind of simple accident are we talking about?'

But Serena merely shrugged. 'You may as well ask her, she's so much better at lurid detail than I am. She's upstairs, putting the children to bed. Probably giving them nightmares, too, with that neurotic imagination of hers . . .'

Chapter 30

Janey was working in the shop three days later when Guy Cassidy came in. Having been kept bang up to date with the goings-on at Trezale House by Maxine gleefully relaying each new instalment over the phone, Janey could almost have timed his entrance to the second.

'He's leaving now,' Maxine had shrieked, minutes earlier. 'Put in a good word for me, Janey, and tell him I deserve a pay rise.'

In order not to give the game away, however, she looked dutifully surprised to see him.

'I've come to thank you,' Guy said simply. Then, breaking into a grin, he added, 'But I have a bit of a problem. If it had been anyone else, I would have brought them flowers . . .'

If there was one major drawback to this job, thought Janey, it was that nobody ever brought you flowers.

'The story of my life,' she replied with a good-humoured shrug. 'But you don't need to thank me, anyway. You helped me when I had a problem; all I did was return the favour.'

'Rather more than that,' said Guy. 'And I'm still grateful. I was going to bring you chocolates but Maxine insisted they'd wreck your slimming campaign.' Studying her figure for a moment he frowned and added, 'Are you really on a diet?'

'Oh dear.' Janey looked amused. 'Does that mean it isn't working?'

'It means you don't need to lose weight.'

Acutely aware of his speculative gaze still upon her, Janey flushed with embarrassment. It was all very well for Guy Cassidy to say she didn't need to diet, but she couldn't help noticing that men like him only ever chose girlfriends as thin as sticks, the kind who could step out of a size-fourteen skirt without even undoing the zip.

'How is Ella?' she said, changing the subject.

'Recovering nicely.' Guy smiled. 'And passionately attached to the bandage. She doesn't really need it any more but whenever we suggest taking it off, the limp gets worse.'

'And Josh?'

This time he pulled a face. 'You mean my modest son? He's cast himself in the role of rescuing hero. By the time he goes back to school next week he'll probably have awarded himself an OBE at the very least.'

Janey laughed. 'So everything's all right then, at home. Business as usual.'

'Well, I wouldn't quite say that.' He gave her an ambiguous look. 'And it's nice of you to ask, but I'm sure you know all the latest developments. Every time I've picked up the phone during the last few days,' he added pointedly, 'it's wafted Maxine's perfume back at me. And the receiver's always warm.'

Caught out, she said, 'Ah.'

'So I'll just say the situation has been dealt with.'

At that moment a customer entered the shop behind him. Guy, leaning against the counter, lowered his voice. 'And since flowers and chocolates are out of the window, how about a couple of theatre tickets instead?'

'You really don't have to,' protested Janey.

'I want to. And the tickets are for Saturday night. Do you have someone you'd like to take with you?'

Flustered by the unexpectedness of the question, she said, 'Um . . . well. Maybe Maxine?'

'What a shame, she has to stay at home and babysit,' Guy replied briskly. 'Never mind, perhaps I'll do instead.'

Behind him, the woman customer waved a bunch of dripping gladioli. Distracted, wondering whether he had just said what she thought he'd said, Janey stammered, 'Y-you mean . . .?'

'Well you can hardly invite Bruno, can you?' Guy grinned. 'So that's settled. I'll pick you up on Saturday. What time do you close the shop?'

'Um . . . f-five o'clock.'

'Good. It doesn't take you too long to get ready, does it? I'll pick you up at six.'

From her upstairs window, Janey watched as Guy expertly reversed the Mercedes into a parking space just outside the shop. As she had suspected, he was bang on time. Her stomach squirmed, the jitters refusing to subside. It was silly to be nervous, since it wasn't even a proper date, but still the adrenaline coursed through her bloodstream, working overtime practically of its own accord.

It would be far easier, she thought, if only Guy Cassidy

weren't so physically attractive. Such exceptional good looks were downright intimidating. Talking to him the other night in the privacy of her own home had been one thing, but this evening they were going to be seen out together in public, looking for all the world like a *real* couple. She was only too well aware of how she measured up against such willowy exotic beauties as Serena Charlton. In the back of her mind lurked the nightmare scenario that other people, observing them together, might be sniggering behind her back at such an unlikely pairing.

But it wasn't a real date, and at least she knew that even if they didn't. As Maxine had carelessly remarked, upon learning of the outing, 'I expect he just feels sorry for you because you never have any fun.'

My sister, thought Janey, such a comfort to have around. At least with Maxine to remind her of her failings, she wasn't likely to get ideas above her station. And, as she had done with James, she was trusting to fate that they wouldn't bump into anyone they knew at the theatre. Then, she had been the embarrassed one. This time, she thought ruefully, the tables of justice had been well and truly turned. If anyone was going to be embarrassed tonight, it was Guy.

When she opened the front door, however, he looked both surprised and pleased to see her.

'You're ready! Amazing.'

He was used to being kept waiting, of course, by glamorous women incapable of leaving the house until their three-hour beauty routines were complete. Janey, who had showered, changed and done her face in less than thirty minutes because she hadn't been able to close the shop before five-thirty, felt intimidated already.

But it wasn't a proper date, she reminded herself for the tenth time in as many minutes, so it really didn't matter. All she had to do was relax, stop feeling nervous and enjoy the evening for its own sake.

'Well, I hate to say it,' she said, as Guy opened the passenger door for her, 'but aren't we going to be horribly early? What time does the play start?'

'Ah.' He smiled. 'I have a favour to ask.'

Oh, that disarming smile. Like magic, Janey's butterflies disappeared. The prospect of seeing Guy again might have been nerve-racking but she'd forgotten how good he was at putting her at her ease. Now, miraculously, her anxieties melted away.

'A favour?' She gave him a deadpan look. 'Don't tell me. You want me to pay for the tickets.'

'Much worse than that.' Guy grinned. 'Some friends of mine are having a party and I promised I'd drop in on them. We'd just stay for an hour or so, then go on to the theatre for eight.' He paused and gave her a swift sidelong glance. 'Would that be OK with you, or is it a complete pain?'

It wasn't what she'd expected, that was for sure. Pulling a face, Janey said, 'Parties aren't exactly my favourite thing at the moment. Look, why don't I wait here? You could go on to the party on your own, see your friends and meet me at the theatre later.'

'Don't be such a wimp.' Guy was already putting the car briskly into gear. 'It isn't that kind of party, anyway.

Mimi and Jack are extremely nice people. You'll love them.'

He hadn't been asking her whether she'd like to go with him, Janey realized. He'd been telling her.

'Won't they mind, when you turn up with me in tow?' she protested.

'Mind?' He laughed. 'They'll be thrilled to bits. They're expecting me to bring Serena.'

Chapter 31

Mimi and Jack Margason lived in a splendid old rectory on the outskirts of Truro. Mimi, welcoming them at the door, gave Guy an immense hug and did a delighted double-take when she saw Janey.

'My darling man! Come along now, make my day and tell me you've dumped dreary Deirdre for good.'

Guy, turning to grin at Janey, said, 'Told you they didn't like her.'

'Serena? Ghastly girl,' Mimi declared, planting a big kiss on his cheek. 'As skinny as a string bean and about as interesting to talk to. Or is that an insult to string beans?'

Having steeled herself for the worst – because with a name like Mimi the very least one could expect was glamour, glitz, drop-dead chic and probably a French accent to boot – this Mimi came as a marvellous surprise to Janey. It wasn't hard to understand, either, why Mimi considered Serena dreary and thin. At a conservative estimate, she had to weigh all of fifteen stone herself. Her long, extremely yellow hair was piled up and loosely secured with blue velvet bows, two biros and a chopstick. A billowing pink-and-silver blouse was worn over a long violet skirt. Mimi's round, laughing face was dominated by a wide mouth, many chins and a great deal of haphazardly applied violet eyeshadow. Her age wasn't easy to gauge but she was probably in her late fifties. She was also wearing the largest, most elaborate silver earrings Janey had ever seen in her life.

'This is Janey,' said Guy, performing the introductions. 'And she's just a friend so spare her the in-depth cross-examination because it won't get you anywhere. Janey, this is Mimi Margason, my very own Beryl Cooke character come to life. She's also the nosiest woman in England, so hang on to your secrets . . .'

'Oh, don't be so boring.'With a chuckle, Mimi ushered them into the house. 'But since you're the first guests to arrive, it's lovely to see you anyway. Now come through to the kitchen – oops, mind those wellies – and let Jack get you a drink. If he offers you the elderflower champagne,' she murmured furtively, 'for Pete's sake smack your lips and look appreciative. It might taste like old pea pods but it's his pride and joy.'

The kitchen was vast, rose-scented and hugely untidy. Mimi had evidently raided the garden that day; upon the twelve-foot-long windowsill stood three enormous, unmatched vases.The poor roses themselves, jammed in willy-nilly irrespective of size and colour, looked like far too many strangers squashed uncomfortably together in a lift.

'I know!' said Mimi cheerfully, having intercepted Janey's glance in their direction. 'I can't organize flowers to save my life. Poor Jack spends all his spare time in the garden, pruning and chivvying them along, and then I have to do that to them. Ruined, in ten minutes flat.'

'They aren't ruined.' Moving closer, Janey admired the blooms which had evidently been tended with devotion. 'They're beautiful. All they need is a bit of . . . sorting out.'

'I suppose I'm just not the sorting-out type.' With an unrepentant shrug, Mimi indicated the rest of the chaotic kitchen where, at the far end, the two men were already deep in conversation. She elaborated, 'We love this house, but let's face it – we're never going to be featured in *House & Garden*. Now come along, let's find you that drink and then we can get down to some serious gossip. I can give you all the dirt on dreadful Deirdre.'

'Actually,' said Janey, 'I did meet her a few times. I already know how dreadful she is.'

Mimi's eyes gleamed. 'In that case, you can tell me how you got yourself involved with gorgeous Guy.'

'Oh dear, this is going to come as such a disappointment to you.' Janey gave her an apologetic smile. 'But I'm afraid we really aren't involved.'

Mimi, however, was not easily swayed. 'You mean it's early days yet and you don't want to say too much about it,' she stage-whispered with the smug air of one who knows better.

'I mean there's nothing to say too much about.' Janey, beginning to realize that the more she protested, the more convinced Mimi would become that something delightfully illicit was going on, decided that this was a problem only Guy could sort out. Glancing once more at the poor, half-suffocated roses on the windowsill, she said suddenly, 'Look, why don't you find me a nice sharp knife—?'

'Help!' Mimi burst out laughing. 'Who are you thinking of using it on – me for asking too many questions? Or Guy, just to prove you aren't madly in love with him?'

Janey grinned. 'Your flowers. Let me do something to them before the rest of your guests arrive. And if you could lay your hands on some old newspapers and a couple more vases . . .'

'Amazing.' Having rummaged in a drawer, Mimi handed her a well-used Sabatier boning knife. Eagerly, she grabbed the bowls of roses and lined them up in front of Janey. 'The lengths some people will go to in order to get out of sampling my husband's beloved elderflower champagne. I say,' she added admiringly as Janey set to work with the knife, 'you really know what you're doing, don't you!'

With deft fingers, Janey separated a dozen or so deep, creamy yellow Casanovas from a tangle of coppery pink Albertines, trimmed their stems and stripped them of their waterlogged lower leaves. 'Plenty of practice,' she said, with a brief smile. 'I'm a florist.'

'How marvellous,' Mimi cried. 'At last, a girlfriend of Guy's who can actually do something besides flick her hair about and pose for a stupid camera.'

'Except I'm not a girlfriend of Guy's,' Janey patiently reminded her.

'Of course you aren't, darling.' Mimi, her silver earrings tinkling like sleighbells, shook her head and gurgled with laughter. 'But just think of the advantages if the two of you *should* decide to get married! Guy could take the photographs, you'd organize the flowers . . . how much more DIY can a bride and groom get?'

'Goodness.' Janey kept a straight face. 'I hadn't thought of it like that. We could get my brother the bishop to perform the ceremony, my sister Maxine could play "Here comes the bride" on her mouth organ and Josh and Ella could stab all the sausages on to little sticks . . .'

Jack Margason, having evidently decided that in the immediate-impact stakes he couldn't even begin to compete with his wife, wore a pale grey shirt and oatmeal trousers which exactly matched his pale grey hair and oatmeal skin. Tall and thin, with liquid, light brown eyes, an apologetic smile and a very long, perfectly straight nose, he reminded Janey of an Afghan hound.

And she wasn't going to get away with it after all, she realized. He had brought her a drink.

'You deserve one,' he told her, 'for doing justice to my poor, beloved roses. I can't tell you how grateful I am.'

Janey, putting the finishing touches to the final arrangement of blush-pink Fritz Nobis and creamy Pascali, tweaked a couple of glossy leaves into position in order to hide the chipped rim of the terracotta bowl in which they stood. Stepping back, she smiled and accepted the glass he offered her. It was the infamous elderflower champagne, and it definitely had character. Manfully she swallowed it.

'Go on then,' said Guy, having given her a ghost of a wink. 'What's the old bag been saying about me?'

'Don't flatter yourself.' The taste of old pea pods clung to Janey's teeth. 'She's been far too busy. Organizing the honeymoon.'

'The brazen hussy; she's already married.'

'Not her honeymoon.' Janey had been so entertained

by Mimi's endless suppositions and fantasies that it hadn't even occurred to her to be embarrassed. 'Ours.'

'Really?' Guy's eyebrows shot up. 'Where are we going? Somewhere nice, I hope?'

Evidently finding nothing strange in the idea that less than a week after Serena's departure Guy should have found himself a new future wife, Jack glanced with regret at the half-empty glass in his hand.

'What a shame, I only have three bottles of elderflower left. But if you think you might be interested, Guy, I could let you have three cases of last year's damson and crab-apple. That would certainly make the wedding party go with a swing.'

By seven-thirty the house was overflowing with guests, an eclectic mixture of smart, arty and downright Bohemian types complete with children and dogs for added informality. Janey, proudly introduced by Mimi as 'a whizz with flowers', almost had to forcibly restrain her from adding, 'She's Guy's new girlfriend but I'm not allowed to tell you because it's all terribly hush-hush.'

What struck Janey about the assortment of guests was their friendliness. Mimi and Jack clearly had no time for the kind of people who might turn up their noses at terrible wine or gaze askance at a messy home.

Two or three of them she even knew slightly, through the shop, whilst others, on hearing about it, bombarded her with questions. There was always someone desperate to learn how a wilting yukka could be sprung back to life, exactly how to go about preserving beech leaves with glycerine, when and how to trim a bonsai . . .

Mischief

She was in the middle of demonstrating the method of putting together a *pot-et-fleur* arrangement to the glamorous wife of a pig farmer when Guy reappeared at her side.

'I'm thinking of setting up evening classes,' Janey told him with a grin.

'It looks to me as if you've already started.' He showed her his watch. 'Eight o'clock. Definitely evening.'

'Eight o'clock already?' The play started at eight thirty; he had come to tell her it was time to leave. Janey, feeling like a six-year-old at a birthday party, looked crestfallen.

'We shouldn't be late,' said Guy. 'Apart from anything else, I can't stand being glared at when I'm trying to squeeze past all the people already in their seats.'

'This play,' she said in neutral tones. 'Is it . . . good?'

'Oh, terrific. Riveting. Unmissable.'

'And these tickets. Expensive?'

'Cost an absolute fortune.'

'Do we have to go?'

Guy shook his head. 'We don't *have* to.'

Feeling guilty, she said, 'Do you want to?'

He smiled. 'Of course I don't. I hate the bloody theatre.'

The party was proving to be a great success. An enormous game of charades was interrupted at nine o'clock by the arrival of a caterer's van bringing Chinese food for sixty. At ten o'clock, everyone was ushered out into the garden for the firework display.

'I haven't had a chance to ask you yet how you've been getting on.' Guy led Janey towards a wooden bench from which they could view the proceedings in comfort. When she shivered in the chilly September night air he removed his green sweater and draped it across her shoulders.

Janey breathed in the scent of aftershave emanating from the soft folds of wool. It was a curiously intimate sensation, wearing an item of clothing still warm from someone else's body. Glad of the darkness she said, 'You mean meeting your friends tonight?'

'I mean sorting yourself out and getting Parry-Brent out of your system.'

'Don't worry, he's well and truly out.' She gave him a rueful smile. 'A little public humiliation works like a charm.'

'It didn't exactly make him look good, either,' Guy reminded her. 'A scene like that won't improve his street-cred.'

'I suppose not.' Janey thought about it for a moment. 'Well, good.'

'And you haven't seen him since?'

'Not at all. He's doing his own flowers from now on . . . or sweet-talking some other gullible female into doing them for him.' She fidgeted with the sleeves of the sweater, twisting them around her cold hands. 'But that's enough about my failed relationship. How about you? Does it feel strange, not having Serena around any more?'

'Ah.' Guy sounded amused. 'You mean it's time to talk about *my* failed relationship.'

Janey laughed. 'Well, it seems only fair. And it's so encouraging, knowing I'm not the only one who makes mistakes.'

Maxine had told her, of course, about Guy's return from Holland and the subsequent departure – amid a flurry of Louis Vuitton suitcases – of Serena and all her worldly goods. There had been no question of either forgiveness or reconciliation; such overwhelming lack of concern for the safety of his children was unforgivable.

'What can I say?' He shrugged, to indicate his own misjudgement. 'I've spent the last three years getting myself involved with unsuitable women and Serena turned out to be the icing on the cake. She was beautiful and she didn't try to suck up to Josh and Ella. Somehow I'd got it into my head that it was how my wife would have behaved if I'd already had children in tow when I first met her. Véronique would never have used them in order to get to me. She'd have taken her time getting to know them and allowed them to make up their own minds about her in return. When I met Serena she said much the same thing and it struck a chord. I was impressed by her honesty.' Pausing for a second, Guy added ruefully, 'I even managed to persuade myself that at last I'd found someone whom Véronique would approve of.'

The first fireworks were being set off, exploding against the night sky in a dazzle of colour and light, each rocket climbing higher than the last. The children squealed with delight. After watching them for a few moments, Guy spoke again. 'A couple of years ago I took the kids to a bonfire-night party,' he said in a low voice, 'and Ella asked me if her mother could see the fireworks from Heaven. The thing is, nobody ever teaches you the answers to questions like that.'

Janey was no longer cold but she shivered anyway.

Brushing a leaf from her black trousers she tucked her feet up on the bench and hugged her knees.

'Now you've really made me feel ashamed of myself. The only person I have to look after is me. If I make a pig's ear of things, at least I'm the only one who has to suffer the consequences. I can't imagine how much more difficult it must be for you, always having the children to consider as well.'

'Hmm,' said Guy. 'The trouble is, it doesn't stop you making the mistakes. You just feel a hell of a lot guiltier afterwards, and hope to God your kids don't say "I told you so".'

In an attempt to cheer him up, Janey said, 'Oh well, you're bound to meet the right girl sooner or later. Who knows, by this time next year you could be married and living happily ever after with someone who adores children . . .'

'You're beginning to sound like Mimi.' With mock-severity he demanded, 'Have you been reading her books?'

'Mimi writes books?' Janey was instantly diverted by this piece of news. 'What kind?'

'The kind where you end up married and living happily ever after with someone who adores children,' said Guy dryly. 'She sat me down and forced me to read an entire chapter, once. Real fingers-down-the-throat stuff it was too. I told her they ought to be sold with detachable sick bags.'

'That's because you're a man,' she explained in comforting tones. 'Women love that kind of thing because the men in the books are so much nicer than any in real life. We call it escapism.'

'The trouble with Mimi is she's written so many she's started believing them,' he protested. 'You wouldn't believe the problems I had with her when she heard about Maxine coming to work for me. She was practically uncontrollable. Pretty-nanny-meets-widowed-father, it seems, is one of her all-time favourite plots.'

It was one of Maxine's, too, thought Janey with secret amusement. But the opportunity to tease him was too good to pass up. 'These things do happen,' she said mildly. 'Who knows how your feelings might change?'

'Oh *please*.' He heaved a great sigh of despair. 'Not you as well. Maxine? Never. Not in a million years!'

'That's what they always say in the books,' Janey replied cheerfully. 'All the way through. Right up until the very last chapter . . .'

Chapter 32

Maxine's high hopes for the lucrative toilet-roll commercial – founded on the basis of having once slept with the casting director – had been cruelly scuppered by his decision to give the job to the actress with whom he was currently sleeping instead. The disappointment of losing out was made all the harder to bear by the almost universal lack of sympathy.

'What a waste,' said Guy, straight-faced. 'All that talent down the pan.'

'If you'd got it,' Josh innocently enquired, 'would it have been a leading rôle?'

Ella, who didn't get the so-called jokes, said loyally, 'Well I'm glad you aren't doing it. I told my teacher Mrs Mitchell that you were going to sit on the toilet on television with your knickers down and she said it sounded horrible.'

'I was not going to sit on the toilet with my knickers down,' said Maxine through gritted teeth. No wonder Mrs Mitchell had given her such a sour look when she'd picked Ella up from school yesterday.

'Josh said you were.'

'Josh is a little toad about to get his Gameboy confiscated.'

'That's not fair!' protested Josh. 'Dad was the one who told me the joke.'

'Ah, you mean the hysterically funny leading rôle joke.' Maxine glared across the breakfast table at Guy. 'I suppose it took you hours to think that one up.'

He looked modest. 'Not at all. As a matter of fact, it came to me in a flush.'

Josh fell about laughing. Even Ella cottoned on to that one.

Maxine realized she was hopelessly outnumbered. 'You'll be sorry when I'm famous,' she snapped. 'In fact you're going to be sorry a lot sooner than that.'

There was a familiar glint in her eye. Recognizing it, Josh said weakly, 'Oh no, she's going to cook dinner. Not the fish pie, Maxine. Please, anything but that.'

'Oh yes.' She smiled, because revenge was so wonderfully sweet. 'Definitely the fish pie.'

Disappointment gave way to delight, however, when the director phoned Maxine a week later. Katrina, the actress whom he'd intended to favour, had somehow managed to fall out of his bed and break her arm in three places. Shooting started tomorrow. Could Maxine possibly get away at such short notice and step into the breach . . .?

Guy was busy in the darkroom. Since she wasn't prepared to risk life and limb opening the door – limbs being a precious commodity just now – Maxine yelled the news from outside.

'Oh, what next,' she heard him sigh. Hardly the encouraging response she might have hoped for. A minute passed before the door opened and Guy, frowning as his eyes adjusted to the light, emerged irritably.

'No,' he said, before she could even open her mouth to begin. 'This is too much, Maxine. Especially after what happened last time. You're either working for me or you're not, but you can't expect me to allow this kind of thing to carry on. I need someone who's reliable.'

What a pig, thought Maxine, outraged by his selfish, uncompromising attitude. The fact that Serena was a hopeless incompetent was hardly *her* fault. Guy had seemed to be so much more good-humoured during the past couple of weeks. And now here he was, reverting to type all over again.

'But this could be my big break,' she pleaded, silently willing him to pick up on the pun. If he smiled, she was halfway there.

Guy, however, saw through that little manoeuvre in a trice. He had no intention of smiling, either. 'Don't be obvious,' he said shortly. 'The answer's still no.'

'But it's fate . . . a chance in a million . . . and the kids are back at school now,' gabbled Maxine, bordering on desperation. In four days she would be earning almost as much as Guy paid her in an entire year. 'Oh please, let me find you a really and truly one-hundred-per-cent reliable nanny . . .'

'Maxine, forget it. You aren't going.'

'But—'

'No.' He spoke with a horrible air of finality.

Both Josh and Ella attended the local village school, which made it easy for Janey to pick them up at three-thirty and return them to Trezale House. Paula, thrilled to have been entrusted with the responsibility of visiting the flower market and running the shop single-handedly during Janey's absence, was almost more excited than Maxine at the prospect of watching her on television when the commercial was finally aired. Janey, less easily impressed, was nevertheless prepared to take care of the children for a few days whilst her sister was away. It was no hardship unless you counted having to sleep in Maxine's pigsty of a bedroom, and she was glad to be able to do a favour for Guy.

When she pulled up outside the school, Josh and Ella seemed equally pleased to see her.

'You're looking after us until Friday,' Ella declared, and promptly handed her a rolled-up sheet of paper. 'Here, Janey. I painted a picture of you in class. It's good, isn't it? What you have to do is say "How lovely" and pin it up on the kitchen wall when we get home.'

Janey studied the portrait. Ella had given her yellow hair, an unflattering purple face and fingers like tentacles. Next to her on a two-legged table stood a vast crimson cake complete with a staggering number of candles.

'Whose birthday is it?'

'Nobody's,' said Ella. 'But Maxine said you were good at cakes and they're my favourite, so I thought you might like to make some.'

'Tell Janey what else you thought,' prompted Josh slyly.

Ella beamed. 'I said Maxine was thin and she doesn't like cooking, but you aren't thin so that means you must like doing it a lot.'

Guy, who had spent the day working in Somerset

photographing an ancient countess and her fabulous jewels for a county magazine, arrived home at seven-thirty. The unfamiliar aroma of gingerbread hit him the moment he opened the front door. The sight of Janey, sitting at the kitchen table with Josh, Ella and practically an entire army of gingerbread men lined up on cooling racks was unfamiliar, too.

Nobody else, however, appeared to have noticed anything out of the ordinary.

'Hello, Daddy,' Ella greeted him airily, over her shoulder. 'We're just waiting for them to get cold enough to eat. I did the tummy buttons myself, with real currants.'

'I'm going to eat the arms and legs first,' Josh told him with ghoulish pride. 'Then the heads, until there's only bodies left.'

Janey, unaware of the smudge of flour on her forehead, smiled and said, 'Hi. Don't worry, I made them a proper tea at six. It's only chicken casserole and mashed potatoes, but there's some left if you're starving . . .'

It hadn't been the best of days as far as Guy was concerned. The countess, who was over eighty, had examined the preliminary Polaroids and haughtily demanded to know why someone reputed to be so clever with a camera couldn't even manage to take a moderately flattering snap.

The raddled old bag, it transpired, had delusions of passing for fifty, which not even all the soft focusing in the world could hope to achieve. It had been a long and tiresome session, throughout which Guy had endured being addressed as 'That boy'.

And now, this.

It didn't take a genius to work it out, but he said it anyway. 'Where's Maxine?'

Janey, evidently the innocent party, looked surprised. 'What? She caught the ten o'clock train this morning. Did you think she wasn't leaving until tonight?'

'Bloody hell,' said Guy. The girl was uncontrollable. Was there anything she wouldn't do in order to get her own way? '*Bloody* Maxine.'

'Oooh!' Ella squealed with delight. When she'd said bloody the other day it had caused all kinds of a fuss. Just wait until the next time her father tried to tell her off for saying it.

'What?' repeated Janey, bewildered by Guy's response. 'I'm sorry. I don't understand. Is there a problem?'

'Go on then,' he said heavily. 'Tell me how she managed to talk you into it.'

It didn't take long for realization to dawn. Maxine had done it again. 'You didn't know she was going,' Janey sighed.

'Damn right I didn't know,' said Guy icily. 'But then she was hardly likely to tell me, was she? My God, I told her she couldn't just waltz off . . .'

Damn, registered Ella, beside herself with glee. Surely that was another bad word? She wondered whether it was worse than 'sodit', which was what Maxine had said when she'd burnt the scrambled eggs the other night.

For once, however, Janey was on Maxine's side. Had she stopped to think about it, she supposed she wouldn't have agreed to take over if she'd known the full story, but she also knew how much the job offer meant to Maxine.

Besides, she was here now, and it wasn't as if she was a crazed axe-murderer.

'Look,' she said reasonably, 'there really isn't a problem. I'm enjoying myself, Paula's going to be looking after the shop . . .'

'Maxine asked me if she could go and I said no,' Guy repeated defiantly. 'And I don't know how you can even begin to defend her. She can't seriously expect to do this kind of thing and get away with it.'

Josh and Ella watched, enthralled, as Janey squared up to their father.

'If you didn't have any intention of allowing her to take the job, you should never have let her go up for the audition. That's unfair.'

'If she'd given me enough warning, I wouldn't have objected.' Guy found it hard to believe that Janey was defending Maxine. 'But I employ her to look after my children. She cannot expect to skip off at a moment's notice, leaving them in the care of God-knows-who . . .'

'She only found out yesterday that she'd got the job,' Janey countered hotly. 'And I'm not God-knows-who. I'm her sister. I'm sorry if that isn't good enough for you, but—'

'Don't be ridiculous.' Realizing that the situation was getting out of hand, he made an effort to calm down. Removing his leather jacket, he tipped Ella off her chair, sat down in her place and pulled her on to his knee.

'And don't look at me like that,' he told Janey. 'You know I'm not criticizing you. This is all Maxine's fault, as usual. That girl is enough to drive any man to distraction.'

And she'd even been flattered when she'd thought Guy had wanted her to look after the children. Janey, still indignant on Maxine's behalf, didn't return his smile. When he reached past Ella and helped himself to a gingerbread man, she hoped it would burn his mouth.

It did. Guy pretended it hadn't.

'These are brilliant,' he said, in an attempt to mollify her. 'Oh come on, Janey. Cheer up. Have a gingerbread man.'

'Is the tummy button nice, Daddy?' asked Ella.

The currant tummy-button was molten. Swallowing valiantly, Guy gave her a squeeze. 'Sweetheart, it's the best bit.'

'Look, you're back now,' said Janey in level tones. 'You don't need me here. Why don't I just go home and leave you to it?'

Belatedly, Guy realized just how affronted she really was. The expression in his dark blue eyes softened. 'OK, I'm sorry. I know you think I'm an ungrateful bas— person, but I'm not really. And of course you can't leave; we want you to stay. How could I not want someone to stay when they can make gingerbread men like these?'

'She did mashed potato with real potatoes, too,' offered Josh.

'And washed my hair,' Ella put in helpfully, 'without getting shampoo in my eyes.'

Janey was threatening to smile. Guy, glancing around the kitchen and counting on his fingers, continued the list.

'*And* she's made a chicken casserole. *And* she's ironed my denim shirt. *And* she's managed to tear Josh away from his Gameboy without even having to handcuff him to the kitchen chair . . .'

Josh, ever-hopeful, said, 'And she's promised I can stay up to watch *Bride of Dracula*.'

'No I haven't!' Janey started to laugh.

'That settles it,' declared Guy. 'I can't possibly watch *Bride of Dracula* on my own. It'll remind me of Maxine and give me hideous nightmares. You're going to have to stay.'

Ella, reaching across him, picked up one of the gingerbread men. To her dismay the all-important currant rolled on to the floor.

'Oh, sodit,' she squealed indignantly. 'What a little bugger. His bloody tummy button's come off.'

Chapter 33

Discretion was all part and parcel of a florist's job, Janey had discovered. When a man who had been married for twenty years began placing a regular order for white freesias to be delivered to an address several miles away from his own home, you kept your mouth shut and delivered them. When your very own middle-aged bank manager suddenly spruced himself up, discovered after-shave and took to popping in for single long-stemmed red roses, you kept a straight face at all costs. And on Valentine's day, when any number of men might request two – or even three – identical cellophane-wrapped bouquets of mixed spring flowers, you didn't bat so much as an eyelid.

Which was how she was managing not to bat an eyelid now. But there could be no doubt about it; the man standing before her was definitely the same man she had seen with her mother all those weeks ago. And the gold American Express card she was holding definitely bore the name 'Oliver J. Cassidy'.

Which was why, of course, he had looked so familiar to her when she'd spotted him at the Grand Rock Hotel.

'I'd like to write the message on the card myself, if I

may,' said Oliver Cassidy with a brief smile.

Janey, who had only popped into the shop for a couple of hours whilst Josh and Ella were at school, watched him uncap a black and gold Mont Blanc fountain pen. She felt like a voyeur.

'There.' The task completed, he passed the card back to her and smiled once more. The brief message: *You have all my love. Counting the days,* was written in a courtly, elegant hand. 'Will they be sent this afternoon?'

'Don't worry, they'll reach her before two o'clock,' Janey assured smoothly. 'I shall be delivering them myself.'

'Darling, what a lovely surprise!' Thea, opening the front door, kissed Janey on both cheeks. Her eyes lit up at the sight of the enormous cellophane-wrapped bouquet. 'And what heavenly lilies . . . how kind of you to think of your poor old mother.'

'They aren't from me,' said Janey dryly. 'They're from an admirer. I'm just the delivery girl.'

Thea, evidently in a buoyant mood, said, 'Oh well, in that case I won't invite you in for a drink.'

'Yes you will.' Handing over the bouquet, Janey headed in the direction of the kitchen and switched on the kettle. By the time she'd spooned instant coffee into two mugs, Thea had opened the envelope, read the message written on the card and slipped it into the pocket of her blue-and-white striped shirt. It was an extremely well-made man's shirt, Janey noted. No prizes for guessing the identity of the original owner.

She waited until the coffee was made before saying anything.

'So who is he, Mum?'

'Good heavens,' countered Thea, a shade too brightly. 'You're the one who sold him the flowers, sweetheart. Surely you know who he is. Or did he run off without paying and you're desperate to track him down?'

'I know who he is. I wanted to know if you did.'

Thea laughed. 'Well of course I do, darling! His name is Oliver and he's madly in love with me.'

'I meant do you know *exactly* who he is?' Janey paused and sipped her coffee. 'But it's pretty obvious now that you do. For goodness sake, Mum, whatever do you think you're doing? What's going on?'

'I don't know why you're making such a fuss,' said Thea crossly. 'There's absolutely nothing to get dramatic about. OK, so his name is Oliver Cassidy and he just happens to be the father of the photographer Maxine's working for. Is that so terrible? Am I committing some hideous crime?'

'You tell me.' Janey, inwardly amazed at her ability to remain calm, sat back and crossed her legs. 'Were you the one who came up with the idea of abducting his grandchildren?'

'Of course I wasn't. And there's no need to make it sound like some kind of kidnapping,' Thea countered. 'He wanted to see them; he knew Guy would kick up all kinds of a fuss if he asked his permission, so he waited until he was away. Those children had a splendid afternoon, Oliver did what he came to Cornwall to do and nobody came to any harm.'

'So you do know all about it,' said Janey accusingly.

'Maxine nearly lost her job as a result of that little escapade. And did dear Oliver tell you how he came to be estranged from his son? Did he explain exactly why Guy would have kicked up such a fuss?'

'It was all a misunderstanding.'Thea dismissed it with an airy gesture. 'Oliver realizes now that he made a mistake, but it's only gone on as long as it has because Guy overreacted. All families have disagreements, unfortunately. Oliver was unlucky enough to have his turned into some ridiculous, long-running feud. Darling, he was heartbroken about it! Seeing those dear little children, even if it was only for a few hours, did him all the good in the world.'

'It wouldn't have, if Guy had found out about it. He would have called the police.'

If there was one thing Thea couldn't bear, it was being criticized by her own children. 'And you're on his side of course,' she countered irritably. 'Despite knowing nothing about what really happened. Just because he no doubt has a pretty face.'

Janey, determined not to rise to the bait, gritted her teeth. 'But it's OK for you to defend his father, just because he's mad about you and stinking rich? Mum, what he did was *wrong!*'

'Oh Janey, don't get your knickers in a twist.' Thea banged her coffee mug down on the table. 'What happened wasn't tragic. The real tragedy is Guy Cassidy's pig-headed refusal to let bygones be bygones, because the children are the ones who suffer. All Oliver was trying to do was make it up to them.'

'Really?' Janey remained unimpressed. 'And what's he

planning to do for an encore? Whisk them out of the country for a few months?'

This was ridiculous. Thea's expression softened. 'Oliver would never do anything like that. He's a wonderful man, darling.'

Janey, who had thought Bruno was wonderful, replied unforgivingly, 'I'm sure he is. As long as he's getting his own way.'

There was a long silence. Finally, Thea said, 'All right, so what happens now? What are *you* going to do for an encore?'

Janey, having already considered the options, shrugged. 'You mean am I going to tell Guy? I don't know, Mum. The thing is, can you be sure his father isn't, in some obscure way, just using you? I'm serious,' she went on, when Thea started to smile. 'It's all highly coincidental, after all. You're Maxine's mother, and Maxine looks after Josh and Ella. How do you know he hasn't hatched some sinister plan?'

'Dear me.' Her mother shook her head and gave her an indulgent look. 'And I thought Maxine was the drama queen of the family. Janey, take it from someone old enough to know. There's nothing even remotely sinister about Oliver Cassidy, and there are no ulterior motives on his part. He loves me, and I love him. I'm sorry if that doesn't meet with the approval of Maxine's employer but as far as I'm concerned, my private life is none of his business anyway. And if you feel you have to tell him, then do it, though personally I can't see the point. From what I hear, hugs and smiles and forgiveness-all-round is pretty much off the cards, so all you'd be doing would be stirring it up again for no useful reason. Still,' she concluded with a take-it-or-leave-it gesture, 'Those are just my thoughts. As I said, it's entirely up to you.'

Janey was now more undecided than ever. What her mother had said made sense. Keeping quiet, on the other hand, meant assuming responsibility for the secret. And it also meant not telling Maxine, who would be sure to tell Guy herself. If anything should ever go wrong, she thought with unease, she would be at least partly to blame.

But Oliver Cassidy had seemed charming, and imprinted in her mind was the expression on his face as he'd written the brief message to accompany Thea's flowers.

'How do you know he loves you?' she asked, gazing into her mother's dark eyes.

'I've had nearly thirty years to learn from my mistakes in that field,' Thea replied simply. 'This time it's the real thing. Trust me, darling. When it happens like this, you *do* know . . .'

In that case, thought Janey as memories of Alan and Bruno flooded back, why don't I?

Torrential rain the next day meant an early wrap for the fashion shoot Guy had been working on in the Cotswolds. Home by four-thirty, he found Janey on the phone in the kitchen, the receiver tucked under her chin whilst she mashed parsnips with one hand and stirred a pan of gravy with the other. Her blond hair was loosely pinned up and the violet sweatshirt she wore over white jeans was slipping off one shoulder. Her cheeks, pink from the heat of the oven, turned pinker still when she realized he was back.

'Oh, I didn't hear you come in. Dinner won't be ready for another hour yet . . . but there's tons of hot water if you'd like a bath.'

Maxine, on the other end of the phone, groaned. 'Uh oh, enter the dragon. Don't tell him it's me.'

'Who are you talking to?' said Guy, his tone deceptively mild.

'Nobody.' Janey's innocent expression was foiled by the tell-tale deepening flush. 'A friend.'

'Did anyone ever tell you you're a hopeless liar?' With a brief smile he crossed the kitchen, took the phone from her and said, 'Hello, Maxine.'

'Oh God.' In London, Maxine sighed. 'Are you still mad at me?'

'What do you think?'

'You're still mad,' she said penitently. 'And I know that what I did was wrong, but you just didn't understand how important this job is to me. I'm sorry Guy, but I really was desperate . . .'

'Hmmm.' Glancing across at Janey, who was frenziedly tackling the parsnips and trying to look as if she wasn't listening, he drawled, 'Lucky for you you've got an understanding sister. I hope you appreciate the favour she's done you.'

'I do, I do.' Maxine's tone was fervent. Much to her relief, the expected bawling-out hadn't happened. Not yet, anyway. Deciding to chance it, she added, 'And aren't *you* glad she's there, too? She's so much better at cooking than I am.'

'She could hardly be any worse.'

'And Josh and Ella think she's terrific!'

'Carry on like this and you'll end up talking yourself out of a job. Or was that what you had in mind?' he enquired evenly. 'If you've landed the lead in some dazzling West End production, Maxine, I'd rather you told me now.'

'Oh, but I haven't! And I really don't want to leave, Guy. I like working for you.'

'But?' he prompted, when it became apparent that Maxine hadn't the courage to say the word herself.

She crossed her fingers, hard. 'But we aren't going to finish shooting until Saturday, so I won't be able to get back before Sunday morning.' The words came out in an apologetic rush. 'I've already asked Janey and she doesn't mind a bit, but is that OK with you?'

If he was ever going to blow his top, it would happen now. As the silence lengthened, Maxine realized she was holding her breath.

'Why,' drawled Guy finally, 'do I feel like a schoolboy who's just found out the summer holidays are carrying on for an extra week?'

'Was he furious?' asked Cindy, who was wallowing in the jacuzzi. It was nice having Maxine as a temporary house-guest whilst her husband was abroad; it was almost like being single again, sharing a flat and gossiping until three in the morning over bottles of wine, about men.

'He wasn't furious at all.' Maxine, perching on the edge of the bath, looked distinctly put out. 'He was delighted.'

'Isn't that what you wanted?'

'There's a difference between agreeing to let me stay

and being delighted,' said Maxine moodily. 'It would be nice to feel a little bit missed. From the sound of it, they're having a whale of a time down there without me.'

'Who knows?' said Cindy, holding out her glass for a top-up. 'Maybe something's going on between them. They could be having a rip-roaring affair.'

'Janey and Guy?' Maxine laughed. 'Now I know you've had too much to drink.'

'I don't see why it's so funny. You told me he'd taken her to a party the other week,' Cindy reminded her. 'And he's pretty irresistible, after all. Are you seriously telling me your sister would turn down the opportunity of a fling with Guy Cassidy?'

'I'm telling you that I spent a good couple of months trying to persuade him to have a fling with me,' said Maxine, tossing back her long blond hair and admiring her reflection in the full-length mirror. 'And it didn't bloody work. Boasting aside, darling, if he can ignore an offer like that, he's hardly likely to be interested in Janey.'

Chapter 34

The phone rang again whilst Guy was taking a shower. Janey, picking it up, recognized titian-haired Charlotte's voice at once. She could almost smell the perfume, too, oozing down the line at her from St Ives.

'He's upstairs in the shower,' she told Charlotte, who had asked to speak to Guy in deeply husky tones. 'Can I take a message?'

'That isn't Maxine.' Huskiness gave way to suspicion. 'Who am I speaking to?'

For a moment, Janey was tempted. Then, deciding that that would be cruel, she said, 'Maxine's taken a few days off. I'm just here looking after the children whilst she's away.'

Charlotte, however, sounded unconvinced. 'And you are . . .?'

'Janey. Maxine's sister.' She wondered whether an apology might be expected, for having been the cause of Charlotte's abandonment at Bruno's party. But she hadn't dragged Guy away; if anything, he had dragged her.

'Oh. Right.' Thankfully, Charlotte didn't mention it either. She sounded unflatteringly relieved, though, to hear that she wasn't facing Serena-standard competition. 'Well in that case, maybe you could ask Guy to call me back.'

'Will do.' Josh had crept barefoot into the kitchen behind her. Janey watched his reflected image in the window as he surreptitiously reached for the biscuit tin. 'No more Jaffa cakes.'

Startled, Charlotte said, 'I beg your pardon?'

'Sorry, I was speaking to somebody else.'

'How did you know I was there?' Josh protested. 'I didn't make any noise.'

'I heard the Jaffa cakes screaming for help.'

'Good Lord.' Charlotte sounded amused. 'Look, whilst you're there, would you happen to know whether or not Guy has anything on tonight?'

'Nothing at all at the moment,' said Janey. 'He's in the shower.'

'I mean any plans.'

'I don't think so. He told me I could go out for the evening if I wanted, so he must be staying in.'

'Oh. And where are you going, somewhere nice?'

The CIA had nothing on Charlotte. Smiling to herself, Janey replied, 'I don't have any plans either. I'll probably just stay here.'

'That sounds nice.' Charlotte sounded immeasurably cheered by the news. 'OK then, if you could just ask Guy to ring me back as soon as he's out of the shower. You won't forget now, will you?'

'Oh hell.' Guy looked bored. 'That means she's going to invite me round for dinner.'

'Stop eating, then,' scolded Janey, because he'd already helped himself to three sausages and she hadn't even dished up yet.

'But I don't want to go. No, I can't face it.' He shook his head. 'She'll float around in some kind of negligée and try to get me drunk so I won't be able to drive home. When she phones back, say I've gone out.'

'Then I'll get the blame for not passing on the message,' she protested. God, men were callous beasts. 'No, you've got to ring her.'

Guy shrugged. 'OK, I'll tell her I've already made other arrangements.'

Janey looked shamefaced. 'I said you hadn't.'

'Then I'll tell her I have to stay in and look after the kids because you're going out.'

'Oops,' said Janey. 'She's already asked me that. I told her I wasn't.'

He mimed mock despair. 'So how long have you been taking this truth drug?'

'I can't help it,' Janey protested with a grin. 'I'm just a naturally honest person.'

'One of you must have been adopted then. You can't be Maxine's sister.'

'And you can't keep changing the subject like this.' In order to spur him into action, she whisked his plate out of reach. 'She's sitting at home, waiting for you to call her back. Do it.'

'Now who's being bossy?' he grumbled, pinching yet another sausage from Ella's plate as he headed for the kitchen phone. 'You're far nicer to my children than you are to me.'

Janey gave him a guileless smile. 'You pay me to be nice to your children.'

'She'd be nicer,' Josh told his father, 'if she didn't make us help with the washing up.'

Just listening to Guy's side of the phone call was uncomfortable enough. Janey, squirming on the other woman's behalf, decided that if she were Charlotte she would have died of embarrassment. But still it went on, Guy tactfully saying no and Charlotte – clearly not embarrassed at all – shooting one excuse after another down in flames.

'Look, maybe another time,' he said eventually, several toe-curling minutes later. 'But not tonight, Charlotte. Really. I have to be in London first thing tomorrow morning and it's been a tough few days. Yes, I know that's what I said last week, but that doesn't mean it isn't still true.'

More muffled protests ensued. Guy glanced across at Janey for help. She, unable to look at him, picked up the pepper mill and over-seasoned her baked tomatoes.

'OK.' He lowered his voice to a conspiratorial whisper. 'If you must know, I *have* to stay here tonight. It's Janey; she's absolutely petrified of being left alone in this house. Yes, I know it sounds ridiculous but she has this thing about burglars breaking in with shotguns. We're so isolated here, you see; I only have to mention going out for the evening and she starts gibbering with fear. Charlotte, I'm sorry but you have to understand, I can't possibly abandon her . . .'

'Thanks a lot,' said Janey, when he returned to the table. 'Why are all men such shameless liars?'

'The first four excuses were true.' He gave her a what-can-you-do shrug. 'And she didn't believe any of them. Sometimes you have to resort to a little elaboration.'

It was certainly instructive, seeing the situation from a male point of view. Curious, she said, 'But if you aren't, you know . . . well, interested in her, why don't you just say so?'

Josh and Ella, evidently accustomed to such goings-on, were unfazed by the conversation.

'He tried doing that last week,' Josh explained kindly. 'But all she did was cry. Then she phoned Dad back, right in the middle of *Coronation Street*, and cried some more.'

'So he took the telephone off the hook,' said Ella. 'But that didn't work either. She got into her car and came here, *still* crying. It was really mean of her,' she added, her expression indignant. 'It was only eight o'clock and it wasn't even our fault, but we had to go up to bed.'

'You see?' protested Guy. 'I get the blame for everything. I can't do anything right.'

Janey, still acutely aware of the fact that she had made almost as much of an idiot of herself with Bruno, couldn't help feeling sorry for Charlotte who was probably weeping buckets right now.

'You must have led her on.' She tried to look disapproving. 'If you really don't want to see her again, it would be far kinder to say so and put her out of her misery.'

He looked surprised. 'Rather than let her down gently?'

'There's nothing worse than not knowing where you stand.' Janey spoke with feeling. She lowered her voice, although Josh and Ella had by this time lost interest. 'You should tell her, you know. It'll be easier all round if you do. Even Charlotte will appreciate it in the long run.'

'Oh hell.' He gave a sigh of resignation. 'I hate these emotional showdowns. This is going to be no fun at all.'

At least he wasn't the one being dumped. Janey wondered if he'd ever been on the receiving end of a verbal 'Dear John'. Somehow, she seriously doubted it.

'You'll go and see her then? Tonight?'

With reluctance, he nodded. Then grinned. 'Only if you're sure you can cope with being left alone in the house for an hour or so?'

'Oh, I think I can stand it,' said Janey bravely. 'If any burglars turn up, I'll just send them into Maxine's bedroom. That should be enough to put them off looting and pillaging for life.'

By the time he got back it was almost nine-thirty. Janey had put Josh and Ella to bed and was finishing the washing up.

'Leave that,' said Guy, opening a bottle of wine and taking two glasses out of the cupboard. 'Come and help me drink this. I need it.'

'Was it awful?'

He ran his fingers through his dark hair and pulled a face. 'Pretty much. Shit, I feel like such a bastard. She said she wished she'd never met me.'

'She didn't mean it,' said Janey consolingly. 'She just feels let down. Charlotte liked you more than you liked her, that's all. And when it ends, it hurts.'

'That's what she said,' mused Guy. 'The trouble is,

she blames me. But you have to get to know someone before you can decide whether or not you're suited. By the time you realize the relationship doesn't have a future, it's too late. They like you, so they end up getting hurt.' He paused, then added, 'Hardly an earth-shattering revelation, I know. It's just that I've never really discussed it with anyone before.'

'Whereas we women discuss it all the time,' said Janey with a grin. 'I told you, you should have stuck at those books of Mimi's. They'd have taught you everything you needed to know.'

'I thought you were supposed to be having an early night,' she protested three hours later.

This was an altogether different Janey from the one he had taken away from Bruno's party, Guy reflected. Now, relaxed and perfectly at ease, interested in hearing what he had to say yet at the same time totally unpushy, she had managed to make him forget the time completely. And he, too, was relaxed; it was such a relief to be able to talk to someone who wasn't even attempting to flirt with him or advance her own cause.

But despite Janey's apparent conviction that she was less attractive than her younger sister, he didn't agree. Tonight, wearing virtually no make-up, with her honey-blond hair loosely held up with combs and her violet sweatshirt still slipping off one shoulder, he found her uncontrived beauty infinitely more attractive. Her summer tan showed no signs of fading, her complexion was flawless and those conker-brown eyes, alight with humour, didn't need shadows and eyeliners to make them spectacular; just as the soft, perfectly shaped mouth had nothing to gain by being plastered with lipstick.

He found himself comparing their manner with the children too, for although Josh and Ella adored Maxine and her slapdash, highly individual ways, her wit was on occasions too acute for comfort, leaving them unsure whether or not she had actually meant it. Maxine could be unpredictable, which in turn made Ella edgy and Josh mildly resentful. Young children appreciated continuity and the security of knowing just where they stood. Berenice, of course, had been stability personified, whilst Maxine was all fun and back-chat, but if he could choose the ideal nanny, Guy realized, it would be someone like Janey, who tempered control with gentle humour. She was also easy on the eye – unlike poor Berenice, he thought with a stab of guilt – extremely good company and not the least bit interested in shooting off at short notice to star in toilet-roll commercials.

'Any more news about your father?' she said suddenly.

Guy, who had been pouring out the last of the Beaujolais, gave her a stern look.

'And there I was, just thinking what a nice person you were.'

'I'm still a nice person,' said Janey innocently. 'I wondered whether there'd been any developments, that's all.'

'None. Every time I rang his home number the answering machine was switched on. In the end I stopped trying.'

'What would you have said, though? If you had spoken to him?'

'I'd have told him to keep away from my home and my children.' Guy's expression was stony, unforgiving. 'I'd have told him that if he ever tries a stunt like that again I'll call the police.'

'But if he apologized,' she persisted, tucking her bare feet beneath her and leaning forwards to reach for the refilled glass, 'and begged you to forgive him, do you think you could?'

'Oh yes.' His eyes darkened. 'Highly likely.'

'I mean it,' said Janey. 'Come on, think it through. He might really regret what happened and now all he wants to do is get to know his grandchildren and make up for lost time.' Her expression was oddly intense.

Guy, however, had made his own mind up long ago. 'You've been watching too much *Little House on the Prairie*,' he told her, before she could open her mouth and say more. 'No, Janey. I never want to see my father again and I don't want the children to have anything to do with him either, so don't even try and talk me round. This is one happy family reunion that definitely isn't going to happen.'

Oh well, thought Janey. Sorry, Oliver. At least you can't say I didn't try.

Chapter 35

Every year in the second week of October the travelling fair came to Trezale, setting up its comfortingly familiar pattern of stalls, side-shows, candy-floss stands and mechanical rides along the high street with the dodgems, ghost train and big wheel taking pride of place at the top end.

Everyone went to the fair; it was a landmark event on the social calendar. Josh and Ella, in a frenzy of excitement at the prospect of spending all their money and spinning themselves sick on the waltzers, were practically counting the minutes until Friday night.

Janey was stunned, however, by Guy's reaction when he called her from his car phone on the M5 on his way back from a fashion shoot in Bath.

'Josh says you've promised they can stay out until midnight,' she told him. 'I need a voice of authority here. What time do they have to be home?'

'What do you mean, they?' Guy demanded. '*We* go home whenever we like.'

'You mean you're coming with us?'

'Why else would I complete a six-hour shoot in three and a half hours?' He sounded amused. 'And skip dinner with Kate Moss. Of course I'm coming with you.'

'Gosh,' said Janey. 'Somehow I hadn't imagined you as a fairground lover.'

'No? What kind of lover had you imagined me as?'

'I meant—'

'I know what you meant.' Guy laughed. 'And it's OK, you can stop blushing now. Look, I'll be home by six, so just tell the kids to hang on. Don't you dare leave without me.'

Josh and Ella had, over the years, grown used to it. Since it was practically the entire reason Maxine had taken the job in the first place, she would have enjoyed every minute. Janey, however, cringed. It was a frosty evening, her nose was probably pink with cold and her hair had been whisked to a frenzy on the Octopus. It was all right for Guy; he was the one taking roll after roll of film with the new camera, but she wasn't used to finding herself on the receiving end of a lens. As far as she was concerned, it was a distinctly nerve-racking experience.

And he was using up film at a rate of knots.

'Haven't you finished yet?' It sounded ungracious, but she wished he would stop. Being asked to test out the latest Olympus was all very well, but this was downright off-putting. She didn't know where to look.

'No need to panic,' said Guy. 'It isn't as if I'm asking you to pose and smile. Just ignore me.'

Janey scowled. 'How can I ignore you when I know my nose is red?'

'Don't be so vain,' he chided briskly. 'I'm trying out a new camera, not using you for the cover of *Vogue*. So relax...'

'Quick, Daddy!' Ella, who wasn't the least bit camera-shy, screamed with delight. 'Take one of me with candy floss all over my face.'

Janey was eating a toffee apple when a male voice behind her said, 'Well, hello. Having fun?'

Swinging round, she saw that it was Alexander Norcross, Mr Presentable himself, looking very smart in a charcoal-grey Crombie and with a plump, shivering brunette in tow.

'Oh hi.' She probably had bits of toffee stuck to her teeth but she smiled anyway. 'Yes, we're having a great time.'

Ella tugged at her arm. 'Janey, can you lend me fifty pence for the hoop-la?'

'Rip-off, these places.' Alexander glanced down at Ella, who had just proved his point. 'How these people have the nerve to charge fifty pence for the opportunity to win something that costs ten, I don't know. If you ask me, there should be a law against it.'

Smart but mean, recalled Janey, pressing a pound coin into Ella's gloved hand. With exaggerated politeness she said, 'Oh dear, does that mean you aren't enjoying yourself?'

'I'm not saying that,' protested Alexander. 'Fairgrounds can be entertaining, so long as you don't waste your cash. We've been here for almost two hours now,' he added with evident pride, 'and it hasn't even been necessary to open my wallet. Now that's what I call real value for money.'

The brunette didn't just have a red nose, she was almost blue with cold all over.

'You mean he hasn't bought you a cup of coffee?' Janey

looked shocked. 'Alexander, this poor girl is going to end up with frostbite. What she needs is a hot espresso and a couple of stiff brandies to warm her up.'

The girl, looking almost pathetically grateful, said, 'That would be nice. Alex, could we do that?'

'Are you cold?' He sounded surprised. 'Well, maybe it is time we made a move. I know. We'll get back to my house and have a nice cup of tea.'

Janey had the urge to scream: 'Make him take you to an expensive restaurant! Better still, tell him to take an almighty running jump into the sea . . .'

But she didn't, and the next moment Josh and Guy arrived back from the shooting gallery. Guy, realizing that she was talking to someone she knew, hung back and maintained a discreet distance. Josh, who was far more interested in money than discretion, charged up to Janey and yelled frantically, 'Quick, I've run out of change!'

'Two kids,' Alexander remarked, when Josh had pocketed another pound coin and shot off to join Ella. 'Well, well. So you found yourself a family man. Bad luck, Jane.'

Janey risked a glance over his shoulder. Ten feet away and eavesdropping shamelessly, Guy grinned.

'Bad luck?'

'Oh well, maybe you get on well with them.' Alexander shuddered with disapproval. 'Some girls don't mind that kind of set-up, after all. But you do want to be careful, Jane. Single mothers are bad enough, but single fathers are an even dodgier prospect. Is he interested in you, or is he just desperate to find someone to look after the house and kiddies?'

'Gosh.' Not daring to meet Guy's gaze, Janey bit her lip and looked worried. 'I hadn't thought of it like that. You mean all he's really after is some kind of substitute nanny?'

'That's exactly what I mean,' Alexander declared with a knowledgeable nod. 'You see, nannies don't come cheap and they aren't always one hundred per cent reliable. As far as the man's concerned, it's simpler and more economical in the long run to find himself a new wife.'

Guy, approaching them, gave Janey a ghost of a wink. She didn't even flinch when he slipped his arm around her waist and gave her a fleeting kiss on the cheek.

'Darling, I thought I'd lost you. We really should be getting home, you know. It's way past Ella's bedtime.'

Janey gave him a cold stare. 'Oh dear, is it? Well in that case we'd better run.'

'What's the matter?' Guy raised his eyebrows. 'Is there a problem?'

'I don't know,' she replied evenly. 'But I think I'm about to find out. Let me ask you a question, Guy. Did you invite me to move in with you because you loved me or because you needed someone to take care of your children?'

His smile faded. After some consideration he said, 'Well, sweetheart. If you think back, I didn't actually invite you to move in with me at all. As far as I recall, I arrived back from Amsterdam one night and there you were, unpacking your suitcases and generally making yourself at home. Not that I'm complaining of course, but—'

'But you do *love* me?' A note of hysteria crept into Janey's voice. 'If we're going to get married next week I need to know if you really love me.'

Alexander and the brunette stood in fascinated silence. Janey prayed Josh and Ella wouldn't pick this moment to come back.

'Sweetheart, of course I do.' Guy gave her a placatory hug. 'We all do. In fact the kids are so smitten, I've decided to sack the nanny. From now on you can look after them all by yourself. Now isn't that just the most wonderful surprise?'

'That's it,' she said flatly. 'The wedding's off.'

The brunette, who had been staring at Guy, snapped her fingers. 'I know who you are. You're Guy Cassidy, the photographer.' Her eyes widened. 'You're famous.'

'Doesn't stop him being a cheapskate double-crossing toad,' Janey snapped.

'Guy Cassidy?' said Alexander, deeply impressed. '*The* Guy Cassidy? Of course you are! Hey, it's really nice to meet you.'

'I don't believe I'm hearing this.' Janey glared at Alexander. 'You've just told me not to marry him and now you're fawning all over him like some kind of groupie!'

Guy frowned. 'He told you not to marry me? Why ever would he say a thing like that? Janey, you're making it up.'

'Look, I'm sorry.' Alexander shook his head. 'I didn't know it was you.'

'Too late,' declared Janey, prising Guy's hand from her arm. 'I wouldn't marry him now if he was Mel Gibson.'

Chapter 36

'And I thought Maxine was the actress.' He caught up with her by the win-a-goldfish stall, where Ella and Josh were engrossed in the task of flipping rubber frogs on to lily pads. 'Carry on like that and you'll end up starring in toilet-roll commercials.'

Janey grinned. The expression on Alexander's face had been superb. It was a shame Guy couldn't have captured it on film.

'You started it.'

'Couldn't resist it. My God, when I heard what he was saying to you; no wonder you're wary of men.' He shook his head in disbelief. 'I must say, you certainly know some extraordinary people.'

At least he didn't know how she'd met Alexander, Janey thought with some relief. He'd already caught her out once, and that was enough.

'My *bloody* frogs keep falling in the water!' complained Ella, unaware of Guy behind her.

He tapped her on the shoulder.

'Oh, sorry Daddy.' She gave him an angelic, gap-toothed smile.

'Good.' Guy winked at Janey. 'Because we don't

want any bloody goldfish anyway.'

'My feet ache,' said Janey as they made their way back to the car two hours later.

Josh and Ella, clutching helium balloons, armfuls of Day-Glo furry toys and an inflatable giant squid, were running on ahead, the squid's pink plastic tentacles wrapping themselves around Ella's legs as she struggled to keep up with Josh.

'My wallet aches.' Guy gave her a rueful look. 'I'm financially destitute. And all because my daughter fell in love with a squid.'

'And you didn't enjoy trying to win it?' Janey mocked. 'Come on, you loved every minute on that rifle range.'

'I would have loved it even more if the sights hadn't been ninety degrees out. Fifteen quid for a squid,' he groaned. 'And what's the betting that by tomorrow morning it'll have a puncture.'

'Stop complaining. You've had a wonderful time.'

'OK, so maybe I have.' He grinned. The next moment, he grabbed her arm and pulled her towards him, so abruptly that Janey almost lost her footing.

'Wha—'

'Sorry, dog shit on the pavement,' said Guy romantically. 'You almost stepped in it.'

'My hero,' Janey murmured, because although she had regained her balance he hadn't released his hold on her. If she moved away she would feel silly – it was hardly the romantic gesture of the decade, after all – but at the same time she couldn't help wondering what Josh and Ella would make of it if they should choose this moment to turn round. Why, she thought with some embarrassment, was he doing this? Why wasn't he saying anything? And why didn't he just let go?

Guy was deep in thought. He wasn't normally slow off the mark but something had just occurred to him, something quite unexpected, and it needed some serious thinking about.

The big stumbling block, he now realized, had been the fact that Janey's unfortunate past had rendered her so totally off-limits from the start. With a history like hers, the last thing she needed was the kind of involvement which could only bring more pain. And when you were a man with a history like his, thought Guy grimly, it was easier simply to steer clear. As he'd told her himself only days earlier, his relationships had a habit of coming to grief. He didn't do it deliberately but it happened anyway. He always seemed to be the one at fault. And it was always the other person who got hurt.

But although he hadn't even allowed the possibility to cross his mind before, Guy now acknowledged the fact that he had been deluding himself. Throughout the past week he'd been telling himself what a great nanny Janey was. In truth, he realized, it was the simple fact of her being there that had been great.

One of the major points in her favour, however, was also one of the major drawbacks, and it was something else with which he was woefully unfamiliar. Janey didn't flirt, and he didn't know if that was because she simply wasn't a flirtatious person, or if it meant she didn't find him worth flirting with. Consequently, he had no idea whether or not she was even faintly attracted to him. Their relationship up until now had been entirely platonic. Over the months – and not without the occasional hiccup along the way – a friendship had been forged. Aside from that, he just didn't know how Janey felt about him.

And all of a sudden it mattered terribly. The idea that she might not return his feelings was galling to say the least. It wasn't the kind of problem he'd ever had to deal with before; he wanted Janey to like him, but how on earth was he going to find out if she did?

Belatedly, Guy realised he was still holding on to her arm. Now he felt plain stupid. Should he carry on and see if she objected, or oh-so-casually let go? It was the kind of dilemma more normally faced by teenagers.

It was his own daughter who came to the rescue. Ella, struggling to disentangle her legs from the tentacles of the squid, slipped off the kerb and landed, with a piercing shriek, flat on her face in the gutter.

She was shaken but not hurt. As he lifted her to her feet and brushed a couple of dry leaves from her white-blond hair, Guy was reminded of his first meeting with Véronique, in another gutter all those years ago. She hadn't flirted with him either, he recalled; she had simply been herself, take it or leave it, and allowed him to make all the running. Falling in love with her had happened so fast, and had been so easy, he would never have believed at the time that waiting for it to happen again could take so long. But finding someone else to fall in love with, he reflected ruefully, hadn't been easy at all.

'You're all right,' said Janey, wiping a lone tear from Ella's cheek with her knuckle. 'No damage, sweetheart. The squid broke your fall.'

'He's hissing.' Ella stopped crying in order to listen. 'I

can hear him making a funny noise.'

'That's because he's a hero,' Janey replied gravely. 'He saved you from being hurt, and punctured a tentacle in the process. Don't worry, we'll stick a plaster on it when we get home.'

By the time they reached the car, Guy had come to a decision. He didn't want to risk rocking the boat whilst Janey was looking after the children. But Maxine would be back on Sunday, and it would be perfectly in order for him to take Janey out to dinner on Sunday night by way of thanking her for having stepped into the breach. This meant he had two days in which to plan what he was going to say . . .

The traffic was nose to tail along the high street where the fair had set up, so he took a left into the road which would take them past Janey's shop and up out of the town. He would take her somewhere really special on Sunday, he decided; maybe the new restaurant in Zennor that everyone was talking about. Would vintage champagne impress or alarm her? Should he take the car or would a cab be better? Or how about flying to Paris, would she think he was being flash? Was that too over-the-top for—?

'Stop!' shrieked Janey. 'Oh my God, stop the car!'

So wrapped up in his own thoughts that for a fraction of a second it seemed as if she had read his mind, Guy slammed on the brakes and screeched to a halt at the side of the road. Janey, white-faced, was staring back at the darkened shop. Guy followed her gaze; something was evidently wrong but he didn't know what. The windows were still intact, the door hadn't been smashed down, the building wasn't going up in flames . . .

'What is it?'

He put out his hand but she was already struggling out of her seatbelt, still staring and apparently unable to speak. As she fumbled for the door handle he saw how violently her hands were shaking.

'Janey, what's the matter?' He spoke more sharply than he had intended. In the back seat, Josh and Ella were craning their necks in order to see what was going on.

'Is it a burglar?' Josh sounded excited. He had glimpsed a figure sitting in the shadows of the recessed entrance to the shop, but burglars, he felt, didn't usually stop for a rest.

'It isn't a burglar.' Janey's voice sounded odd, as if she hadn't used it for a long time. The handle of the passenger door having defeated her, she said numbly, 'Can you open this for me please?'

'Who is it?' Guy had already figured it out for himself but he asked the question anyway.

'My husband. Alan. It's . . . my husband.'

She was evidently in a state of deep shock. Guy hesitated, wondering what he should do. At this moment he doubted whether Janey could even stand upright, let alone cross the road unaided.

He was also seized, quite abruptly, with the almost overwhelming urge to cross the road himself and batter Alan Sinclair to a pulp. Because he wasn't dead, he'd never been dead, and he had no right to put Janey through two years of hell and still have the nerve to be alive.

'Why don't you wait here?' He spoke in soothing tones,

as if she were a child. 'Just stay in the car and let me speak to him.'

But Janey turned to stare at him as if he had gone irredeemably mad. '*What*?'

Josh and Ella, in the back seat, listened in dumbstruck silence.

'I said, let me just—'

'I heard you,' she replied through gritted teeth. 'And I can't believe you have the bloody nerve to even think of such a thing. If you saw your wife, Guy, what would you do? Sit in the car and let *me* go and have a word with her?'

As a counter-attack it was horribly below the belt, but Janey didn't even stop to consider what she was saying.

'Véronique is dead,' Guy murmured. 'Your husband is alive.'

'Of course he's alive,' shrieked Janey, almost beside herself with rage. 'That's why I'd quite like to see him, you stupid bastard, except that I can't bloody see him because you won't switch off the stupid child-lock on this stupid bloody door!'

He flicked the switch.

'There. Janey, all I'm saying is be careful. Ask yourself why he left and why he's decided to come back.'

But it was too late. She was already out of the car.

'Oh Dad!' wailed Ella, as he put the car into gear. 'This is exciting! Can't we stay and watch?'

'No.' Guy's jaw was set, the expression in his eyes unreadable. 'We can't.'

Chapter 37

'My God, I don't believe it,' sighed Maxine. 'What is this, some kind of sick joke? Did they move April Fool's day?'

Bruno put his hand out to steady her glass, which was tilting alarmingly.

'Careful,' he said, at the same time admiring her cleavage. 'Didn't you read the government health warning on the bottle? Red wine on a white dress can seriously damage your night.'

The dress, which had cost a scary amount of money, was an Azzedine Alaia. Moreover, it belonged to Cindy, who had threatened her with certain death if anything untoward happened to it. Mindful of the warning, Maxine placed the glass on a table out of harm's way.

'My night's already been damaged,' she said rudely. 'What the hell are you doing here?'

Bruno grinned. 'Just one of those fateful coincidences, I suppose. Jamie Laing's an old friend of mine. When he called last week and invited me to the party I didn't even think I'd be able to get up here, but my new assistant manager was keen to work this weekend, so . . .' He shrugged and gestured around the room. 'It seemed like a nice idea. Now why don't I ask how you came to be invited to this party? Or maybe it isn't a coincidence at all. Maybe you're following me.'

'Oh, absolutely,' declared Maxine, the words dripping sarcasm. But the urge to show off was simply irresistible. Glimpsing a semi-familiar face in the crowd, she waved over Bruno's shoulder, realizing too late that the face belonged to an actor whom she had only seen on television. At least Bruno hadn't witnessed the actor's blank stare. 'Sorry, so many old friends,' she said airily. 'Me? Oh, Jamie's a darling, isn't he? I've been up here all week, shooting a commercial with him. It's all gone wonderfully well, he's predicting great things for me if I decide to give the acting business another go.'

'So you'd leave Trezale?' Bruno, equally unable to resist putting her down, looked sympathetic. 'Oh dear, you mean persuading Guy Cassidy that you were the woman of his dreams didn't work out? Must have been a bit of a kick in the teeth for you.'

'A kick in the teeth for *me*?' Maxine gave him a condescending smile. 'Bruno, men like you are the reason women like me wear stiletto heels. Is being obnoxious a hobby of yours, or are you just particularly miffed because I turned down your own touching little offer of a quickie in the back seat of your car?'

She was wonderful, he thought, filled with silent admiration. He adored almost everything about Maxine Vaughan, from those fabulous bare shoulders right down to that pair of ridiculously high heels. But if the body was terrific, the mind was even more entrancing. She could trade insults like no female he had ever met before, she was sharp and funny, a talented liar, and out for everything she could possibly get. They were alike in every way. Best of all, he thought with a barely suppressed smile, she was as mad about him as he was about her.

'I wasn't miffed,' he replied easily, leaning against the wall and running his fingers carelessly through his hair. The emerald-green wallpaper matched his eyes and offset his deep purple jacket to perfection. 'You were being loyal to your sister; an admirable quality in any girl, but especially you.'

He thought he looked so great, thought Maxine, with all that streaky blond hair and that toffee-brown tan. He was only resting against the wall because the colour of it went so well with his jacket. And he had some nerve, too; you had to be unbelievably un-gay in order to get away with wearing a jacket like that over an ochre tee-shirt and pale yellow trousers. She was only surprised it wasn't smothered in bloody sequins . . .

'I told Janey she should never have got involved with you,' she declared, ignoring the last jibe. 'I knew exactly what would happen and I was right. Tell me, does it give you some kind of thrill, finding some vulnerable female and tearing her to pieces like that?'

'I didn't actually set out to hurt her,' Bruno protested with a good-humoured shake of his head. 'Believe it or not Janey couldn't accept the way I am, that was all.'

'You mean she couldn't accept the fact that you're such a bastard?' There was derision in Maxine's eyes. 'Or that you deliberately humiliated her in front of two hundred people at your stinking rotten party?'

'Maybe I went a bit far.' Despite the admission, Bruno

was still smiling. 'But she started it. All I did was retaliate and she didn't even fight back. Let's face it, Janey's too nice.' He shrugged. 'We really weren't suited at all.'

'You can say that again.'

'Ah well, these things happen. I suppose she hates me now.'

Cindy, who had appeared behind Bruno, was wriggling her eyebrows in a gesture of deepest appreciation. Maxine, pretending she hadn't noticed, snapped, 'You can definitely say that again.'

'Good.' He glanced over his shoulder, winked at Cindy, then returned his attention to Maxine. 'So loyalty is no longer an issue. You can stop pretending, sweetheart. We just take it from here.'

As he said the words he moved closer, lowering his voice accordingly. For something to do, Maxine reached for her drink and took a great slug of red wine. The glass remained in her hand, between them, on a level with Bruno's trousers.

'Armani versus Alaia,' he observed in conversational tones. 'We're talking serious money.'

'You think you're so irresistible,' Maxine drawled. 'Don't you?'

'Not at all.' Bruno removed the glass from her hand, drained it and put it out of reach. 'I'm just honest. Maxine, I admire you enormously for your loyalty towards your sister, but it's different now. You can relax. We're both three hundred miles from home. Janey hates me. As far as I'm concerned, you are the most delectable female I've ever known and as far as you're concerned, you fancy me rotten. So why don't we stop playing games and simply admit how we feel about each other? OK,' he conceded, 'so it's a massive coincidence, but since we're both here in London at the same party, why waste time? Why don't we just take advantage of the situation and enjoy it?'

Coincidence had had precious little to do with it, other than the fact that Jamie Laing really was a friend of Bruno's. Upon hearing from his new waitress that according to her son – who attended the same school as Josh Cassidy – Josh's nanny was doing a TV commercial with someone called Jamie, all it had taken was a phone call. He had practically invited himself along to the end-of-ad party at Jamie's elegant, three-storey Chelsea home. His appearance there tonight might have caught Maxine off-guard but he had been rehearsing these lines for days.

Maxine fixed him with an unswerving gaze. Beneath a great deal of gold eyeshadow and at least three coats of mascara, her dark eyes were serious.

'You really think,' she said, very slowly, 'I fancy you rotten?'

'I don't think.' Bruno gave her a modest smile. 'It's a fact.'

'Shit!' howled Maxine. 'That is just so unfair. How could you possible *know*?'

The fact that she was wearing those ludicrous high heels didn't bother Bruno in the least; he didn't care that at this moment she was a couple of inches taller than him. Leaning across, he kissed her very lightly on the mouth.

'I'm an expert,' he said, then broke into a grin. 'But even if I hadn't been, I would still have known. It was obvious from the start, angel. You might be able to act but even you aren't that good.'

This was unbelievable. Talk about one-upmanship, thought Maxine, torn between admiration for such a talent and annoyance because if there was one thing she couldn't stand, it was being seen through. And she had thought she'd done so well, too. Damn, damn, damn!

'You don't even know me.' She looked cross. 'Not properly, anyway.'

'Don't sulk,' Bruno chided. 'And of course I know you, as well as I know myself. I told you before, we're alike. I've never met anyone as much like me before in my life. That was why it was so easy. Looking at you is like looking into a mirror.'

'Except I wear more make-up.' Hopelessly unprepared for such a turn of events, Maxine resorted to flippancy. It gave her time to think.

But she had reckoned without his ability to read minds.

'You're also more nervous,' Bruno replied, sliding his arm around her waist. 'And there's no need to be. Stop trying to analyse it, sweetheart. It's happened, whether you like it or not. Some things are just out of our control. All we have to do now is enjoy it.'

He was breathtakingly self-confident. Maxine decided with some regret that he was also right.

'Has it even occurred to you that I might say no?' she asked, because it went against the grain to be too much of a pushover.

Bruno grinned. 'What would be the point? We both know you're going to say yes.'

Everything seemed to be happening in ultra-slow motion.

Just crossing the street was like climbing Everest. Janey, dimly aware of Guy's Mercedes accelerating away behind her, felt the muscles in her legs contract with each step. She listened to the sound of her own uneven breathing and she saw the figure in the shop doorway turn in her direction, tilting his head in that achingly familiar way.

Still numb with shock, she tried to formulate some kind of plan. It was so strange, she had no idea what she was going to say. All she could think of was the fact that her hands were cold. Alan had always hated being touched by cold hands. If she touched him, would he wince and draw away? Should she just keep her hands jammed in her pockets? God, was this really happening?

'Janey.'

It had taken forever but somehow she had made it across the street. Her heart was pounding in her ears and she still couldn't speak but to Janey's immense relief she didn't need to because Alan was saying it all for her, pulling her into his arms and hugging her so tightly she could hardly breathe. Over and over again, as he covered her face with kisses, he murmured 'Janey, oh Janey, I've missed you so much . . . you don't know how long I've dreamt of this day.'

'You're alive,' she murmured finally, touching his face as if to prove it beyond all doubt. His cheek was warm and her hands were cold but he didn't flinch away. She had almost forgotten how good-looking he was. The sun-bleached hair was shorter; the face, confusingly, looked both older and younger and a new, pale scar bisected his left eyebrow. But the eyes, light blue and fringed with long lashes, were as clear as they had always been. They, at least, were unchanged. The eyes, and that hypnotically reassuring voice . . .

'Oh my poor darling,' Alan whispered tenderly, taking her icy fingers and pressing them to his lips. 'Don't say that; I can't bear to imagine what I must have put you through. All I can say is that at the time I thought I was making the right decision for both of us. The trouble was,' he went on, breaking into a sad smile, 'no matter what I did or how hard I tried, and God knows I tried, I could never stop loving you.'

Chapter 38

Stupidly, she had almost forgotten that the flat had been Alan's home too. It seemed odd, watching him walk into the kitchen and know without having to ask where things were.

'It should be champagne, of course,' he said cheerfully, uncapping the half-empty bottle of cooking brandy that was all Janey had in the way of something to drink, 'but you look as if you could do with warming up, so . . . cheers.'

He had filled her balloon glass almost to the brim. With a trembling hand Janey raised it to her lips and gulped down several eye-watering mouthfuls, willing it to have some kind of effect on her numbed brain. She had fantasized over this scene a thousand times, her fevered imagination running riot as she covered every possible eventuality. It had never even crossed her mind that she might be so lost for words she would barely be able to say anything at all.

There were still too many questions to be answered. Alan had disappeared from her life and she didn't know why. Now he was back and she was still none the wiser. The brandy, however, was beginning to make its presence known; she could feel that much, at least.

'Sit down,' she said haltingly, when Alan had switched on the gas fire and paused to admire the new painting above the mantelpiece. 'You'd better explain everything. Right from the start. I need to know why you did it.'

She had chosen the armchair for herself. Alan sat on the sofa opposite, nursing his drink and looking contrite.

'I want you to know, Janey, that I'm desperately ashamed of myself. I took the coward's way out, I realize that now, but it really didn't seem like that at the time. I was under pressure, confused, I couldn't figure out any other way of going about it without causing you even more pain.'

As far as Janey was concerned, even more pain was a physical impossibility. She had hit the threshold and stayed there, trapped like a bluebottle stuck to flypaper.

'Go on,' she said briefly, her eyes clouded with the unbearable memories of those first months. 'What are you trying to tell me, that you'd met someone else?'

'No!' He looked appalled. 'Janey, absolutely not. Oh God, is that what you thought?'

Impatience began to stir inside her. 'I didn't know what to think,' she replied evenly. 'I tried everything, but there were never any answers. And you weren't there to ask.'

Alan had known this wasn't going to be easy. He shook his head and tried again. 'I know, and it was all my fault. What's the expression? Be careful what you wish for, because you may get it.'

Janey stared at him.

'Don't look at me like that, sweetheart, please. The truth is, I loved you too much. You were what I wished for, and I got you.' He hesitated for a second, then went on, 'And it scared the hell out of me. It became a kind of obsession, you see; I managed to convince myself that sooner or later you would fall out of love with me. It's a terrible feeling, Janey, to think you aren't good enough for your own wife. It was all right for you; you knew how much you meant to me, but all I felt was more and more insecure. Every single morning I'd wake up and ask myself whether this would be the day you'd decide you'd had enough of being married. To someone,' he concluded brokenly, 'who didn't deserve you.'

He'd stopped speaking. It was Janey's turn. Her glass was empty and she'd almost forgotten how to breathe.

'But that's crazy,' she managed to say, her voice barely above a whisper. Of all the possible reasons she had come up with, this was one she had never for a moment even considered. 'We were married, we were happy together.'

'Yes, it was crazy.' Alan nodded, his expression regretful. 'I know that now, but at the time I think I was a little bit crazy myself. It was a kind of self-torture, and I couldn't break the cycle. The more I thought about it, the more real it became. And the fact that you seemed happy no longer counted for anything, because I'd convinced myself that you were only putting on some elaborate act for my benefit. You read about it all the time in the papers; it happens every day, for God's sake. Perfect couples with apparently perfect marriages, except they aren't perfect at all. Suddenly, out of the blue, the wife or husband says they can't stand it any more; they hire a hit-man or simply up and leave with their secret lover. Janey, it got so bad I had to get away. I didn't want to go, but it seemed like the only option left to me. You have to try and understand, sweetheart. I was desperate.'

Wordlessly, she held out her glass and watched Alan refill it. He still wore Pepe jeans, still moved with that same casual, confident grace. He had always exuded such an air of confidence; how could she possibly have known that beneath the surface lurked a maelstrom of insecurity and self-doubt?

The brandy was no longer lacerating her throat. This time it slipped down like warm honey. 'You should have asked me,' she said, tears prickling the back of her eyes. 'If you'd told me how you felt, I could have—'

'I didn't want to hear it,' Alan interjected, his own eyes filled with pain. 'Don't you see, Janey? If you'd reassured me, I would only have convinced myself you were lying. And that would have been almost as unbearable as hearing you say you didn't love me.'

'Oh God.' With a trembling hand, Janey covered her face. What he was telling her made an awful kind of sense. Such paranoid beliefs, once they took a hold, made reassurance impossible. 'You should have gone to see a doctor.'

'I did. After I'd, um, left.' Alan gave her a crooked half-smile. 'And a world of good that did me, too. He said that, in his experience, any man who harboured suspicions about his wife most probably had every right to do so. Then he told me that his own wife had walked out on him three weeks earlier and it wasn't until she'd gone that he found out she'd been having an affair with their dentist for the past five years.'

'I wasn't having an affair,' said Janey, her voice

beginning to break. 'I would never have done anything like that. Never.'

'Yes, well.' He dismissed the protest with a shrug. 'You can understand it didn't help.'

Janey could understand that such a bloody useless doctor should be struck off the medical register. She shuddered at the thought of the damage he might have inflicted on countless innocent people.

'Are you still cold?' Alan patted the empty cushion on the settee. 'Why don't you come over here, sweetheart? Sit by me.'

But Janey needed to hear everything first. There were nearly two whole years separating them, two blank years in which anything might have happened. She couldn't relax until she knew it all. She also needed more brandy . . .

'Where did you go?' she pleaded, suddenly desperate to get it over with. 'Where have you been living? What have you been doing?'

His smile was bleak. 'Existing. Trying to stop loving you. Telling myself a million times that I'd been a complete fool who'd made the worst mistake of his life, but that it was too late to go back.' He stopped for a second, gazing into space and swallowing hard. 'I'm sorry, Janey. Here I go again, moaning on about my own stupid feelings when what you want to hear are the facts. OK, well they aren't exactly riveting but here goes. I hitch-hiked to Edinburgh, did a bit of bar work, got myself a filthy little bed-sitter and spent most of my spare time shaking cockroaches out of the duvet. After a few months, when I couldn't stand the place a moment longer, I travelled down to

Manchester. That was just as awful, but the customers had different accents and at least the pub employed bouncers to break up the fights, instead of expecting me to tackle them myself.'

Janey shuddered. 'That scar on your forehead . . .?'

'A bloody great Scotsman with fourteen pints of lager inside him and a broken bottle in each fist.' He touched the scar as if to remind himself. 'I was lucky. One of the other barmen almost died.'

Janey bit her lower lip. Alan could have died. She had thought he was dead . . .

'Go on. How long were you in Manchester?'

He thought for a moment. 'Three, four months? Then I moved down to London. Another lousy bed-sit, another family of cockroaches to get to know. I did some casual work here and there when I could get it, but it was pretty much of a hand-to-mouth existence. Not to mention lonely.'

'But you must have met people, made new friends?'

'I didn't want to,' he replied simply. 'I didn't think I deserved any. Unless I was working, there were times when I didn't even speak to a soul for days on end. London's like that; you can almost begin to believe you no longer exist.'

'Girlfriends?' said Janey, needing to know. It had been almost two years, after all.

But Alan smiled and shook his head. 'Hadn't I suffered enough? Janey, my feelings for you were what got me into this mess in the first place. I was hardly going to risk it again, was I? Besides,' he added sadly, 'I was still in love with you. I didn't want anyone else. And even if I had, it would have been too much of a betrayal.'

'And now you're back.' Janey still felt as if she were in suspended animation. It was a curious feeling, like one of those near-death experiences people reported, when they hovered on the ceiling and gazed down at their own lifeless bodies. She had no idea of the time, no conception of what she might say or do next. It was as if all this were happening to somebody else.

Alan nodded. Again, the hesitant half-smile. 'I'm back.'

'Why?'

He took a deep breath. 'Please let me get it all out in one go. Wait until I've finished before you say anything. I haven't been able to stop loving you, Janey. I tried, but it didn't work. I've no idea how you feel about me, now. I don't know, maybe you've put the past behind you, met someone else and forgotten you even knew me . . . but I had to find out. I need to know if you do still care for me. And if you can ever forgive me. I have to know whether there's a chance for us to carry on as we were before. As husband and wife.'

He looked so unsure of himself, so scared of what she might say. Only sheer desperation had given him the strength to admit his own weakness and declare his feelings for her with such heart-wrenching honesty. And he had always been the stronger partner in the past, thought Janey, so seemingly secure and laid-back with his devil-may-care attitudes and freewheeling lifestyle.

But he hadn't been secure at all, she realized; he had needed her, more than she had ever imagined. He hadn't abandoned her for another woman, either. Nor had he ever stopped loving her. And now he needed understanding, love and forgiveness in return.

It's like a dream come true, Janey realized hazily. Tears were beginning to roll down her cheeks and she thought how stupid, to cry now. This is the happiest night of my life.

'Of course we can carry on,' she said, rising unsteadily to her feet. The tears fell faster as Alan came towards her, his expression one of joy mingled with relief.

'You don't know how much this means to me,' he murmured, his mouth grazing her wet cheek. 'I wouldn't have been able to bear it if you'd said no. The scariest part was not knowing whether you'd met someone else.'

Janey, breathing in the wonderful familiarity of him, closed her eyes. 'There's no one else,' she whispered, stroking his hair and revelling in the sensation of his warm hands against her back. 'There's never been anybody else. Only you.'

Chapter 39

'Oh good!' said Maxine, when Cindy finally picked up the phone. 'You're there.'

'It's four o'clock in the morning,' Cindy replied in arch tones. 'Of course I'm here. The question is, where are you? More to the point, who is that man lying stark naked in the bed next to you?'

Maxine grinned. 'That's two questions.'

'And that's no answer,' said Cindy briskly. 'Besides, I haven't finished yet. You were seen tiptoeing away from the party at midnight, sweetie, and that was four long hours ago. The thing is, what on earth could you possibly have been doing since then that's kept you so busy you couldn't call your oldest and dearest friend to let her know about it?'

'Gosh.' Maxine sounded deeply impressed. 'You mean you were worried about me?'

'Worried? Of course I wasn't worried. I was jealous!' Abandoning all self-control, Cindy screeched down the phone. 'So stop buggering about and tell me who he is before I explode!'

'OK, OK,' sighed Maxine. 'His name's Jim Berenger and he's an actor. We're here at his flat in Belsize Park and I just rang to let you know that I'll be back tomorrow morning. Well, this morning,' she amended, glancing up at the clock. 'If you're good, I'll give you all the girly gossip then.'

Cindy was still screaming, 'Oh my God, is he spectacular in bed?' when Bruno leaned across and seized the phone.

'Hi,' he said, lying back against the pillows and daring Maxine to stop him. 'Actually, my name is Bruno Parry-Brent; I'm a restaurateur and we're in my hotel room at the Royal Lancaster. And yes, since you ask, I am most definitely spectacular in b—'

'Stop it!' hissed Maxine. Struggling to her knees, she wrenched the receiver back from him and slammed it down, cutting Cindy off in mid-shriek. 'How could you do that?'

'Relax darling.' Effortlessly, Bruno fended her off. 'We have nothing to hide. We're going legit.'

'I don't want to go legit,' Maxine howled. 'This is a one-off, an aberration, a never-to-be-repeated—'

'It's been a two-off already,' Bruno reminded her, his green eyes glittering with amusement as he surveyed her in all her naked glory. 'Play your cards right and we can make it three.'

'Bastard.' She threw a pillow at his head.

'And it isn't an aberration, either. I thought it was rather nice.'

'This is stupid, cried Maxine, wrapping a sheet around herself and debating whether to risk tipping the contents of the ice bucket over him. Somehow, she didn't quite dare. The prospect of retaliation was too awful. 'Cindy's the biggest gossip in the world, she's got a mouth like a megaphone . . . and you think it's funny!'

'Not at all. I'm quite serious.'

'So am I bloody serious.' Maxine looked fierce. 'I have a sister who will probably never speak to me again if she ever hears about this. Even more to the point,' she added heavily, 'you have Nina.'

Bruno said nothing for a while. No longer smiling, he studied Maxine's face for several seconds, his own expression oddly intense. Then, reaching out, he traced the line of her cheek with a warm forefinger.

'I told you I was serious,' he said eventually. 'This is it, Max. We were always meant to be together. I love you.' He paused, then added, 'I'm going to leave Nina.'

'Go on,' persisted Bruno, pinning Maxine down on the bed and expertly avoiding her flailing limbs. 'Say it. You won't get any breakfast until you do.'

The tray was outside the door, tantalizingly out of reach. Maxine, who was starving, made another hopeless bid for freedom before falling back, exhausted, against the pillows. She ached too much to put up a decent fight and it was all Bruno's fault. He was the most insatiable man she had ever known.

'Say what?'

'Tell me that you love me.' He enunciated the words slowly and clearly, as if addressing a dim child.

Maxine's brown eyes narrowed. 'Why?'

'Because I've said I love you, and it's only fair. And if you don't,' he added with an air of triumph, 'well, no breakfast. I shall just have to seduce you all over again.'

Desperate to eat, Maxine said in a small voice, 'I love you.'

'Louder.'

'I love you.'

'Come on, don't be shy,' Bruno persisted. 'Much louder than that.'

She sighed. Then, at the top of her voice, screamed, 'I LOVE YOU!'

'Tell us something we don't know,' came the shouted reply from the room adjoining theirs. 'You've been proving it all bloody night. Bloody honeymooners!'

Maxine burst out laughing.

'Honeymooners,' Bruno mused. 'Now there's an idea.'

'I think you have to be married to come into that category.' Still grinning, Maxine ruffled her hair and glanced at her reflection in the mirror. Not bad, considering the excesses of the past nine hours. Thank goodness for smudge-proof mascara.

But Bruno was giving her an odd look. For the first time he no longer seemed entirely sure of himself. 'That's what I mean.'

'Oh,' she mocked. 'So now you think we should get married?'

'That's exactly what I mean.'

Maxine's eyebrows shot up. The next moment she started to laugh once more, so uncontrollably that the bed shook.

'Don't do that,' Bruno retaliated crossly. Jesus, would she ever take anything he said at face value? 'I'm serious.'

It was a while before she could manage to speak again. 'Oh please! Bruno, you just aren't the marrying kind.'

He looked offended. 'Nobody is, until they meet the person they want to marry. Think about it, Max, you and me, together.'

'How can I think about it?' she gurgled. 'It's the most ridiculous idea I ever heard. Look at our track records; we were born to cheat! Can you imagine the chaos it would cause if we ever tried to stay faithful to each other?'

He watched her fling back the bedclothes, and make her way to the door. Naked, she briefly checked that the coast was clear before reaching for the breakfast tray.

'But that's just it,' Bruno protested, meaning every word and willing her to take him seriously. 'We're the same, so we understand each other. God, you're such a pig,' he added, as Maxine tore into a croissant. Within seconds it was gone and she was starting on the toast, slathering it with butter and honey and sprinkling brown sugar on top before stuffing it greedily into her mouth.

'There, you see?' she countered between mouthfuls. 'You're going off me already.'

He watched her set to work on the second slice; she looked like a bricklayer on speed, and the butter was going on thicker than cement. It didn't stop him loving her, but it was a miracle she wasn't the size of a Sherman tank.

'I'm a restaurateur,' he reminded her. 'I like to see people enjoying their food, not shovelling it down like porridge.'

'I am enjoying it.' With immense satisfaction, Maxine licked her fingers one by one. Then, with a determined smile she added, 'And there's another good reason why you can't leave Nina. You love that restaurant. Imagine how she'd react if you told her about us – she'd have you out of there like a shot.' She fired an imaginary pistol into the air for emphasis. 'Boom. And then what would you be? An ex-restaurateur.'

Bruno shrugged. It wasn't a welcome forecast, but it was fairly accurate, given the circumstances. The restaurant belonged to Nina; giving her up would mean giving up his livelihood. Until now, such an action had been unthinkable.

It was a measure of his feelings towards Maxine that it no longer even seemed to matter. 'Sacrifices have to be made,' he said lightly. 'I can always get another job. The lifestyle may take a bit of a dive, but . . . well, I happen to think you're worth it.'

'Don't.' Maxine felt suddenly afraid. This was so unlike Bruno, so totally out of character for him. 'In five minutes you could be telling me it's all a joke.'

But when Bruno reached for her, the expression in his eyes was deadly serious. 'No joke. I've waited nearly twenty years for this. I don't even know if I like it, yet. I love you more than you love me, and that makes me the vulnerable one. This has never happened to me before.'

More moved than she dared admit, Maxine said briskly, 'Evidently not. Rule number one is never tell people you love them more than they love you. It's asking to get kicked in the teeth.'

'I know.' Bruno kissed her collarbone. 'But it's the only way I can think of to convince you I'm not bullshitting.'

A shudder of sheer longing snaked its way down her spine. 'OK,' she said simply. 'I believe you. But it still isn't going to be easy.'

'And I'm going to be poor. Well,' he amended with a forced smile, 'relatively poor, anyway. Is that a major problem for you?'

To her absolute horror, Maxine realized she was in danger of bursting into tears. Staring hard at the tops of the trees outlined against a pale grey sky, which was all she could see from their third-floor window overlooking Hyde Park, she willed the lump in her throat to subside. Nobody made her cry and got away with it. Least of all, she thought crossly, a bloody man.

But Bruno, misinterpreting her silence, was growing impatient. 'Is it?' he persisted. 'Are you only interested in men with money? Is that what you're trying to tell me?'

Maxine hit him with a pillow.

'You bastard,' she howled. 'What do you think I am, some kind of bimbo gold-digger? How dare you!'

'Ouch.' Bruno dodged out of reach as she lunged at him again. Overcome with relief, he broke into a grin. 'Look, I wasn't accusing, I was asking. And it's a perfectly reasonable question, anyway. Lots of people are attracted to money. What about that ex-fiancé of yours?' he added in ultra-reasonable tones. 'Janey told me about him. He was loaded, and you can't tell me you didn't enjoy it.'

Just for a second, Maxine experienced a pang of longing for those lost luxuries. Of course she had loved living in a splendid house, swanning around in smart cars, flashing a diamond ring the size of a beech nut at anyone who came within a two-mile radius, never having to worry about the next gas bill . . . But it hadn't been enough. And, having left that life behind her, she had never even for a moment regretted doing so.

'Oh yes, it was nice,' she said. 'But I gave it all up, didn't I? *And* I gave the engagement ring back to him, in case you were wondering. It cost nine thousand pounds but I still did it.'

'Pity,' murmured Bruno. 'That's one noble gesture you might live to regret.'

'Yes, well.' Maxine couldn't help agreeing with him there, but a girl had to have some scruples. Brown eyes flashing, she said proudly, 'At least it proves I'm not a fortune hunter.'

Unable to resist making the dig, he countered, 'What about Guy Cassidy? Would you have lusted after him if he'd been penniless and unknown?'

'Guy doesn't count,' Maxine declared flatly. 'I wanted to work for him because he could have boosted my career. Not that it did the slightest bit of good,' she grumbled. 'Do you know, in all the time I've been there he hasn't taken so much as a single photograph of me? I'm sure that's out of spite.'

'Don't worry.' Bruno gave her a hug. 'I've got a Kodak Instamatic. I'll take thousands of photos of you.'

'You aren't influential and famous.'

'I'm not rich either.'

She smiled. 'I don't care. Really.'

'So what's the verdict?' Bruno realized that he was holding his breath. There are only a few moments in a lifetime when real decisions have to be made. This was one of those moments. 'Do we give it a whirl?'

Maxine, both exhilarated and afraid, said in a low voice, 'It isn't going to be easy, you know. Being poor is the least of our worries. We're going to upset quite a few people. You have Nina to deal with. I have Janey.'

'What are you,' Bruno demanded, 'a bloody politician? Answer the question, Max. Does that mean yes or no?'

'You idiot.' Fondly she caressed his tanned arm. 'How can you even ask? You saw through me right from the start. You knew I loved you almost before I knew it myself.'

'You're going to have to say it,' he persisted evenly. 'Yes, Maxine? Or—'

'Darling!' she exclaimed, loving him even more for his insecurity and hurling herself into his arms. 'Don't panic! I *am* the original girl who can't say no.'

Chapter 40

'This is terrible,' said Janey, looking at her watch and seeing that it was almost ten o'clock. 'There are so many things we should be doing. We really ought to get up.'

'What could be more important than this?' Alan, who didn't want to move, kissed the top of her head. 'Making love, catching up on lost time, getting to know one another all over again . . .'

'Phoning the police,' she continued dryly.

'What?'

Janey smiled. 'You're on the missing persons' register. One of us is going to have to let them know you're no longer missing.'

'Oh God.' Alan shuddered. 'You can do that. What do you suppose they'll do . . . come round and rap my knuckles for running away without leaving a note?'

'I haven't the faintest idea, but we still have to phone them.' Janey, wriggling out of reach, slid out of bed and grabbed her dressing gown. 'And Paula's downstairs, running the shop on her own. She doesn't even know I'm up here. If she starts hearing footsteps, she'll think we're burglars.'

'Why?' Alan's eyes narrowed. 'Where does she think

you spend your nights? Come to that,' he added with growing suspicion, 'who were you with last night? That was a pretty smart car you leapt out of. Are you sure there isn't something you aren't telling me?'

Janey hadn't given Guy Cassidy so much as a thought until now. Belatedly she realized that she must have caused him considerable inconvenience. He had been due to fly up to Manchester at seven for a photo session with the much sought-after, deeply temperamental supermodel, Valentina di Angelo. She prayed that in letting him down at such short notice he wouldn't have had to cancel the entire shoot.

'There's nothing to tell,' she said in reassuring tones, still mindful of the unfounded suspicions which had prompted Alan's disappearance in the first place. 'Maxine moved back down here a few months ago and took a nannying job up at Trezale House, but for the past week she's been in London making a TV advert. I offered to look after the children whilst she was away, so I've been staying at the house and Paula's taken over in the shop. Everyone's been doing everyone else's job,' she added cheerfully. 'It's been fun.'

'You always liked children.' Alan's expression grew bleak. 'That was something else that scared me. I knew you wanted a family of your own, but I was afraid you'd love them more than you loved me.'

Janey stared at him, appalled. 'It doesn't work like that.'

'Sometimes it does.' A note of urgency crept into his voice. 'Look, sweetheart. I've come back and we're going to make it work this time, but I still wouldn't be happy if you suddenly announced you were pregnant. So, no little accidents. No "Surprise, surprise, darling, I can't think how it happened, but . . ." announcements. Because that's something I just couldn't handle. OK?'

'No little accidents,' Janey repeated numbly, stunned by the bombshell and by the suddenness with which it had been dropped. She would never have dreamed of intentionally becoming pregnant without Alan's knowledge and approval, but neither would she ever have guessed the strength of his own feelings on the subject. He was evidently deadly serious.

Having got that bit of information off his chest, however, he cheered up and changed the subject.

'So Maxine's been working as a nanny, you say? Heaven help *those* poor kids! What mother in her right mind would employ someone like Maxine, anyway?'

Janey picked up her hairbrush and sat in front of the mirror. 'It isn't a mother, it's a father. A widower.'

'Oh well.' Alan stretched and yawned. 'That explains it. Old or young?'

'Thirtyish.' Janey set about restoring some semblance of normality to her hair. 'Coming up to thirty-five, I think.'

'Really,' he drawled, watching her reflection in the mirror. 'And is he good-looking?'

Janey carried on brushing. 'I suppose so. If you like that sort of thing,' she added, her tone deliberately off-hand.

'And do you like that sort of thing?'

'Stop it.' As she swivelled round to face him, the dressing gown fell open to reveal her bare legs. Her knuckles were white as she gripped the brush. 'Don't try and read something into a perfectly innocent situation. I was doing Maxine a favour, that's all. I'm not interested in Guy and he certainly isn't interested in me.'

'Why not? Is he gay?'

'Of course he isn't gay.' Janey replied wearily. 'He has women coming out of his ears. And he isn't interested in anyone unless they're drop-dead gorgeous, OK? You'd have to have at least half a dozen covers of *Vogue* under your belt before Guy Cassidy would even notice you. Even Maxine didn't qualify, which really pissed her off.'

'Guy Cassidy the photographer? Is that who you're talking about?' Alan sat up and took notice. Evidently impressed, he said, 'And he's the one whose kids you've been looking after?'

Janey nodded. He was also the one she'd been hideously rude to last night. She would have to phone and apologize.

'Oh well, that's all right then.' Alan grinned with relief. 'And there I was, thinking I had a rival on my hands. I see what you mean now about the gorgeous girls. He can have just about anyone he wants.'

And although it was undoubtedly true, Janey couldn't help feeling a bit miffed. Having allayed Alan's suspicions, she now had to bite her tongue in order not to blurt out: 'Yes, but he held my hand last night, and he kissed me . . .'

But that would be childish and it had only been a jokey kiss anyway, not a real one. Instead, feeling very second-best, she said lightly, 'Of course he can have anyone he wants. So he's hardly likely to be interested in me, is he?'

'Exactly.' Nodding in vigorous agreement, Alan then leaned over and gave her bare knee a consoling pat. 'Sorry, sweetheart, it isn't very flattering, but you know what I mean. He's had some of the best in the world, lucky sod. I even heard he had a bit of a thing going with that dark-haired model, Serena Charlton. Christ,' he added, rolling his eyes in deep appreciation, 'if that isn't drop-dead gorgeous, I don't know what is.'

Maxine, guiltily in love and desperately confused, wasn't looking forward to the next twenty-four hours.

'I don't know what you're getting so worked up about,' said Bruno, as their train drew into Trezale station. He had insisted they travel back together, and Maxine had grown more and more jittery by the mile. 'It isn't like you. Here, d'you want to finish this?'

She took the lukewarm gin and tonic from him, swallowed and pulled a face. 'The whole thing isn't like me. Look, I may have been involved with married men before, but they were just flings. Nobody's ever done anything as drastic as leaving their wife on my behalf. And even if they'd wanted to, I wouldn't have let them.'

The breathe-if-you-dare Alaia dress had gone back into Cindy's walk-in wardrobe. Now, wearing her own jeans and a striped shirt knotted at the waist, she looked younger and infinitely more vulnerable.

'Relax. Let me take care of Nina.' Bruno grinned. 'And how many times do I have to tell you, anyway? She isn't my wife.'

Maxine gazed gloomily out of the window as the train creaked to a halt. 'That doesn't make me feel any less guilty. It's still going to be horrible.'

'Ah, but I'm worth it.'

She thought of Janey, whose fragile self-confidence was about to be shattered, and of Guy's disdainful reaction to the news. Even people she only vaguely knew were going to disapprove, on principle. But she really did love Bruno, and he loved her. Besides, she no longer appeared to have any choice in the matter.

'You'd better be worth it,' she murmured, rising to her feet and mentally preparing herself for the fray. 'For everyone's sake, you'd better be.'

It was nine o'clock when she let herself into the house. Guy, of all people, was cooking in the kitchen. Highly diverted by the spectacle, Maxine watched him pile burnt oven chips and enormous fillet steaks on to three plates. Ella, cringing at the sight of blood, was wailing, 'Ugh, I hate fillet steak. Why can't we have proper food instead?'

'I like fillet steak!' announced Maxine, from the doorway. 'Is there enough for me? And where's Janey?'

Ella, sensing salvation, ran over and gave her a hug. 'Hooray, you're back. If you cook me some beefburgers you can have my steak. Janey went home after the fair last night. She called Daddy a bastard and jumped out of the car because she wanted to see her husband. Actually, I'd rather have fish fingers than beefburgers but not burnt like the chips. Daddy's a terrible cook. I'm really hungry,' she added boastfully, 'because I've been up in a helicopter to Manchester.'

Where convoluted storytelling was concerned, thought Maxine, Ella could give Ronnie Corbett a run for his money. Thoroughly confused, she turned to Guy. 'I think I need a translator. So what really happened last night?

You and Janey had an argument and she stormed off in a huff?'

Guy threw the frying pan into the sink, which was already overflowing with washing-up. 'Her husband came back.'

'What!' Maxine gazed at him in disbelief. 'You mean Alan? Are you sure?'

'I already said that,' Ella complained. Having rifled the freezer, she now shoved three icy fish fingers into Maxine's unsuspecting hands. 'Why didn't you listen to me? Shall I tell you all about the helicopter while you cook my tea?'

'He's back,' continued Guy evenly. 'I don't know any more than that. We were driving past the shop and he was waiting outside.'

Still stunned, Maxine said, 'So what did you argue about?'

'I told her to be careful, to find out why he'd turned up after all this time.' He shrugged. 'Maybe I wasn't very subtle. It didn't go down well.'

'I still can't believe it.' Maxine sank into the nearest chair. 'My God, that man has a nerve! Poor Janey.'

'Quite. I was going to phone her this evening, but I'm not exactly flavour of the month.' Guy picked up an overdone chip, gazed at it for a second and put it down again. 'Maybe you should do the honours. Make sure everything's all right.'

'How can it be all right?' Maxine, who had never had much time for Alan Sinclair, looked gloomy. 'He's back, isn't he? It's bad news all round, if you ask me.'

But she found herself faced with a moral dilemma. As

the news gradually sank in, it became more and more obvious that since Alan had returned, telling Janey about herself and Bruno was going to be an awful lot easier if Janey was happy. Telling Janey that in her opinion Alan was a no-good, selfish sonofabitch who deserved a boot up the bum, on the other hand, wasn't going to make her very happy at all.

'Haven't you phoned her yet?' Guy, coming into the kitchen at ten-thirty, found her half-heartedly tackling the mountain of washing-up.

'I tried,' fibbed Maxine, who had been putting it off as long as she could. 'No answer. She must be out.'

'Out of her mind.' Guy picked up a Day-Glo pink fluffy rabbit – one of Ella's trophies from last night's trip to the fair – and placed it on the dresser next to a cross-eyed furry pig. 'My God, hasn't he done enough damage already?'

'All this concern,' she said in lightly mocking tones, 'when you don't even know him.'

'I've heard enough. And you aren't exactly his greatest fan yourself.' He gave her a sharp look. 'You were the one who told me what a bastard he was in the first place.'

'I know, but I've been thinking.' Maxine concentrated on the washing-up, scrubbing furiously at Josh's cornflake-encrusted breakfast bowl. 'You know how stubborn Janey can be. If you ask me, the more critical we are of Alan, the more likely she is to dig her heels in and take his side. I really think the best thing we can do is pretend to be pleased he's back. That way, she can make up her own mind, in her own time, without sacrificing her pride.'

Guy nodded in grudging agreement. 'Maybe you're right.'

'Of course I'm right.' That had gone well. Maxine, pleased with herself, said, 'I always am.'

'And it makes things so much easier for you,' he continued smoothly. 'What a happy coincidence.'

Damn. She raised her eyebrows. 'A happy coincidence? Sorry, I'm not with you.'

'I know you aren't,' said Guy. 'You're with Bruno Parry-Brent.'

'Oh.' Maxine gave up. So he had recognized Bruno's car when he'd dropped her off earlier, after all.

No more deceit, Bruno had told her. *No need for denials. We're going public.* Well, here goes. She raised her chin in defiance. 'Yes, I'm with Bruno. I wasn't before, when you thought I was. But I am now.'

'Dear God.'

'Is that a problem?'

Guy looked amused. 'I expect so, but at least it isn't mine. One thing I will say, about you and Janey.'

'What?' Maxine bristled, aware of the fact that it wasn't going to be flattering.

He grinned. 'You really do have the most extraordinary taste in men.'

Chapter 41

In the event, Janey rang the house first.

'Oh, hi. It's me,' she said hesitantly when Guy picked up the phone. 'Look, I know it's late but I wanted to apologise for last night. I said some horrible things and I'm really sorry.'

'No problem.' Guy couldn't help smiling to himself because Janey's idea of horrible things was on a par with Maxine's scathing off-the-cuff one-liners. 'Believe me, I've been called worse.'

'And I let you down,' she continued, clearly racked with guilt. 'I know how important the Manchester trip was, and I feel terrible about it. Were you able to find a babysitter?'

'No.'

'Oh God, I'm sorry.'

'But it didn't matter. The kids came up with me. So if you ever want to be bored rigid for thirty minutes by a seven-year-old describing what it's like to fly in a helicopter,' he added wryly, 'just ask Ella.'

'Really?' Immeasurably relieved, Janey started to laugh. 'I didn't ruin the whole day, then.'

'Well, the pilot may take a while to recover, but all in

all it was a great success.' Guy paused, then said casually, 'And am I allowed to ask how you are? Is everything . . . sorted out?'

'Everything is completely sorted out.' Her voice grew guarded, as if in anticipation of more *Are you sure you know what you're doing?* remarks. With some awkwardness, she went on, 'Look, it's a bit complicated and I can't really explain over the phone, but I understand now why he did what he did. Now he's back and we're giving it another go. Starting afresh. And I know what you're probably thinking, but it's my life, he's my husband, and no, he didn't run off with another woman . . .'

'Sshh,' said Guy, as her voice rose. 'Calm down. You don't have to justify yourself to me. I'm not going to criticise your decision, Janey. I'm hardly in a position to, considering the lousy mistakes I've made over the past few years. Besides,' he added, choosing his words with care, 'it was what you wanted, wasn't it? And now you've got it; a second chance of happiness. For heaven's sake, it's what anyone would want.'

'I know.' Relief was tinged with caution, as if she still couldn't quite believe he wasn't going to put the boot in. 'And I am happy. Look, I have to go now, Alan's coming downstairs. Could you ask Maxine to phone me tomorrow as soon as she gets back from London?'

At that moment Maxine came into the sitting room carrying two cups of tea and a packet of Jaffa cakes.

'Well actually—' said Guy, but Janey wasn't listening.

'And give my love to Josh and Ella,' she continued hurriedly. 'Tell them I'll see them soon. I really must go . . . bye.'

'She wants you to phone her tomorrow,' Guy told Maxine, when he had replaced the receiver. 'She thinks you're still in London. She was in a hurry to hang up.'

'And?' Maxine demanded, avid for details. 'What did she say?'

'Not a lot. Just that she understands why he left, and that they're making another go of it.' He shook his head in disbelief. 'Oh yes, and she's happy.'

Considering the almost total lack of interest he'd shown in her own love life, thought Maxine, he was displaying an astonishing amount of concern for Janey's. It really seemed to have got to him. But that, she supposed, was because he knew she was capable of looking after herself. Janey, far less experienced where men were concerned, was a sitting target for unscrupulous males like Alan Sinclair. Why, she had even been hopelessly out of her depth with Bruno, and he was a pussy cat . . .

'I wonder what his excuse was,' she mused, offering Guy a Jaffa cake. 'It must have been spectacular. My God, when you think of the hard time some married men have if they just nip into the pub for a quick drink after work. They get home two hours late and their wives give them merry hell. Yet Alan gets home two *years* late and Janey's thrilled to bits.'

It was certainly ironic. Guy, who had also been giving the matter some thought, said, 'She almost expects to be treated badly. I suppose you get used to it, if all the men you've ever known are bastards.'

'You've said it.' Maxine grinned. 'And then to top it

all, she had to spend a week living here with you. Talk about the final straw.'

'I haven't treated her badly.' He looked offended. 'I was perfectly nice.'

'You!' Maxine choked on a mouthful of Jaffa cake. 'You're never nice!'

'I am when I want to be. It all depends on the company I keep.'

'You're never nice to me.'

'Exactly.' Guy was staring into his cup. 'And is it any wonder? This is the most disgusting tea I've ever drunk in my life.'

Maxine tried hers. 'Oh bum,' she said crossly. 'The sugar isn't sugar. It's salt.'

'I never thought I'd hear myself say this.' He shook his head in mock despair. 'But I'm actually beginning to feel sorry for Bruno Parry-Brent. Does the poor sod have any idea what he's taking on?'

For Bruno, it was a first. Total honesty, not something which had ever featured particularly heavily on his personal agenda before, was what was called for now.

But if it was harder than he'd imagined, it was also necessary. Maxine had turned his entire world upside down. He wanted to spend the rest of his life with her. For as long as he could remember, he had been a committed philanderer. Infidelity had come as naturally to him as breathing. But that was in the past. His mad, bad days were behind him. The only person he wanted from now on was Maxine.

351

It was two o'clock in the morning and Nina was sitting at the kitchen table drinking camomile tea. Her long white fingers, wrapped around the cup, appeared almost luminous in the muted glow of the shaded wall lamps. Her face, bare of make-up, seemed paler still, but her voice remained calm.

'So it was Janey Sinclair's sister all the time.' She nodded thoughtfully. 'How interesting. Janey talked to me about you, you know. I thought she was the one you were involved with.'

'Not my type,' said Bruno, because total honesty was all very well but some things were undoubtedly better left unsaid. He wasn't concerned about his own reputation, but at least he could protect Janey's.

'And Maxine is?'

'Yes.'

'You're absolutely sure?'

He nodded. 'Absolutely.'

'Oh well.' Nina shrugged and recrossed her legs. 'It was bound to happen sooner or later. If I'm honest, I didn't expect us to last this long.'

She was taking it well, thought Bruno with gratitude. But then nothing ever fazed Nina. It was what he'd always liked about her. 'I didn't expect it to happen like this,' he admitted with a rueful smile. 'And to me, of all people.'

'Where will you live?'

'I'm going to see Don Hickman tomorrow. Now the summer season's over he should be able to find me a cheap holiday cottage. I suppose I'll have to start looking out for another job, too.' He paused, then added, 'Unless you want me to carry on here . . .?'

'No.' Nina shook her head. 'Better not. I think we need a clean break.'

'Right.' Bruno gave her a concerned look. 'Are you sure you'll be OK?'

She smiled. 'Of course I will. We had a good partnership, and now it's over. It's hardly the end of the world.'

Leaning across the table, he kissed her pale forehead. 'Thank you. For making it easy.'

'My pleasure.' Nina returned the kiss, stroking his streaky-blond hair for a moment before rising to her feet and placing her empty teacup in the sink. 'But it isn't going to be quite so easy for you, financially. Does Maxine have plenty of money?'

'No.'

'Oh dear,' she said with affectionate amusement. 'In that case, it really must be love.'

Bruno, fast asleep in the spare room, lay spread-eagled across the bed with one foot dangling over the side. With tears streaming silently down her cheeks, Nina stood in the doorway and watched the man she had loved for the past ten years dream of the girl he loved.

Sadly, that girl wasn't herself. But she had done absolutely the right thing, Nina reassured herself. Breaking down and begging him to stay – maybe even attempting to bribe him with yet more money – would only have earned his contempt. Instead she had been cool, calm and understanding, and it was much the best way because now they could part as friends. More importantly, it kept the door open. Bruno would know he could always return.

You're leaving me now because you're besotted with someone called Maxine Vaughan, thought Nina, who is undoubtedly beautiful and who makes you laugh. She's probably brilliant in bed, too. But she can't possibly love you as much as I do, and that's why I'm letting you go. Because it doesn't matter how long it takes. I'm prepared to wait for you to come back.

Chapter 42

'Oh Janey, I'm so happy for you!' Maxine enveloped her sister in a bear hug and swung her round in the narrow hallway, trampling all over the Sunday papers which had only just been pushed through the letterbox. 'Look, I've brought champagne to celebrate. Where's Alan, still in bed? Tell him to get up this minute and come and give his long-lost sister-in-law an enormous kiss!'

Janey, abandoning the mangled newspapers, followed her up the stairs. 'You've missed him. He's gone to the surfing club. He'll be back at around midday.'

Inwardly relieved, Maxine squeezed Janey's hand. 'Oh well, never mind. There'll be plenty of time for that later. Maybe it's nicer this way; we can have a proper talk without interruptions, and drink all the champagne ourselves. Come along, grab a jacket and a couple of glasses; it's time to hit the beach.'

It was cold but sunny, and the tide was on its way out. Down at the water's edge, Janey held up the glasses while Maxine eased the cork from the bottle, aiming it into the glittering turquoise sea.

'To you and Alan,' she said with a grin when their

glasses had been filled as they walked along. 'May you live happily ever after. Cheers!'

'Cheers,' Janey responded with a dutiful smile. She was pleased Maxine was pleased, but it had also come as something of a surprise. Having anticipated suspicion, criticism and a million questions laced with Maxine's own particular brand of sarcasm, she was still very much on her guard. Champagne on the beach and wholehearted approval weren't what she'd been expecting at all.

'This is from Guy, by the way.' Maxine waved the bottle. 'He sends his best wishes. Oh, and something else.' Rummaging in the inner pocket of her ancient leather flying jacket, she produced a crumpled cheque. Your wages for last week.'

Janey was almost embarrassed to take the cheque. It seemed odd, accepting payment for something which hadn't even seemed like work. But since refusing the money would appear even odder, she stuffed it into the back pocket of her jeans. 'Thanks, I enjoyed it.'

'So did they.' Maxine rolled her eyes in mock reproach. 'Although I'm beginning to seriously regret sending you there. Josh and Ella actually expect me to bake cakes now! And I mean real cakes,' she added darkly, 'with flour and stuff. Not even the kind you make from a packet.'

Both intrigued and amused, Janey waited to see how long Maxine could hold out. She was clearly making a heroic effort not to get down to the nitty-gritty and ask all the questions she would normally have blurted out within milliseconds. Janey, guessing that Guy must have had a stern word with her on the subject, made a silent bet with herself that Maxine would crumble somewhere between the smugglers' cave and the rock pools.

The smugglers' cave was still two hundred yards ahead of them, however, when Maxine, in the middle of prattling on about the hideous little brat with whom she'd co-starred in the toilet-roll commercial, suddenly stopped dead and ripped off her sunglasses.

'OK, that's enough,' she declared, fixing her dark eyes on Janey and daring her to move. 'You've had your fun but this is downright cruel. It's all very well for Guy bloody Cassidy to warn me against giving you the third degree but I am your sister, after all. So stop pretending to be interested in my glittering career and tell me everything, before I explode!'

Janey glanced at her watch. Nine whole minutes; whoever would have thought Maxine would be capable of restraining herself for that length of time?

'Everything you need to know?' she said innocently. 'Right. Well, first of all you sieve the flour into a bowl. Don't forget to add a pinch of salt. Then you—'

'Stop it!' Maxine shrieked, picking up a dripping, slippery mass of seaweed and advancing towards her. 'Tell me about Alan. Tell me why he left . . . why he came back . . . what he's been doing . . . what *you're* going to do.'

The trouble was, by the time Janey had finished telling her, Maxine was no longer so sure she wanted to know.

What she found almost impossible to understand was the fact that Janey actually seemed to believe the incredible line her bastard of a husband had been stringing her. As far as Maxine was concerned, she'd never heard such a heap of total and utter bullshit in her entire life.

'. . . So that's it,' Janey concluded, reaching for the Bollinger and tipping the last of it into their empty glasses. With a sidelong glance in Maxine's direction, she said with a trace of defiance, 'Go on then, your turn. You must have an opinion.'

Mere words couldn't even begin to convey her opinion of Alan Sinclair, thought Maxine, almost beside herself with silent rage. But she also realized she'd been right about Janey, who clearly wouldn't tolerate even the mildest of criticisms. One wrong word and she would leap to Alan's defence. Any suggestion that he might have been less than honest and it would be champagne corks at thirty paces.

But she was an actress, thank goodness, and she could out-act even her unspeakable brother-in-law any day of the week. For the sake of her pride, Janey was going to have to make the discovery of just how unspeakable he really was, in her own time.

For the past week, Maxine's dramatic talent had been stretched to the limit, pronouncing – in entirely convincing tones – 'When you have Babysoft in your bathroom, you know you have the best.' Now, perched on a cold rock at the far end of Trezale beach, she stretched it that little bit further and said simply, 'Oh Janey, what on earth were you expecting me to say? You're happy, and that's good enough for me. I'm *glad* he's back.'

They were making their way back along the shoreline when Janey unwittingly asked the question Maxine had been gearing herself up for.

'So what else happened in London? You must have gone to a few parties; did you meet any nice men?'

Janey was carrying the glasses. Maxine, who had stuffed the empty Bollinger bottle inside her jacket, was skimming pebbles across the water. She watched the last pebble collide with a wave and disappear from view. A gust of wind blew her hair into her eyes and she used the extra seconds it gave her to compose herself.

'I went to *a* party,' she said finally, 'and met *a* nice man.'

'And now it's my turn to be kept in suspense?' Janey protested. 'Come along now, don't be shy! Give me the gory details.'

'I've known him for a while.' Maxine took a deep breath and wished she could have persuaded Guy to part with two bottles of champagne. A little extra Dutch courage would have come in useful. 'But until the party I didn't even know I liked him. You know him too; quite well, in fact. And I don't think you're going to like it much when I tell you who it is.'

Janey thought hard for a moment. With a perplexed shrug she said, 'Well, you've got me. But if it's an actor . . .' Her eyes widened in mock amazement and she clapped her free hand to her chest. 'You don't mean . . . Mel—'

'Look, he loves me and I love him,' said Maxine rapidly. 'It's serious stuff. I know you hate him, but you have to believe me . . . for the first time in my life I really do feel—'

'Mel Gibson?' shrieked Janey, and several seagulls beat a panicky retreat.

'Bruno.' Maxine's shoulders stiffened in an unconscious gesture of defiance. There, she'd said it. Now all she had to do was pray Janey didn't burst into tears.

But Janey was starting to laugh. 'Is this a joke? Max, that's not fair. Come on now, I told you everything!'

'And now I'm telling you. It really isn't a joke.' The words spilled out fast, jerkily. Maxine took another steadying breath. 'He turned up at the party on Friday night and practically kidnapped me. Except I wanted to be kidnapped,' she amended, a shiver running down her spine even as she recalled the sheer romance of it all. 'He wants to marry me. He's leaving Nina. Oh Janey, it was as much of a shock to me as it is for you, but it just happened! I can't even begin to describe how I feel . . .'

'Well,' said Janey as the gulls continued to wheel frantically overhead. 'I'm stunned.'

'I'm sorry.'

'You're sorry I'm stunned, or sorry it's Bruno?'

'You know what I mean.' Maxine bit her lower lip. 'I've been dreading telling you. Do you absolutely hate me?'

'I don't hate you. I can't believe you're being so incredibly stupid,' sighed Janey, 'but of course I don't hate you. Max, the last time I came for a walk along this beach, *somebody* gave me the most almighty lecture. I can't remember it word for word, but it had something to do with keeping well away from Bruno Parry-Brent because he was an unprincipled, sex-crazed, triple-timing shit-gigolo-bastard who would bring me nothing but everlasting grief.' Pausing, she tilted her head to one side. 'Now does that ring any bells with you, or do you have a twin sister I don't know about?'

'Oh hell,' said Maxine uncomfortably. She braced

herself once more. 'Look, I know I said all those things but that's the whole point; he would only have made you miserable. You're a nice person and you expect everyone else to be nice, too. You're trusting, unselfish, honest; as far as people like Bruno are concerned, it's practically an open invitation to behave badly. They can't resist it. And I know,' she added with passion in her voice, 'because I'm like Bruno too. I don't trust men, I'm a selfish bitch and I lie like the clappers. Don't you see, Janey? Bruno and I were made for each other! We're a perfectly matched pair.'

Janey frowned. 'I thought you loathed him.'

'I did.' Maxine gave her an apologetic look. 'Well, I thought I did. But what I really loathed was the fact that I knew he'd end up hurting you. You see, it was like watching a re-run of me and Maurice. You know what I'm like, Janey. I simply can't handle nice, dependable men. The better they treat me, the worse I behave. If a man's going to keep me on my toes, keep me interested, he needs to be a bastard, someone I can fight with. I don't mean getting beaten up,' she added hastily, as Janey's eyebrows rose. 'I'm not into black eyes and teeth flying in all directions. I just need someone I don't trust enough to take for granted.'

Maxine was rattling on at a furious pace, putting across every argument she could think of. Strangely, thought Janey, it rang true. It might be weird, but it made sense.

'I know it's masochistic,' Maxine went on. 'I'm a hopeless case. But if it's easy, there's no buzz. And I need that buzz . . .'

Uncomfortably aware that she was once again echoing Maxine's own words to her, Janey said, 'There's still Nina.

You say Bruno's going to leave her. What makes you think he will?'

'I don't have to think.' The gulls were still wheeling noisily overhead. Maxine suppressed an urge to hurl the champagne bottle at them. Meeting Janey's concerned gaze, she recalled Bruno's phone call earlier this morning. 'I know,' she said simply. 'He already has.'

They had finished retracing their steps. Janey's white beach shoes were awash with sand. By the time they'd made their way back up the high street, it was almost midday.

'Alan will be home any minute now,' she said, fishing in her pocket for the front-door key. 'If you'd like to stay for lunch, you're very welcome. Or is Guy expecting you back?'

'Special dispensation,' Maxine replied with an unnecessary glance at her watch. She had already arranged to meet Bruno at the Dune Bar at twelve-thirty. Somehow a cosy foursome didn't seem appropriate. 'Guy's given me the afternoon off; he's taking the kids over to Mimi Margason's house for lunch. She's the woman whose party you went to, isn't she? I've never met her, but she sounds wild.'

'She is.' Janey wondered if she would ever see Mimi again. She had the uncomfortable feeling that bridges were being burnt. Unless they came into the shop, she might never even see Guy and the children again, either. 'She's outrageous. And very, very nice.'

'Ah well, in that case I probably wouldn't like her,' Maxine replied. 'As I said, nice people make me nervous. Apart from you,' she added cheerfully. 'Sisters don't count.'

'So will you stay for lunch?'

'I can't.' By this time they had reached the shop. Taking a step forward, Maxine kissed Janey's cold cheek. 'I'm seeing Bruno. It's a bit of an awkward situation, isn't it?'

'It's certainly unusual.' Janey smiled. 'I dare say we'll get used to it.'

'We're both happy,' said Maxine, wishing she didn't feel so guilty. 'We've both got the men we really and truly want. There's only one thing left to do now, to round it off.'

'What's that?'

Maxine grinned. 'Find some poor long-suffering female for Guy.'

Chapter 43

Bruno evidently didn't believe in wasting time. Maxine, only a few minutes late, arrived at the Dune Bar to find him deep in conversation with an extremely pretty brunette, pouring her a glass of Chardonnay with one hand and jangling two sets of keys in the other.

'And about time too,' he complained when Maxine joined them. 'I don't think you know Pearl, do you? I've just been telling her how madly in love with you I am, and how you've changed my life for ever. Think what an idiot I'd have looked if you hadn't turned up.'

'He's definitely a changed man,' Pearl declared, eyeing Maxine with undisguised curiosity. 'I only came over to invite him to a party tomorrow night and he hasn't stopped talking about you for the last twenty minutes. He won't even come to the party.'

Bruno, eyes glittering with amusement, slid his arm around Maxine's waist. 'I'd only get chatted up by women with designs on my body,' he complained. 'There's only one woman in my life from now on. Who needs parties, when we have each other?'

'Boring old fart,' said Maxine, helping herself to wine. 'I like parties. If I was invited to one, I'd go.'

'You can both come.' Pearl scribbled the address on the back of a beer mat. Grinning at Maxine, who evidently met with her approval, she said, 'It'll be fun.'

Bruno had picked up the beer mat. Maxine promptly whisked it from his grasp.

'I'll definitely be there, but Bruno might not,' she said smoothly. 'He doesn't need parties any more, you see. He'd only get chatted up by women with designs on his body.'

'Thanks,' said Bruno, when Pearl had left.

'What's the problem?' Maxine demanded. 'Afraid you won't be able to resist a bit of temptation?'

'Look, we both know you aren't going to any party tomorrow night. Guy's away and you're looking after the kids. I only said no because I didn't think you'd want me to go on my own,' he said with a trace of exasperation. 'I thought you wouldn't trust me.'

'So what are we supposed to do?' Maxine countered. 'Trot along to the nearest hospital and ask to be surgically joined at the hip? Sweetheart, we're just going to have to *learn* to trust each other. I'm not going to try and stop you doing anything you want to do and you're certainly not going to stop me. You can chat up Michelle Pfeiffer if you like. All you have to remember is that if I ever find out you've been unfaithful to me, it's over.' With her index finger, she drew a swift, clean line across his throat. 'Finito. Kaput. Down the pan.'

Bruno kissed her. 'I love you.'

'Hmm.' People were staring, but Maxine didn't care. 'Just as well. We're going to be gossiped about from here to Land's End.'

He picked up one of the sets of keys and dangled them in front of her. 'In that case, let's really give them something to gossip about. Here, take them. Don showed me round a few properties this morning. I'm now the proud tenant of Mole Cottage.'

'You don't waste much time,' said Maxine admiringly. 'Is it nice?'

'Nice?' Bruno launched into brochure-speak. 'Mole Cottage is an *eminently* desirable seventeenth-century residence complete with *stunning* sea view, *two* charming bedrooms, *spacious* shower and delightful beamed ceilings throughout. The living room's actually smaller than the shower cubicle, the wallpaper is unspeakable and the garden's buried beneath six feet of weeds,' he added with a rueful shrug, 'but if we can ignore the décor we'll survive. At least it was dirt cheap.'

Maxine took the keys. 'I suppose these are the modern-day equivalent of a diamond ring.'

'You've done the diamond-ring bit before. You can't keep getting engaged; it's tacky.' Bruno grinned. 'Besides, I'm *nouveau pauvre*. As from today, a key-ring's about as much as I can afford.'

It was Maxine's turn to kiss him. 'I don't care. When are you going to move in?'

'As soon as you finish your drink. My suitcases are in the car.'

She experienced another spasm of guilt. 'How was Nina?'

'Fine.' Bruno drained his glass. 'Absolutely fine. She even helped me pack.'

Frowning slightly, Maxine twisted the stem of her glass

between her fingers. 'Wasn't she even a little bit upset?'

'No.' He had privately come to the conclusion that Nina felt he was in the grip of a wild passion which would be out of his system by Christmas. It wouldn't, of course, but it had certainly made leaving a whole lot easier. 'She takes things in her stride. There's only one major drawback to my leaving, as far as Nina's concerned.'

'Oh yes?'

'Bruno's Restaurant.' He pulled a face. 'She spoke to the new chef this morning and he says if he's going to take full charge, it should be named after him.'

Maxine, who had only briefly glimpsed the thin, carroty-haired individual with the bobbing Adam's apple and alarmingly pointed ears, said, 'I can't remember what he's called.'

Bruno broke into a grin. 'Wayne.'

'I'm late, I'm sorry.' Alan, bursting through the door at ten past one, gave Janey an enormous, conciliatory hug. 'I lost all track of time. All the old crowd were there; you can't imagine how much catching up we had to do.'

And you can't imagine how terribly afraid I've been, thought Janey, willing herself to stay calm. Punctuality had never been one of Alan's strong points, but that didn't mean she hadn't suffered agonies of uncertainty as each minute had ticked by. She wondered if she would ever truly be able to relax and overcome the fear that each time he left the house she might never see him again.

But that was something she was just going to have to come to terms with, she told herself firmly. Shrieking like a fishwife wouldn't solve anything, and whingeing on about how worried she'd been would only burden him with guilt.

'Don't worry, I expected you to be late.' With a casual gesture, she wiped her damp palms on her jeans. 'They're your friends; you must have had lots to talk about.'

'It was still thoughtless of me.' He stroked her blond, just-washed hair. 'But you really don't have to worry, sweetheart. I'm not going to disappear into thin air again. This time I'm here for good.'

She smiled. 'Good.'

'And to make up for being late home, I'm cooking lunch.' He began to roll up the sleeves of his denim shirt in businesslike fashion. 'You can put your feet up and relax. I'll do everything myself.'

Janey started to laugh, because the smell of lamb roasting in the oven permeated the entire flat. 'It's all done,' she said, recalling how often in the past they had gone through this routine.

True to form, Alan looked appalled. 'All of it? Roast potatoes, onion sauce, all the vegetables?'

She nodded, brown eyes sparkling. 'Afraid so.'

'Oh well, in that case . . .' Alan took her hand and pulled her gently in the direction of the bedroom '. . . maybe we should both put our feet up.'

Janey raised a quizzical eyebrow. 'And relax?'

'Hmm.' Sliding his arm around her waist beneath the fleecy lilac sweatshirt she wore, he edged towards the zip on her jeans. 'Maybe we'll leave the relaxing until later . . .'

'Oh shit.' With a groan, Janey ducked away from the window. 'I don't believe it. Oh *hell*!'

'Who is it?' Alan demanded irritably, as she wriggled across the bed and made a grab for her yellow-and-white towelling robe. Whoever it was, they certainly had a lethal sense of timing.

'Quick, get some clothes on,' hissed Janey. 'It's my mother.'

Thea Vaughan was proud of the way she had brought up her children, teaching them to be independent from an early age, allowing them to make their own decisions and never saying 'I told you so' when those decisions turned out to be mistakes. But enough was enough. This time, Janey had gone too far. And no mother, she felt, could be expected to sit back and watch her daughter make a mistake quite as monumental as the one Janey was making now.

'Mum.' Flushed and dishevelled, Janey opened the front door. 'What a surprise! You usually phone.'

'What a coincidence,' mimicked Thea briskly. 'So do you. When you have something to tell me, that is,' she added in meaningful tones. 'Some small item of news you think I might be interested in hearing.'

Janey had known it wouldn't be easy. Thea was clearly on the warpath, outraged at having been left out and determined to make a monumental drama out of the event. It was precisely why she hadn't made more than a token effort to contact her mother in the first place.

'I did try to phone you,' she insisted. 'Yesterday. There was no reply.'

'Stuff and nonsense,' retorted Thea, her crimson cape billowing out as she stomped up the stairs. 'I was out of the house for less than fifteen minutes. No doubt you were too busy to try again,' she continued scathingly. 'Which is why I have to hear the news from that nosey baggage Elsie Ellis, who from the sound of it has spent the last couple of days with her ears pinned against your adjoining wall. I dare say she's also been broadcasting the news of your husband's return to everyone who has set foot inside that bakery of hers. Personally, I'm amazed she hasn't stood on the steps of the bloody town hall with a megaphone.'

'Look, I'm sorry.' Janey's heart was pounding uncomfortably against her ribs. This was even worse than the time Maxine and the cricketers had turned up out of the blue, catching her with Bruno. 'But I don't understand why you're so angry that Alan's back. Aren't you at least happy for me?'

'My God, you are naïve.' It came out as a snort of derision. 'And I thought I was stupid, marrying your father! At least I had the guts to get out of the marriage before he ruined my entire life.'

'It isn't the same thing.' Outraged by the accusation, Janey's voice rose. 'That was completely different! You told us yourself he had non-stop affairs, Alan didn't do that. My father made you miserable for years; you can't possibly compare your marriage with mine. It's all very well for you to come storming round here with your mind already made up, but you don't even know why he left.'

She cringed as Thea reached the top of the stairs and flung open the door to the flat. If Alan had decided to hide in the bedroom, her mother's scorn would know no bounds.

But he was there, pouring Chablis into glasses and –

thank heavens – standing his ground.

'Don't be angry with Thea,' he said calmly, evidently having overheard the furious exchange on the stairs. 'She has your best interests at heart. I've turned off the oven, by the way. Why don't we sit down and discuss this whole thing in a rational manner?'

It was what Alan was best at. Janey, drinking far too much wine far too quickly, said nothing and allowed him to get on with it.

Thea, however, remained stonily unimpressed. 'Such a touching tale,' she remarked, her expression sardonic, the light of battle in her brown eyes. 'Forgive me if I don't break down in tears, but I'm less of a soft touch than my daughter.'

Alan shrugged. 'I'm sorry, I know how you must feel. But it happens to be the truth.'

'Balls,' said Thea.

Janey winced. 'Mum!'

'Oh grow up!' her mother snapped. 'I've never heard such codswallop in all my life. If he'd had the guts to say he ran off with another woman I could almost forgive him, but this . . . this complete and utter claptrap is just despicable. Janey, he's making a fool of you and I'm not going to let it carry on.'

'I can't help what you think,' said Alan, reaching for Janey's hand and squeezing it. With a sorrowful shake of his head, he met Thea's withering gaze. 'And there's no way in the world I can ever prove it, but there was no other woman. That's the absolute truth, and Janey believes me. Maybe in time you'll come to believe it too. I certainly hope you will, for Janey's sake if not for mine, but—'

'But nothing!' declared Thea with venom. 'Do I look as if I have a mental age of six? You're a liar and a cheat, and you all but wrecked my daughter's life. If you think I'm going to stand by and let you do it again, my lad, you most certainly have another think coming.'

'Right, that's enough,' Janey shouted. Red-faced, she leapt to her feet, narrowly avoiding the coffee table, and wrenched open the living-room door. 'You're treating *me* like a six-year-old, and it isn't even any of your damn business. Alan's my husband and you're just jealous because he came back and yours didn't. What's the matter, don't you want me to be happy?'

'For God's sake,' sighed Thea, frustrated by her daughter's hopelessly misguided loyalty. 'Of course I want you to be happy. That's why I came here, to try and make you see sense.'

'Well let me tell you what would make me happy,' yelled Janey, trembling all over and clutching the door handle for support. 'You leaving. Because I won't be bullied and I won't stand here and listen to another word of this garbage. You're interfering with my life and I don't need it. I don't need you, either,' she concluded with intentional cruelty. 'So why don't you do us all a favour and just get out of here, now?'

Chapter 44

After a late lunch, Mimi walked with Guy around the garden. Ahead of them, Josh and Ella were spinning around like tops in a race to see who could make themselves dizziest and fall over in the most spectacular fashion. Within seconds, her arms flailing and her legs buckling drunkenly beneath her, Ella staggered sideways into a flowerbed.

'Masochistic little sods,' said Mimi fondly as Ella let out a scream of delight and Josh, not to be outdone, careered head first into a mass of overgrown rhododendrons. 'They'll keep going until they feel sick, then run to you for sympathy.'

'If anyone needs sympathy, it's me.' Pausing for a moment, Guy took a photograph of Ella as she emerged from the flowerbed. 'Nothing seems to be going according to plan at the moment. God knows what's going to happen next,' he added, adjusting the shutter speed and taking aim once more, 'but I'm pretty sure I'm not going to like it.'

Poor Guy. Mimi, who had heard all about Alan Sinclair's return over lunch, tucked a companionable arm through his. 'Ah, but that's the thing about masochism,' she said with the air of one who knows. 'We might grow up, but that doesn't mean we automatically grow out of it. Look at me,' she exclaimed, gesturing towards her hips. 'I wasted ten years of my life trying to diet! All that miserable calorie-counting and jumping on scales, and what did it achieve? I'd lose a stone, gain a stone, and bore everybody rigid into the bargain . . . My God, was there ever anything more pointless? I was *miserable,* darling . . . a slave to fashion. Giving up dieting and saying to hell with size twelve was the best decision of my entire life!'

Since Mimi was currently wearing a pink mohair cardigan trimmed with sequins, a mauve organza blouse and a blue-and-white gingham skirt, it was hard to imagine her ever having been a slave to fashion.

Thoroughly mystified, Guy responded with a cautious nod. 'I see.'

'And it's the same with Janey,' she continued triumphantly. 'She might think she's hooked on this wretched husband of hers but all he is, really, is a habit she hasn't broken. You have to be patient, darling. Given time, she'll come to her senses and realize she can do without him after all. Mind you, I bet you wish now you'd made your move a bit earlier,' she added with a smug, I-told-you-so smile. 'She would have had to think twice then, wouldn't she, before rushing off without so much as a backward glance? In that respect, I'm afraid you have only yourself to blame.'

'Really.' Guy struggled to keep a straight face. 'Well, this is all very interesting, but I'm afraid you're on completely the wrong track. Janey's a friend, nothing more. She's a very nice girl, but that's as far as it goes. She just isn't my type. When I said I didn't know what was going to happen next,' he explained, 'I was referring to Maxine. If this new affair of hers turns out to be more than a nine-day wonder, it's going to mean trouble for me. Before long, she'll be wanting to move in with Bruno Parry-Brent and I'll have to start looking for a new nanny.'

'Of course you will,' said Mimi blithely. 'And who would be absolutely perfect for the job? Janey.'

'You're shameless.' This time he was unable to hide his smile. 'Do you know that? Quite apart from the fact that she has a shop to run, I've already told you, Janey isn't my type.'

Mimi, not believing him for a second, pulled the mohair cardigan more tightly around her vast bosom as a sudden gust of wind whistled down her cleavage.

'You're only a man,' she said, her tone comforting. 'What would you know? You thought Serena was your type.'

'I have to get back,' said Maxine regretfully, stirring the surface of the water with her big toe and transferring an artful dollop of foam on to Bruno's shoulder. 'We can't spend the rest of our lives lying in the bath. Besides, I'm starting to prune.'

He reached for her hand and kissed her wrinkled fingertips, one by one. 'I don't want you to go. Why don't you give in your notice and come and live here with me?'

'What, leave my job?'

'I left Nina,' Bruno reminded her. 'And my job. I'm not going to enjoy sitting around waiting for you to dash over here whenever you can manage to get a couple of hours off.'

She grinned. 'You've done it to enough women yourself, haven't you? Now you can find out how it feels to be the one on the receiving end.'

'I want us to be together,' he said crossly. 'All the time.'

He was sounding more and more like a fretful mistress. Leaning forward, Maxine gave him a kiss. 'So do I, but then we'd both be unemployed. Besides, Guy's been good to me – in his own way – and I can't leave him in the lurch. Why don't we just see how things go for a while before doing anything drastic?'

'Well thanks,' murmured Bruno, who felt he had already acted pretty drastically. But Maxine, in a hurry to get back to Trezale House, was climbing out of the bath and reaching for the larger of the two towels.

'Don't glare at me like that,' she said cheerfully. 'You know what I mean. Look, I'll have a word with Guy and see if we can't come to some kind of arrangement. If he's at home, maybe he'll let me spend my nights here. And the kids are at school during the day . . .'

'Such concern all of a sudden, for Guy Cassidy,' Bruno complained, watching as she eased herself into her jeans and bent to pick up her crumpled white shirt. 'He's hardly likely to go out of his way to make things easier for us. He doesn't even like me.'

'Don't worry.' Maxine winked. 'I have ways of getting round Guy. Don't you trust me?'

'No.' He wasn't used to feeling jealous and he didn't much like it. 'That's why I want you to come and live here.'

'I don't trust you, either,' countered Maxine sweetly, doing up the last couple of buttons and knotting the shirt tails around her waist. 'So forget it. Because I'm not moving anywhere until you manage to persuade me that I can.'

Guy was leafing through a mound of contact sheets and eating a Marmite sandwich when Maxine rolled into the sitting room at seven.

'You look as if you've just crawled out of bed,' he observed, taking in her tousled hair, bright eyes and distinctly rumpled white shirt.

'It's what you do when you're in love.' She gave him an unrepentant smile.

Josh and Ella were sprawled in front of the fire, their blond heads bent over a game of Monopoly. Glancing up, Josh said hopefully, 'If you've been asleep all afternoon, I expect you'd like to play Monopoly now. I've nearly finished beating Ella.'

Guy pushed the contact sheets to one side. 'How was Janey?'

'Happy.' Maxine rolled her eyes. 'What can I say? He fed her some terrible line and she fell for it. I just went along with the whole thing and pretended to be pleased for her.' Collapsing on to the floor next to Ella, who was biting her lip at the prospect of having to mortgage the Old Kent Road, she added, 'But it was definitely the right thing to do. At the moment, she won't hear a word against him.'

'Hmm,' said Guy. 'So I gathered. Your mother phoned earlier, wanting to speak to you.'

Maxine pulled a face. If Thea had somehow heard about Bruno leaving Nina from outside sources, it was entirely possible that she was in for a lecture. Her mother was sensitive about such matters. 'Oh.' She looked wary. 'Did she say what about?'

'In Technicolor detail.' Guy glanced across at the children to make sure they weren't listening. 'And it isn't good news. She went round to Janey's place this afternoon and told Alan exactly what she thought of him. It didn't go down well at all,' he explained. 'She and Janey had a screaming row and Janey ended up booting her out of the flat.'

'Hell.' Maxine heaved a gusty sigh. 'Poor Mum. I suppose I should have warned her. Now we've got a family feud on our hands. Was she upset?'

'Upset, no. Angry, yes.' He half smiled, recalling the colourful language Thea Vaughan had employed during the course of their forty-minute conversation. 'But with herself as much as anything. She realizes now that she made a mistake.'

'Daddy, can you lend me two thousand pounds?' asked Ella in desperation. 'To stop me going bankrupt.'

'She also warned me that I had all this to come,' Guy went on, shaking his head wearily. 'Apparently, raising daughters is the pits. One calamity after another.'

'That means no,' declared Josh, merciless in victory. 'Good, you're bankrupt. You've lost and I've won. Come on, Maxine, you're next. I'm the racing car and you can be the old boot.'

'Good old Mum,' said Maxine. 'She always was about as subtle as Bernard Manning.'

'She certainly has character.' Guy grinned. 'She sounded fun though. I'd like to meet her.'

'Now there's a thought! Janey and I were only saying this morning that what you need is a woman in your life.' Maxine's dark eyes glittered with mischief. 'Maybe I should introduce you to my mother.'

Chapter 45

Janey was in the shop putting the finishing touches to a congratulations-on-your-retirement bouquet when Guy came in.

'They're nice.' He nodded at the autumnal flowers.

'For Miss Stirrup, with love from Class 2C.' Having trimmed and curled the bronze and gold ribbons holding the bouquet together, Janey reached for the staple gun and clipped the accompanying card to the cellophane wrapper. 'She's a complete dragon; she was my English teacher, always sticking the whole class in detention when the weather was good and all we wanted to do was go tearing off down to the beach. I was tempted to write out "Have a Happy Retirement" a hundred times,' she added with a grin. 'And spell "retirement" wrongly, just to annoy her.'

She was looking well and happy, Guy realized. The habitual working uniform of jeans and tee-shirt had been replaced by a pastel pink wool dress which flattered both her figure and colouring. She was wearing make-up too, not a great deal but enough to make a difference. The overall effect was one of renewed confidence and cheerfulness. So far, he decided, everything appeared to be going well.

But he still couldn't bring himself to raise the subject of the long-lost husband's miraculous return. Instead, sticking to safer ground, he placed a large Manila envelope on the counter.

'I'm just on my way up to London. I thought I'd drop this in before I left. Go on, open it. It's for you.'

'Really?' Janey gave him a playful look. 'What is it, more wages?'

Guy smiled. 'Afraid not.'

'Oh!' As the photograph slid out of the envelope, she caught her breath. 'Oh, my God . . . this is amazing. I can't believe it's really me.'

As soon as he had developed Friday night's films, taken purely in order to test out the latest Olympus, Guy had known he had something special. The particular miracle of photography, he always felt, was the fact that although technical expertise played a part, it was never everything. The best camera in the world, coupled with perfect lighting and the most compliant subjects, could produce adequate but ultimately disappointing results, whereas occasionally – and for no apparent reason – an off-the-cuff, unplanned snap of a shutter succeeded in capturing a mood, an expression, a moment in time to perfection.

He had felt at once, even as he pegged up the still-dripping print in the darkroom, that this was one such success. It didn't happen often but it had happened last Friday, and the result was almost magical. Unaware of the camera, Janey had hoisted Ella into her arms in order to give her a clear view of Josh on the dodgems. Their faces, close together, were alight with shared laughter. Ella's small fingers, curled around Janey's neck, conveyed love and trust. The only slightly out-of-focus background managed to capture both the excitement and noise of the fairground. Ella's childish elation and Janey's pride and delight in Josh's prowess at the wheel of his dodgem car were reflected with such astonishing clarity, it almost brought a lump to the throat. Unposed, unrehearsed and using only natural available light, it was the kind of one-in-a-million shot all photographers seek to achieve. Guy, having achieved it, had known at once where its future lay.

'I don't know much about this kind of thing,' said Janey, who was still studying the print intently. She hesitated, then glanced up at him. 'But it is good, isn't it? I mean seriously good.'

'I think so.'

'It has . . . impact.' The fact that she was featured in the picture was irrelevant. Shaking her head, she struggled to express herself more clearly. 'You can . . . *feel* it. I don't think anyone could look at this photograph and not respond. And how strange, we look like—'

'Like what?' Guy prompted half-teasingly, but she shook her head once more and didn't reply. Against the darker background, which had created a kind of halo effect, both Ella's hair and her own appeared white-blond and the camera angle had managed to capture a similarity in their bone structure; but the fact that they looked like mother and daughter was sheer chance, a mere trick of the lens and far too embarrassing to voice aloud.

Instead, she said simply, 'I love it. Thank you.'

'And now I have a favour to ask.' Guy, who knew exactly what had been going through her mind, was amused by her reluctance to comment on the apparent resemblance between Ella and herself. 'I was approached by a children's charity a couple of weeks ago. They're mounting a national appeal and they've asked for my help.'

'Raising money?' He had given her the photograph. Janey, happy to return the favour, was eager to help. 'What can I do, keep a collecting tin here on the counter? I did a stint once, rattling a tin on a street corner for the RSPCA.' With a grin, she added, 'I did brilliantly, too. It wasn't until three hours later I realized most of my shirt buttons were undone. All those men stuffing pound coins into my tin had been getting an eyeful of my boobs and there I was saying thank you and thinking what lovely caring people they were.'

'All these months I've known you,' Guy drawled. 'And I never figured you for a topless model.'

'It was almost worse than topless.' Janey cringed at the memory. 'I was wearing a really awful old bra held together with a safety pin. Talk about mortifying.'

'Well you can rattle a tin if you want to, but that wasn't what I had in mind.' Leaning against the counter, Guy tapped the photograph with a forefinger. 'You see, they asked me to come up with the advertising poster for the campaign. With your permission I'd like to use this.'

She stared at him. 'You're joking.'

'Why would I joke? It's perfect. As you said yourself, you can't look at this picture and not feel something. With any luck,' he added with a wink, 'the public will look at it and feel compelled to donate pots of money.'

At that moment the door to the shop opened behind

him. Guy could almost have guessed without turning around that the waft of Paco Rabanne aftershave and accompanying footsteps belonged to Alan Sinclair. Janey had gone two shades pinker and her hand reached automatically to her hair.

But he turned anyway, taking his first look at the man who had caused her such untold grief. He saw what he had expected, too; blond, boyish good looks, an air of laid-back charm, the kind of features typical of a man who knew he stood a greater than average chance of taking risks and getting away with them. The urge to launch right in and tell Alan Sinclair exactly what he thought of him was compelling, but it was a luxury he was unable to allow himself. Thea had tried, and failed spectacularly. For once in her life, he reflected, Maxine had been right.

'Darling . . . I wasn't expecting you back so soon.' Janey sounded both pleased and flustered. 'Guy, this is Alan, my husband. Alan, meet Guy Cassidy . . . um, Maxine's boss.'

Guy was not a vain man. He nevertheless knew from experience that other men, upon meeting him for the first time, instinctively mistrusted him with their own wives or girlfriends. Even if the women didn't appear overtly interested – although, he had to admit, they frequently did – the men grew jealous. It was going to be interesting, he decided, to see how Janey's husband would react.

Alan, however, appeared disappointingly unfazed. There were no gritted teeth behind the cheerful smile as he shook Guy's hand.

'Of course,' he said easily. 'It's really nice to meet you, Janey's told me all about you and your family. I'm also a great admirer of your work.'

'Thank you.' The boy had charm, thought Guy. And since he must be almost thirty he wasn't even a boy; it was simply the impression he gave of being not altogether grown up.

'Look, darling. Guy dropped by to show me this picture.' Touching the back of Alan's wrist in order to regain his attention, Janey pushed the photograph into his hand. 'He wants to use it for a poster advertising a charity fund-raising campaign. What do you think, isn't it marvellous?'

Alan studied the print for several seconds, clearly impressed. Finally, flicking back his blond hair, he nodded. 'It is. Maxine must be over the moon. Fame at last.'

Guy bit his lip. That was always the trouble with deserting your wife, he thought with derision. When you eventually came back you didn't always recognize her.

'You idiot,' giggled Janey. 'This isn't Maxine. It's me.'

'Oh, right.' Unperturbed by his mistake, Alan took another look and nodded. Turning to address Guy he said casually, 'Very flattering. That's why you're so in demand as a photographer, of course. It's all clever stuff.'

Guy barely trusted himself to speak. No wonder Janey was so lacking in self-confidence, he thought bitterly. Between the pair of them, Alan and Bruno had sapped her of every last ounce of the stuff.

'Flattery doesn't come into it.' He had observed Janey's crestfallen expression. His dark blue eyes glittered as he removed the photograph from Alan Sinclair's grasp. 'The picture was there, waiting to be taken. All I did was capture it on film.'

'Of course,' Apparently realizing his mistake, Alan shrugged and smiled once more. 'I'm sorry, I wasn't implying otherwise. And I think it'll make a great campaign poster.'

'I still can't believe it,' sighed Janey. 'This is so exciting.'

'Not to mention well timed.' Slipping his arm around her waist, Alan gave her a brief, congratulatory hug. 'Maybe now we'll be able to take that holiday after all.' He turned to look at Guy. 'How much will she be getting for this?'

Guy stared at him. Janey, whose colour had only just reverted to normal, went bright pink all over again.

'Alan, it's for a charity campaign! The idea is to raise money. I wouldn't be paid!'

'Oh.' The disappointment was evident in his voice. This time, when he glanced down at the print, it was without interest. 'Shame.'

'I have to go.' Guy looked at his watch. Janey was embarrassed, which was maybe no bad thing, although if anyone should be ashamed it was her husband. 'Look, I'm presenting the idea to the organizers this afternoon. When they make their final decision I'll be in touch.'

'Oh dear,' said Alan, when Guy had left the shop. 'Did I put my foot in it?'

'Both feet.' Janey busied herself with a bucket of moss. She had two wreaths to complete before lunch. 'I can't believe you said that. God knows what Guy must have thought.'

'It was a simple enough mistake.' He looked injured. 'These models get paid thousands for a couple of hours' work, don't they? I was only looking after your interests. Why should you be ripped off, just because you're a friend?'

'Well nobody's being ripped off.' Shuddering at the memory of the look on Guy's face, she began packing the damp moss around the wire base of the first wreath. 'It's for a children's charity. Nobody's getting paid.'

Alan had almost entirely lost interest by now. 'In that case I can't imagine why you're so excited about it. God, I'm starving. Is there anything to eat upstairs?'

'Not unless you've bought some food.' Irritated by his manner, Janey's reply bordered on sarcasm. 'Since I've been working since five o'clock this morning, I'm afraid I haven't had time to visit the supermarket.'

He was immediately contrite. 'I didn't mean it like that. Sorry, sweetheart.'

'Well.' In her agitation, she narrowly missed slicing her finger on a protruding wire. 'Just don't expect gourmet meals, OK? I'm not Superwoman.'

'You are to me.' Alan gave her his most beguiling smile. Leaning across the counter and pulling her towards him, he kissed her soft, down-turned mouth. 'Don't be cross, Janey. You know how much I love you.'

She was still tense. He really had upset her. When she didn't reply, he smoothed a wayward strand of blond hair from her cheek and said, 'Come on, sweetheart. What is it? Is there something going on that I should know about?'

Janey hesitated. 'Like what?'

'Like the possibility that there could be more to this

so-called friendship between you and Guy Cassidy than meets the eye?'

Oh God, she thought wearily. Not again.

'Well?' he persisted.

'No.' She shook her head for added emphasis. 'Of course there isn't.'

'Hmm,' said Alan, not sounding entirely convinced. His eyes narrowed as he studied her evident discomfort. 'There'd better not be.'

The discord had unnerved Janey. It was their first semi-argument and the knot of tension in the pit of her stomach had stayed with her all afternoon. Easy-going by nature, she wished now she hadn't snapped at Alan, but at the same time she didn't feel she'd acted too unreasonably. As long as he wasn't working, she didn't see why she should put in a sixty-hour week in the shop and knock herself out cooking three-course dinners in her precious free time.

It was with some trepidation that she climbed the stairs to the flat at six-thirty. She was hungry and her feet ached. She definitely didn't feel up to an evening of verbal sparring and unease.

As she began to turn the door handle, however, she heard Alan's voice shouting from inside: 'Stop! Don't come in!'

For a fraction of a second, Janey felt her heart lurch. It was ridiculous, but the memory of a recent TV drama came flooding back to her. The wife, arriving home early from work, had been commanded to wait outside the front door in just such a manner whilst the husband's mistress, fetchingly wrapped in a bed sheet, had made her escape through the kitchen door at the back of the house. It had struck a chord at the time, because she had experienced the same situation when Maxine and the cricketers had been hammering on the door and she had been caught with Bruno. The difference, of course, was that in this flat there was no back door from which one could safely escape, only windows and an ankle-snapping fifteen-foot drop.

The next moment, Alan opened the door himself. He grinned. 'OK, you can come in now. All ready.'

She hadn't seriously doubted him, of course, but the sight that greeted her still managed to bring a lump to Janey's throat. There were no semi-naked females in the dimly lit living room. Instead, the small dining table had been set for two. Flickering candles cast an auburn glow over the tablecloth, and he had unearthed the crystal glasses she so seldom used. An unopened bottle of champagne stood in an ice-packed Pyrex bowl.

'Surprise,' murmured Alan, in her ear. 'I hope you're hungry.'

Unbelievably touched by the gesture, Janey could only nod. The fact that it was so unexpected made it all the more special. This, she reminded herself, was why she loved him.

'I'm sorry about this morning.' Taking her hand, he led her towards the table. 'My stupid jealousy. But I'm going to make everything up to you, sweetheart. Here, sit down. Didn't I say we should celebrate my return with champagne?'

It was actually '*méthode champenoise*', Janey observed,

glancing at the label. But that was just as nice as the proper kind . . .

Watching him ease the cork from the bottle, she held her breath as she always did in anticipation of the moment of release. When it finally happened, however, it was sadly lacking in oomph. The cork, instead of ricocheting off the ceiling, toppled limply to the floor. The accompanying silence was deafening.

Alan looked disappointed. 'Story of my life,' he said with a regretful grimace. 'I suppose it was bound to happen. I always seem to get everything wrong.'

'Don't be silly.' Janey's eyes filled with tears as she leap to her feet and hugged him. 'You do everything *right*. You've cooked a stupendous dinner, haven't you? Why don't I dash down to the off-licence and pick up another bottle whilst you're serving up?'

'Actually,' he said, 'it might be a better idea if you give me the money and I get the bottle. You can take a look at the food. I've done my best, but you aren't the only one who isn't Superwoman,' he added defensively. 'It may not be stupendous.'

Janey smiled. 'Why, what's the problem?'

'Well, I don't know.' Alan shook his head and looked perplexed. 'I've never cooked a stupid chicken before. Is it really supposed to have a plastic bag full of squishy bits up its bum?'

Chapter 46

Valentina di Angelo was only temperamental when she wanted to be. Her fame had been founded upon the highly public rows between herself and her first husband, a hard-drinking but undoubtedly talented actor. Following their even more public divorce, Valentina had come to the reasonable conclusion that while displays of temperament were newsworthy, sweet, quiet, nice girls who liked sewing, reading and watching *EastEnders* were not.

She was always careful, though, to ensure that the temperamental outbursts didn't affect her work. As far as the *paparazzi* were concerned, Valentina di Angelo never turned up anywhere less than three hours late, but her modelling career was something else altogether. Always cheerful, always punctual, she worked like a trooper and never complained about anything. No supermodel, after all, was ever that indispensable. Hurling insults at chat-show hosts, journalists and horrible hangers-on, and generally acting the drama queen, was a strictly after-hours occupation.

It worked, too, like a dream. She was famous for being a beautiful, acid-tongued bitch, and only the people she cared about knew any different.

And although she'd only just met Guy Cassidy, she had already placed him on the list of people she cared about. They had worked well together, she felt, but it was the tantalizing distance he'd kept which intrigued her more than anything else. Even during the shoot itself – during which she'd been wearing not very much at all – he hadn't seemed to notice the lush perfection of her body in the way most top photographers did. The end results had been faultless of course, but as far as Valentina was concerned there was a certain amount of unfinished business to be taken care of. With two short-lived marriages and seven broken engagements behind her, she also felt she had plenty of experience. She'd met her share of Mr Wrongs and got them out of her system. Now, at twenty-five, she was ready for Mr Right. And Guy Cassidy, with his talent, toe-curling good looks and enigmatic personality, was without a doubt right up her street. Better still, he had unceremoniously dumped her arch rival Serena Charlton. It therefore stood to reason, she thought happily, that the man had impeccable taste.

If Guy was surprised to receive her phone call, he didn't show it. He was, however, curious to know how she had managed to track him down to a small hotel in Leicester Square.

'Ah, you're talking to a girl with two and a half GCSEs,' said Valentina. She wasn't entirely brainless. Not like Serena, she thought with a smirk of pride.

'I'm still intrigued.'

'I knew you were a friend of Mac Mackenzie,' she explained. 'So I rang him. He gave me your home phone number. Then I phoned your home and spoke to someone called Maxine. She told me you were staying at the Randolph and gave me the number for that. I called the Randolph, asked to speak to you . . . and here I am!' She giggled. 'There, does that put you out of your misery?'

Guy, sounding amused, said, 'Oh, absolutely. Thanks.'

'Which is nice, because I didn't even expect you to be here in London,' Valentina continued, her tone artless. 'But since you are, how would you feel about having dinner with me?'

He hesitated for a second. 'You mean tonight?'

'No, New Year's Eve, 2005.' This time she laughed. 'Of course, tonight. What's the problem, are you already booked? Tell them you've had a better offer . . .'

Guy had run across more than his fair share of up-front women in his time, but even he was taken aback. Valentina, he thought, was forward with a capital 'F'.

'I know, I know,' she said good-naturedly, reading his mind. 'I'm a pushy cow. Go on, you can say no if you want to. My ego will be crushed but I dare say I'll get over it. In a few years or so.'

It had been a long day. Guy hadn't been planning anything more arduous than a hot bath and maybe a quick drink in the bar downstairs before grabbing the opportunity of an early night and eight hours of uninterrupted sleep.

But Maxine's joking remark the other day, that what he needed was a woman in his life, had stayed in his mind. Faintly put out at the time to think that she and Janey had been discussing his imperfect love life, it had nevertheless struck a semi-painful chord. Maybe he should be making more of an effort. All he had to do, after all, was say yes.

'OK,' he said, before she started to wonder if he had hung up. 'Dinner sounds good. Where would you like to go?'

Bed, thought Valentina with a triumphant smile. But even she wasn't that blatant.

'The Ivy,' she replied. 'Nine o'clock sharp. I'll meet you outside.'

'I'd better give them a ring first.' Reaching across the bed, Guy picked up the phone directory. 'They may be fully booked.'

'Don't worry.' Valentina laughed, because she was practically their resident tourist attraction. 'They always find room, for me.'

Heads turned when Valentina di Angelo entered the restaurant. Heralded all over the world as the new Audrey Hepburn, she took the expression 'gamine' to its limits. Despite having been born and raised in Tooting, her southern Italian parentage clearly showed; skilfully cropped black hair framed an immaculate, olive-skinned face, conker-brown eyes three times bigger than Bambi's and possibly the most sensual red mouth on the planet. Around her long, impossibly slender neck she wore a narrow satin choker, a Valentina trademark copied by teenagers everywhere. And if anyone had ever thought it was impossible to look fabulous in a pink leather jacket, lime green Lycra cycling shorts and red trainers, Valentina proved otherwise.

She looked positively angelic, thought Guy, despite the bizarre, Mimi-esque outfit. Everyone else in the room was covertly watching her. He only hoped she didn't take it into her head to object and start creating her usual mayhem.

But Valentina was in high spirits. She was hungry, too. Over a dinner of watercress soup, lamb cutlets and sinfully rich chocolate pudding she set out to prove to Guy Cassidy just how much of a perfect partner she could be. The sense of distance she had noted last week was still there, but it was definitely lessening. Another bottle of Chablis, she felt, could well be all that was needed to do the trick.

'So how old are your kids?' she asked, resting her chin in her cupped palm and fixing him with her liquid brown eyes. When a man looked this good in a plain white linen shirt and dark blue chinos the prospect of checking out the body underneath was positively enthralling. 'It's a boy and a girl, isn't it? Have you got any photos I can see?'

'Josh is nine. Ella's nearly eight. And photographs of other people's children are boring.' Guy, who had a couple in his wallet, kept them there.

'Don't be so defensive,' Valentina scolded, almost disappearing under the table as she reached for her bag. After rummaging energetically, she pulled out a battered leather wallet of her own. 'Come along now, don't be shy. I'll show you mine if you show me yours.'

He smiled. 'You don't have any children.'

'Ah, but I do have an extremely fertile family. Two brothers, three sisters, five nephews and eleven nieces. So grit your teeth,' said Valentina happily, 'and prepare to be bored out of your skull.'

'Tell me if it's none of my business,' she said twenty

minutes later, 'but wasn't it weird being with Serena, knowing how much she hated kids?'

The fact that there was no love lost between Serena and Valentina was no secret. Guy, however, had no intention of providing additional fuel for gossips. There had been enough speculation already about the ending of his affair with Serena.

'She doesn't hate kids,' he replied easily. 'She just doesn't swoon over the idea of them.'

Idly, Valentina swirled her spoon through the double cream and chocolate sauce on her plate. 'How can anyone not love children?' Then, observing the expression on Guy's face – the distance was returning – she shook her head and grinned. 'I suppose you get this kind of thing all the time. Eager women dying to get their claws into you, banging on about how much they adore kids because they think it'll make you like them more.'

'Pretty close.' He found her perception and honesty appealing. 'Do you always say what you think?'

'Oh, always!' This time her eyes glittered with amusement. She had a tiny smudge of chocolate on her lower lip. Instinctively he reached across the wiped the smudge away with his thumb. Smiling, Valentina kissed it. 'There, I did warn you. Say what I think, do what I want. That's my motto.'

According to Maxine and Janey, he needed a woman in his life. They hadn't had much time for Serena; maybe Valentina would meet with their approval. Guy was entertained by the idea of parading her before them like a prospective champion at Crufts. At least she was about as far removed from Serena as it was possible to be.

'And what do you want?' he said, entering into the spirit of the game. Beneath the table Valentina had slipped off her trainers. One bare foot was now lazily caressing his thigh.

'More chocolate pudding,' she answered and the famous smile widened. 'Then you.'

The *paparazzi* were waiting outside on the pavement. The moment Valentina emerged from the restaurant with her pink leather jacket draped casually over her shoulders Italian-style, flashbulbs began exploding like fireworks.

'No pictures. I said no fucking pictures!' she yelled, glaring at them with disdain. 'We're having a private evening out, for God's sake. What are you, a bunch of animals?'

They loved her, of course. She made them a fortune. Seldom did a week go by without Valentina di Angelo featuring centre stage in the celebrity montages of the Sunday supplements. An encounter with Valentina was guaranteed to line their pockets and brighten their day. The public, it went without saying, lapped it all up like cream.

'Come on, Val, give us a smile,' one of them shouted. 'You know you can do it!'

'And you know what you can do,' she retorted, tossing her inch-long black hair.

'How about a quote then?' another ginger-bearded freelancer said hopefully. 'Are you and Guy Cassidy an item?'

'Are your legs breakable?'

'Hey, Guy! What's the idea? Did you take her out for a bet or something?'

Guy simply grinned and said nothing. He was content to leave the insults to the experts.

'Hey, Val. show us what you're hiding under that cheap jacket!' goaded one old hand who knew her well. 'Is it true you've had your tits fixed?'

This was the moment Valentina had been waiting for. This was the man who had started the rumour a fortnight ago, and she was ready for him.

'Why don't you come and take a closer look?' she said sweetly, and the other men grinned. Guy, who knew what was about to happen, took a discreet step to one side.

'Yeeuch, you bitch!' howled the photographer as the bowl of ice cream she had been concealing beneath the folds of the pink leather jacket cascaded down his face and chest. It was particularly splendid ice cream, honey and walnut, but well worth wasting on such a good cause and wonderfully photogenic against a black polo-neck sweater. Serve him right, Valentina thought happily, for being too stupid to tell the difference between plastic surgery and a tissue-packed Wonderbra.

Another volley of flashbulbs exploded, another feature in the tabloids was instantly guaranteed. Having made her mark, Valentina handed the empty bowl to one of the other members of the pack and reached for Guy's arm.

'Come on,' she murmured under her breath, as they moved towards their waiting cab. 'That's the business taken care of. Now for the pleasure . . .'

Chapter 47

'No?' Valentina shrieked, scarcely able to believe what she was hearing. In her agitation, she almost catapulted off the bed. 'No? What the hell do you mean, *no?*'

The realization that he was making a huge mistake had crept up on him even as they made their way up to his hotel room. Having initially fended her off with a drink from the mini-bar, Guy had spent the last fifteen minutes searching for an acceptable way out of the situation he'd so stupidly got himself into. And it was a supremely ironic situation, he couldn't help thinking, because ninety-nine per cent of men would no doubt drool like dogs at the prospect of a night of passion with Valentina di Angelo.

It wasn't even as if she had done anything wrong. Beauty apart, she was funny and honest, great company and altogether about as engaging a person as anyone – *paparazzi* excluded – could wish to meet. But he just couldn't go through with it. For some unfathomable reason, he knew he would be making a terrible mistake.

'I'm sorry.' Guy shook his head, forcing himself to look at her. There was resignation in his dark blue eyes. 'I really am. It's been a great evening, but . . .'

'But what?' wailed Valentina, overcome with a sudden

rush of fear. 'What have I done wrong? What's the problem, for God's sake?' Casting around for a reason . . . *any* reason . . . she said helplessly, 'Am I too fat?'

'Don't be ridiculous.' It was every model's greatest fear. What was worse, he thought with an inward sigh and a glance at her stick-thin legs, was that she really meant it. 'You aren't fat and you haven't done anything wrong. It's me.'

Relief mingled with suspicion. Valentina's fingers continued to clench and unclench against the bedspread. 'What, then? If you're going to try and tell me you're impotent,' she warned, 'I may have a bit of trouble believing you.'

Guy had to smile. If he had been impotent, it would have been so much simpler. She would have felt sorry for him and he would have been off the hook. But 'won't play' was harder for Valentina to bear than 'can't play', and now thanks to him she was feeling sorry for herself.

'No,' he said gently. 'Look, you're a gorgeous girl and I'm probably going to kick myself in the morning, but right now I just know it would be . . . well, the wrong thing to do.'

Valentina didn't. As far as she was concerned it was the most absolutely right thing to do in the entire world. Her brown eyes clouded; what the hell was the big deal anyway, she thought with renewed frustration. It wasn't as if she was asking him to hitch-hike barefoot across bloody Antarctica. It was only sex, after all.

'More like you get a kick out of leading girls on,' she retaliated, still smarting from the humiliation of being rejected for no good reason at all by the most attractive man she'd clapped eyes on in years. And after such a promising start, too.

'It's not that, either.'

'Bastard,' murmured Valentina under her breath.

She wasn't taking it at all well. Guy pushed his fingers through his hair in a gesture of mild despair. 'Look, that's just what I'm trying not to be. If we spent the night together, I'd be a *real* bastard. You see, there's . . . somebody else,' he admitted with reluctance. 'I'm already involved with someone, and it wouldn't be fair to either of you if I . . .'

His voice trailed away. He took a slug of brandy, swallowed and shrugged.

'Oh.'Valentina's fingers began to unclench. A man with a conscience was something of a novelty in her experience. It was just a shame, she thought sorrowfully, he was so intent on being faithful to someone else rather than her. 'Who is it, anyone I know?'

Guy shook his head. As far as he was aware it wasn't anyone at all, but it appeared to be doing the trick, which was all that really mattered. He still didn't understand why the idea of sleeping with Valentina should suddenly have become such an undesirable proposition. It just had. Maybe, he thought with a mixture of resignation and alarm, there really was such a thing as the male menopause and it had arrived a decade ahead of schedule. Damn, what filthy rotten luck. Of all the nights to be hit with it . . .

'Well, she's a lucky girl.' Acknowledging defeat with as much good grace as she could muster, Valentina smiled and reached for her jacket. 'Whoever she is. No, don't worry, I can find my own way out. I'll ask the night porter to get me a cab.'

'I'm sorry,' said Guy, meaning it. Opening the door for her, he planted a brief kiss on her cheek. 'I was tempted, you know. This monogamy thing is pretty new to me.'

'Invite me to the wedding,' Valentina quipped. 'I'll tell her what a hero she's married. After all, I can personally vouch for your fidelity.'

He grinned. 'Thanks.'

But she was still wildly curious. Guy wasn't giving much away. Unable to resist it, she paused in the doorway.

'Is she beautiful?'

'Yes.'

'Is it . . .' – a stab in the dark, now – 'the girl I spoke to on the phone? What's her name, Maxine?'

Guy started to laugh. 'No,' he said, patting her shoulder. 'Nice try, sweetheart. But it definitely isn't Maxine.'

Thea, lying in bed with Oliver's arm around her, was looking pensive.

'What is it?' Pulling the duvet up to her shoulders, for the central heating in Thea's house was about as predictable as Thea herself, he gave her bare shoulder a squeeze. 'Worried about Janey?'

She was, of course, but that wasn't what was uppermost in her mind right now. Indirectly, she thought, the problem was Oliver himself. The trouble with being in love was the fact that it was so time-consuming. Whilst this might not be a problem for

Oliver, who could easily afford to have his time consumed, it was an undoubted drawback when you were a not altogether successful sculptress with work to do and bills to pay. The sale of the Ballerina had temporarily stalled the boring letters from the bank droning on about her overdraft, but the increasing displeasure of Tom Sparks, the owner of the studio, was somewhat more ominous. She was falling behind with the rent in a big way, and he wasn't amused. Sadly, not working meant not selling. And whilst at first it hadn't seemed to matter – how, after all, could financial security even begin to compare with all-consuming happiness? – the prospect of losing her beloved studio was fast becoming a real possibility.

All she had to do, of course, was mention this inconvenient dilemma to Oliver. Without so much as a second thought he would sign the necessary cheque like the proverbial good fairy and make everything right again. As far as he was concerned, there was no dilemma: Thea needed money and he had plenty of it. He would be happy to help out. No big deal.

But there lay the crunch. For it was a big deal. It hadn't been easy, but one way or another she had been self-supporting for the last twenty-five years, and whilst the idea of becoming a kept woman had always appealed, she now realized that some fantasies were better left unfulfilled. Maybe it was a salutary lesson, a kind of punishment for ever having wished it in the first place. Or maybe, she thought dryly, it was just sheer bloody bad luck. Because Oliver Cassidy, erupting into her life, had changed her. Here he was, the proud and generous owner of all that gorgeous money . . . and she loved him too much to take it.

It was no good, Thea decided, she was simply going to have to *make* time to work. If necessary – ugh, what a hideous prospect – she would even get up a couple of hours earlier each morning and sculpt whilst Oliver slept.

'Yes,' she lied, dragging her mind back to that other dilemma: Janey. Propping herself up on one elbow, she sighed. 'I ballsed it up completely. I should have tackled Alan on his own, of course. She was bound to take his side.'

Oliver kissed her warm shoulder. It was ironic, he felt, that they should both have been through virtually the same ordeal. In his own case, however, Véronique's untimely death had effectively prevented him from ever being able to be proved right.

'Of course she was,' he said consolingly. 'I know how hard it is; we do our best for our children, God knows, but sometimes they have to make their own mistakes. Give her time, darling, and maybe she'll come to her senses.'

'I bloody hope so.' Thea's tone was fretful; she still nurtured a fearsome longing to corner Alan Sinclair and slap him senseless. 'But how much longer is she going to need and how much more damage can he do in the meantime? Janey's so stubborn it almost frightens me,' she added, her tone bleak. 'I wouldn't put it past her to get herself pregnant, just to spite us all.'

Chapter 48

Janey was looking wonderful, thought Bruno, watching from a distant corner as she entered the party on Alan Sinclair's arm. In a billowing white silk shirt tucked into white jeans, and with her blond hair left loose to fall past her shoulders, she exuded an air of careless glamour he had never seen in her before. The self-esteem which had been at rock-bottom for the past two years had clearly been revitalized by her husband's return, he decided, impressed by the almost magical transformation. It was as if she had been brought back to life, like a desperately wilted flower plunged into a bucket of water in the nick of time.

Hastily, Bruno pulled himself together. What was the matter with him anyway? Nauseating similes weren't his bag at all. Talk about un-macho . . .

Janey looked good because she was happy and in love, he decided, firmly banishing all thought of wilting flowers from his mind. It was as simple as that. Whether she would deign to speak to him when she realized he was here, however, was another matter altogether.

In the event, Janey didn't have a lot of choice. Having resolutely decided to ignore Bruno her plans were scuppered within minutes by Pearl, who dragged him into the kitchen. Janey, leaning against the fridge, was still waiting for Alan to uncork a bottle of Australian white. Gazing at a heavily doodled-on Chippendales calendar above the cooker, she assumed a fixed, I'm-not-listening expression. But the kitchen wasn't that big and nobody had ever called Pearl subtle.

'. . . I still don't believe you, darling!' she cried, clinging to Bruno's arm and waggling an admonitory finger at him. 'It's all very well saying you've fallen madly in love with this Maxine character, but does this mean you're actually planning to stay faithful to her, forsaking all others and all that gloomy stuff? You realize of course the whole town's laying bets on how long you'll manage to stick it out,' she added gleefully. 'So far nobody's dared risk their money on anything more than a month.'

Behind her, Alan glanced across at Janey. Eyebrows raised, he mouthed, 'Maxine?'

Nodding, she forced herself to smile as Bruno turned to face her. If she didn't, Alan would wonder why.

'Oh, I'm a reformed character.' Bruno grinned. 'It can happen, you know, even to me. Although if the odds are that good, maybe I should think about placing a bet myself.'

'So you're Bruno.' Stepping forward, Alan shook his hand. 'Hi, I'm Alan Sinclair, Maxine's brother-in-law. I've been hearing quite a bit about you.'

'That's a coincidence,' said Bruno easily. 'I've heard about you too.'

Pearl, who had been drinking double tequila slammers to celebrate the success of her party, was in high spirits.

Bruno was the greatest fun; she loved him to death. And although she hadn't actually been introduced to Alan Sinclair before, he had been one of the crowd at the surf club when she'd popped in and issued an open invitation to tonight's bash. The fact that he was deeply attractive hadn't escaped her notice at the time, either. It was just a shame, Pearl thought, that he should have chosen to turn up with a sleek blond girlfriend in tow.

'Everyone's heard about Bruno,' she told Alan with a giggle. 'Maybe I shouldn't be saying this if you're related to Maxine, but it's my party so what the hell! This man is wicked. Gorgeous,' she admitted, clinging to Bruno's arm and giving it an affectionate squeeze, 'but seriously wicked . . . possibly the wickedest man in all Cornwall.'

Janey cringed. She still couldn't believe she'd never heard so much as a single word of gossip about Bruno before getting involved with him herself. As far as everyone else was concerned, she thought bitterly, his conquests were practically the stuff of legend. And Pearl, whom she'd never met before in her life, was moving perilously close to the knuckle . . .

'You are looking at a seducer *extraordinaire*,' she continued, blithely unaware of Janey's unease. 'He's been doing it for years, you know. None of us can figure out how he manages to keep on getting away with it.'

'Thank you,' said Bruno with mock gravity. Janey, standing behind Alan, was looking positively stricken. Feeling sorry for her, he attempted to steer the conversation on to safer ground. 'But that was in the bad old days. From now on I'm a changed man, I promise you. How's your father, by the way? Has he managed to sell that yacht of his yet?'

But Pearl hadn't finished. Yachts were boring. The idea that Bruno Parry-Brent had turned over a new leaf, on the other hand, was simply too entertaining for words.

'In the bad old days!' she shrieked, gurgling with laughter and only narrowly missing the sleeve of Alan's faded denim shirt as tequila sloshed haphazardly out of her tilted glass. 'How long ago was your birthday, you old fraud? I might have missed the party but Suzannah told me all about it. She said you had the most terrific showdown with some poor girl you'd been seeing on the quiet until she found out what you were really like. Who did Suzie say she was, now?' She hiccuped, tried to think, and shook her head. 'No, I give up. Come on Bruno, remind me! I can't remember her name, but apparently she runs the flower shop in the high street . . .'

'Oh for goodness sake, will you stop going on about it.' Janey, stepping out of her clothes, left them in a heap on the bedroom floor. As she made her way through to the bathroom she added crossly, 'It was embarrassing for me too, you know.'

'I should think it was.' Alan's eyes were narrow with anger. 'You must be the laughing stock of Trezale . . . and you expect me to forgive you, just like that? Jesus, you aren't making it easy for me! You told me there hadn't been anyone else and I was stupid enough to believe you. Now I find out you've not only been screwing another man' – he spat the words out in disgust – 'but you had to make a complete fool of yourself and choose the town fucking stud.'

Not trusting herself to speak, Janey slammed the bathroom door and cleaned her teeth so hard her gums bled. Finally, taking a deep breath, she returned to the bedroom.

'Look,' she said, eyes ablaze with defiance, 'I wish it hadn't happened, but it did. And I'm not going to apologize. I said there hadn't been anyone else because that was what you wanted to hear, but what the hell did you seriously expect me to do . . . lock myself into a chastity belt and become a born-again virgin for the rest of my life? Be realistic,' she snapped, no longer caring what he thought. 'You were the one who left, for God's sake. And if sleeping with Bruno makes me the laughing stock of Trezale, so what? I'm used to it. People have been talking about me behind my back for the last two years, ever since my husband vanished off the face of the bloody earth. So if it's an apology you're waiting for,' she went on, 'you can forget it, because I've only slept with one man in two whole years . . . and that's not bad. If I'd known I was going to get this kind of grief,' Janey concluded bitterly, 'I would have slept with fifty.'

The ensuing silence seemed to go on for ever. Alan, sitting up in bed, stared at her. Finally he said, 'You've changed.'

It was late and Janey was tired but she didn't want to climb into the bed beside him. Leaning against the wall, she replied, 'I had to. When you're on your own you have to learn to look after yourself.'

Alan shook his head. 'And it's all my fault. I'm sorry,

409

sweetheart, I can't help it. It was the shock of finding out like that; I felt so damn jealous. Janey, come here. Please?'

He was holding his arms out to her. To her shame it was physical exhaustion rather than the prospect of reconciliation that propelled her towards the bed. Wearily, she submitted to his embrace.

'It's bound to take a while,' Alan murmured into her hair, 'getting used to being together again.'

'Mmm.'

'What are you doing?' He frowned as she adjusted the pillows and rolled on to her side, facing away from him.

Janey closed her eyes. 'Going to sleep.'

Chapter 49

'Oh no, not you.' Sighing, Maxine wished now that she'd ignored the doorbell. 'I nearly got the sack last time you played this trick.'

Oliver Cassidy smiled. 'I'm sorry.'

'I should bloody well hope so,' she countered with indignation. 'Guy was furious with me. I was lucky to escape in one piece. And you were pretty lucky yourself,' she added. 'He was all for calling out the police. You could have been charged with kidnapping.'

She looked like her mother, Oliver realized. And although she was giving a good impression of a woman deeply outraged, he guessed it was more for effect than anything else.

'I could,' he admitted, his eyes crinkling at the corners as his smile broadened, 'but it wouldn't have been exactly fair, would it? Kidnappers have a tendency to demand ransoms. I gave Josh and Ella money.'

'You almost gave me a heart attack,' grumbled Maxine, shivering as a gust of wind rattled round the porch. Her bare feet on the stone step were icy. 'You shouldn't have lied to me, it was a rotten thing to do.'

'Growing old and never being allowed to see your

grandchildren is pretty rotten too.' Oliver, well wrapped up against the cold, in a beige cashmere overcoat, also shivered. 'Sometimes, desperate measures are called for. Maxine, I really am sorry you had to bear the brunt of my son's anger, but . . . goodness, this wind is bitter, isn't it?'

Maxine, standing her ground, forced herself not to smile. 'I expect it's nice and warm though, inside your car.'

'Go on,' said Oliver. 'Live a little. If you invite me in for a quick cup of coffee we can both relax. Guy's away, Josh and Ella are still at school; nobody need ever know I've been here.'

'What are you, the king of the door-to-door salesmen?' Maxine started to laugh. 'OK, you can come in. Just don't try and sell me any floor mops.'

'. . . So you see, Guy never forgave me for speaking my mind,' Oliver concluded fifteen minutes later. 'I felt he was too young to be married, that he was making a huge mistake, but he was too stubborn to take my advice. When Josh and Ella are grown up and he finds himself faced with the same problems, maybe he'll understand I had only his best interests at heart.' He shrugged and pushed his empty cup to one side. 'But by then it'll be too late, of course. I'll be dead.'

Maxine was well able to understand how he felt. Hadn't Thea reacted in exactly the same way upon hearing that Janey's decidedly unprodigal husband had breezed back into Trezale? And hadn't Janey reacted just as Guy had done, refusing to accept for even a single moment that her mother's opinion of him might be right?

'You might not be dead,' she ventured, struggling to say something reassuring. 'Look, I do sympathize but you must realize I'm in an impossible position here. I can't help you. And if you think I can persuade Guy to see reason, well . . . I'd have about as much chance of getting him to believe in Father Christmas.'

'I want to see my grandchildren again,' said Oliver Cassidy.

'No.'

He was no longer smiling. The expression in his eyes, she realized, was one of ineffable sadness.

'Maxine, listen to me.' Speaking without emotion, he leaned back in his chair and rested his clasped hands on the kitchen table. 'By the time Josh and Ella are grown up, I will certainly be dead. If my doctor is to be believed, I'll be dead by Christmas. I don't believe him of course – he's a notorious scaremonger – but I have to accept that there may be something in what he says. Maybe next year people can cross me off their Christmas card list but not this year.' He paused, then shrugged. 'Anyway, let's not get maudlin. I'm only telling you this because I need you to understand why I'm so anxious to see my grandchildren again.' Fixing his steady gaze upon her, he added, 'And why I need you to help me.'

'Oh hell.' Maxine shook her head in despair. 'Now I do wish you were a door-to-door salesman. Then I'd be able to say no.'

Josh and Ella were safely tucked up in bed by the time Bruno arrived at Trezale House. Since Maxine's idea of a romantic dinner *à deux* was spaghetti hoops on toast, he had brought the ingredients for a decent meal with him. Whilst he busied himself in the kitchen, slicing onions and mushrooms for the stroganoff, she sat happily drinking lager and relaying to him the events of the afternoon.

'Yeeuk! What are you doing?' she screeched as Bruno, having listened in silence for a good ten minutes, abandoned washing the leeks in order to cup wet, cold hands over her ears.

'The rest of your brain,' he explained carefully. 'I thought maybe we should save it. These medical experts can do wonders nowadays . . . if you're lucky they might be able to slide some of it back in.'

'Ha ha, very funny.' Unabashed, Maxine wriggled out of reach. 'OK, so when Guy finds out he'll have me hung, drawn and quartered, but wouldn't anyone else in my position have done the same?'

'You still don't get it, do you?' Standing back, gazing down at her with a mixture of amusement and disbelief, Bruno drawled, 'You really are full of surprises, my angel. How can anyone so smart be so incredibly dumb? How could you – of all people – fall for a line like that?'

'Like what?' The tiniest of frown lines bisected her eyebrows. Confusion registered in her dark brown eyes. 'What are you talking about?'

'And you told me Janey was the gullible one.' He couldn't resist it. The fact that razor-sharp Maxine had a hitherto unsuspected weak spot was totally, blissfully endearing. She was, he thought with a triumphant grin, never going to live this down.

'Oh come on,' she protested, as realization finally dawned. 'Bruno, no! That's sick.'

'*Maxine, yes!*' Mimicking her outraged tone, he stepped smartly back to avoid a kick on the shin. 'Look, I might not have met the man but you've already told me what he's like. What did Guy say – his father was a ruthless businessman who'd stop at nothing to get what he wanted? If he wants to see his grandchildren and you're telling him he can't, then he's going to have to come up with something spectacular to make you change your mind. What could be simpler than the old imminent-death routine? It might not be terribly original, but it usually does the trick. And it worked, didn't it?' he concluded with a cheerful I-told-you-so grin. 'My poor darling, you'd better dig out that bulletproof vest and superglue yourself into it. There's no telling how Guy Cassidy's going to react when he finds out what you've done this time.'

'Oh shit!' wailed Maxine, appalled. What she'd done this time had undoubtedly cost her her job. Travelling with Oliver Cassidy in the unimaginable luxury of his silver-grey Rolls, she had longed to ask more questions about the illness which was soon to rob him of his life. But she hadn't, for fear of appearing nosey and because it simply wasn't the kind of thing you discussed with a virtual stranger. Instead they had talked abut Josh and Ella; her soon-to-be-screened toilet-roll commercial; the wild beauty of the Cornish coastline; the stupid, sodding totally uninteresting weather . . .

Josh and Ella had been thrilled, of course, to see their grandfather waiting at the school gates. Maxine, quite choked by the poignancy of the situation, had almost been forced to blink back tears. How could anyone with even half a heart, she thought, possibly deny a dying man the chance of a last meeting with his only grandchildren?

They had returned to Trezale House to spend four blissfully happy hours together. Oliver Cassidy had even professed to adore the fish fingers and alphabetti spaghetti she'd served up, although he hadn't been able to eat a great deal of it. At the time, she had assumed his lack of appetite must be connected with the illness.

And at eight o'clock in the evening he had left. With heartbreaking innocence Ella had cried, 'Will we see you again soon, Grandpa?' and Maxine, a lump in her throat the size of an egg, had turned away. Josh, handling yet another fifty-pound note with due reverence, had said, 'When I buy my computer, Grandpa, I'll teach you to play Pokémon. If you practise long enough you might even get as good as me.'

'Maxine, how can I ever thank you?' Oliver Cassidy had smiled and rested his hand on her shoulder as she walked with him to the front door. Tilting his grey head, planting a brief, infinitely gentle kiss on her cheek, he added quietly, 'You're a very special girl and I'm truly grateful. You'll never know how much this afternoon has meant to me.'

And the fact that Guy was bound to find out what had happened – because with the best will in the world Ella was too young to keep a secret for anything exceeding fifteen seconds – didn't bother Maxine in the least. She knew she'd done the right thing, and furthermore she was going to tell him about his father's fatal illness. Surely, she thought as she stood on the step and watched Oliver Cassidy disappear down the drive in his Rolls, surely even Guy would be jolted into remorse when he learned the truth.

'Oh shit,' said Maxine again, as the irony of the situation struck her. For the last eight hours she had thought over and over again how desperately unfair it was that such a charming man should have to die. Now, riddled with self-doubt and the growing fear that maybe, after all, she had been conned in the most underhand manner possible, she found herself almost hoping he would. At least then, she thought fretfully, she'd be proved right.

On the way to school a week later, Maxine – hardly daring to raise the subject for fear of breaking some miraculous spell – turned to Josh and Ella and said in ultra-casual tones, 'You didn't tell Guy about your grandfather's visit, did you?'

It was a statement rather than a question. Maxine knew they couldn't have told him. She was still alive.

Behind her, Ella promptly erupted into fits of giggles. Josh, in the passenger seat, looked immensely proud. 'No.'

'Why not?'

He shook his head. 'It's a secret.'

'Oh come on, you can tell me,' said Maxine.

Emma mimed zipping her mouth shut. 'We can't tell anybody. It's an even bigger secret than the one about you smashing Daddy's car into the gatepost.'

'Look, I'm glad it's a big secret,' Maxine explained patiently. 'But I should be in on it. I was there, wasn't I?'

Josh considered this argument for a moment. After exchanging glances with Ella, he said, earnestly, 'OK, but you mustn't tell anyone else. Swear you won't, Maxine.'

'Bum,' said Maxine, and Ella giggled again. It was her favourite word.

'Grandpa said it had to be a secret,' Josh explained, 'because if we ever told anyone else, you'd get the sack and we'd never see you again for the rest of our lives.'

'Oh.' Overcome with emotion, Maxine's eyes abruptly filled with tears. Thankfully, they had by this time reached the school so she didn't risk killing them all.

'Well, it's nice to be appreciated,' she said gruffly, curbing the urge to fling her arms around them and smother them in noisy kisses. If she did that in front of their schoolfriends, Josh would certainly die of shame. She cleared her throat instead and attempted to turn the situation into a joke. 'So that must mean you like me a little bit, then?'

'I do,' Ella declared lovingly. 'And Josh was glad too.'

Maxine smiled. 'Was he, sweetheart?'

'Ella,' Josh murmured, his expression furtive.

But the sheer relief of having finally been allowed to break the silence proved too much for Ella. Having extricated herself from her safety belt she climbed forward between the front seats and adopted a noisy stage-whisper. 'Because Grandpa gave us extra money for not saying anything,' she confided, blue eyes shining. 'Lots of money you didn't even know about, but if we told the secret to anyone . . . except you, now . . . we'd have to give it all back.'

'Oh.' So much for thinking she'd been the one they couldn't bear to lose, thought Maxine. Mercenary little sods.

'Josh is going to buy a computer.' Ella's nose wrinkled in evident disgust. 'Ugh, computers are stupid. I don't want one!'

'That's because you're a girl,' he sneered. 'You want a stupid horse.'

Ella pushed him, then turned to Maxine, her smile angelic. 'A real, live horse,' she said happily. 'Called Bum.'

Chapter 50

Janey, lying in the bath, told herself she was being stupid. She was a mature adult, after all, not a child for whom a birthday was a real landmark. The importance of birthdays worked according to a sliding scale; as you grew older, their significance decreased. Heavens, it was almost fashionable to forget your own birthday . . .

It was downright depressing, on the other hand, if everyone else forgot it too.

But she had dug herself into a hole from which, it now seemed, there was no face-saving escape, because her birthday was tomorrow and to mention it casually in passing at this late stage would be too humiliating for words. The trouble was, Janey thought with a pang of regret, she hadn't bothered earlier because she'd stupidly assumed everyone else would remember.

She was still in the bath when the telephone rang. Seconds later, Alan opened the bathroom door.

'Phone, sweetheart. It's Maxine.'

Superstition told Janey that if she climbed out of the water and went to answer it, Maxine wouldn't have remembered her birthday. If she stayed where she was, on the other hand, it might suddenly click.

'Ask her what she wants.' Slowly and deliberately she began to soap her shoulders. 'Take a message, or say I'll call back.'

He reappeared after a couple of minutes. 'She asked if you could babysit tomorrow evening. Guy had already said she could take a couple of days off and she and Bruno have arranged to go up to London,' he recited. 'But now Guy has to be somewhere tomorrow night, so he wonders if you wouldn't mind doing the honours. He says he'll definitely be home by midnight.'

So much for superstition. Wearily, Janey nodded. 'OK. I'll call her back in a minute.'

'No need.' He sounded pleased with himself. 'I've already told her you'll do it. She says can you be there by seven-thirty.'

Janey stared at him. 'Well, thanks.'

'What?' Alan looked surprised. 'I knew you'd say yes. All I did was say it for you. Why, have you made other plans?'

'No.' She closed her eyes. 'No other plans.'

'There you are then,' he chided, tickling the soles of her feet. 'Stroppy.'

Janey forced herself to smile. It was only a birthday after all. Not such a big deal.

'How about you? Are you doing anything tomorrow night?'

'Ah well, I was planning a quiet romantic evening at home with my gorgeous wife.' He rolled his eyes in soulful fashion. 'Just the two of us . . .'

'You could always come and help me babysit.'

'. . . but since you won't be here,' Alan concluded

cheerfully, 'I may as well meet the lads for a drink at the surf club.'

Janey, curled up on the sofa with a can of lager and a packet of Maltesers, was so engrossed in the book she was reading she didn't even hear the car pull up outside. When Guy opened the sitting-room door she jumped a mile, scattering Maltesers in all directions.

'Sorry.' He grinned and bent to help her pick them up. 'So which is scariest, me or the book?'

'You said you'd be back at midnight.' Still breathless, Janey glanced up at the clock. 'It's only half past nine. Oh no,' she said accusingly, 'you haven't walked out on her again. Tell me you didn't dump her at the hotel . . .'

When Charlotte had phoned Guy the night before and begged him to partner her at the firm's annual dinner, he had made strenuous efforts to get out of it. But Charlotte had been truly desperate. Everyone else was taking someone, she explained, evidently frantic, and she'd been let down at the last minute by her own partner who'd thoughtlessly contracted salmonella poisoning. 'Oh please Guy, I can't possibly go on my own,' she had wailed down the phone at him. 'It's not as if I'm asking you to sleep with me; I know it's over between us, but just this one last favour? Pleeease?'

He hadn't had the heart to refuse. But fate – for the first time in what seemed like years – appeared to be on his side. Within minutes of arriving at the hotel, Charlotte had disappeared to the loo. Finally emerging half an hour later, pale and obviously unwell, she clung to Guy's arm and groaned pitifully, 'Oh God, I think I'm going to have to go home. Tonight of all nights, as well. Bloody chicken biryani. *Sodding* salmonella.'

Guy, hiding his relief, had said goodbye to all the people he hadn't even had time to be introduced to, helped Charlotte out to the car and driven her home. Mortified at the prospect of throwing up in front of him, she had vehemently refused his offer to stay for a while and make sure she was all right. Food poisoning was a singularly unglamorous illness and all she wanted was to be left alone.

'Oh poor Charlotte!' Janey tried hard not to laugh at the expression on Guy's face. 'She doesn't have much luck, does she?'

'Every cloud,' he replied with an unrepentant grin. 'I didn't even have to give her a goodnight kiss.'

Janey looked at her watch; it was still only twenty to ten. Now that Guy was here, she supposed she could go home too. But Alan wouldn't be there, and the prospect of sitting alone in the flat on her birthday was infinitely depressing.

Sensing her hesitation, Guy said, 'Do you have to get back straight away?'

'Well, no.'

'Good. I'll open a bottle.'

When he had finished pouring the wine, he picked up the paperback Janey had been so wrapped up in. 'Hmm, so I was right. No wonder you nearly jumped out of your skin, reading horror stories like this.'

She laughed. 'I found it buried under a pile of comics in your downstairs loo. You should give it a try; it's actually very well written. I was really enjoying it.'

'As if Mimi didn't have enough fans.' With a shudder he dropped the book into her open handbag. 'Take it home with you. She always sends me a copy of her latest best-seller, though God knows why. The covers alone are enough to give me a headache.'

'You're such a chauvinist,' said Janey cheerfully. 'I like them.'

'You shouldn't need them.' Guy's expression was severe. 'Alan's back; you've got your own happy ending now.'

Janey fiddled with a loose thread on the sleeve of her pastel pink cotton sweater. 'Mmm.'

Guy decided to chance it. Very casually he said, 'Although I suppose it can't be easy. Two years is a long time. Getting used to living together again must take a while.'

She hadn't breathed so much as a word to anyone about the difficulties they'd been having. She'd barely been able to admit them to herself, Janey realized. But there were only so many excuses you could make on someone else's behalf. Alan was charming, funny and affectionate. But the flipside was beginning to get to her. Despite having been back for over a month now, he had made no real effort to find work. The amounts of money he borrowed from her in order to 'tide him over' were only small, but with no way of repaying them they soon mounted up. Janey, watching her own bank balance dwindle, was at the same time having to spend twice as much as usual on groceries, whilst Alan appeared to spend his money buying drinks for all his old friends down at the surf club.

'No, it isn't easy.' Janey attempted to sound matter of fact about it. There was no way in the world she would admit the true extent of her problems to Guy, but she was tired of pretending everything was perfect.

'I expect it's me,' she went on, taking fast, jerky sips of wine. 'When you've lived alone for a while you become selfish. It's always the silly things, isn't it? Like suddenly having to make sure there's food in the house; remembering not to use all the hot water; the toilet seat always being up when you want it down.'

'Tell me about it,' Guy raised an eyebrow. 'I share my home with Maxine. She might not leave the toilet seat up, but she drives me insane. You can't move in that bathroom for cans of industrial-strength hair spray. At the last count there were eleven different bottles of shampoo up there, and she leaves great blobs of hair mousse all over the carpet.' He shook his head in despair. 'It's like walking through a field of puffball mushrooms.'

'Why do you suppose I sent her up here to work for you?' Janey laughed. 'I've been through that mushroom field. I was desperate.'

She was starting to relax. Even more casually, Guy said, 'But at least Maxine and I aren't married.'

Janey looked uncomfortable. 'No.'

'Look.' Taking a deep breath, he decided to risk it. 'I'm on your side, Janey. Maybe this is none of my business but I can't help feeling there's more to it than hot water and toilet seats. Alan was away for two years. You've both changed. There are bound to be problems. Just because he's come back, you aren't automatically obliged to be happy.' He paused for a second, his eyes serious. 'These things don't always work out. There's no shame in that. Nobody would blame you.'

Janey bit her lip. What he said made so much sense, but she still couldn't bring herself to admit quite how torn she felt. Alan loved and needed her, after all. How on earth would it affect him if she were suddenly to announce that she had changed her mind?

Feeling horribly disloyal just thinking about it, she willed herself to remain calm. She wasn't going to pour her heart out to Guy; he'd suffered quite enough of that after the Bruno fiasco. He might be on her side, she thought, but she still had some pride. She didn't want him to think she was a completely hopeless case.

'We're fine,' Janey assured him, as convincingly as she knew how. She smiled. 'Really. I was just having a bit of a moan, that's all.'

Shit, thought Guy, not believing her for a second. He'd blown it. And he had thought he'd been doing so well.

'Shit!' Maxine yelled practically simultaneously, in London.

Bruno gave the maître d' an apologetic grin and hoped he wouldn't change his mind about giving them the last table in the restaurant.

'She's from Iceland,' he confided. 'Doesn't speak a word of English. I think she's saying "hello".'

But Maxine, staring at the reservation diary lying open on the desk before them, was too appalled to enter into the spirit of the game.

'It's the fifteenth,' she groaned. 'Oh hell, I can't believe it's really the fifteenth!'

Of November, thought Bruno, following her gaze. Big deal. Unless she'd suddenly realized her period was late, in which case it would definitely be a big deal . . .

'Quick, I need a phone!' Maxine launched herself across the mahogany desk. 'Can I use this one?'

But the maître d', who had quick reflexes, had already clamped his hand firmly over the phone. The last time someone had tried that trick, they'd called their mother in South America. 'This one is reserved for table bookings, madam. We have a pay phone for customers at the far end of the bar.'

'What is it?' Bruno demanded, as Maxine rifled his pockets for change. To his alarm, there were tears glistening in her eyes.

'That bastard,' she seethed. 'I asked him what she was doing tonight and he told me she didn't have any plans. 'I suppose *he's* gone out . . .'

'Who?'

'Bloody Alan bloody Sinclair.' The words dripped with contempt. 'Who else?'

Bruno raised his eyebrows. 'Why, what's he done now?'

'Oh, nothing much,' snapped Maxine. 'At least, not by his standards. It's only Janey's birthday, after all.'

Chapter 51

Right, that's it, thought Guy.

Janey, watching him replace the receiver, was unnerved by his grim expression.

'Bad news?'

He nodded. 'Very bad news.'

'Oh no.' Her heart lurched. 'What is it?'

'It's November the fifteenth,' Guy replied slowly. 'Your birthday. Don't tell me you'd forgotten too.'

'The nerve of that man,' cried Maxine, flushed with annoyance. 'He wouldn't even let me speak to her!'

Bruno frowned. 'Alan? Why not?'

She looked at him as if he was being deliberately obtuse. 'Not Alan, stupid. Guy. She's babysitting up at the house. I thought he'd be out, but he's back.'

By this time thoroughly confused and too hungry to care much anyway, Bruno had begun studying the menu. But Maxine was still muttering to herself, twirling her hair round her fingers in a frenzy of indignation. He sighed. 'OK, so why wouldn't Guy let you speak to her?'

'I don't know, do I?' She glared at him across the table. 'He told me to leave everything to him; he'd deal with it.

428

What the bloody hell is that supposed to mean?'

'I'd have thought it was pretty obvious.' Bruno grinned. 'He's going to make sure Janey's birthday goes with a bang.'

'I know it's my birthday.' Janey felt unaccountably nervous. 'Who was that on the phone? Is that the very bad news, or is there something else?'

'It was Maxine, ringing from a call box.' Guy bent to refill their glasses. 'She's mortified at having forgotten, but she sends her love and says she'll bring you back a mega-stupendous present. Her words,' he said dryly. 'I wouldn't get your hopes up if I were you. She bought Josh a mega-stupendous present the other week; it turned out to be a bouncing rubber brain. When you throw it against the wall,' he added with a look of resignation, 'it screams *Ouch.*'

'I could probably do with one of those.' Janey smiled. 'So that's really the bad news, Maxine forgetting my birthday?'

But the humour had vanished from his eyes once more. Really, she thought, he was incredibly hard to keep up with.

'No,' said Guy. 'The bad news is Alan forgetting your birthday.'

Janey, opening her mouth to protest, had no chance.

'Don't even say it,' Guy warned. 'For God's sake, Janey! Why do you always have to defend him? The way he's treated you is sickening enough, but not even being able to remember your birthday – this year of all years – is downright despicable!'

'Lots of husbands forget their wives' birthdays.' She couldn't help it; now he was being unfair. 'Thousands do, all the time. It's practically a condition of marriage.' Janey realized she was shaking.

Guy's dark eyes, glittering with derision, bored into her. 'Don't be such a coward,' he drawled unpleasantly. 'Stop covering up for him. Why can't you just admit the fact that he's a selfish bastard and he's making you miserable? Why don't you give yourself a rest, Janey, say what you really think and stop being so fucking *nice*?'

This was too much. Something snapped inside her. Guy, launching into a totally unprovoked attack, was somehow managing to make her feel she was the one at fault.

'How dare you!' The words came tumbling out of her mouth but it was as if someone else was saying them for her. 'How dare you try and heap the blame on me? If you want to know what I really think, it's that you're just as much of a bastard as my husband!' She was trembling violently but the voice doing the talking didn't falter. 'OK, if you want the dirt I'll give it to you. It isn't working out because he's a selfish, idle sponger who expects me to do everything for him because that's how it used to be, and he doesn't see why it should be any different now. He's using me . . . taking advantage of me. I know he's doing it. I hate him doing it, but I don't have any choice!'

Janey paused, gulping for breath, panting as if she'd just run a marathon. But he had goaded her into this exorcism and now it was all spilling out. Her chest hurt, her throat ached and her fingernails were biting into her palms like fish hooks. But she had almost finished and she was going to force him to understand the kind of hell she'd been through if it killed her.

'I don't have any choice.' She repeated the words in a low voice. 'Because Alan needs me. I'm afraid of what he might do if I tell him it's over. I don't think he could handle it. He's dropped hints, and they scare me witless. I really believe he would harm himself: how can I possibly afford to take that risk? How could I ever live with myself if I called his bluff and he did commit suicide?' She shook her head and shuddered helplessly at the mere mention of the word. 'It would be on my conscience for the rest of my life. It would be my fault. I'd be the one who had killed him.'

'Oh Janey,' Guy gave her a ghost of a smile. 'I'm sorry I shouted at you. Do you understand now why I had to do it?'

He had been goading her deliberately, of course; forcing her to lose her temper with him and spill it all out. With a weary nod, she said, 'I understand, but it isn't as if there's anything you can do to help. You knowing about my problems isn't going to make them go away.'

'Well,' persisted Guy, 'do you at least feel better?'

'I don't know.' It was a lie. She did feel better, Janey realized, but how long was that likely to last? She would probably wake up tomorrow morning and kick herself. Ungraciously, she said, 'I suppose you do, now you've weaseled that little confession out of me. At least your curiosity's been satisfied.'

'Don't be bitchy.'

'*Don't be bitchy*?' Echoing the words, she mimed frustration. 'Five minutes ago you told me to stop being so fucking nice. You really do know how to shower a girl with compliments, Guy.'

He grinned, because there weren't many people on the planet less adept at handling a compliment than Janey. When he'd once tried admiring her new trousers she had replied, 'At least they hide my legs.' When on another occasion he had said her hair looked nice, she'd promptly told him it needed cutting. If he displayed appreciation of her chicken casserole she invariably shook her head and said either, 'Too much tarragon,' or 'Not enough salt.'

If he thought for one minute it would help, Guy told himself, he would shower her with compliments. He would tell her she was beautiful, that she had stunning legs, wondrous eyes, a deeply kissable mouth . . .

He could also tell her that the prospect of spending the night with Valentina di Angelo had left him utterly cold, whereas the thought of spending the night with Janey Sinclair was infinitely desirable.

Guy smiled, because at least he could stop worrying about the male menopause. He also, finally, understood why he hadn't wanted to sleep with Valentina. It was *because* he wanted Janey.

But it was hardly the time to make his feelings known. If anything was guaranteed to send her screaming out of the house, he decided, it was a declaration of lust from some bastard who had just bullied her into revealing the innermost secrets of her hopeless marriage to another bastard. Oh yes, that would really restore her faith in men.

'What are you thinking?' Janey demanded in accusing tones, because Guy was miles away and there was a hint of a smile around his mouth. If he was laughing at her, she would slap him.

'Nothing. Sorry.' Hastily, he composed himself. 'Look, I understand how you must feel about Alan, but this rubbish about killing himself is emotional blackmail. Janey, nobody has the right to do that to you. It's ludicrous. If he wants to jump off a cliff, that's his decision. You wouldn't have made him do it, and you wouldn't be responsible.'

'But—'

Guy's expression was severe. 'No, this time you're just going to have to sit there and let me have my say. What he's doing is sick. It's also selfish. And people who will stoop to such depths in order to get whatever they want are way too selfish to top themselves, believe me. He's threatening to do it because it's the only way he knows of making sure you don't dump him. If he really loved you as much as he says, he wouldn't dream of putting you through this kind of hell. Janey, if I thought for one moment you'd take me up on it I'd bet my house, my car – my *kids*, for God's sake – that he's bluffing. If you tell him to take a running jump, believe me, the last place he's going to visit is a handy clifftop.'

'It's so easy for you to say that.' Just listening to him made Janey's stomach squirm. 'You don't even know him. It's different when it's your own husband. I can't gamble with his life.'

More's the pity, thought Guy. But she clearly wasn't going to change her mind. At least he had forced her to admit the problem; it might not be much but it was a start.

'No. OK.' He had to agree she had a point. Maxine, faced with a similar threat, would doubtless hand the poor chap a Stanley knife and run him a nice hot bath.

But Janey was Janey, and that wasn't her style. She considered other people's feelings, had probably never deliberately hurt anyone in her entire life, and was prepared to sacrifice her own happiness in order to avoid upsetting Alan bloody Sinclair.

That was the trouble with nice girls, he thought ruefully. They had a conscience. Sometimes it was bloody infuriating.

'Now what?' Janey glared at him, because he was doing it again. She never knew what he was thinking and it unnerved her.

He grinned. 'We've finished the bottle. Shall I open another one?'

'What, so that you can lecture me for another hour?' She was only half joking. When Guy set his mind to it, he could be horribly persistent. Especially when he was determined to prove that he was right.

'We could change the subject.'

Janey looked at her watch; it was gone eleven-thirty. 'I can't drink any more and still drive home,' she said with a note of regret. 'And it's later than I thought. I'd better be making a move.'

'You don't have to drive. You could always spend the night here. In Maxine's room,' he said, before she had a chance to become flustered. 'It wouldn't do Alan any harm to wonder where you'd got to,' he added slyly. 'Serve him right for forgetting your birthday.'

But Janey was unfolding her legs, searching around

434

for her shoes and stuffing Mimi's book into her bag. 'And tomorrow morning I'd go to work with a raging hangover.' She pulled a face. 'Thanks for the offer, but I have to be at the market by six.'

She had ignored the dig, resolutely refusing to rise to the bait.

'Let me just go and check on the kids,' said Guy, good-naturedly accepting defeat. 'Then I'll see you out.'

Janey was waiting in the hall when he returned downstairs. She wound a red cashmere scarf around her neck. 'Are they all right?'

'Well away.' Guy nodded and grinned. 'How about you, after all that interrogation? Are you OK?'

'I'll live.' With a smile, she flipped the tasselled ends of the scarf over her shoulders. 'At least you didn't pull my fingernails out.'

'I do have something else to say,' he warned. 'Before you go.'

Janey braced herself. She might have guessed he would. 'Oh. What is it?'

'Happy birthday.' The red scarf was covering the lower half of her face. Before she realized what was happening Guy was gently pushing it down, out of the way. There was her mouth, wonderfully soft and inviting. When you wished someone a happy birthday, he reasoned, it was perfectly in order to give them a kiss to go with it.

But he didn't want to alarm her. Instead, exercising almost superhuman control, he cast one last regretful glance at those slightly parted lips and aimed, instead, an inch to the left.

'Except it hasn't been too happy,' he murmured.

Ridiculously, his heart was pounding like a schoolboy's. 'I'm sorry about that.'

Janey, startled by her own reaction to what was, after all, only a polite gesture, was deeply ashamed of herself. Just for a fraction of a second she had thought Guy was going to kiss her properly. What was even more awful was the fact that she had wanted him to.

'It isn't over yet.' Flustered, she resorted to feeble humour. 'I've still got Maxine's present to look forward to, haven't I? If Josh's brain says "Ouch", she'll probably find one for me that yells "Dimwit".'

Guy, who was still wearing his dinner jacket, reached into the inner pocket and withdrew a small, green leather box.

'Well, I can't compete with a bouncing brain.' As he took Janey's hand and placed the box in her palm, his eyes silently dared her to object. 'But at least this won't hurl insults at you.'

Inside lay a slender rose-gold bangle engraved around the outer edge with delicately entwined leaves and flowers. It was old, simple and breathtakingly beautiful. Janey, who had never been more embarrassed in her entire life, said, 'Oh for heaven's sake, you don't want to give me something like this.'

'Don't be silly. Call it making amends for giving you such a hard time tonight.' Since she evidently had no intention of taking the bracelet out of the box, Guy did it himself and pushed it over her trembling hand.

'But where . . . who . . . ?'

'I spotted it in an antique shop in St Austell a few months ago,' he lied. 'I was going to give it to Serena, then I decided it wasn't her style. You may as well have it,' he added casually. 'It's no use to me.'

Janey flushed with pleasure. It was still embarrassing to be on the receiving end of such generosity but Guy clearly wouldn't take it back. The engraved flowers were forget-me-nots, she realized, studying the bangle in more detail and loving the way it gleamed rather than glittered in the light, showing its age and quality.

'Definitely not Serena's style.' She gave him a mischievous smile. 'I'm glad you didn't give it to her. I love it, Guy. Thank you.'

This time she reached up and kissed him, her warm lips brushing his cheek a decorous inch from his mouth just as he had done earlier. The same tingle of longing zipped through her. Janey, fantasizing wildly, wondered what Guy would do if she moved towards him . . . moved her mouth to his.

The image flashed into her brain. ready-made, as if in answer. Pushy, eager Charlotte, throwing herself at Guy. Guy, good-humoured but resigned, wondering how the hell to fend her off without hurting her feelings. And Janey herself, hearing all about it, wondering how Charlotte could bear to make such an idiot of herself when he was so plainly uninterested.

No upturned bucket of ice-cold water could have shocked her to her senses more abruptly. So much for wild fantasies, Janey decided, and prayed that Guy hadn't been able to read her mind.

'Thanks again for the bracelet.' She took a hasty step backwards, pulling the scarf up over her chin once more and making a clumsy grab for the front door. 'Gosh, it's freezing outside! Look at all those stars . . . there's even ice on your bird table . . . poor old birds . . .'

One stupid kiss on the cheek, Guy realized, shaking his head in disbelief, and she'd managed to give him a severe erection. Never mind the poor birds, he thought, watching Janey as she jumped into the van, anxious to get home to her undeserving pig of a husband. To *hell* with the wildlife. What about me?

Chapter 52

'Janey, it's me. Can you come over here right away?'

At the sound of her mother's voice, Janey felt the muscles of her jaw automatically tighten. Confiding her marital problems to Guy had been one thing, but she still considered Thea's outburst in front of Alan to have been totally out of order. Even if she had been right, it was an unforgivable action.

They hadn't spoken to each other since. And now here was Thea on the other end of the phone, expecting her to drop everything and rush over to see her. To add insult to injury, it was pouring with rain.

Squish, went the mister spray in Janey's hand as she aimed it at a three-foot yucca plant. 'I'm busy,' she said, stretching past the yucca and giving the azaleas a shower. *Squish, squish.* 'What do you want?'

'I need to see you.' Thea sounded quite unlike her usual self. 'Please, Janey.'

Suspecting some kind of ulterior motive, Janey kept her own response guarded. 'Why?'

'Because Oliver is dead,' said Thea quietly, and replaced the receiver.

★   ★   ★

He had died the previous evening, without warning, in her bed. Thea, having slipped out of the house at eight o'clock, had gone to the studio and worked for three hours on a new sculpture. Returning finally with arms aching from the strenuous business of moulding the clay over the chicken-wire framework of the figure, and a glowing sense of achievement because it had all gone so well, she had climbed the stairs to her bedroom and found him. His reading glasses were beside him, resting on her empty pillow. The book he had been reading lay neatly closed on the floor next to the bed. It appeared, said the doctor who had come to the house, that Oliver had dozed off and suffered the stroke in his sleep. He wouldn't have known a thing about it. All in all, the doctor explained in an attempt to comfort Thea, it was a marvellous way to go.

Thea, wrapped up in a cashmere sweater that still bore the scent of Oliver's cologne, was huddled in the corner of the tatty, cushion-strewn sofa drinking a vast vodka-martini. There were still traces of dried clay in her hair and beneath her fingernails; her eyes, darker than ever with grief, were red-rimmed from crying.

Having left Paula in charge of the shop, and feeling horribly helpless, Janey helped herself to a vodka to keep her mother company. Their differences forgotten, because her own unhappiness paled into insignificance compared with Thea's, Janey sat down and put her arms around her.

'Bloody Oliver.' Thea sniffed, continuing to gaze at the letter in her lap. 'I keep thinking I could kill him for doing this to me. How could he keep this kind of thing to himself and not even warn me? Typical of the bloody man . . .'

She had found it in his wallet, neatly slotted in behind the credit cards. The plain white envelope bore her name. The contents of the letter inside had come as almost more of a shock than his death.

'Are you sure you want me to read it?' Janey frowned as her mother handed it to her. 'Isn't it private?'

'Selfish bastard,' Thea murmured, fishing up her sleeve for a crumpled handkerchief as the tears began to drop once more down her long nose. 'Of course I want you to read it. How can any man be so selfish?'

Janey recognized the careful, elegant writing she'd noted on Oliver's visit to her shop as she now read his farewell.

My darling Thea,

Well, if you're reading this you've either been snooping shamelessly or I'm dead. But since I have faith in you, I shall assume the latter.

Now I suppose you're as mad as hell with me for doing it this way because, yes, I knew it was going to happen in the not-too-distant future. My doctor warned me I was a walking time-bomb. And no, there was nothing that could be done either medically or surgically to prevent it happening. This time even money couldn't help.

But think about it, sweetheart. Would you really have been happier, knowing the truth? I'm afraid I developed an all-consuming fear that you might try and persuade me to take things easy, maybe even not allowing me to make love to you as often as I liked for fear of over-exerting myself. What a deeply depressing prospect that would have been. Now perhaps you can begin to understand why I didn't tell you!

Right, now for something you do already know. I love you, Thea. We may not have had a vast amount of time together but these last months have been the very happiest of my life. When I came to Cornwall, it was to see my grandchildren. How could I ever have guessed I would meet and fall so totally in love with a beautiful, bossy, wonderful woman who loved me in return? And for myself rather than for my money.

If, on the other hand, you're reading this letter because you stole my wallet and were riffling through my credit cards, I trust you're now ashamed of yourself.

That was a joke, sweetheart. No need to rip this letter to shreds. If I can keep my sense of humour, so can you.

I don't know what else to say. I'm sorry if I've upset you, but even though my motives were selfish I still feel my decision was the right one to make. If you contact my solicitor (details in the black address book) he will organize the reading of my will. Maybe this will go some way towards making amends.

My darling, I love you so very much.

Oliver.

'Well,' said Janey, clearing her throat as she folded the pages of the letter and handed them back to her mother. 'I think he was right.'

'Of course he was right.' With an irritable gesture, Thea wiped her wet face on her sleeve. 'But that doesn't mean

I have to forgive him. Did he think I wouldn't want anything to do with him if I'd known he was about to keel over and die?'

'He's explained why he didn't want you to know,' Janey reminded her. 'He wanted to enjoy himself without being nagged. He didn't want you endlessly worrying about him. He didn't want you to be miserable.'

'Well I am,' Thea shouted. 'Bloody miserable! After all these years I finally meet the man I've waited for all my life, and he has to go and do this to me. It isn't fair!'

Nothing she could say, Janey realized, was going to help her mother. All she could do was be there.

'At least you met him,' she said, giving Thea another hug. 'If you hadn't, think what you would have missed. Surely a few months with Oliver was better than nothing at all?'

'In a couple of years, maybe I'll think that.' Thea passed Janey her empty glass. 'All I know right now is that it hurts like hell. Get me another drink, darling. A big one. On second thoughts, just give me yours. You have to drive.'

'It's OK, Mum. I don't have to go anywhere.'

'Yes, you do,' said Thea. 'Someone has to tell Guy Cassidy his father is dead. He might not care,' she added bitterly, 'but he still has to know.'

Guy couldn't believe what he was hearing. And from Janey, of all people. So much, he decided, for mutual trust.

Maxine had gone to the supermarket and the children were at school. Janey, sitting bolt upright on a kitchen chair with her wet hair plastered to her head, had refused his offer of coffee and had come straight to the point. She was also, very obviously, on Thea's side.

'So what you're telling me,' said Guy evenly, 'is that your mother has been having an affair with my father. They've practically been living together. And you knew all about it.'

He was clearly angry. And Thea had been right, thought Janey. The fact that Oliver was dead wasn't what was bothering him. The anger was directed solely at her.

'I found out about it, yes.' Struggling to curb her impatience, she pushed a damp strand of hair away from her eye. 'But is that really important? OK, so you had a quarrel with him years ago but that's over now. Guy, your father died last night. Josh and Ella will be upset even if you aren't.'

'You knew where he was all the time.' It was as if he hadn't heard her. 'And you didn't tell me.'

Janey's dark eyes flashed. The contrast between Thea's terrible grief and this total lack of concern couldn't have been more marked. 'I thought about telling you,' she said coldly. 'And I decided against it. I'm glad now that I did.'

'Did what?' Maxine, buckling under the weight of six carrier bags, and even more sodden and bedraggled than Janey, appeared in the doorway. 'Am I interrupting something personal here?' Her eyebrows creased in suspicion. 'Are you talking about me?'

Guy, assuming that Maxine was in on it too, didn't say anything.

'Oliver Cassidy died last night,' Janey told her.

'Oh my God, you're not serious!' For a moment, Maxine looked as if she didn't know whether to laugh or cry. One of the carrier bags dropped to the floor with an ominous crash.

'No, it's a joke,' snapped Guy.

'So he wasn't lying,' Maxine wailed. 'I knew he wouldn't lie to me! Bloody Bruno . . . !'

'What?' Guy demanded, sensing that he hadn't heard anything yet. He glared at Maxine. 'Come on, out with it! What else has been going on that I don't know about?'

'Jesus,' he sighed, when she had finished telling him.

'Oh calm down.' Maxine, having rummaged energetically through every carrier, finally located the chocolate digestives. 'He's dead now, so what does it matter? I'm just glad I let him see the kids,' she added with renewed defiance. 'Go on, have a biscuit.'

It was like a jigsaw puzzle, thought Guy. Everyone had been holding different pieces. Maxine's story was clearly news to Janey.

But the oddness of Janey's presence in the house had apparently only just struck Maxine. Turning to her sister and speaking through a mouthful of biscuit, she said, 'I don't understand. Why *are* you here?'

'Janey came to tell me about my father.' Guy couldn't resist it. It was, he decided, his turn to spring a surprise.

Maxine frowned. 'But how did she know?'

'Your mother sent her over here.' His eyes glittered with malicious pleasure. 'My father, you see, was in her bed when he died.'

The funeral took place three days later. With typical thoroughness and attention to detail, Oliver Cassidy had made all the arrangements himself. Even he, however, hadn't been able to organize the weather, which had gone from bad to atrocious. Trezale churchyard, cruelly exposed to the elements, was awash with freezing rain. The small funeral party had to struggle to stay standing against the force of the bitter, north-westerly gales as Oliver's coffin was lowered slowly into the ground.

Back at Thea's house afterwards, the sitting room was warm but the atmosphere remained distinctly chilly. Guy, barely speaking to anyone, looked bored. Douglas Burke, Oliver's solicitor, had travelled down from Bristol to preside over the reading of the will as instructed by his late client and was anxious to get it over with so that he might return home to his extremely pregnant wife. Thea was desperately trying to contain her grief. Only the presence of Ella and Josh, who had insisted on attending the funeral, brightened the proceedings at all.

'At least the food's cheerful,' Maxine murmured in Janey's ear. Oliver had organized that too, making a private arrangement with the head chef from the Grand Rock where he had retained a room until the end though seldom visiting it. The hors d'oeuvres, arranged on silver platters, were ludicrously over the top; each stuffed cherry tomato had been precision carved, each quail's egg painstakingly studded with caviar. The sculptured smoked-salmon mousse, a work of art in itself, could have graced a plinth in the Tate Gallery. The champagne was Taittinger.

'There's only us,' Janey fretted. 'It doesn't seem right, but the solicitor insisted it was what Oliver wanted.'

She had phoned him herself, on her mother's behalf. Her suggestion that an announcement should be placed in the *Telegraph* had been firmly rebuffed. Not until after the funeral, Oliver had apparently instructed. He didn't want his gaggle of ex-wives descending on Trezale and upsetting Thea.

'Look at Guy,' whispered Maxine, giving him a mischievous wink just to annoy him. 'Moody sod.'

'I don't think he's ever going to speak to me again.' Janey tried to sound as if she couldn't care less. 'He said I'd betrayed him.'

'I suppose we all did.' Maxine grinned. 'I still think it's funny. It was like a mass conspiracy, except none of us realized we were all separately involved.'

'Poor Oliver. Poor Mum,' sighed Janey, toying idly with an asparagus canapé she didn't have the heart to eat.

'At least you're back on speaking terms,' Maxine consoled her. 'That's one family feud nipped in the bud. Speaking of which,' she added, 'how are things going with you and Alan?'

Speaking of conspiracies, thought Janey dryly . . .

Aloud she said, 'Oh, fine.'

The will reading lasted less than fifteen minutes. Simply and concisely, Oliver had divided his amassed fortune into three equal parts, making Thea, Josh and Ella instant millionaires. Thea, by this time beyond tears, called Oliver a bastard and said she didn't want his stinking, lousy, rotten money. Josh and Ella, entranced both by her thrilling choice of words and by the prospect of such unimaginable riches, were less than overjoyed to learn that their own inheritances were to be held in trust until they were twenty-one.

'Bugger,' pouted Ella, because if Thea could swear, so could she. 'Twenty-one's *ancient*. I'll be too old to ride a horse by then.'

'Don't worry.' Maxine, fastening her into her emerald-green coat, winked at Janey. 'You'll be able to treat yourself to a solid gold Zimmer frame.'

'Dad didn't get any money.' Josh looked thoughtful. 'Does that mean we're richer than he is now?'

Guy, darkly handsome and decidedly impatient, was already waiting at the front door to take them home. Janey, pretending she hadn't noticed him there, bent down and gave Josh a hug. 'Probably. Just think, you may have to start giving him pocket money in future.'

'But only if he makes his bed and washes the car.' Josh beamed at her, highly diverted by the prospect. Then, sounding startled, he said, 'Oh!'

His gaze had dropped. He was no longer looking at her face.

Janey, smiling, said, 'What?'

'Um . . . nothing.' Josh's long-lashed blue eyes clouded with confusion as natural good manners vied with surprise. Tentatively, he reached out and touched the sleeve of her ivory silk shirt. 'You're wearing Mummy's bracelet, that's all.'

'Janey!' wailed Ella, barging past and almost knocking him down. 'Maxine won't tell me. What's a Zimmer frame?'

Chapter 53

It was ten o'clock in the evening by the time Janey let herself into the flat. Alan, for once not out at the surf club, had fallen asleep in front of the television with the gas fire blazing and both living-room windows wide open. Three empty lager cans and the remains of an Indian takeaway littered the coffee table upon which his feet were propped.

In the dim light, his enviable cheekbones seemed more pronounced and the corners of his mouth appeared to curve upwards as if in secret amusement. His blond hair gleamed and his eyelashes, not blond but dark, cast twin shadows upon his cheeks. Watching him sleep, Janey wondered how anyone could look so beautiful – almost angelic – and still snore like a pig.

He woke with a start when she switched off the television.

'Oh. You're back.' Rubbing his eyes, he pushed himself into a sitting position. As Janey bent to pick up the empty cans, he added, 'Leave that, I'll do it in a minute. So how did it go this afternoon?'

'Like a funeral.' Since Alan's idea of 'in a minute' was more like next weekend, she continued piling the empty curry and rice containers on to his dirty plate. In the kitchen the sink was crammed with more unwashed plates and coffee mugs, and the sugar bowl had been tipped over, spilling its contents on to the floor. Sugar crunched beneath her feet as she chucked the lager cans one by one into the bin.

'Don't worry, I'll clear it up,' Alan called from the living room. 'How's Thea, OK now?'

'Oh, absolutely fine.' Janey wondered if he had any idea what a stupid question that was. 'She's almost forgotten what he even looked like.'

Alan appeared in the doorway, looking shamefaced. 'Hey, no need to snap. You know what I meant.'

'She'll get through it,' said Janey briefly.

'Come on, sit down and relax. You look exhausted.' He took her hand and the bracelet – Véronique's bracelet, thought Janey – brushed against his wrist. When Alan had remarked upon it last week she'd simply told him that it had been a birthday present and he had assumed she'd had it for years.

'So what's the news?' he asked, when Janey had shrugged off her coat. 'You said the solicitor was coming down to read the will; that's unusual nowadays isn't it? Did Thea get anything?'

She looked at him. 'Any what?'

'Sweetheart, you aren't even listening to me!' Smiling and shaking his head in gentle reproach, Alan opened another can of lager. 'I asked you if he left Thea anything in the will. After all, from what you told me he seemed pretty smitten. The least he could do was show his appreciation with a nice little legacy.'

'He did,' said Janey tonelessly.

'Well, how much?'

'About one and a half.'

'Thousand?' Alan looked faintly disappointed. 'That's not much. I thought he was supposed to be loaded.'

'One and a half million,' said Janey.

After the endless, churning turmoil of the past weeks, finally making the decision was easy. Having listened to Alan for over an hour now, Janey knew it couldn't go on any longer. Whilst he had been crowing over her mother's inheritance and excitedly planning how they should spend the money Thea was bound to hand out to Maxine and herself, she had reached the point of no return. His shameless assumptions both appalled and sickened her. His greed revolted her. The realization that she was about to do what she had told Guy Cassidy she could never risk doing, left her feeling . . . well, Janey wasn't quite sure how she felt; presumably that would come later. Right now, all she had to do was say the words.

'. . . and we could do with a decent car,' he went on, waving dismissively in the direction of the window overlooking the high street. 'The van's OK for carting flowers around but it's hardly what you'd call stylish. How about a soft-top for next summer, sweetheart? Something with a bit of go in it?'

'Look.' Janey, unable to contain herself any longer, said evenly, 'Oliver Cassidy left that money to my mother. Not to me, and not to you. I don't know how you can even think you have any right to a share in it.'

'Janey, all I'm saying is that Thea is bound to want

you to share her good fortune!' Alan looked hurt. 'You need a holiday, you need a decent car; I'm just trying to advise you.' He paused, then broke into a grin. 'And of course you'll want to take somebody to Barbados with you, to rub all that Ambre Solaire on to those gorgeous shoulders of yours . . .'

Her heart began to race. 'Alan, I don't want my mother to give me any money and I'm not planning any holidays. But if someone came up to me in the street tomorrow and handed me two free tickets to Barbados, I wouldn't take you anyway. I'd take Maxine.'

'You're upset.' He nodded understandingly. 'This funeral's taken it out of you. Come on, you should be in bed.'

'I'm not upset.' Janey was starting to shake. 'I just don't want this to go on any longer. It isn't working, Alan. You said we needed time to get used to each other again. Well, I've had enough time to know that it isn't going to happen.'

He stared at her. As stunned, she realized, as if he had found her walking stark naked down the high street.

'Sweetheart,' he protested finally, 'what are you talking about?'

'Us.' The time had come to be brutal. She mustn't allow him to wheedle his way around her. 'This marriage. I don't want to carry on. I don't want to be married to you any more. You told me I'd changed, and I have. I'm sorry, Alan, but that's it. You're going to have to find somewhere else to stay.'

And somebody else to support you, she thought wearily. Guy had been right; Alan was a user and a taker. She just hoped he had been right about the other matter, too . . .

'I can't believe I'm hearing this.' Alan was very still, his eyes narrowed, his voice scarily low.

I can't believe I'm saying it, Janey thought, biting her lip and wishing he wouldn't stare at her like that. But she had to stick to her guns.

'I mean it.'

'Good God, woman! I came back here because I couldn't live without you! You welcomed me back with open arms . . . how can you change your mind just like that? What have I done that's so terrible?'

'Nothing.' Janey fought to stay calm. 'You haven't done anything terrible. I don't love you any more, that's all.'

But he was shaking his head. 'No. no. It doesn't work like that. I want the real reason.'

'OK, fine.' She held up her hand and began counting the real reasons off on her fingers. 'You haven't bothered to look for a job. You expect me to pay for everything. You endlessly take me for granted. You want my mother to give me money so you can spend it. And,' she concluded heavily, 'you forgot my birthday.'

He blinked. 'Any more?'

'Yes,' snapped Janey, for the hell of it. 'You snore.'

'I see.' Alan's smile was bleak. 'Oh yes, I definitely see. Your mother's the one behind all this, isn't she? That old bitch put you up to it. What did she do, threaten to cut you off without a penny if you didn't dump me?'

'Don't be ridiculous.' Enraged by his nastiness, yet at the same time almost welcoming it because it was so much easier to deal with than threats of suicide, Janey rounded on him. Her brown eyes blazed. 'You're the one who was so intent on getting your hands on that money! And no,

Mum hasn't so much as mentioned your name, so don't even think she has anything to do with this. My mother has more important things on her mind than you, just at the minute.' She paused, then added icily, 'This is *my* decision. All my own work. And since I've already made up my mind, there's no point in even trying to argue. As far as I'm concerned, the sooner you leave, the better.'

Alan's shoulders slumped. The anger in his eyes faded, to be replaced by resignation. 'So that's it,' he murmured with infinite sadness. 'It's all over.'

Janey, scarcely daring to breathe, nodded.

'Oh well, it was always on the cards, I suppose. Stupid of me.' He shook his head. 'I geared myself up to this before coming back, and now I have to get used to the idea all over again. Somehow it's even harder, this time . . .'

Guy had been right, Janey reminded herself, gritting her teeth. It was emotional blackmail, pure and simple. Alan wouldn't really do anything drastic.

'. . . like thinking you're going to the electric chair, being reprieved, then being told that it was just a joke, you're going to get it after all.'

'I'm not sending you to the electric chair,' she said quietly.

'Aren't you?' He reached for her hand. 'Janey, I love you. Where would I go, what kind of future do I have without you? What would be the point of *anything*?'

'Stop it.' Sick with fear that he might actually mean what he was saying, Janey prayed she was doing the right thing. 'You mustn't say that.'

'Why not? I'm thinking it. Jesus,' Alan sighed,

squeezing her hand so hard she felt her fingers go numb. 'I've thought of nothing else for the past two years. All I wanted was to be with you, Janey. God knows, I'm not perfect . . . I've tried to get a job, but there just haven't been any around. And I'm sorry about that. And I know I don't always do the washing up, but it's hardly a reason to end a marriage! Maybe I don't deserve you,' he murmured brokenly, 'but I do love you. Let me prove it, sweetheart. Give me one last chance and I'll turn over a new leaf, I swear I will. I'll make you happy.'

'No,' said Janey. 'I told you, I've already made up my mind. I don't care what you do from now on. I'm not responsible for you any more. The answer's still no.'

'You callous bitch.' Abruptly, he dropped her hand and pushed it away, his jaw set and a vein thudding in his cheek. 'OK. If that's what you want, I'll go. But I hope you realize what you're doing. You could end up regretting this, Janey. In a very big way indeed.'

Maxine, stretched out across Janey's settee with her hands behind her head, wiggled her toes in time to the jingle advertising a new chocolate bar. Nobody was allowed to watch BBC any more. Every time the commercials came on, her attention began to wander in anticipation. When the Babysoft commercial was shown, she stopped whatever she was doing in order to gaze, entranced, at herself on the television screen.

'Damn, the film's starting again! Maybe it'll be on in the next break. Now what was I saying . . . ?'

'You were telling me to relax,' said Janey helpfully, 'and to stop worrying about Alan.'

'Exactly. Look, kicking him out was the best thing you ever did. This should be the happiest time of your life, darling! You came to your senses, gave him the old heave-ho and now you can start afresh. He's out of your system,' she added forcefully. 'You're free at last! I can't understand why you should even care what happens to him. When did that bastard ever show any consideration for you, after all?'

Janey hadn't expected her sister to understand. When she had tried to relay her fears, Maxine had howled with laughter and said, 'You should be so lucky.'

The trouble was, wanting to put the whole miserable affair behind her was easier said than done. How could she even begin to relax when every time the phone rang she leapt a mile, petrified it might be the police . . . the hospital . . . Alan himself, with a stomachful of pills?

It had been a week now since he'd left. He was staying with Jan and André Covel, sleeping on the living-room floor of their tiny flat. Conditions, it appeared, were less than ideal; Jan wasn't happy about the set-up, he had grimly informed Janey when he had returned to pick up the last of his few possessions. Still, it was better than a sleeping bag on the beach. And it probably wouldn't be for very long . . .

'You're well rid of him,' Maxine declared, stretching out for the remote control and flipping over to Channel 4 in search of more commercials. 'And think how nice it is to have the place to yourself again. Got any more chocolate Hobnobs, Janey, or was that the last packet?'

Janey couldn't help smiling. Maxine, draped across the sofa like Cleopatra, waving an empty biscuit wrapper and hogging the remote control, could almost be Alan. And since Bruno had started work at the Grand Rock ten days earlier – his shifts clashing cruelly with Maxine's own precious time off – she had been turning up more and more often at the flat.

'Oh yes, it's great, having the place to myself,' Janey said mildly. 'And yes, we're out of Hobnobs. What time does Bruno finish tonight?'

Maxine, busy emptying crumbs into the palm of her hand, looked gloomy. 'When the last punter leaves. You wouldn't believe how long some people can just sit there, nursing a lousy cup of coffee. I'm sure they do it out of spite.'

'But you two are still OK?' She couldn't imagine how Maxine's chaotic ways must be affecting Bruno.

'More than OK.' Maxine, having licked up the last of the crumbs, stretched luxuriously. 'We're talking blissful. It's like being on a permanent honeymoon without the bother of being married . . . except he keeps wanting us to *get* married. Now will you look at that – one pink sock and one orange one. Why on earth didn't I notice that before?'

'Are you going to marry him?' asked Janey curiously.

'I don't know. We'll see.' Maxine shrugged and flicked back her blond hair. 'It's going well, but I don't see the point of rushing into anything drastic. It doesn't do him any harm to keep him in suspense. Besides, who knows what might happen now my career's taking off? The last thing I need is to be tied down . . .'

And Alan called me a callous bitch, thought Janey, marvelling at her sister's *laissez faire* attitude.

'So when he asks you to marry him and you refuse,' she said, deeply intrigued 'what does Bruno *do*?'

'What can he do?' Maxine countered with a casual shrug. 'Apart from hope for better luck next time. Don't get me wrong, I love him to death, but he's hardly in a position to argue. My career comes first and he knows that.' She hesitated, looking thoughtful. 'Does that sound selfish?'

Janey, filled with admiration, said, 'Yes.'

'Oh well.' Maxine broke into an unrepentant grin. 'Never mind. A bit of suffering never hurt anyone, especially Bruno.'

Chapter 54

The build-up to Christmas was starting. Business in the shop was brisk and orders were already flooding in. Janey, thanking her lucky stars for ever-reliable Paula, was snowed under with requests for Christmas wreaths, table decorations and *pot-et-fleur* arrangements. Mistletoe was going down a bomb with teenagers whom she otherwise never saw from one year to the next.

Paula was out making the morning's deliveries and Janey, armed with leather gloves and secateurs, was battling her way through a mountain of holly when the shop door opened and a tall, dark-haired girl came in carrying a baby. The girl, elegantly attired in an expensive caramel leather jacket, black trousers and low-heeled black and tan boots, sported a great deal of make-up and reeked of perfume. The baby, presumably a boy, was bundled up in a navy snowsuit and a blue-and-white striped bobble hat. Wisps of ash-blond hair were plastered to his forehead and he had the most adorable blue eyes Janey had ever seen.

The girl, who looked to be in her mid-twenties, seemed nervous. It was with some relief that Janey abandoned the holly and peeled off her gloves.

'Hi.' She waved at the little boy and smiled at his mother. 'Can I help you?'

'Um . . . well, I hope so.' Long, heavily mascaraed eyelashes batted with agitation. Stalling for time, she glanced around at the hanging baskets strung from the ceiling. The baby, sensing inattention and seizing the moment, made a grab for a nearby trailing ivy frond. The terracotta pot from which it grew was dragged with an ominous grating sound from its shelf. The next moment, before anyone had a chance to move, it had crashed into a bucket of freesias, scattering leaves and compost over the tiled floor. Startled, the baby promptly let out an ear-splitting wail.

'Oh no,' cried his mother. 'Oh hell! I'm so sorry . . .'

'It doesn't matter.' Gently, Janey disentangled the long tendril of ivy from the baby's chubby clenched fist. By some miracle the terracotta pot hadn't broken. There was a mess, but not an expensive mess.

'I'll pay for the damage.' Shifting the baby from one hip to the other, the girl rummaged frantically in her shoulder bag for her purse. 'I really am sorry. Are the freesias a write-off too?'

She was shaking, Janey noticed. Bending down, swiftly retrieving the pot from its resting place amongst the poor battered freesias, she shook her head and smiled.

'It's OK, they were on their last legs anyway. I was going to bin them tonight. And look, the pot's fine.' She held it up for inspection. 'No problems, honestly. You don't have to pay for anything.'

The baby had by this time stopped yelling. After regarding Janey for some seconds with solemn intensity, he broke into a sudden beaming grin.

'Oh God,' said the girl, still distressed. 'You're being so nice about this. It doesn't make it any easier for me.'

'It was an accident,' Janey protested. 'What were you expecting me to do, dial 999?'

'I don't mean the pot.' She hesitated, flicking back her glossy dark hair. 'It's taken me weeks to pluck up the courage to come here . . . and I'm afraid you aren't going to like the reason why.'

Janey frowned. 'I don't understand.'

'You are Mrs Sinclair, aren't you?' said the girl nervously, and Janey nodded again.

'Well my name's Anna Fox.' She waited, then shook her head. 'I suppose that doesn't ring any bells?'

The baby, apparently entranced by the gold buttons on Janey's sweater, squealed with delight and made a futile grab for them.

'Sorry?' said Janey, puzzled.

'Oh dear, this is even more difficult than I thought.' Two spots of bright colour appeared on the girl's cheeks. 'Look, it was Alan I really came to see. Your . . . um . . . husband. Maybe it would be easier if he explained.' She blinked rapidly. 'Is he around at the moment?'

In less than a split second it all became clear. Stunned, Janey clutched the counter for support. The baby, chuckling with delight, revealed two pearly teeth and vast amounts of pink gum. How curious, she thought irrelevantly, that such a grin could be so irresistible. Any adult with only two teeth in his head would never get away with it.

Anna Fox bit her lip, her dark eyes bright with a

mixture of pride and regret. 'I really *am* sorry,' she sighed. 'I did say it wasn't going to be easy. You must think I'm a complete bitch.'

The door swung open. Paula, like the cavalry, had arrived in the nick of time.

'Dear old Mrs McKenzie-Smith burst into tears when I arrived with her bouquet,' she announced cheerfully. 'It's her golden wedding anniversary and this is the first time her husband's ever given her flowers. Hello, gorgeous,' she went on, wiggling stubby fingers at the wide-eyed baby. 'Oh I say, what a lovely smile! What's your name then?'

'Good, you're back,' said Janey hurriedly. 'Paula, can you take over here? We're going upstairs for a while . . .'

'His name's Justin,' said Anna, fumbling with the zip as she struggled to get him out of his snowsuit. With a defensive glance in Janey's direction she added, 'He's ten months old.'

Janey, who had switched the kettle on, was now leaning in the kitchen doorway whilst she waited for it to boil.

'Does he say anything yet?'

Anna pulled a face. 'Only "Da".'

'Da!' Justin exclaimed in delighted recognition. 'Da da da. *Da!*'

'Ma,' prompted Anna, embarrassed, and he beamed. 'Mmm . . . Da!'

'This is crazy,' said Janey, giving up on the kettle and sitting down. 'Here you are feeling sorry for me, and I'm feeling sorry for you. Look, Alan doesn't live here. We

462

aren't . . . together, anymore. I can't say I'm not stunned by all this, but you haven't upset me. In a weird kind of way, it's the best news I've had in years.'

'Really?' Anna's eyes promptly filled with tears as astonishment mingled with overwhelming relief. 'Oh my goodness, I'm so glad . . . oh dear, now my mascara's going to run.'

Janey passed her a box of tissues. The baby, half in and half out of his snowsuit, was wriggling like an eel.

'Here, let me take him,' she offered, as Anna struggled to blow her nose and hold him on her lap at the same time. 'You don't have enough hands.'

'You really and truly don't mind?' said Anna, sniffing loudly.

Janey smiled. 'Of course not. I like babies.'

'I mean about me and Alan.' She bit her lip. 'I still feel dreadful, springing this on you.'

'I can't tell you how glad I am that you did,' Janey assured her, from the heart. 'Listen, I kicked him out. He didn't want to leave . . .' She hesitated, then shrugged and said simply, 'Well, now I know, I don't have to feel guilty any more. You can't imagine what a relief that is.'

'We only went along as a kind of joke,' Anna explained, clutching her cup of coffee and looking defiant. 'It wasn't as if I was desperate or anything, but my friend Elaine had been answering ads in the Personal columns without much luck, and I said why didn't she try a singles bar instead. Well, she found this new one advertised in *Time Out* and dragged me along to keep her company. I didn't even want to go, but she's such a nag. That's probably why her boyfriends never last longer than a week,' she added with a smile. Janey, who privately felt Personal columns and singles bars had a lot to answer for, gave her an encouraging nod.

'Well, the moment we got to this place in Kensington she spotted Alan and liked the look of him. He came over, started chatting . . . and that was how it all started. Elaine was furious with me of course, but what could I do? He was so handsome and charming that when he asked for my phone number at the end of the night I gave it to him. He wasn't the least bit interested in Elaine.' She looked at Janey. 'Now, of course, I wish he had been.'

'And that was when?' Janey silently marvelled at the story Alan had concocted about Glasgow and Manchester.

'The February before last. Nearly two years ago.'

Janey nodded. He hadn't wasted much time, then. So much for the Scottish cockroaches and seedy bedsitters. 'OK, go on.'

'Well, he just kind of moved in with me.' Anna looked helpless. 'I suppose I was pretty gullible but somehow I didn't even twig that he might be taking advantage of me. When you're madly in love, you don't think of things like that. My house, you see, was left to me by an aunt, so money wasn't a problem. I had a good job in advertising, and it was just so lovely having someone to come home to at the end of the day. To begin with, he used to do odd bits around the house: chucking clothes into the washing machine, cooking the occasional meal. And I thought that was so great! After a few months, of course, it started petering out.' Anna paused, then took a deep breath. 'Elaine had been making sarcastic remarks all along, but I'd dismissed them as jealousy. Just as I was beginning to think maybe she had a point after all, I found out I was pregnant.'

'Great timing,' said Janey sardonically.

'Yes, well. Blame it on the hormones, but the idea of coping with a baby on my own scared me witless. I managed to persuade myself that Alan wasn't so bad after all. I wanted him to marry me,' she said with a self-deprecating shrug. 'That was when I found out he wasn't actually divorced.'

'So he talked about me?'

'Not really. He just told me you were separated.'

Janey, amazed how easy it was to remain calm, murmured, 'What a shame he couldn't have told me.'

'You didn't *know?*' Anna's dark eyebrows shot up. 'I mean . . . he was your husband! What did you think, that he was working abroad or something?'

'I didn't know what to think,' Janey replied. 'He just disappeared. I thought he was dead.'

Shaking her head in disbelief, Anna reached into her bag and took out a packet of cigarettes. 'Oh well, why should that surprise me?' She gestured wearily with the box of matches. 'He did the same to me, after all.'

'Finish the story,' said Janey. 'He couldn't marry you because he wasn't divorced. So what happened after that?'

'Nothing much.' Anna gazed at the smoke spiralling towards the ceiling. 'We didn't get married. I gave up work and had the baby. Alan started going out more and more often because he said he couldn't stand the bloody noise of bloody crying, and eight weeks ago he upped and left. We'd had an awful row the night before,' she explained. 'The next morning, I took Justin to the clinic for one of his routine check-ups. By the time we got back two hours later, Alan had moved out.'

'No note?'

Anna, smiling briefly, shook her head. 'No note. But he'd threatened to leave and his clothes had gone. So I knew he wasn't dead.'

'But you did know where to find him?' Janey was deeply intrigued. Hadn't it even occurred to Alan that, for whatever reason, Anna might want to get in touch with him? Did he seriously expect to get away with it a second time when there was a baby to consider?

'Ah, but he didn't know I knew.' Folding her half-smoked cigarette into the ashtray, Anna pushed back her hair and glanced across at Justin to make sure he'd fallen asleep. 'All Alan ever told me about you was that you had a flower shop, and that you lived above it. When I asked where, he just said somewhere in Cornwall. One night though, he came home really drunk. We had a massive argument and Alan said if I wasn't careful he'd go home to Trezale. The next morning,' she added, 'he had a thumping hangover and couldn't even remember the row. I don't know why I did it but I wrote "Trezale" down in the back of my diary.'

'So you came all the way down here from London, just on the off-chance?'

'Gosh no. I did a bit of Miss Marpleing first.' Anna smiled. 'I called Directory Enquiries, got the numbers of all the Sinclairs and started ringing them, asking if they were the florist. The third person I spoke to told me the name of your shop, which meant I could phone Enquiries again and get your number . . . which in turn matched up with the next one on my list. All I had to do then was call you and ask to speak to Alan. Actually, I spoke to your assistant. But she just said Alan had gone out for the afternoon, so then I knew he was living back here, with you. That was a few weeks ago, of course,' she concluded. 'Before you booted him out.'

'Clever,' said Janey. 'He's still living in Trezale, by the way. I can give you the address.' She paused, still curious. 'So why have you come down here? Do you want him back?'

The baby stirred in his sleep, stretching his arms and briefly clenching his tiny fists.

'God no,' said Anna, running a gentle finger over his cheek. 'I just didn't want him to think he could get away with it.' Her eyes bright with defiance, she added, 'I wanted *you* to know what a bastard he was, too. For your own protection, not just to be mean. I suppose I needed to make him realize he couldn't go around treating women like dirt.'

'Well, thanks.' Janey smiled. 'I'm glad you did. I only wish you could have turned up a few weeks earlier.'

'You were really feeling guilty?'

She nodded. 'He's a convincing liar, as well as a bastard. He *made* me feel guilty. Oh . . . the relief of knowing I can stop!'

Anna said mischievously, 'Do you want to come with me when I go to see him? Would that be fun?'

'I've got an even better idea.' Janey broke into a grin. Reaching across the table, she picked up the phone. 'Why put ourselves out? Why don't I give him a ring and ask him to come over here?'

It was like exorcizing a ghost, only more fun. Janey, who hadn't enjoyed herself so much for years, made the phone call and issued the invitation in a voice overflowing with sultry promise. Alan, instantly assuming that she had come to her senses and realized she couldn't live without him, was delighted and only too happy to forgive her.

Within twenty minutes of putting the phone down he arrived, jaunty, freshly showered and bright-eyed with anticipation, on her doorstep. Janey and Anna, peeping out from behind the curtains, marvelled at the indestructible nerve of the man and struggled not to laugh out loud.

'Come on up,' Janey called huskily down the stairs when Alan had rung the bell. 'Door's open.'

The next moment, having rushed upstairs two at a time, he appeared in the living-room doorway. The expression on his face when he saw who else was waiting for him was out of this world. Indescribable, thought Janey. Better than sex . . .

'Surprise, darling,' said Anna brightly. Lifting her face, she sniffed the air. 'Oh how sweet,' she added, turning to Janey. 'He's wearing my favourite aftershave. Isn't that a thoughtful touch?'

Alan looked like a cornered animal, Janey decided, the flickering narrowed eyes reflecting his fury at having been caught out. Having come here expecting recon-ciliation, he had been made to look foolish instead. In a small way, they had succeeded in turning the tables. This time, he was the one facing humiliating rejection.

'What the hell are you doing here?' he hissed at Anna, but the trembling, nerve-racked girl who had entered the shop an hour earlier, inspired by Janey's lead, had undergone an almost magical transformation.

Now, casually confident, she gave him a sweet smile. 'It was urgent, darling. Remember that competition I entered you for? Well, they phoned. You've been short-listed for the finals.'

This was so far removed from the reply he'd been expecting, Alan couldn't take it in. 'What?' He stared at her, confused. 'What competition?'

'Don't you remember, sweetheart?' Anna protested good-naturedly. 'Father of the Year.'

Caught yet again, made to look even more foolish, he snarled, 'Oh, clever. Ha bloody ha. How did you find me, anyway?'

'Easy,' Janey murmured in an undertone. 'Just follow the trail of aftershave.'

Alan rounded on her. 'And you can shut up, spiteful bloody bitch. Was this your idea? I suppose you think it's funny.'

Janey's gaze fell briefly on the still-sleeping Justin. If she had her way, Alan would be indelibly tattooed – in the appropriate place – with a government health warning so that in future at least other women could be spared. Any minute now, no doubt, he would storm out of the flat.

Oh well, she thought, at least they could make the most of the opportunity while they still had it.

'*Funny?*' With a quizzical glance in Anna's direction,

she shook her head. 'Oh no, Alan; you're way too sad to be funny. In fact I'd probably call you pathetic. How about you Anna, any other suggestions spring immediately to mind?'

'Gosh!' declared Anna, her dark eyes alight with enthusiasm. 'I can think of *loads* . . .'

'Goodness, I enjoyed that,' Anna said happily when Alan had left, almost taking the door off its hinges as he went. 'How do you feel?'

Janey heaved a sigh of pleasure. 'Free.'

'Me too. Here we are, young, free and single. Not to mention starving . . .'

The baby, who had slept peacefully through the whole showdown, began to stretch and stir.

'Come on,' said Janey, feeling the need to celebrate. 'My treat. Let's go somewhere wonderful for lunch.'

Chapter 55

The first week of January was always the quietest of the year. Nobody wanted to buy flowers, nobody was getting married . . . or even dying. Janey, alone in the empty shop, was perched on a stool twiddling her hair around her fingers and reading an old magazine when the door bell went and Guy walked in.

It was awful; her heart almost leapt into her throat at the unexpected sight of him. Having taken Josh and Ella to Klosters for a fortnight's skiing over Christmas and the New Year, he was incredibly tanned. The contrast between grey Trezale and Guy Cassidy – brown and breathtakingly handsome in a white shirt and faded, close-fitting Levi's – couldn't have been more marked. His eyes seemed bluer than she remembered, the teeth whiter, those faultless cheekbones more pronounced. Damn, be even smelled wonderful . . .

Hastily shovelling the magazine under the counter, Janey prayed she didn't look as overawed by his glamour as she felt. Not having seen Guy since the day of his father's funeral, when she had made the excruciating discovery about the bracelet, she had no idea what to expect now.

His smile was brief. 'Hi. Good Christmas?'

'Fabulous,' said Janey. She hadn't meant to sound sarcastic but that was how it came out. With Guy and family away in Switzerland, Maxine and Bruno had closeted themselves in Mole Cottage and – according to Maxine – had spent the week screwing themselves into a blissful stupor. With only a grieving mother for company, it hadn't been the jolliest of times for Janey. As far as she was concerned it had been a festive season to forget.

Guy, however, detected the raw edge to her voice.

'Well,' he said, softening slightly, 'maybe this will cheer you up. Childsafe are launching their campaign next week. They're holding a charity ball at the Grosvenor House Hotel. The organizers chose to go with the shot I submitted so if you can stand the thought of being surrounded by a million posters of yourself, you'd better start thinking what to wear.'

He handed Janey a thick, silver-embossed invitation. Gazing at it, the words 'For two people' leapt out at her.

'Um . . . I don't have anyone to take with me.' Hating having to say it, she mumbled the words in an apologetic undertone.

Guy smiled. 'Actually this is my invite. It seemed only fair to ask you to be my partner.'

'Oh.' Her stomach took a spiralling dive.

'It's next Friday,' he pointed out. 'You'll have to get Paula to take over here. I thought we'd fly up around lunchtime, spend the night at the hotel and come back on Saturday morning.'

'I see,' said Janey cautiously, 'How much are the rooms?'

Guy's eyes glittered with amusement. 'Don't panic, that's already been taken care of. All you have to do is chuck an evening dress into a suitcase.'

She hesitated. 'Right.'

'You do have an evening dress?' He looked concerned. The thought had evidently only just struck him.

Janey, feeling more and more like a decidedly second-rate Cinderella, experienced a surge of resentment. Maybe, she thought crossly, he'd like to take care of that too.

'Of course I do,' she lied smoothly, lifting her chin in defiance. 'No need to panic. I won't turn up in anything Crimplene.'

Whilst it was perfectly acceptable for Maxine to drool over Mel Gibson, developing a crush on someone you knew was somehow infinitely more embarrassing. Janey, unhappily contemplating her own schoolgirlish infatuation with Guy, couldn't believe how juvenile she was being. She didn't even know why it should suddenly have happened, anyway. For months she'd been fine, then . . . wham! . . . one full-blown crush, sprung up from nowhere, threatening to make her look even more of an idiot than she already felt.

It must be because of Alan, she told herself; some bizarre kind of reaction to being properly single again. Whatever, it was deeply and horribly humiliating.

'Who's that?' said Paula, peering over her shoulder. Janey, who hadn't realized she'd come up behind her, jumped a mile.

'Just some old magazine.' Hastily, she tried to turn

the page. 'I found it under the counter.'

'It's Guy!' Paula, ever helpful, pointed him out. 'Oh look, he's with Valentina di Angelo . . . isn't she stunning? You must be so excited about Friday,' she added dreamily. 'Imagine, going to a ball with Guy Cassidy. Everyone will think you're a couple. By this time next week, *you* could be splashed across the pages of some gossip column . . . what are you wearing, by the way? Have you decided yet? Not lime-green cycling shorts, I hope, like vampy Valentina!'

Janey, who had imagined nothing but going to a ball with Guy Cassidy for the last six days, and who knew only too well that he had felt morally obliged to invite her, closed the magazine and chucked it into the bin.

'I'm not wearing anything,' she murmured wearily. It really was the only answer. Turning, she caught Paula's goggle-eyed expression and forced a smile. 'Because I'm not going.'

Guy, who had been up half the night working in the darkroom, was still in bed when Janey phoned at eleven o'clock on Thursday morning.

'Hi, it's me,' she said quickly. 'Um, I'm in a bit of a rush, so I'll just say it. I'm sorry, but I won't be able to make it tomorrow after all. Paula's gone down with terrible flu so she won't be able to look after the shop, and there's no one else who can do it so I'm going to have to stay here. I really am sorry,' she gabbled, not sounding it, 'but I thought I'd better let you know as soon as possible. I'm sure you've got dozens of other girls to choose from . . .'

Guy, barely awake, propped himself up in bed.

'I chose you.' He sounded distinctly put out. 'I thought you'd enjoy it. Look, we could fly back on Friday night if it would help. Surely there's somebody capable of holding the fort for a couple of hours in the afternoon? What about your mother?'

'No, nobody.' Janey was firm. 'So it was kind of you to ask me, but I'm afraid that's it. I know you'll still have fun there, anyway. Just ring up someone else . . . oh God, more customers coming in . . . I really must go . . .'

Damn, thought Guy, when she had hurriedly hung up. Bloody Paula. Bloody flu. *Bloody hell.*

Paula, who had been lugging bottle gardens the size of coffee tables in from the back of the shop, stopped to lean against the counter and catch her breath. Bright-eyed and pink-cheeked, she said, 'I haven't got flu.'

'One little white lie.' Janey, just glad to have done the deed, excused herself with a shrug.

'What happens when he asks my mum if I'm better yet? She'll think he's gone off his rocker.'

'Your mother only works for Guy on Mondays and Wednesdays,' Janey replied evenly. 'By then it won't matter any more.'

'Hmm.' Paula looked unconvinced. 'Well *I* don't know why you won't go to the do anyway. It sounds brilliant. If anyone's off their rocker around here,' she added darkly, 'it's you.'

'Oh darling, you'll never believe it . . . the best news in the world!' Maxine, erupting through the front door of the cottage, flung herself into Bruno's arms. 'My agent just rang to tell me I've landed a part in *Romsey Road*! You're hugging the next Bet Lynch . . . the future queen of the soaps . . . the biggest new name in television since Miss Piggy!'

'Thank God.' Bruno, who loathed every minute of his job at the unbelievably stuffy Grand Rock, heaved a sigh of relief. 'You can take me away from all this. They film it in Manchester don't they? When do we leave?'

'Well . . .' Maxine hesitated. '*I* start next week, but don't hand your notice in yet. It's only a walk-on . . . or rather, a mince-on part,' she amended with a grin. 'I play a white-stilettoed trollop with a severe case of dangly-earring who tries to proposition the local vicar. He turns me down and I flounce off in a huff. But at least I'm in it!' Her brown eyes danced as she gave Bruno another almighty hug. 'And once they see how brilliant I am they're bound to want me to stay.'

'Next week?' He frowned. 'How does Guy Cassidy feel about this?'

'Oh, he's fed up with the weather. He decided this morning to take the kids to St Lucia. Some friends of his have a massive house there. I said I wanted to go too, so he was as thrilled as I was when the call came through this afternoon.' She grinned. 'Now he doesn't have to pay for my plane ticket.'

Bruno digested this in silence. If he had been offered the choice between a week in St Lucia without Maxine and a week at home with her, he would have stayed. The idea of passing up a free holiday, however, evidently hadn't so much as crossed her mind.

And although the thought of Maxine spending a week

on a tropical Island with Guy Cassidy was bad enough, the idea of her socializing with a television crew in Manchester was somehow even more menacing. He might love her, but he still didn't trust her an inch. Particularly, thought Bruno, when she was so hellbent on furthering her career.

He frowned. 'How long will you be gone?'

'Only a week.'

'A whole week? For one lousy walk-on?'

Maxine nuzzled his neck and smiled to herself. 'Hmm, I know. But I straddle two episodes. That's the kind of trollop I am.'

Bruno said nothing. That was just what he was afraid of.

'You've got a ladder in your stocking.'

Maxine, shaking back her hair and almost knocking herself senseless with her extravagantly gaudy earrings, said, 'Oh, bum.' From her seat in the studio canteen she grinned up at Zack Morrison, star of *Romsey Road* and heart-throb to millions. 'I'm supposed to have two.'

He nodded. He had a great nod. The way that lock of dark hair flopped over his left eyebrow, Maxine decided, was positively mesmerizing.

'I spotted you earlier, down on the set,' he said casually. 'You're good.'

'I know.' Maxine, too excited to eat, abandoned her Danish pastry. The part he played was that of the womanizing dodgy dealer, irresistibly wicked and altogether dangerous to know. In truth he wasn't actually that good-looking, just a damn sight better than the rest of the males in the cast. It was his character, Robbie Elliott, that really set the female pulses racing, as each woman secretly wondered whether she could be the one to tame him.

'I've seen you in the Babysoft ad, too,' he told her, and Maxine shrugged.

'Stepping stones,' she replied, crossing her legs and idly swinging one scuffed white stiletto from her toes. 'Why don't you sit down, before your salad falls off its plate?'

Zack Morrison, currently between wives, was captivated by Maxine's honesty. The rest of her wasn't bad either, he admitted to himself. He tended to go for brunettes, so blonde made a nice change. The smile was stunning. And even the terrible outfit she was wearing couldn't disguise the fact that beneath it, aching to get out, was a stupendous figure.

It was the honesty, however, which appealed above all. Women, throwing themselves at him, invariably told him how unhappy they were with the men they were currently either involved with or married to. It was their way of letting him know how available they were.

But although he was pretty certain Maxine Vaughan was throwing herself at him, practically all she'd talked about throughout lunch was her idyllic relationship with somebody called Bruno Parry-Brent.

This Bruno character, according to Maxine, was outrageously attractive, a superb chef, seriously wealthy and the best company in the world. Zack, accustomed to being made to feel he was the one with all these attributes –

apart from the cooking, of course – was almost jealous. She was practically implying that he didn't match up, he thought, feeling absurdly put out. He was Robbie Elliott, for Christ's sake, more than a match for any man.

And the more extravagantly she sang the unknown Bruno's praises, the more intrigued be became. Maxine Vaughan both mystified and intrigued him. Unable to resist such a challenge, Zack heard himself say, 'Ah, but he isn't one of us, is he? He isn't in the business. It's not as if he could pull any strings to help you in your career.'

'Of course he couldn't.' Maxine shrugged and spooned sugar into her cold coffee. 'But that doesn't matter. If I'm good enough, I'll make it on my own merit. Plenty of people do, don't they?' She brightened and added proudly, 'After all, I've got this far!'

'One toilet-roll ad and a walk-on.' Zack Morrison dismissed her dazzling achievements-to-date with a languid gesture. 'It's who you know in this game, darling. OK, this Bruno chap might be able to whip up a terrific omelette but that isn't going to put your name in lights.'

Maxine looked him. 'That's hardly his fault.'

'Whereas with the right man behind you,' Zack drawled. 'Well . . .'

'Oh come on,' she remonstrated, giving him a good-humoured smile. 'It isn't that straightforward.'

'Look, let me give you an example.' He leaned across the table towards her and lowered his voice. 'Just a for-instance. I'm what makes *Romsey Road* one of the top-rated shows on TV. I have clout. If I went to the script-writers tomorrow and suggested they expand your character . . . really bring her into the storyline . . . they'd listen to me.' He nodded, amused by the expression of disbelief in her eyes. 'Seriously. If I wanted to do it, I could. Now wouldn't you agree that's simpler than slogging round endless auditions in search of the next measly job?'

'Of course it is,' said Maxine quietly. The brightness in her eyes had faded and she was shifting almost imperceptibly away from him. She looked, thought Zack, disappointed.

'And I *could* do it,' he boasted.

'I'm sure you could.' Maxine bit her lower lip. 'Look I'm sorry, but I'm beginning to think I've been a bit naïve here. What are you saying, that if I do you a . . . favour, you'll do one for me in return? Is this the old casting-couch routine?'

Zack Morrison grinned, bewitched all over again both by her troubled expression and forthright manner. 'Why, would you go to bed with me if I asked you to? In exchange for a part in *Romsey Road?*'

'No.' Maxine shook her head. 'I wouldn't. I really am sorry, Mr Morrison, but I'm just not that sort of girl.'

She was terrific, thought Zack, filled with admiration. What a cracker! What an irresistible challenge.

'In that case I won't ask.' Giving Maxine the benefit of the famous Robbie Elliott smile, he glanced down at his watch. 'And I don't know about you, but I have to be back on set in ninety seconds. How are you fixed for this evening? Are you free for dinner?'

Maxine looked wary. 'I don't know whether I should.'

'No strings,' he assured her, still smiling.

'Well, OK.' With a trace of defiance, she added, 'But I

have to phone Bruno at eight-thirty.'

'Give me the address of where you're staying later.' Zack rose swiftly to his feet. 'I'll pick you up at nine. Wear something smart,' he added, deciding that Maxine Vaughan deserved the full works, no expense spared. 'We'll really hit the town.'

When he had gone, Maxine sipped her coffee. It was scummy, stone cold and unbelievably disgusting but that didn't matter. Her lips curled up at the corners as she allowed herself a small, triumphant smile.

Next year the Oscars, she thought happily. God, I'm good!

Chapter 56

St Lucia had been spectacular, but it would have been more spectacular if Guy could have got Janey out of his mind.

He still didn't know why she had refused to go with him to the charity ball at the Grosvenor, either. All he knew, he thought dryly, was that as he had been driving through Trezale on his way to the airport that Friday lunchtime, he had overtaken Paula, giving a very poor impression of a flu-ridden invalid, pedalling furiously uphill on her bike.

But Janey had evidently had her reasons for standing him up, he concluded, and whilst half of him had longed to go round to the shop and shake them out of her, the other half had told him it wasn't the greatest idea in the world. She'd had a hell of a year, after all. The best thing he could do was back off for a while and give her time to sort herself out. It was infuriating, but undoubtedly necessary.

It had also been the reason why – out of sheer desperation – he had carted Josh and Ella off for a time-wasting week in St Lucia. Janey, Guy concluded, had cost him a goddamn fortune. She would have an absolute fit if she only knew.

But now he was back. And he had a few bridges to mend. Ready, steady . . .

Waiting silently in the doorway, Guy watched her at work. She had her back to him, and her shoes were off. Smiling to himself, he observed the holes in the elbows of her baggy, charcoal-grey sweater. The long white flowing skirt, made of light cotton, was more suited to July than February and her bare brown legs were mottled with cold. The temperature was positively arctic but so engrossed was she that it evidently hadn't occurred to her to turn on the heating. Neither did she seem to have noticed that her long white hair, having escaped from its combs on one side of her head, was trailing over her left shoulder in a tangled, clay-streaked and lop-sided mane.

'Oh,' said Thea, finally sensing his presence and swivelling round to look at him. When she saw who it was she said 'Oh,' again, this time an octave lower.

'It's OK,' Guy told her. 'I haven't come here to shout at you.'

'I should bloody well hope not.' Her eyebrows lifted. 'And I certainly wouldn't recommend it, young man. Because I'd shout right back.'

Guy believed her. 'As a matter of fact I came here to apologize,' he said. 'I was pretty uptight at the funeral, but that's no excuse for bad manners. I should at least have offered my condolences . . .'

'I didn't realize you hadn't.' Thea's expression softened slightly. 'I'm afraid the entire day passed in a bit of a blur. Goodness only knows what that poor young solicitor must have thought of me . . . according to Janey I was swearing like a sailor.'

That had been almost three months ago. Guy nodded. 'So how are things now? How are you feeling?'

She shrugged, wiping her hands on her skirt. 'Well, not full of the joys of spring . . . but I'm back at work, which has helped. It's stupid; now that I no longer need to do it to earn a living, I find I'm spending more time here than ever before.' Hesitating for a second, she added, 'I suppose it takes my mind off other things. I actually believe these latest sculptures are the best I've ever done. It's just a shame Oliver isn't here to see them and tell me how brilliant I am.'

'At least the studio's your own, now.' Maxine had told him about that. Guy smiled. 'My father would definitely approve. He always loathed the idea of paying rent and never getting the chance to own anything at the end of it.'

Thea gazed at him. 'Does it bother you, the fact that he left me so much money?'

'Absolutely not.' Guy shook his head very firmly indeed. 'You deserved it. If anything, it bothers me that he left my children so much money,' he countered. 'They're in danger of becoming insufferable. Hardly a day goes by without one or other of them drawing up a new list of things-to-buy-when-I'm-twenty-one.'

'And did they enjoy their holiday?' Thea smiled. 'You're very brown. Janey told me you'd taken them somewhere hot but I can't remember where.'

'St Lucia.' Ridiculously, the mere mention of her name lifted his spirits. 'Janey was talking to you about . . . us?'

'I think she was missing your children,' she replied with unconscious cruelty. 'She's extremely fond of them, you know.'

'They're very fond of her.' Guy pretended to study the half-finished figure she was currently working on. 'How is Janey, by the way? It's been a while since we've seen her.'

Thea, itching to get back to work, smoothed her thumb fondly across the ridge of the figure's cheekbone. Not quite yet, but soon, she would attempt a bust of Oliver.

'Well, what can you expect?' She spoke the words absently, her thoughts elsewhere. 'Considering her abysmal taste in men. Oh, she's getting over it now; the decree nisi comes through next week, thank God, but I can't help wondering what's going to happen next. She's a lovely girl, even if I do say so myself, but her confidence has taken a bit of a battering. What she needs is a decent man who isn't going to muck her about.' Screwing up her vision, she leaned forward to check the symmetry of the figure's eyelids. 'Although personally I dread meeting the next one she brings home. If her track record's anything to go by, I'll loathe him on sight.'

Guy didn't bother to hide his amusement. 'Are there many men you do like?'

Thea's gaze flickered in his direction. 'I liked Oliver,' she said with pride. 'As far as I was concerned, he was about as perfect as a man could get.'

'Well, that's one.'

'And I suppose you aren't bad,' she conceded with a brief smile. 'A bit too good-looking for my taste, maybe. But I dare say you'll improve with age.'

Janey howled with laughter. Tears streamed down her face and her sides ached but she was quite unable to stop. Maxine, unable to find the tissues, chucked across a piece of kitchen roll instead and waited patiently for the hysteria to subside.

'You never laugh that much when I tell you one of my jokes,' she complained eventually. 'And it's not even supposed to be funny. Poor Bruno; I'm *dreading* telling him.'

'Poor Bruno?' gasped Janey, wiping her eyes and gasping for breath. *'Poor Bruno! I love it . . . !'*

'And he loves me.' Maxine looked glum. 'He's not going to be thrilled, I can tell you.'

Janey struggled to compose herself. If she breathed really slowly and kept her mind a total blank, she told herself firmly, she could do it. No more laughing; this was serious stuff. Bruno was about to be dumped and she wanted to hear every last glorious detail. If she didn't get a grip, Maxine might decide not to tell her and that would be just too cruel.

'So what did he do wrong?' she asked, pressing her lips together and looking suitably concerned.

'Nothing.' Maxine sounded gloomier than ever. 'That's why it's going to be so difficult.'

'OK. In that case, why are you dumping him?'

'Oh Janey,' wailed Maxine suddenly, 'he got nice! You know what I'm like with men; I can't handle it when they're nice. Look at Maurice; it was running away from him that brought me back here in the first place. He was so nice I thought I was going to die of boredom.' She paused, shaking her head in despair. 'And that was what was so brilliant about Bruno. He had such a reputation . . . he was so wicked! I really thought I'd found someone I'd never get tired of.'

'You mean you thought you'd met your match?'

'Well, I had, then.' Maxine looked resigned. 'But somehow it all changed. I began to feel as if I'd got myself a housewife. Bruno wanted to prove I could trust him. He stopped being wicked. And I don't know . . . I suppose I stopped being interested.'

Janey struggled to keep a straight face. Oh dear, falling in love for possibly the first time in his life had turned Bruno into a bore.

'I bet he leaves Trezale,' she mused. The shame of it would undoubtedly be too great for a man of his reputation to bear. 'He won't be able to handle the prospect of bumping into you.' Grinning, because it was what Alan had done, she added, 'Maybe he'll skulk off down the coast to St Ives.'

'Ah.' Maxine blinked. 'Well he wouldn't actually need to move away. You see, I am.'

'What?'

'I am. Moving away. To Manchester,' said Maxine rapidly. 'They've given me a six-month contract to appear in *Romsey Road:* the white-stilettoed trollop is going to have a steamy affair with the vicar. And if they decide to get her pregnant I'll be sticking a cushion up my jumper and signing up for another year on top of that. Oh Janey, it's happening at last,' she sighed, her eyes glistening with tears of joy. 'I'm going to be Mandy Blenkinsop.'

'You're changing your name to *Blenkinsop?*'

'That's her name, stupid! The trollop's.' Maxine grinned. 'She didn't have one before, you see, because it was only a walk-on. But from next month she becomes a real character.' Dreamily she added, 'And I'll be a bona

487

fide member of the cast. I'll probably have my own fan club.'

Bruno was forgotten. It was as if he had never even existed. Stunned, Janey said, 'What about Guy?'

Maxine shifted uneasily in her chair. 'Well, he knew it was on the cards. It isn't as if it's going to come as a huge surprise, is it? And when you think how many times he's almost sacked me, he'll probably be glad to see me go.'

'But you haven't quite plucked up the courage to tell him yet?' Janey spoke in faintly admonishing tones. 'Max, you must. Look at the trouble he had last time, finding a replacement for Berenice. He doesn't want any old nanny looking after his children. If it comes to that,' she amended, 'Josh and Ella won't want any old nanny either. They're going to miss you terribly.'

'Shame they didn't show a bit more appreciation, then, while they still had me.' Resorting to flippancy in order to cover up the guilt, Maxine said, 'Those little brats are forever telling me how much more fun they had when you were looking after them. Seriously, Janey, if you ever felt like selling the shop and switching careers . . . You could even have a crack at Guy while you're there, see if you don't have better luck with him than I did!'

It was like Pavlov's dogs. Maxine was only joking, but even the most frivolous of insinuations was enough to bring the colour surging into Janey's cheeks. Silently cursing her inability to keep it at bay and desperate to change the subject, she resolutely ignored the jibe and instead launched a bold counter-attack.

'Come on, Max. I'm your sister, remember? Do you seriously expect me to believe that's all there is to it?'

Maxine blinked. 'To what?'

'This whole *Romsey Road* business.' It hadn't been an innocent blink. Janey, pleased with herself for having guessed, moved in for the kill. 'Because I can't help thinking what an extraordinary coincidence it is, you getting the part and at the same time losing interest in Bruno. Call it a shot in the dark,' she suggested lightly, 'but would there happen to be any seriously wicked men in Manchester?'

This time even Maxine had the grace to look embarrassed. 'Well,' she murmured vaguely, 'now you come to mention it, maybe one or two . . .'

Chapter 57

The fact that the weather had finally taken a dramatic turn for the better did nothing at all to lift Bruno's spirits. Outside Mole Cottage – which Maxine had insisted on calling Toad-in-the-Hole Cottage following the discovery of a mouldy cooked sausage under the bed – the sun shone with enthusiasm for the first time in months. Tiny clouds drifted across a clear blue sky, the sea – turquoise fading to aqua – glittered in the distance and daffodils had sprung up en masse, their yellow heads nodding in the warm breeze. Even the hopelessly overgrown front garden was sprouting an assortment of yellow blooms; but since he had no interest in flowers Bruno didn't have a clue what they were.

He didn't care, either. He didn't care much about anything at all right now, except the fact that forty-eight hours earlier Maxine had left him.

Standing at the living-room window, he gazed blindly out to sea as tears pricked the back of his eyes. She hadn't even let him down gently, dammit. Instead, with typically selfish haste, she had just come out with it – no, there was nobody else and he hadn't done anything wrong, it simply wasn't working. After that she'd slung the few clothes and bits of make-up she had left at the cottage into a pink raffia bag, and said gaily, 'Sorry, darling, but these things happen. Wish me luck. Bye!'

The lying bitch, he thought, pressing his lips together and turning the postcard over and over in his hands. She hadn't even bothered to cover her tracks properly. That was what you got for loving and trusting someone, Bruno concluded bitterly. They took fucking advantage of you and didn't even stop to think of the pain they were inflicting . . .

He had found the postcard stuffed into the breast pocket of his denim shirt. Maxine, who had borrowed it the previous weekend, had spilt chocolate milkshake down the sleeve and chucked it into his laundry basket. That way, of course, he could wash and iron it himself before she borrowed it again.

And it was such a naff card, Bruno thought, blinking hard and staring down at the scene depicting *Romsey Road* in all its grubby glory. Turning it over, he read for the fifteenth time the brief message scrawled on the other side: 'Don't I *always* deliver the goods? Ring me! Zack.'

Even Bruno, who didn't watch television, recognized the name. Zack Morrison might not be the most talented actor on the planet, he thought sourly, but he was renowned for his ability to deliver the fucking goods . . .

Bruno dressed with care, deliberately choosing the pink-and-grey striped shirt she had bought for him and teaming it with immaculately pressed charcoal-grey trousers. It was warm enough outside not to bother with a jacket.

Studying himself in front of the bedroom mirror Bruno nodded, satisfied with what he saw. He could still turn it on when he wanted to, he thought with renewed pride. How many women, after all, had told him he had the sexiest green eyes in the world? How many had called his smile irresistible? How many had begged him to take them away from their husbands?

Paco Rabanne, Bruno decided, reaching for the bottle standing on the chest of drawers. No, *Eau Sauvage.* She had bought that for him too. If that was what she liked best, it was what he would wear.

Nina was sitting up at the bar drinking tomato juice and chatting to one of the lunchtime regulars when Bruno walked into the restaurant. The good weather had brought with it an influx of customers and they all seemed to be enjoying themselves. What Wayne Simmonds lacked in personal magnetism, Bruno decided, he evidently made up for with his skill in the kitchen. At least the business hadn't suffered whilst he'd been away.

'Goodness,' said Nina shyly, her eyes lighting up when she spotted him. 'Look who's here! Bruno, how lovely to see you after all this time. And you're looking so well; working at the Grand Rock obviously suits you.'

Smiling, Bruno bent and kissed her pale cheek. Nina hadn't changed at all; that was what he'd always liked about her. Even the floppy, floral, Laura Ashley dress was utterly predictable. She'd been wearing it for the past six years.

'You're looking pretty good yourself.' Standing back, studying her shining, unmade-up face and breathing in the comfortingly familiar scent of patchouli oil, he took her hand and gave it a gentle squeeze. 'Are you busy or can we go upstairs and have a proper chat? It feels odd being down here and not having the right to insult the customers.'

The sitting room, flooded with sunlight, was less tidy than before but otherwise just as he remembered it.

Nina, intercepting his glance, smiled and said, 'You were the one who put things away around here. I'm still as hopeless as I ever was.'

'You aren't hopeless.' His tone was affectionate. 'Just . . . relaxed. Oh Nina, it really is good to see you. Tell me how you've been keeping. Tell me how you've really been.'

The dozen or so silver bracelets tinkled as she pushed her hair behind her ears. 'Well, fine. Busy at Christmas, of course, and New Year's Eve was as chaotic as ever. January was steady. We've changed the menu around and the customers seem to approve.'

'I meant how have *you* been.' Leading Nina to the sofa, he sat down next to her without letting go of her hand. 'I don't suppose it's been that easy for either of us . . .'

'Oh, you know.' She shrugged and examined a fraying hole in her skirt. 'As you said at the time, these things happen. Life goes on.'

'Nina.' Bruno's voice softened. 'I said some very stupid things at the time. And I've lived to regret them. You—'

'How's Maxine?' she said suddenly, her eyes bright with interest. 'I saw her in that toilet-roll commercial on television. I thought she was very good.'

Bruno sighed. 'Maybe she was. But Maxine isn't you,

sweetheart. She doesn't even begin to compare with you. I realize that now. I don't want Maxine any more,' he said simply. 'I want you to forgive me for behaving like a fool. I want *you*.'

For a moment Nina looked as if she were about to burst into tears. Gazing at him, hesitantly touching the sleeve of his shirt, she whispered, 'This is the one I bought you last summer.'

He nodded and gave her an encouraging smile.

'Oh Bruno, I wanted you back so badly it hurt,' Nina said softly. 'I dreamed of this happening; it was practically the only thing that kept me alive . . .'

'And now I am back.' Bruno stroked the inside of her thin wrist.

'If only you'd changed your mind sooner.' Nina spoke with genuine distress. The last thing she wanted was to hurt him. 'Oh dear, I don't quite know how to tell you this . . . but I've met someone else. I'm happy with him. We're going to be married in April; nothing flashy, just a small wedding, not even a proper honeymoon.'

'Married?' echoed Bruno, his eyes widening with horror. He stared at her, aghast. 'Who the hell to?'

She flinched. 'Um . . . Wayne.'

'You are joking!' he shouted, unable to believe what he was hearing. 'Don't be so ridiculous, Nina! You can't do that!'

Nina stuck to her guns. She loved Wayne and he loved her. She knew that.

'But we are doing it,' she said nervously. 'It's all arranged. April the twentieth.'

This was like a truly terrible dream. Bruno, not even

realizing that his fingernails were digging into her wrist, howled, 'For Christ's sake, cancel it! He's only marrying you for your money.'

'No he isn't.' Nina pulled free and rubbed her arm. Poor Bruno, he may as well hear all the news in one go. Straightening her shoulders, her face glowing with pride, she said, 'He's marrying me because I'm pregnant.'

Chapter 58

It wasn't much, thought Guy ruefully, but it was all he had. Maxine's throwaway remark last night, when she had teased Josh about his new eight-year-old girlfriend – 'Goodness me, you've gone almost as pink as Janey does whenever I mention your father!' – wasn't a great deal to go on, but it was the most promising sign so far that she might actually feel more for him than she'd been admitting.

It had been enough to persuade him that the moment had arrived to do something, to find out for himself. Not knowing was beginning to get to him, Guy decided. The time had come to act. And if Maxine had been wrong, he thought, he could always strangle her with his bare hands . . .

Two dozen pink roses. Janey winced as one of the thorns ripped into the tender skin between finger and thumb. He'd had to order not one, but *two* dozen long-stemmed pink roses.

Jealousy, pure and simple, surged within her as she tried to imagine whom Guy was so eager to impress. And how tempting it was to choose less-than-perfect blooms, the ones whose petals were beginning to loosen so that within a day or two they would drop off

But pride compelled her to select the finest, just-flowering buds instead, flawless shell-pink tinged with apricot. If whoever-it-was took the trouble to look after them, they would last a good fortnight. Bitchily, Janey wondered if Guy's interest in whoever-it-was would exceed the life of the exquisite roses.

It was sheer pride too, that sent her up to the flat to brush her hair and change into a clean olive-green shirt and white jeans before setting off with the delivery. If the girl – presumably yet another svelte model – was going to be there when she arrived at Trezale House, Janey didn't want to feel any more inferior by comparison than she already did. Knowing that you had a crush on someone was bad enough. Having to face his infinitely more glamorous size-eight girlfriends was downright intimidating.

Stop it, thought Janey wearily, rubbing off the lipstick she had just applied and staring at the little pot of bronze eyeshadow which had somehow found its way into her hand. Now she was being really stupid, she told herself, flinging the eyeshadow back into the drawer of her dressing table and gazing at her reflection in the mirror. As if a bit of make-up was going to help.

Guy opened the front door as she was lifting the flowers out of the van. It would have suited Janey to hand them over to him then and there but all he did was step aside, enabling her to carry the bouquet into the house.

There didn't appear to be anyone else at home, certainly no stunning, semi-naked brunette draped across the kitchen table. In an effort to sound normal, Janey said casually, 'No Maxine?'

'No Maxine, no kids.' He shrugged and smiled. 'She's taken them to some birthday party in Truro. They won't be back for hours.'

'And there I was, thinking the roses were for her.' Janey placed them on the table, suddenly remembering that she hadn't seen Guy since the day he had come to the shop with the invitation to the charity ball. Praying he wouldn't mention it, realizing to her despair that her cheeks were hot, she turned her attention to the ribbons on the bouquet, fiddling with the curly bits and tweaking them into shape.

'Actually' – Guy's voice came from behind her – 'they're for you. And why did you make up that story about Paula having flu, by the way? Was the prospect of spending an entire evening in my company really that awful, or is there another explanation? And don't expect me to count to ten whilst you think of one,' he continued, his tone even, 'because you've had eight weeks already.'

This time Janey blushed with a vengeance. She couldn't help it. She didn't know what to say either.

'Look,' she said finally, and with at least semi-truthfulness, 'I just thought you'd enjoy yourself more if you took somebody else.'

'Janey, if I had thought I would have enjoyed myself more with somebody else, I would have asked them to be my partner in the first place.' His tone registered both amusement and impatience. 'And you aren't admiring your flowers. You're supposed to say "How lovely, you shouldn't have".'

'Well, you know what I mean.' Aware that she was gabbling, she took a step back. 'There were those photos in the paper of you and Valentina, and that's the kind of partner people expect you to turn up with. They'd wonder what on earth you were doing—'

'They might even think I was coming to my senses at last.' Guy, a million times more nervous than he was letting on, said quietly, 'Janey, did you hear what I said just now?'

'Of course I heard you.' Flustered, hopelessly confused, Janey shook her head. 'I just don't know why you're saying it. You phoned me up and ordered these flowers. You can't give them *back* to me . . .'

'Why on earth not?' He raised his eyebrows. 'I've paid for them. I gave you my Access card number over the phone.'

'But this is stupid.'

'No it isn't, it's sensible.' Guy started to smile. 'It got you here, didn't it?'

She bit her lip. 'I still don't understand.'

'You could try saying thank you,' he suggested, his eyes glittering with amusement. 'It's how people generally express their appreciation when they've been given two dozen ruinously expensive pink roses.'

Janey gave up. 'In that case, thank you. They're beautiful. How-very-kind-you-really-shouldn't-have. And they weren't that expensive,' she added with a faint answering smile. 'I thought they were very reasonable.'

It was now or never, Guy decided. He took a deep breath.

'Another way of expressing your appreciation when

you've been given two dozen very reasonably priced pink roses,' he said slowly, 'is with a kiss.'

Janey stared at him. Was this some kind of hideous practical joke? Was Maxine hiding behind the Welsh dresser, camcorder at the ready? Was Jeremy Beadle lurking inside the fridge?

Finally, she said, 'You want me to kiss the *roses*?'

But the expression on Guy's face was quite serious. No longer smiling, there was almost an air of apprehension about him. Janey, suddenly light-headed, felt her heart begin to race. Her stomach did a loop and disappeared.

'It's up to you,' said Guy, 'but I'd prefer it if you kissed me.'

As if in a dream, inwardly amazed that her legs were still capable of carrying her, she stepped forward and with infinite caution brushed her lips against his tanned cheek.

'OK?' she said stupidly, when it was done.

But Guy, half smiling down at her, shook his head. 'Terrible,' he murmured. 'Very poor attempt. I'm sure you can do better than that.'

He put his arms around her. Janey, no longer in any condition to protest, closed her eyes as his mouth found hers. Caution abandoned, this time the receiver, she gave herself up to him. This time the kiss seemed to go on for ever.

'Big improvement,' said Guy at last, speaking the words into her hair and not releasing his hold on her.

Janey, glad to be held – she needed all the support she could get – took a deep, steadying breath.

He smiled. 'All right?'

'I'm not sure.' Raising her brown eyes to his face, she said shakily, 'Is this a joke? Because if it is, I think I shall have to kill you.'

'You could always set Maxine on to me. That would be a fate far worse than death.' Guy, overjoyed by the success of his plan, broke into a broad grin. 'Except it isn't a joke, so you don't need to. My God, Janey, do you have any idea what you've put me through, these past months?'

Bewildered, still unable to take in the fact that this was happening to her, she said, 'I'm sorry.'

'So you bloody well should be.' He kissed her again, breathing in the faint scent of her perfume. 'You don't give away *any* clues; I didn't know whether you found me even remotely attractive; you *wrecked* my sex life . . .'

'What are you talking about?' Janey demanded, trembling all over and clutching the front of his shirt. Able to feel the warmth of his skin through the cotton, she suppressed an incredible urge to start undoing buttons.

'You were involved with that terrible husband of yours so I couldn't have you,' Guy complained. 'And I didn't want anyone else. It's been sheer torture.' He rolled his eyes in mock reproach. 'You aren't exactly forgettable just now either; everywhere I go, I'm haunted by that damn charity poster. I was seriously beginning to regret using that photograph, I can tell you. How was I to know they were going to plaster your face across just about every hoarding in the country?' With an extravagant sigh, he concluded, 'All in all, you're one difficult lady to fall in love with, Janey Sinclair, and I think you should apologize for all the trouble you've caused.'

'Do you really mean it?' She shivered. He had just said he was in love with her. Somewhere out there in the real world, Paula was expecting her back to close the shop, and here she was, standing in the middle of Guy Cassidy's kitchen listening to this.

'Of course I bloody well mean it,' Guy declared indignantly.

'It's just that I still keep expecting Jeremy Beadle to leap out of the fridge,' Janey murmured, glancing over her shoulder to make sure. 'What time did you say Maxine was bringing Josh and Ella back?'

'Not for ages.' He grinned. 'This was a carefully planned campaign, sweetheart. You don't seriously think I'd risk being interrupted by that rabble, do you?'

'Hmm.' Janey, her fingers still unsteady, touched his mouth. 'Just as well I didn't ask Paula to deliver the flowers.'

Guy kissed her again. 'I seem to be making all the running here.' His tone was gently admonishing. 'You haven't even told me yet how you feel about all this. Is it OK with you or do you have strong feelings about getting seriously involved with a bad-tempered photographer, two noisy juvenile delinquents and an out-of-control nanny?'

Janey's thoughts flew back to the night of the fair, when Alexander Norcross had warned her of the dangers of one-parent families.

'I don't know,' she said lightly. 'Are you only doing this because it's easier than finding a replacement for Maxine?'

Guy laughed. 'Brilliant idea. I haven't threatened to sack her for weeks. Do you really think she'd go, if we asked nicely?'

Janey breathed a guilty sigh of relief. So Maxine hadn't told him yet. She hadn't seriously suspected he would do such a thing but it was nice to know for sure.

Then she smiled, because 'nice' was such a hopelessly inadequate word to describe how it felt, knowing that Guy really did love her for herself. Not all men had ulterior motives, Janey reminded herself. Alan was a bad experience she could put behind her now. No two men in the world, after all, could be more different than Alan and Guy.

'No, I'm not looking for a cheap childminder,' he told Janey, stroking her hair away from her face and gazing into her eyes. He was looking for a wife, but there was no need to alarm her with that just now. There was no need to hurry; they had all the time in the world to get to know each other properly . . .

'Good,' said Janey, 'because I'm not cheap.'

'Unlike your very reasonably priced roses.'

'Nobody's ever given me flowers before.' She gazed lovingly at them, her eyes bright with tears of happiness. 'Oh dear, I've got a terrible confession to make.'

Guy looked at her. 'Go on.'

'I thought you were buying them for some horrible new woman in your life. I almost chose the not-so-good ones that I knew wouldn't last.'

'You'd have been sorry.' He grinned. 'So you were jealous? That's encouraging.'

'Of course I was jealous.' Janey looked ashamed. 'All

right, I'll admit something else. I couldn't face going to London with you because I was too afraid of making a fool of myself. I thought you'd be able to tell how I felt.'

If only she'd realized, thought Guy, how badly he had wanted to know how she felt.

But that was all in the past. Smiling, he stroked her cheek. The flawless skin, as soft to the touch as warm silk, was positively addictive.

'Never mind,' he murmured. 'I know now. And you feel just about perfect to me.'